At the Sign of the Cat and Racket

"COULDN'T YOU GET OUT OF THE WAY?"

At the Sign of the Cat and Racket

THE COMEDY OF HUMAN LIFE, VOLUME VII

Honoré de Balzac

NONSUCH

First published 1901

Nonsuch Publishing Limited
The Mill, Brimscombe Port, Stroud, Gloucestershire, GL5 2QG
www.nonsuch-publishing.com

British Library Cataloguing in Publication Data.
A catalogue record for this book is available from the British Library.

ISBN 1-84588-051-X

Typesetting and origination by Nonsuch Publishing Limited
Printed in Great Britain by Oaklands Book Services Limited

CONTENTS

INTRODUCTION TO THE MODERN EDITION

HONORÉ DE BALZAC was born to middle-class parents in 1799 in Tours, a place he describes in 'The Vicar of Tours' as 'one of the least literary towns of France'. He was educated at the college of the Oratorians at Vendôme before moving to Paris in 1816, where he studied law and worked as clerk to an advocate. Balzac began his literary career by contributing to journals and reviews, as well as writing historical novels under pseudonyms. When the publications for which he wrote began to look for short stories he wrote what were to become the first stories in *The Comedy of Human Life.* A collection of these, under the title *Scenes from Private Life,* was published in 1829 and was well-received.

Balzac was greatly influenced by France's political climate. After Napoleon's final defeat at Waterloo in 1815 the country had been ruled by the restored Bourbon monarchy. The July Revolution of 1830 swept the last Bourbon king, Charles X, from the throne and installed Louis Philippe, the so-called 'bourgeois monarch,' who had the support of the middle classes, in his place. Louis Philippe's reign would last until the Revolution of 1848, just two years before Balzac's death, and the effect that the Revolution, Napoleon's Empire, the Bourbon Restoration and the July Monarchy had on the lives of the French would dominate his work.

Devoting himself to his writing, he is said to have worked for fifteen hours a day, but continued to have an active social life, which provided material and inspiration for his stories. Although he also produced five plays and a collection of humorous tales, most of his writing formed part of *The Comedy of Human Life*, a vast project depicting French society after 1815, which he intended to consist of 137 connected short stories, novellas and novels, although he only completed ninety-one. He divided the *Comedy* into groups of stories with similar themes: 'Studies of Manners' which includes many of his most famous works, and is itself divided into *Scenes from Private Life*, *Scenes from Provincial Life*,

Scenes from Parisian Life, *Scenes from Political Life*, *Scenes from Military Life* and *Scenes from Country Life*; 'Philosophical Studies'; and 'Analytical Studies.'

'At the Sign of the Cat and Racket,' 'The Ball at Sceaux,' 'The Purse' and 'Madame Firmiani' are taken from *Scenes from Private Life*, while 'Pierrette' and 'The Vicar of Tours' are part of *Scenes from Provincial Life*. Balzac was motivated to try to understand human society in the way that a biologist would seek to understand a species, and was concerned that post-Revolutionary France was bereft of honour and dominated by money. Money is a motivating force in all of the stories in this collection, from the desire of Emilie de Fontaine to marry a rich Peer of France in 'The Ball at Sceaux' to the unusual attitude of Madame Firmiani towards the fortune of Octave de Camps in the story that bears her name.

His stories made him rich and respected, although he continued to worry about money and status, and he was always ambitious to achieve more. It is possible that this driving ambition was what caused his strength to fail, which it did in 1847. With his health in decline, he travelled to Poland in 1849 to visit a wealthy Polish lady, Eveline Hanska, with whom he had been corresponding for over fifteen years. They married in 1850, but, a mere three months later, Balzac died. At his funeral, his contemporary Victor Hugo said, "henceforth, men's eyes will be turned towards the faces not of those who are the rulers but of those who are the thinkers.'

The following introduction is the work of George Saintsbury (1845–1933), academic and literary critic. A prolific author in his own right, Saintsbury was also regarded as the foremost authority on French literature of his time.

INTRODUCTION

In the very interesting preface, dated July 1842, which Balzac prefixed to the first collection of the *Comédie Humaine*, he endeavours, naturally enough, to represent the division into *Scènes de la Vie Parisienne*, etc., as a rational and reasoned one. Although not quite arbitrary, it was of course to a great extent determined by considerations which were not those of design; and we did not require the positive testimony which we find in the Letters to tell us that in the author's view, as well as in our own, not a few of the stories might have been shifted over from one division to another, and have filled their place just as well in the other as in the one.

La Maison du Chat-qui-Pelote, however, which originally bore the much less happy title of "Gloire et Malheur," was a *Scène de la Vie Privée* from the first, and it bears out better than some of its companions its author's expressed intention of making these "scenes" represent youth, whether Parisian or Provincial. Few of Balzac's stories have united the general suffrage for touching grace more than this; and there are few better examples of his minute Dutch-painting than the opening passages, or of his unconquerable delight in the details of business than his sketch of Monsieur Guillaume's establishment and its ways. The French equivalent of the "Complete Tradesman" of Defoe lasted much longer than his English counterpart; but, except in the smaller provincial towns, he is said to be uncommon now. As for the plot, if such a stately name can be given to so delicate a sketch, it is of course open to downright British judgment to pronounce the self-sacrifice of Lebas more ignoble than touching, the conduct of Théodore too childish to deserve the excuses sometimes possible for passionate inconstancy, and the character of Augustine angelically idiotic. This last outrage, if it were committed, would indeed only be an instance of the irreconcilable difference which almost to the present day divides English and French ideas of ideally perfect girlhood, and of that state of womanhood which corresponds thereto. The *candour adorable* which the Frenchman adores and exhibits in the girl; the uncompromising, though mortal, passion of the woman; are too different from any ideal that we have entertained, except for a very short period in the eighteenth century. But there are few more pathetic and charming impersonations of this other ideal than Augustine de Sommervieux.

All the stories associated with *La Maison du Chat-qui-Pelote*, according to French standards—all, perhaps, according to all but the very strictest and oldest-fashioned of English—are perfectly free from the slightest objection on the score of that propriety against which Balzac has an amusing if not quite exact tirade in one of his books. And this is evidently not accidental, for the preface above referred to is an elaborate attempt to rebut the charge of *im*propriety, and to show that the author could draw virtuous as well as unvirtuous characters. But they are not, taking them as a whole, and omitting the "Cat and Racket" itself, quite examples of putting the best foot foremost. *Le Bal de Sceaux,* with its satire on contempt for trade, is in some ways more like Balzac's young friend and pupil Charles de Bernard than like himself; and I believe it attracted English notice pretty early. At least I seem, when quite a boy, and long before I read the *Comédie Humaine*, to have seen an English version or paraphrase of it. *La Bourse*, though agreeable, is a little slight. I should rank *Madame Firmiani* a good deal higher than these two, though it also is a little slight, and though it is not in Balzac's most characteristic or important manner. Rather, perhaps, does it remind us of the "Physiologies" and the other social "skits" and sketches which he was writing for the *Caricature* and other papers at the time. Still, the various descriptions of the heroine have a point and sparkle which are almost peculiar to the not quite mature work of men of genius; and the actual story has a lightness which, perhaps, would have disappeared if Balzac had handled it at greater length.

As for bibliography, *La Maison du Chat-qui-Pelote*, under the title above referred to, saw the light first with other *Scènes de la Vie Privée* in 1830. But it was not dated as of the previous year till five years later, in its third edition; while the title was not changed till the great collection itself. Of its companions, *Le Bal de Sceaux* was an original one, and seems to have been written as well as published more or less at the same time. It at first had an alternative title, *Ou le Pair de France*, which was afterwards dropped.

La Bourse was early, but not quite so early as these. It appeared in, and was apparently written for, the second edition of the *Scènes de la Vie Privée*, published in May 1832. In 1835 it was moved over to the *Scènes de la Vie Parisienne*, between which and the *Vie Privée* there is in fact a good deal of cross and arbitrary division. But when the full *Comédie* took shape it moved back again.

Madame Firmiani was first published in the *Revue de Paris* for February 1832; then became a *Conte Philosophique*, and still in the same year a *Scène de la Vie Parisienne*. It was in the 1842 collection that it took up its abode in the *Scènes de la Vie Privée*.

Les Célibataires, the longest number of the original *Comédie* under a single title, next to *Illusions perdues*, is not, like that book, connected by any unity of story. Indeed, the general bond of union is pretty weak; and though it is quite true that bachelors and old maids are the heroes and heroines of all three, it would be rather hard to establish any other bond of connection, and it is rather unlikely that any one unprompted would fix on this as a sufficient ground of partnership.

Two at least of the component parts, however, are of very high excellence. I do not myself think that *Pierrette*, which opens the series, is quite the equal of its companions. Written, as it was, for Countess Anna de Hanska, Balzac's step-daughter of the future, while she was still very young, it partakes necessarily of the rather elaborate artificiality of all attempts to suit the young person, of French attempts in particular, and it may perhaps be said of Balzac's attempts most of all. It belongs, in a way, to the Arcis series—the series which also includes the fine *Ténébreuse Affaire* and the unfinished *Député d'Arcis*—but is not very closely connected therewith. The picture of the actual *Célibataires*, the brother and sister Rogron, with which it opens, is in one of Balzac's best-known styles, and is executed with all his usual mastery both of the minute and of the at least partially repulsive, showing also that strange knowledge of the *bourgeois de Paris* which, somehow or other, he seems to have attained by dint of unknown foregatherings in his ten years of apprenticeship. But when we come to *Pierrette* herself, the story is, I think, rather less satisfying. Her persecutions and her end, and the devotion of the faithful Brigaut and the rest, are pathetic no doubt, but tend (I hope it is not heartless to say it) just a very little towards *sensiblerie*. The fact is that the thing is not quite in Balzac's line.

The other and shorter constituent of the book, *Le Curé de Tours*, is certainly on a higher level, and has attracted the most magnificent eulogies from some of the novelist's admirers. I think both Mr. Henry James and Mr. Wedmore have singled out this little piece for detailed and elaborate praise, and there is no doubt that it is a happy example of a kind in which the author excelled. The opening, with its evident but not obtruded remembrance of the old and well-founded superstition—derived from the universal belief in some form of Nemesis—that an extraordinary sense of happiness, good luck, or anything of the kind, is a precursor of misfortune, and calls for some instant act of sacrifice or humiliation, is very striking; and the working out of the vengeance of the goddess by the very ungoddess-like though feminine hand of Mademoiselle Gamard has much that is commendable. Nothing in its well exampled kind is better touched off than the Listomère coterie, from the shrewdness of Monsieur de Bourbonne to the selfishness of Madame de Listomère. I do not know that the old maid herself—cat, and far worse than cat as she is—is at all exaggerated, and the sketch of the coveted *appartement* and its ill-fated *mobilier* is about as good as it can be. And the battle between Madame de Listomère and the Abbé Troubert, which has served as a model for many similar things, has, if it has often been equaled, not often been surpassed.

I cannot, however, help thinking that there is more than a little exaggeration in more than one point of the story. The Abbé Birotteau is surely a little too much of a fool; the Abbé Troubert an Iago a little too much wanting in verisimilitude; and the central incident of the clause about the furniture too manifestly improbable. Taking the first and the last points together, is it likely that any one not quite an idiot should, in the first place, remain so entirely ignorant of the value of his property; should, in the second, though, ignorant or not, he attached the greatest possible *pretium affectionis* to it, contract to resign it for such a ridiculous consideration; and should, in the third, take the fatal step without so much as remembering the condition attached thereto? If it be answered that Birotteau was idiot enough to do such a thing, then it must be observed further that one's sympathy is frozen by the fact. Such a man deserved such treatment. And, again, even if French justice was, and perhaps is, as much influenced by secret considerations as Balzac loves to represent it, we must agree with that member of the Listomère society who pointed out that no tribunal could possibly uphold such an obviously iniquitous bargain. As for Troubert, the idea of the Jesuitical ecclesiastic (though Balzac was not personally hostile to the Jesuits) was a common one at the time, and no doubt popular, but the actual personage seems to me nearer to Eugène Sue's Rodin in some ways than I could have desired.

These things, however, are very much a case of "As You Like It" or "As It Strikes You," and I have said that *Le Curé de Tours* strikes some good judges as of exceptional merit, while no one can refuse it merit in a high degree. I should not, except for the opening, place it in the very highest class of the *Comédie,* but it is high beyond all doubt in the second.

Pierrette, which was earlier called *Pierrette Lorrain*, was issued in 1840, first in the *Siècle,* and then in volume form, published by Souverain. In both issues it had nine chapter or book divisions with headings. With the other *Célibataires* it entered the *Comédie* as a *Scène de la Vie de Province* in 1843.

Le Curé de Tours (which Balzac had at one time intended to call by the name of the Curé's enemy, and which at first was simply called by the general title *Les Célibataires*) is much older than its companions, and appeared in 1832 in the *Scènes de la Vie Privée.* It was soon properly shifted to the *Vie de Province*, and as such in due time joined the *Comédie* bearing its present title.

G. S.

AT THE SIGN OF THE CAT AND RACKET

Dedicated to Mademoiselle Marie de Montheau

HALF-WAY down the Rue Saint-Denis, almost at the corner of the Rue du Petit-Lion, there stood formerly one of those delightful houses which enable historians to reconstruct old Paris by analogy. The threatening walls of this tumbledown abode seemed to have been decorated with hieroglyphics. For what other name could the passer-by give to the Xs and Vs which the horizontal or diagonal timbers traced on the front, outlined by little parallel cracks in the plaster? It was evident that every beam quivered in its mortices at the passing of the lightest vehicle. This venerable structure was crowned by a triangular roof of which no example will, ere long, be seen in Paris. This covering, warped by the extremes of the Paris climate, projected three feet over the roadway, as much to protect the threshold from the rainfall as to shelter the wall of a loft and its sill-less dormer-window. This upper story was built of planks, overlapping each other like slates, in order, no doubt, not to overweight the frail house.

One rainy morning in the month of March, a young man, carefully wrapped in his cloak, stood under the awning of a shop opposite this old house, which he was studying with the enthusiasm of an antiquary. In point of fact, this relic of the civic life of the sixteenth century offered more than one problem to the consideration of an observer. Each story presented some singularity; on the first floor four tall, narrow windows, close together, were filled as to the lower panes with boards, so as to produce the doubtful light by which a clever salesman can ascribe to his goods the colour his customers inquire for. The young man seemed very scornful of this part of the house; his eyes had not yet rested on it. The windows of the second floor, where the Venetian blinds were drawn up, revealing little dingy muslin curtains behind the large Bohemian glass panes, did not interest him either. His attention was attracted to the third floor, to the modest sash-frames of wood, so clumsily wrought that they might have found a place in the Museum of Arts and Crafts to illustrate the early efforts of French carpentry. These windows were glazed with small squares of glass so green that, but for his good eyes, the young man could not have seen the blue-checked cotton curtains which screened the mysteries of the room from profane eyes. Now and then the watcher, weary of his fruitless contemplation, or of the silence in which the house was buried, like the whole neighborhood, dropped his eyes towards the lower regions. An involuntary smile parted his lips each time he looked at the shop, where, in fact, there were some laughable details.

A formidable wooden beam, resting on four pillars, which appeared to have bent under the weight of the decrepit house, had been encrusted with as many coats of different paint as there are of rouge on an old Duchess' cheek. In the middle of this broad and fantastically carved joist there was an old painting representing a cat playing rackets. This picture was what moved the young man to mirth. But it must be said that the wittiest of modern painters could not invent so comical a caricature. The animal held in one of its forepaws a racket as big as itself, and stood on its hind legs to aim at hitting an enormous ball, returned by a man in a fine embroidered coat. Drawing, colour, and accessories, all were treated in such a way as to suggest that the artist had meant to make game of the shop-owner and of the passing observer. Time, while impairing this artless painting, had made it yet more grotesque by introducing some uncertain features which must have puzzled the conscientious idler. For instance, the cat's tail had been eaten into in such a way that it might now have been taken for the figure of a spectator—so long, and thick, and furry were the tails of our forefathers' cats. To the right of the picture, on an azure field which ill-disguised the decay of the wood, might be read the name "Guillaume," and to the left, "Successor to Master Chevrel." Sun and rain had worn away most of the gilding parsimoniously applied to the letters of this superscription, in which the Us and Vs had changed places in obedience to the laws of old-world orthography.

To quench the pride of those who believe that the world is growing cleverer day by day, and that modern humbug surpasses everything, it may be observed that these signs, of which the origin seems so whimsical to many Paris merchants, are the dead pictures of once living pictures by which our roguish ancestors contrived to tempt customers into their houses. Thus the Spinning Sow, the Green Monkey, and others, were animals in cages whose skill astonished the passer-by, and whose accomplishments prove the patience of the fifteenth-century artisan. Such curiosities did more to enrich their fortunate owners than the signs of "Providence," "Good-faith," "Grace of God," and "Decapitation of John the Baptist," which may still be seen in the Rue Saint-Denis.

However, our stranger was certainly not standing there to admire the cat, which a minute's attention sufficed to stamp on his memory. The young man himself had his peculiarities. His cloak, folded after the manner of an antique drapery, showed a smart pair of shoes, all the more remarkable in the midst of the Paris mud, because he wore white silk stockings, on which the splashes betrayed his impatience. He had just come, no doubt, from a wedding or a ball; for at this early hour he had in his hand a pair of white gloves, and his black hair, now out of curl, and flowing over his shoulders, showed that it had been dressed *à la Caracalla,* a fashion introduced as much by David's school of painting as by the mania for Greek and Roman styles which characterized the early years of this century.

In spite of the noise made by a few market gardeners, who, being late, rattled past towards the great market-place at a gallop, the busy street lay in a stillness of which the magic charm is known only to those who have wandered through deserted Paris at the hours when its roar, hushed for a moment, rises and spreads in the distance like the great voice of the sea. This strange young man must have seemed as curious to the shopkeeping folk of the "Cat and Racket" as the "Cat and Racket" was to him. A dazzlingly white cravat made his anxious face look even paler than it really was. The fire that flashed in his black eyes, gloomy and sparkling by turns, was in harmony with the singular outline of his features, with his wide, flexible mouth, hardened into a smile. His forehead, knit with violent annoyance, had a stamp of doom. Is not the forehead the most prophetic feature of a man? When the stranger's brow expressed passion the furrows formed in it were terrible in their strength and energy; but when he recovered his calmness, so easily upset, it beamed with a luminous grace which gave great attractiveness to a countenance in which joy, grief, love, anger, or scorn blazed out so contagiously that the coldest man could not fail to be impressed.

He was so thoroughly vexed by the time when the dormer-window of the loft was suddenly flung open, that he did not observe the apparition of three laughing faces, pink and white and chubby, but as vulgar as the face of Commerce as it is seen in sculpture on certain monuments. These three faces, framed by the window, recalled the puffy cherubs floating among the clouds that surround God the Father. The apprentices snuffed up the exhalations of the street with an eagerness that showed how hot and poisonous the atmosphere of their garret must be. After pointing to the singular sentinel, the most jovial, as he seemed, of the apprentices retired and came back holding an instrument whose hard metal pipe is now superseded by a leather tube; and they all grinned with mischief as they looked down on the loiterer, and sprinkled him with a fine white shower of which the scent proved that three chins had just been shaved. Standing on tiptoe, in the farthest corner of their loft, to enjoy their victim's rage, the lads ceased laughing on seeing the haughty indifference with which the young man shook his cloak, and the intense contempt expressed by his face as he glanced up at the empty window-frame.

At this moment a slender white hand threw up the lower half of one of the clumsy windows on the third floor by the aid of the sash runners, of which the pulley so often suddenly gives way and releases the heavy panes it ought to hold up. The watcher was then rewarded for his long waiting. The face of a young girl appeared, as fresh as one of the white cups that bloom on the bosom of the waters, crowned by a frill of tumbled muslin, which gave her head a look of exquisite innocence. Though wrapped in brown stuff, her neck and shoulders gleamed here and there through little openings left by her movements in sleep. No expression of embarrassment detracted from the candour of her face, or the calm look of eyes immortalised long since in the sublime works of Raphael; here were the same grace, the same repose as in these Virgins, and now proverbial. There was a delightful contrast between the cheeks of that face on which sleep had, as it were, given high relief to a superabundance of life, and the antiquity of the heavy window with its clumsy shape and black sill. Like those day-blowing flowers, which in the early morning have not yet unfurled their cups, twisted by the chills of night, the girl, as yet hardly awake, let her blue eyes wander beyond the neighbouring roofs to look at the sky; then, from habit, she cast them down on the gloomy depths of the street, where they immediately met those of her adorer. Vanity, no doubt, distressed her at being seen in undress; she started back, the worn pulley gave way, and the sash fell with the rapid run, which in our day has earned for this artless invention of our forefathers an odious name.[1] The vision had disappeared. To the young man the most radiant star of morning seemed to be hidden by a cloud.

During these little incidents the heavy inside shutters that protected the slight windows of the shop of the "Cat and Racket" had been removed as if by magic. The old door with its knocker was opened back against the wall of the entry by a man-servant, apparently coeval with the sign, who, with a shaking hand, hung upon it a square of cloth, on which were embroidered in yellow silk the words: "Guillaume, successor to Chevrel." Many a passer-by would have found it difficult to guess the class of trade carried on by Monsieur Guillaume. Between the strong iron bars which protected his shop windows on the outside, certain

AT THE SIGN OF THE CAT AND RACKET

packages, wrapped in brown linen, were hardly visible, though as numerous as herrings swimming in a shoal. Notwithstanding the primitive aspect of the Gothic front, Monsieur Guillaume, of all the merchant clothiers in Paris, was the one whose stores were always the best provided, whose connections were the most extensive, and whose commercial honesty never lay under the slightest suspicion. If some of his brethren in business made a contract with the Government, and had not the required quantity of cloth, he was always ready to deliver it, however large the number of pieces tendered for. The wily dealer knew a thousand ways of extracting the largest profits without being obliged, like them, to court patrons, cringing to them, or making them costly presents. When his fellow-tradesmen could only pay in good bills of long date, he would mention his notary as an accommodating man, and managed to get a second profit out of the bargain, thanks to this arrangement, which had made it a proverb among the traders of the Rue Saint-Denis: "Heaven preserve you from Monsieur Guillaume's notary!" to signify a heavy discount.

The old merchant was to be seen standing on the threshold of his shop, as if by a miracle, the instant the servant withdrew. Monsieur Guillaume looked at the Rue Saint-Denis, at the neighboring shops, and at the weather, like a man disembarking at Havre, and seeing France once more after a long voyage. Having convinced himself that nothing had changed while he was asleep, he presently perceived the stranger on guard, and he, on his part, gazed at the patriarchal draper as Humboldt may have scrutinized the first electric eel he saw in America. Monsieur Guillaume wore loose black velvet breeches, pepper-and-salt stockings, and square-toed shoes with silver buckles. His coat, with square-cut fronts, square-cut tails, and square-cut collar, clothed his slightly bent figure in greenish cloth, finished with white metal buttons, tawny from wear. His grey hair was so accurately combed and flattened over his yellow pate that it made it look like a furrowed field. His little green eyes, that might have been pierced with a gimlet, flashed beneath arches faintly tinged with red in the place of eyebrows. Anxieties had wrinkled his forehead with as many horizontal lines as there were creases in his coat. This colourless face expressed patience, commercial shrewdness, and the sort of wily cupidity which is needful in business. At that time these old families were less rare than they are now, in which the characteristic habits and costume of their calling, surviving in the midst of more recent civilization, were preserved as cherished traditions, like the antediluvian remains found by Cuvier in the quarries.

The head of the Guillaume family was a notable upholder of ancient practices; he might be heard to regret the Provost of Merchants, and never did he mention a decision of the Tribunal of Commerce without calling it the *Sentence of the Consuls*. Up and dressed the first of the household, in obedience, no doubt, to these old customs, he stood sternly awaiting the appearance of his three assistants, ready to scold them in case they were late. These young disciples of Mercury knew nothing more terrible than the wordless assiduity with which the master scrutinized their faces and their movements on Monday in search of evidence or traces of their pranks. But at this moment the old clothier paid no heed to his apprentices; he was absorbed in trying to divine the motive of the anxious looks which the young man in silk stockings and a cloak cast alternately at his signboard and into the depths of his shop. The daylight was now brighter, and enabled the stranger to discern the cashier's corner enclosed by a railing and screened by old green silk curtains, where were kept the immense ledgers, the silent oracles of the house. The too inquisitive gazer seemed to covet this little nook, and to be taking the plan of a dining-room at one side, lighted by a skylight, whence the family at meals could easily see the smallest incident that might occur at the shop-door. So much affection for his dwelling seemed suspicious to a trader who had lived long enough to remember the law of maximum prices; Monsieur Guillaume naturally thought that this sinister personage had an eye to the till of the Cat and Racket. After quietly observing the mute duel which was going on between his master and the stranger, the eldest of the apprentices, having seen that the young man was stealthily watching the windows of the third floor, ventured to place himself on the stone flag where Monsieur Guillaume was standing. He took two steps out into the street, raised his head, and fancied that he caught sight of Mademoiselle Augustine Guillaume in hasty retreat. The draper, annoyed by his assistant's perspicacity, shot a side glance at him; but the draper and his amorous apprentice were suddenly relieved from the fears which the young man's presence had excited in their minds. He hailed a hackney cab on its way to a neighboring stand, and jumped into it with an air of affected indifference. This departure was a balm to the hearts of the other two lads, who had been somewhat uneasy as to meeting the victim of their practical joke.

"Well, gentlemen, what ails you that you are standing there with your arms folded?" said Monsieur Guillaume to his three neophytes. "In former days, bless you, when I was in Master Chevrel's service, I should have overhauled more than two pieces of cloth by this time."

"Then it was daylight earlier," said the second assistant, whose duty this was.

The old shopkeeper could not help smiling. Though two of these young fellows, who were confided to his care by their fathers, rich manufacturers at

Louviers and at Sedan, had only to ask and to have a hundred thousand francs the day when they were old enough to settle in life, Guillaume regarded it as his duty to keep them under the rod of an old-world despotism, unknown nowadays in the showy modern shops, where the apprentices expect to be rich men at thirty. He made them work like negroes. These three assistants were equal to a business which would harry ten such clerks as those whose sybaritical tastes now swell the columns of the budget. Not a sound disturbed the peace of this solemn house, where the hinges were always oiled, and where the meanest article of furniture showed the respectable cleanliness which reveals strict order and economy. The most waggish of the three youths often amused himself by writing the date of its first appearance on the Gruyère cheese which was left to their tender mercies at breakfast, and which it was their pleasure to leave untouched. This bit of mischief, and few others of the same stamp, would sometimes bring a smile on the face of the younger of Guillaume's daughters, the pretty maiden who has just now appeared to the bewitched man in the street.

Though each of the apprentices, even the eldest, paid a round sum for his board, not one of them would have been bold enough to remain at the master's table when dessert was served. When Madame Guillaume talked of dressing the salad, the hapless youths trembled as they thought of the thrift with which her prudent hand dispensed the oil. They could never think of spending a night away from the house without having given, long before, a plausible reason for such an irregularity. Every Sunday, each in his turn, two of them accompanied the Guillaume family to mass at Saint-Leu, and to vespers. Mesdemoiselles Virginie and Augustine, simply attired in cotton print, each took the arm of an apprentice and walked in front, under the piercing eye of their mother, who closed the little family procession with her husband, accustomed by her to carry two large prayer-books, bound in black morocco. The second apprentice received no salary. As for the eldest; whose twelve years of perseverance and discretion had initiated him into the secrets of the house, he was paid eight hundred francs a year as the reward of his labors. On certain family festivals he received as a gratuity some little gift, to which Madame Guillaume's dry and wrinkled hand alone gave value-—netted purses, which she took care to stuff with cotton wool, to show off the fancy stitches, braces of the strongest make, or heavy silk stockings. Sometimes, but rarely, this prime minister was admitted to share the pleasures of the family when they went into the country, or when, after waiting for months, they made up their mind to exert the right acquired by taking a box at the theatre to command a piece which Paris had already forgotten.

As to the other assistants, the barrier of respect which formerly divided a master draper from his apprentices was so firmly established between them and the old shopkeeper, that they would have been more likely to steal a piece of cloth than to infringe this time-honored etiquette. Such reserve may now appear ridiculous; but these old houses were a school of honesty and sound morals. The masters adopted their apprentices. The young man's linen was cared for, mended, and often replaced by the mistress of the house. If an apprentice fell ill, he was the object of truly maternal attention. In a case of danger the master lavished his money in calling in the most celebrated physicians, for he was not answerable to their parents merely for the good conduct and training of the lads. If one of them, whose character was unimpeachable, suffered misfortune, these old tradesmen knew how to value the intelligence he had displayed, and they did not hesitate to entrust the happiness of their daughters to men whom they had long trusted with their fortunes. Guillaume was one of these men of the old school, and if he had their ridiculous side, he had all their good qualities; and Joseph Lebas, the chief assistant, an orphan without any fortune, was in his mind destined to be the husband of Virginie, his elder daughter. But Joseph did not share the symmetrical ideas of his master, who would not for an empire have given his second daughter in marriage before the elder. The unhappy assistant felt that his heart was wholly given to Mademoiselle Augustine, the younger. In order to justify this passion, which had grown up in secret, it is necessary to inquire a little further into the springs of the absolute government which ruled the old cloth-merchant's household.

Guillaume had two daughters. The elder, Mademoiselle Virginie, was the very image of her mother. Madame Guillaume, daughter of the Sieur Chevrel, sat so upright in the stool behind her desk, that more than once she had heard some wag bet that she was a stuffed figure. Her long, thin face betrayed exaggerated piety. Devoid of attractions or of amiable manners, Madame Guillaume commonly decorated her head—that of a woman near on sixty—with a cap of a particular and unvarying shape, with long lappets, like that of a widow. In all the neighborhood she was known as the "portress nun." Her speech was curt, and her movements had the stiff precision of a semaphore. Her eye, with a gleam in it like a cat's, seemed to spite the world because she was so ugly. Mademoiselle Virginie, brought up, like her younger sister, under the domestic rule of her mother, had reached the age of eight-and-twenty. Youth mitigated the graceless effect which her likeness to her mother sometimes gave to her features, but maternal austerity had endowed her with two great qualities which made up for everything. She was patient and gentle. Mademoiselle Augustine, who was but just eighteen, was not like either her father or her mother. She was one of those daughters whose total absence of any physical affinity with their parents makes one believe in the adage: "God gives children." Augustine was little, or, to describe her more truly, delicately made. Full of gracious candour, a man of the world could have found no fault in the charming girl beyond a certain meanness of gesture or vulgarity of attitude, and sometimes a want of ease. Her silent and placid face was full of the transient melancholy which comes over all young girls who are too weak to dare to resist their mother's will.

The two sisters, always plainly dressed, could not gratify the innate vanity of womanhood but by a luxury of cleanliness which became them wonderfully, and made them harmonize with the polished counters and the shining shelves on which the old man-servant never left a speck of dust, and with the old-world simplicity of all they saw about them. As their style of living compelled them to find the elements of happiness in persistent work, Augustine and Virginie had hitherto always satisfied their mother, who secretly prided herself on the perfect characters of her two daughters. It is easy to imagine the results of the training they had received. Brought up to a commercial life, accustomed to hear nothing but dreary arguments and calculations about trade, having studied nothing but grammar, book-keeping, a little Bible-history, and the history of France in Le Ragois, and never reading any book but those their mother would sanction, their ideas had not acquired much scope. They knew perfectly how to keep house; they were familiar with the prices of things; they understood the difficulty of amassing money; they were economical, and had a great respect for the qualities that make a man of business. Although their father was rich, they were as skilled in darning as in embroidery; their mother often talked of having them taught to cook, so that they might know how to order a dinner and scold a cook with due knowledge. They knew nothing of the pleasures of the world; and, seeing how their parents spent their exemplary lives, they very rarely suffered their eyes to wander beyond the walls of their hereditary home, which to their mother was the whole universe. The meetings to which family anniversaries gave rise filled in the future of earthly joy to them.

When the great drawing-room on the second floor was to be prepared to receive company—Madame Roquin, a Demoiselle Chevrel, fifteen months younger than her cousin, and bedecked with diamonds; young Rabourdin, employed in the Finance Office; Monsieur César Birotteau, the rich perfumer, and his wife, known as Madame César; Monsieur Camusot, the richest silk mercer in the Rue des Bourdonnais, with his father-in-law, Monsieur Cardot, two or three old bankers, and some immaculate ladies—the arrangements, made necessary by the way in which everything was packed away—the plate, the Dresden china, the candlesticks, and the glass—made a variety in the monotonous lives of the three women, who came and went and exerted themselves as nuns would to receive their bishop. Then, in the evening, when all three were tired out with having wiped, rubbed, unpacked, and arranged all the gauds of the festival, as the girls helped their mother to undress, Madame Guillaume would say to them, "Children, we have done nothing to day."

When, on very great occasions, "the portress nun" allowed dancing, restricting the games of boston, whist, and backgammon within the limits of her bedroom, such a concession was accounted as the most unhoped felicity, and made them happier than going to the great balls, to two or three of which Guillaume would take the girls at the time of the Carnival.

And once a year the worthy draper gave an entertainment, when he spared no expense. However rich and fashionable the persons invited might be, they were careful not to be absent; for the most important houses on the exchange had recourse to the immense credit, the fortune, or the time-honored experience of Monsieur Guillaume. Still, the excellent merchant's two daughters did not benefit as much as might be supposed by the lessons the world has to offer to young spirits. At these parties, which were indeed set down in the ledger to the credit of the house, they wore dresses the shabbiness of which made them blush. Their style of dancing was not in any way remarkable, and their mother's surveillance did not allow of their holding any conversation with their partners beyond Yes and No. Also, the law of the old sign of the Cat and Racket commanded that they should be home by eleven o'clock, the hour when balls and fêtes begin to be lively. Thus their pleasures, which seemed to conform very fairly to their father's position, were often made insipid by circumstances which were part of the family habits and principles.

As to their usual life, one remark will sufficiently paint it. Madame Guillaume required her daughters to be dressed very early in the morning, to come down every day at the same hour, and she ordered their employments with monastic regularity. Augustine, however, had been gifted by chance with a spirit lofty enough to feel the emptiness of such a life. Her blue eyes would sometimes be raised as if to pierce the depths of that gloomy staircase and those damp store-rooms. After sounding the profound cloistral silence, she seemed to be listening to remote, inarticulate revelations of the life of passion, which accounts feelings as of higher value than things. And at such moments her cheek would flush, her idle hands would lay the muslin sewing on the polished oak counter, and presently her mother would say in a voice, of which even the softest tones were sour, "Augustine, my treasure, what are you thinking about?" It is possible that two romances discovered by Augustine in the cupboard of a cook Madame Guillaume had lately discharged—*Hippolyte Comte de Douglas* and *Le Comte de Comminges*—may have contributed to develop the ideas of the young girl, who had devoured them in secret, during the long nights of the past winter.

And so Augustine's expression of vague longing, her gentle voice, her jasmine skin, and her blue eyes had lighted in poor Lebas' soul a flame as ardent as it was reverent. From an easily understood caprice, Augustine felt no affection for the orphan; perhaps because she did not know that he loved her. On the other hand, the senior apprentice, with his long legs, his chestnut hair, his big hands and powerful frame, had found a secret admirer in Mademoiselle Virginie, who, in spite of her dower of fifty thousand crowns, had as yet no suitor. Nothing could be more natural than these two passions at cross-purposes, born in the silence of the dingy shop, as violets bloom in the depths of a wood. The mute and constant looks which made the young people's eyes meet by sheer need of change in the midst of persistent work and cloistered peace, was sure, sooner or later, to give rise to feelings of love. The habit of seeing always the same face leads insensibly to our reading there the qualities of the soul, and at last effaces all its defects.

"At the pace at which that man goes, our girls will soon have to go on their knees to a suitor!" said Monsieur Guillaume to himself, as he read the first decree by which Napoleon drew in advance on the conscript classes.

From that day the old merchant, grieved at seeing his eldest daughter fade, remembered how he had married Mademoiselle Chevrel under much the same circumstances as those of Joseph Lebas and Virginie. A good bit of business, to marry off his daughter, and discharge a sacred debt by repaying to an orphan the benefit he had formerly received from his predecessor under similar conditions! Joseph Lebas, who was now three-and-thirty, was aware of the obstacle which a difference of fifteen years placed between Augustine and himself. Being also too clear-sighted not to understand Monsieur Guillaume's purpose, he knew his inexorable principles well enough to feel sure that the second would never marry before the elder. So the hapless assistant, whose heart was as warm as his legs were long and his chest deep, suffered in silence.

This was the state of affairs in the tiny republic which, in the heart of the Rue Saint-Denis, was not unlike a dependency of La Trappe. But to give a full account of events as well as of feelings, it is needful to go back to some months before the scene with which this story opens. At dusk one evening, a young man passing the darkened shop of the Cat and Racket, had paused for a moment to gaze at a picture which might have arrested every painter in the world. The shop was not yet lighted, and was as a dark cave beyond which the dining-room was visible. A hanging lamp shed the yellow light which lends such charm to pictures of the Dutch school. The white linen, the silver, the cut glass, were brilliant accessories, and made more picturesque by strong contrasts of light and shade. The figures of the head of the family and his wife, the faces of the apprentices, and the pure form of Augustine, near whom a fat chubby-checked maid, was standing, composed so strange a group; the heads were so singular, and every face had so candid an expression; it was so easy to read the peace, the silence, the modest way of life in this family, that to an artist accustomed to render nature, there was something hopeless in any attempt to depict this scene, come upon by chance. The stranger was a young painter, who, seven years before, had gained the first prize for painting. He had now just come back from Rome. His soul, full-fed with poetry; his eyes, satiated with Raphael and Michael Angelo, thirsted for real nature after long dwelling in the pompous land where art has everywhere left something grandiose. Right or wrong, this was his personal feeling. His heart, which had long been a prey to the fire of Italian passion, craved one of those modest and meditative maidens whom in Rome he had unfortunately seen only in painting. From the enthusiasm produced in his excited fancy by the living picture before him, he naturally passed to a profound admiration for the principal figure; Augustine seemed to be pensive, and did not eat; by the arrangement of the lamp the light fell full on her face, and her bust seemed to move in a circle of fire, which threw up the shape of her head and illuminated it with almost supernatural effect. The artist involuntarily compared her to an exiled angel dreaming of heaven. An almost unknown emotion, a limpid, seething love flooded his heart. After remaining a minute, overwhelmed by the weight of his ideas, he tore himself from his bliss, went home, ate nothing, and could not sleep.

The next day he went to his studio, and did not come out of it till he had placed on canvas the magic of the scene of which the memory had, in a sense, made him a devotee; his happiness was incomplete till he should possess a faithful portrait of his idol. He went many times past the house of the Cat and Racket; he even ventured in once or twice, under a disguise, to get a closer view of the bewitching creature that Madame Guillaume covered with her wing.

For eight whole months, devoted to his love and to his brush, he was lost to the sight of his most intimate friends, forgetting the world, the theatre, poetry, music, and all his dearest habits. One morning Girodet broke through all the barriers with which artists are familiar, and which they know how to evade, went into his room, and woke him by asking, "What are you going to send to the Salon?" The artist grasped his friend's hand, dragged him off to the studio, uncovered a small easel picture and a portrait. After a long and eager study of the two masterpieces, Girodet threw himself on his comrade's neck and hugged him, without speaking a word. His feelings could only be expressed as he felt them—soul to soul.

"You are in love?" said Girodet.

They both knew that the finest portraits by Titian, Raphael, and Leonardo da Vinci, were the outcome of the enthusiastic sentiments by which, indeed, under various conditions, every masterpiece is engendered. The artist only bent his head in reply.

"How happy are you to be able to be in love, here, after coming back from Italy! But I do not advise you to send such works as these to the Salon," the great painter went on. "You see, these two works will not be appreciated. Such true colouring, such prodigious work, cannot yet be understood; the public is not accustomed to such depths. The pictures we paint, my dear fellow, are mere screens. We should do better to turn rhymes, and translate the antique poets! There is more glory to be looked for there than from our luckless canvases!"

Notwithstanding this charitable advice, the two pictures were exhibited. The *Interior* made a revolution in painting. It gave birth to the pictures of genre which pour into all our exhibitions in such prodigious quantity that they might be supposed to be produced by machinery. As to the portrait, few artists have forgotten that lifelike work; and the public, which as a body is sometimes discerning, awarded it the crown which Girodet himself had hung over it. The two pictures were surrounded by a vast throng. They fought for places, as women say. Speculators and moneyed men would have covered the canvas with double napoleons, but the artist obstinately refused to sell or to make replicas. An enormous sum was offered him for the right of engraving them, and the print-sellers were not more favoured than the amateurs.

Though these incidents occupied the world, they were not of a nature to penetrate the recesses of the monastic solitude in the Rue Saint-Denis. However, when paying a visit to Madame Guillaume, the notary's wife spoke of the exhibition before Augustine, of whom she was very fond, and explained its purpose. Madame Roquin's gossip naturally inspired Augustine with a wish to see the pictures, and with courage enough to ask her cousin secretly to take her to the Louvre. Her cousin succeeded in the negotiations she opened with Madame Guillaume for permission to release the young girl for two hours from her dull labours. Augustine was thus able to make her way through the crowd to see the crowned work. A fit of trembling shook her like an aspen leaf as she recognized herself. She was terrified, and looked about her to find Madame Roquin, from whom she had been separated by a tide of people. At that moment her frightened eyes fell on the impassioned face of the young painter. She at once recalled the figure of a loiterer whom, being curious, she had frequently observed, believing him to be a new neighbour.

"You see how love has inspired me," said the artist in the timid creature's ear, and she stood in dismay at the words.

She found supernatural courage to enable her to push through the crowd and join her cousin, who was still struggling with the mass of people that hindered her from getting to the picture.

"You will be stifled!" cried Augustine. "Let us go." But there are moments, at the Salon, when two women are not always free to direct their steps through the galleries. By the irregular course to which they were compelled by the press, Mademoiselle Guillaume and her cousin were pushed to within a few steps of the second picture. Chance thus brought them, both together, to where they could easily see the canvas made famous by fashion, for once in agreement with talent. Madame Roquin's exclamation of surprise was lost in the hubbub and buzz of the crowd; Augustine involuntarily shed tears at the sight of this wonderful study. Then, by an almost unaccountable impulse, she laid her finger on her lips, as she perceived quite near her the ecstatic face of the young painter. The stranger replied by a nod, and pointed to Madame Roquin, as a spoil-sport, to show Augustine that he had understood. This pantomime struck the young girl like hot coals on her flesh; she felt quite guilty as she perceived that there was a compact between herself and the artist. The suffocating heat, the dazzling sight of beautiful dresses, the bewilderment produced in Augustine's brain by the truth of colouring, the multitude of living or painted figures, the profusion of gilt frames, gave her a sense of intoxication which doubled her alarms. She would perhaps have fainted if an unknown rapture had not surged up in her heart to vivify her whole being, in spite of this chaos of sensations. She nevertheless believed herself to be under the power of the Devil, of whose awful snares she had been warned by the thundering words of preachers. This moment was to her like a moment of madness. She found herself accompanied to her cousin's carriage by the young man, radiant with joy and love. Augustine, a prey to an agitation new to her experience, an intoxication which seemed to abandon her to nature, listened to the eloquent voice of her heart, and looked again and again at the young painter, betraying the emotion that came over her. Never had the bright rose of her cheeks shown in stronger contrast with the whiteness of her skin. The artist saw her beauty in all its bloom, her maiden modesty in all its glory. She herself felt a sort of rapture mingled with terror at thinking that her presence had brought happiness to him whose name was on every lip, and whose talent lent immortality to transient scenes. She was loved! It was impossible to doubt it. When she no longer saw the artist, these simple words still echoed in her ear, "You see how love has inspired me!" And the throbs of her heart, as they grew deeper, seemed a pain, her heated blood revealed so many unknown forces in her being. She affected a severe headache to avoid replying to her cousin's questions concerning the pictures; but on their return Madame Roquin could not forbear from speaking to Madame Guillanme of the fame that had fallen on the house of the Cat and Racket, and Augustine quaked in every limb as she heard her mother say that she should go to the Salon to see her house there. The young girl again declared herself suffering, and obtained leave to go to bed.

"That is what comes of sight-seeing," exclaimed Monsieur Guillaume—"a headache. And is it so very amusing to see in a picture what you can see any day in your own street? Don't talk to me of your artists! Like writers, they are a starveling crew. Why the devil need they choose my house to flout it in their pictures?"

"It may help to sell a few ells more of cloth," said Joseph Lebas.

This remark did not protect art and thought from being condemned once again before the judgment-seat of trade. As may be supposed, these speeches did not infuse much hope into Augustine, who, during the night, gave herself up to the first meditations of love. The events of the day were like a dream, which it was joy to recall to her mind. She was initiated into the fears, the hopes, the remorse, all the ebb and flow of feeling which could not fail to toss a heart so simple and so timid as hers. What a void she perceived in this gloomy house! What a treasure she found in her soul! To be the wife of a genius, to share his glory! What ravages must such a vision make in the heart of a girl brought up among such a family! What hopes must it raise in a young creature who, in the midst of sordid elements, had pined for a life of elegance! A sunbeam had fallen into the prison. Augustine was suddenly in love. So many of her feelings were soothed that she succumbed without reflection. At eighteen does not love hold a prism between the world and the eyes of a young girl? She was incapable of suspecting the hard facts which result from the union of a loving woman with a man of imagination, and she believed herself called to make him happy, not seeing any disparity between herself and him. To her the future would be as the present. When, next day, her father and mother returned from the Salon, their dejected faces proclaimed some disappointment. In the first place, the painter had removed the two pictures; and then Madame Guillaume had lost her cashmere shawl. But the news that the pictures had disappeared from the walls since her visit revealed to Augustine a delicacy of sentiment which a woman can always appreciate, even by instinct.

On the morning when, on his way home from a ball, Théodore de Sommervieux—for this was the name which fame had stamped on Augustine's heart—had been squirted on by the apprentices while awaiting the appearance of his artless little friend, who certainly did not know that he was there, the lovers had seen each other for the fourth time only since their meeting at the Salon. The difficulties which the rule of the house placed in the way of the painter's ardent nature gave added violence to his passion for Augustine.

How could he get near to a young girl seated in a counting-house between two such women as Mademoiselle Virginie and Madame Guillaume? How could he correspond with her when her mother never left her side? Ingenious, as lovers are, to imagine woes, Théodore saw a rival in one of the assistants, to whose interests he supposed the others to be devoted. If he should evade these sons of Argus, he would yet be wrecked under the stern eyes of the old draper or of Madame Guillaume. The very vehemence of his passion hindered the young painter from hitting on the ingenious expedients which, in prisoners and in lovers, seem to be the last effort of intelligence spurred by a wild craving for liberty, or by the fire of love. Théodore wandered about the neighbourhood with the restlessness of a madman, as though movement might inspire him with some device. After racking his imagination, it occurred to him to bribe the blowsy waiting-maid with gold. Thus a few notes were exchanged at long intervals during the fortnight following the ill-starred morning when Monsieur Guillaume and Théodore had so scrutinized one another. At the present moment the young couple had agreed to see each other at a certain hour of the day, and on Sunday, at Saint-Leu, during Mass and vespers. Augustine had sent her dear Théodore a list of the relations and friends of the family, to whom the young painter tried to get access, in the hope of interesting, if it were possible,

in his love affairs, one of these souls absorbed in money and trade
genuine passion must appear a quite monstrous speculation, a thin
Nothing meanwhile, was altered at the sign of the Cat and Racket. If Augustine was absent-minded, if, against all obedience to the domestic code, she stole up to her room to make signals by means of a jar of flowers, if she sighed, if she were lost in thought, no one observed it, not even her mother. This will cause some surprise to those who have entered into the spirit of the household, where an idea tainted with poetry would be in startling contrast to persons and things, where no one could venture on a gesture or a look which would not be seen and analyzed. Nothing, however, could be more natural: the quiet barque that navigated the stormy waters of the Paris Exchange, under the flag of the Cat and Racket, was just now in the toils of one of these tempests which, returning periodically, might be termed equinoctial. For the last fortnight the five men forming the crew, with Madame Guillaume and Mademoiselle Virginie, had been devoting themselves to the hard labour, known as stock-taking.

Every bale was turned over, and the length verified to ascertain the exact value of the remnant. The ticket attached to each parcel was carefully examined to see at what time the piece had been bought. The retail price was fixed. Monsieur Guillaume, always on his feet, his pen behind his ear, was like a captain commanding the working of the ship. His sharp tones, spoken through a trap-door, to inquire into the depths of the hold in the cellar-store, gave utterance to the barbarous formulas of trade-jargon, which find expression only in cipher. "How much H.N.Z.?"—"All sold."—"What is left of Q.X.?"—"Two ells."— "At what price?"—"Fifty-five three."— "Set down A. at three, with all of J.J., all of M.P., and what is left of V.D.O."—A hundred other injunctions equally intelligible were spouted over the counters like verses of modern poetry, quoted by romantic spirits, to excite each other's enthusiasm for one of their poets. In the evening Guillaume, shut up with his assistant and his wife, balanced his accounts, carried on the balance, wrote to debtors in arrears, and made out bills. All three were busy over this enormous labour, of which the result could be stated on a sheet of foolscap, proving to the head of the house that there was so much to the good in hard cash, so much in goods, so much in bills and notes; that he did not owe a sou; that a hundred or two hundred thousand francs were owing to him; that the capital had been increased; that the farmlands, the houses, or the investments were extended, or repaired, or doubled. Whence it became necessary to begin again with increased ardor, to accumulate more crown-pieces, without its ever entering the brain of these laborious ants to ask—"To what end?"

Favoured by this annual turmoil, the happy Augustine escaped the investigations of her Argus-eyed relations. At last, one Saturday evening, the stock-taking was finished. The figures of the sum-total showed a row of 0's long enough to allow Guillaume for once to relax the stern rule as to dessert which reigned throughout the year. The shrewd old draper rubbed his hands, and allowed his assistants to remain at table. The members of the crew had hardly swallowed their thimbleful of some home-made liqueur, when the rumble of a carriage was heard. The family party were going to see *Cendrillon* at the Variétés, while the two younger apprentices each received a crown of six francs, with permission to go wherever they chose, provided they were in by midnight.

Notwithstanding this debauch, the old cloth-merchant was shaving himself at six next morning, put on his maroon-colored coat, of which the glowing lights afforded him perennial enjoyment, fastened a pair of gold buckles on the knee-straps of his ample satin breeches; and then, at about seven o'clock, while all were still sleeping in the house, he made his way to the little office adjoining the shop on the first floor. Daylight came in through a window, fortified by iron bars, and looking out on a small yard surrounded by such black walls that it was very like a well. The old merchant opened the iron-lined shutters, which were so familiar to him, and threw up the lower half of the sash window. The icy air of the courtyard came in to cool the hot atmosphere of the little room, fall of the odour peculiar to offices.

The merchant remained standing, his hand resting on the greasy arm of a large cane chair lined with morocco, of which the original hue had disappeared; he seemed to hesitate as to seating himself. He looked with affection at the double desk, where his wife's seat, opposite his own, was fitted into a little niche in the wall. He contemplated the numbered boxes, the files, the implements, the cash box—objects all of immemorial origin, and fancied himself in the room with the shade of Master Chevrel. He even pulled out the high stool on which he had once sat in the presence of his departed master. This stool, covered with black leather, the horse-hair showing at every corner—as it had long done, without, however, coming out—he placed with a shaking hand on the very spot where his predecessor had put it, and then, with an emotion difficult to describe, he pulled a bell, which rang at the head of Joseph Lebas' bed. When this decisive blow had been struck, the old man, for whom, no doubt, these reminiscences were too much, took up three or four bills of exchange, and looked at them without seeing them.

Suddenly Joseph Lebas stood before him.

"Sit down there," said Guillaume, pointing to the stool.

As the old master draper had never yet bid his assistant be seated in his presence, Joseph Lebas was startled.

'What do you think of these notes?" asked Guillaume.

"They will never be paid."

"Why?"

"Well, I heard that the day before yesterday Étienne and Co. had made their payments in gold."

"Oh, oh!" said the draper. "Well, one must be very ill to show one's bile. Let us speak of something else.—Joseph, the stock-taking is done."

"Yes, monsieur, and the dividend is one of the best you have ever made."

"Do not use new-fangled words. Say the profits, Joseph. Do you know, my boy, that this result is partly owing to you? And I do not intend to pay you a salary any longer. Madame Guillaume has suggested to me to take you into partnership.—'Guilaume and Lebas;' will not that make a good business name? We might add, 'and Co.' to round off the firm's signature."

Tears rose to the eyes of Joseph Lebas, who tried to hide them.

"Oh, Monsieur Guillanme, how have I deserved such kindness? I only do my duty. It was so much already that you should take an interest in a poor orph—"

He was brushing the cuff of his left sleeve with his right hand, and dared not look at the old man, who smiled as he thought that this modest young fellow no doubt needed, as he had needed once on a time, some encouragement to complete his explanation.

"To be sure," said Virginie's father, "you do not altogether deserve this favour, Joseph. You have not so much confidence in me as I have in you. (The young man looked up quickly.) You knew all the secrets of the cash-box. For the last two years I have told you of almost all my concerns. I have sent you to travel in our goods. In short, I have nothing on any conscience as regards you. But you—you have a soft place, and you have never breathed a word of it." Joseph Lebas blushed. "Ah, ha!" cried Guillaume, "so you thought you could deceive an old fox like me? When you knew that I had scented the Lecocq bankruptcy?"

"What, monsieur?" replied Joseph Lebas, looking at his master as keenly as his master looked at him, "you knew that I was in love?"

"I know everything, you rascal," said the worthy and cunning old merchant, pulling the assistant's ear. "And I forgive you—I did the same myself."

"And you will give her to me?"

"Yes—with fifty thousand crowns; and I will leave you as much by will, and we will start on our new career under the name of a new firm. We will do good business yet, my boy!" added the old man, getting up and flourishing his arms. "I tell you, son-in-law, there is nothing like trade. Those who ask what pleasure is to be found in it are simpletons. To be on the scent of a good bargain, to hold your own on 'Change, to watch as anxiously as at the gaming-table whether Étienne and Co. will fail or no, to see a regiment of Guards march past all dressed in your cloth, to trip your neighbour up—honestly of course!—to make the goods cheaper than others can; then to carry out an undertaking which you have planned, which begins, grows, totters, and succeeds! to know the workings of every house of business as well as a minister of police, so as never to make a mistake; to hold up your head in the midst of wrecks, to have friends by correspondence in every manufacturing town; is not that a perpetual game, Joseph? That is life, that is! I shall die in that harness, like old Chevrel, but taking it easy now, all the same."

In the heat of his eager rhetoric, old Guillaume had scarcely looked at his assistant, who was weeping copiously. "Why, Joseph, my poor boy, what is the matter?"

"Oh, I love her so! Monsieur Guillaume, that my heart fails me; I believe—"

"Well, well, boy," said the old man, touched, "you are happier than you know, by Gad! For she loves you. I know it."

And he blinked his little green eyes as he looked at the young man.

"Mademoiselle Augustine! Mademoiselle Augustine!" exclaimed Joseph Lebas in his rapture.

He was about to rush out of the room when he felt himself clutched by a hand of iron, and his astonished master spun him round in front of him once more.

"What has Augustine to do with this matter?" he asked, in a voice which instantly froze the luckless Joseph.

"Is it not she that—that,—I love?" stammered the assistant.

Much put out by his own want of perspicacity, Guillaume sat down again, and rested his long head in his bands to consider the perplexing situation in which he found himself. Joseph Lebas, shamefaced and in despair, remained standing.

"Joseph," the draper said with frigid dignity, "I was speaking of Virginie. Love cannot be made to order, I know. I know, too, that you can be trusted. We will forget all this. I will not let Augustine marry before Virginie.—Your interest will be ten per cent."

The young man, to whom love gave I know not what power of courage and eloquence, clasped his hand, and spoke in his turn—spoke for a quarter of an hour, with so much warmth and feeling, that he altered the situation. If the question had been a matter of business, the old tradesman would have had fixed principles to guide his decision; but, tossed a thousand miles from commerce, on the ocean of sentiment, without a compass, he floated, as he told himself, undecided in the face of such an unexpected event. Carried away by his fatherly kindness, he began to beat about the bush.

"Deuce take it, Joseph, you must know that there are ten years between my two children. Mademoiselle Chevrel was no beauty, still she has had nothing to complain of in me. Do as I did. Come, come, don't cry. Can you be so silly? What is to be done? It can be managed perhaps. There is always some way out of a scrape. And we men are not always devoted Celadons to our wives—you understand? Madame Guillaume is very pious . . . Come. By Gad, boy, give your arm to Augustine this morning as we go to Mass."

These were the phrases spoken at random by the old draper, and their conclusion made the lover happy. He was already thinking of a friend of his as a match for Mademoiselle Virginie, as he went out of the smoky office, pressing his future father-in-law's hand, after saying with a knowing look that all would turn out for the best.

"What will Madame Guillaume say to it?" was the idea that greatly troubled the worthy merchant when he found himself alone.

At breakfast Madame Guillaume and Virginie, to whom the draper had not as yet confided his disappointment, cast meaning glances at Joseph Lebas, who was extremely embarrassed. The young assistant's bashfulness commended him to his mother-in-law's good graces. The matron became so cheerful that she smiled as she looked at her husband, and allowed herself some little pleasantries of time-honored acceptance in such simple families. She wondered whether Joseph or Virginie were the taller, to ask them to compare their height. This preliminary fooling brought a cloud to the master's brow, and he even made such a point of decorum that he desired Augustine to take the assistant's arm on their way to Saint-Leu. Madame Guillaume, surprised at this manly delicacy, honored her husband with a nod of approval. So the procession left the house in such order as to suggest no suspicious meaning to the neighbors.

"Does it not seem to you, Mademoiselle Augustine," said the assistant, and he trembled, "that the wife of a merchant whose credit is as good as Monsieur Guillaume's, for instance, might enjoy herself a little more than Madame your mother does? Might wear diamonds—or keep a carriage? For my part, if I were to marry, I should be glad to take all the work, and see my wife happy. I would not put her into the counting-house. In the drapery business, you see, a woman is not so necessary now as formerly. Monsieur Guillaume was quite right to act as he did—and besides, his wife liked it. But so long as a woman knows how to turn her hand to the book-keeping, the correspondence, the retail business, the orders, and her housekeeping, so as not to sit idle, that is enough. At seven o'clock, when the shop is shut, I shall take my pleasures, go to the play, and into company.—But you are not listening to me."

"Yes, indeed, Monsieur Joseph. What do you think of painting? That is a fine calling."

"Yes. I know a master house-painter, Monsieur Lourdois. He is well-to-do."

Thus conversing, the family reached the Church of Saint-Leu. There Madame reasserted her rights, and, for the first time, placed Augustine next herself, Virginie taking her place on the fourth chair, next to Lebas. During the sermon all went well between Augustine and Théodore, who, standing behind a pillar, worshiped his Madonna with fervent devotion; but at the elevation of the Host, Madame Guillaume discovered, rather late, that her daughter Augustine was holding her prayer-book upside down. She was about to speak to her strongly, when, lowering her veil, she interrupted her own devotions to look in the direction where her daughter's eyes found attraction. By the help of her spectacles she saw the young artist, whose fashionable elegance seemed to proclaim him a cavalry officer on leave rather than a tradesman of the neighborhood. It is difficult to conceive of the state of violent agitation in which Madame Guillaume found herself—she, who flattered herself on having brought up her daughters to perfection on discovering in Augustine a clandestine passion of which her prudery and ignorance exaggerated the perils. She believed her daughter to be cankered to the core.

"Hold your book right way up, miss," she muttered in a low voice, tremulous with wrath. She snatched away the tell-tale prayer-book and returned it with the letter-press right way up. "Do not allow your eyes to look anywhere but at your prayers," she added, "or I shall have something to say to you. Your father and I will talk to you after church."

These words came like a thunderbolt on poor Augustine. She felt faint; but, torn between the distress she felt and the dread of causing a commotion in church, she bravely concealed her anguish. It was, however, easy to discern the stormy state of her soul from the trembling of her prayer-book, and the tears which dropped on every page she turned. From the furious glare shot at him by Madame Guillaume the artist saw the peril into which his love affair had fallen; he went out, with a raging soul, determined to venture all.

"Go to your room, miss!" said Madame Guillaume, on their return home; "we will send for you, but take care not to quit it."

The conference between the husband and wife was conducted so secretly that at first nothing was heard of it. Virginie, however, who had tried to give her sister courage by a variety of gentle remonstrances, carried her good nature so far as to listen at the door of her mother's bedroom where the discussion was held, to catch a word or two. The first time she went down to the lower floor she heard her father exclaim, "Then, madame, do you wish to kill your daughter?"

"My poor dear!" said Virginie, in tears, "papa takes your part."

"And what do they want to do to Théodore?" asked the innocent girl.

Virginie, inquisitive, went down again; but this time she stayed longer; she learned that Joseph Lebas loved Augustine. It was written that on this memorable day, this house, generally so peaceful, should be a hell. Monsieur Guillaume brought Joseph Lebas to despair by telling him of Augustine's love for a stranger. Lebas, who had advised his friend to become a suitor for Mademoiselle Virginie, saw all his hopes wrecked. Mademoiselle Virginie, overcome by hearing that Joseph had, in a way, refused her, had a sick headache. The dispute that had arisen from the discussion between Monsieur and Madame Guillaume, when, for the third time in their lives, they had been of antagonistic opinions, had shown itself in a terrible form. Finally, at half-past four in the afternoon, Augustine, pale, trembling, and with red eyes, was haled before her father and mother. The poor child artlessly related the too brief tale of her love. Reassured by a speech from her father, who promised to listen to her in silence, she gathered courage as she pronounced to her parents the name of Théodore de Sommervieux, with a mischievous little emphasis on the aristocratic *de*. And yielding to the unknown charm of talking of her feelings, she was brave enough to declare with innocent decision that she loved Monsieur de Sommervieux, that she had written to him, and she added, with tears in her eyes: "To sacrifice me to another man would make me wretched."

"But, Augustine, you cannot surely know what a painter is?" cried her mother with horror.

"Madame Guillaume!" said the old man, compelling her to silence.— "Augustine," he went on, "artists are generally little better than beggars. They are too extravagant not to be always a bad sort. I served the late Monsieur

Joseph Vernet, the late Monsieur Lekain, and the late Monsieur Noverre. Oh, if you could only know the tricks played on poor Father Chevrel by that Monsieur Noverre, by the Chevalier de Saint-Georges, and especially by Monsieur Philidor! They are a set of rascals; I know them well! They all have a gab and nice manners. Ah, your Monsieur Sumer—, Somm——"

"De Sommervieux, papa."

"Well, well, de Sommervieux, well and good. He can never have been half so sweet to you as Monsieur le Chevalier de Saint-Georges was to me the day I got a verdict of the consuls against him. And in those days they were gentlemen of quality."

"But, father, Monsieur Théodore is of good family, and he wrote me that he is rich; his father was called Chevalier de Sommervieux before the Revolution."

At these words Monsieur Guillaume looked at his terrible better half, who, like an angry woman, sat tapping the floor with her foot while keeping sullen silence; she avoided even casting wrathful looks at Augustine, appearing to leave to Monsieur Guillaume the whole responsibility in so grave a matter, since her opinion was not listened to. Nevertheless, in spite of her apparent self-control, when she saw her husband giving way so mildly under a catastrophe which had no concern with business, she exclaimed:

"Really, monsieur, you are so weak with your daughters! However—"

The sound of a carriage, which stopped at the door, interrupted the rating which the old draper already quaked at. In a minute Madame Roquin was standing in the middle of the room, and looking at the actors in this domestic scene: "I know all, my dear cousin," said she, with a patronizing air.

Madame Roquin made the great mistake of supposing that a Paris notary's wife could play the part of a favourite of fashion.

"I know all," she repeated, "and I have come into Noah's Ark, like the dove, with the olive-branch. I read that allegory in the *Génie du Christianisme*," she added, turning to Madame Guillaume; "the allusion ought to please you, cousin. Do you know," she went on, smiling at Augustine, "that Monsieur de Sommervieux is a charming man? He gave me my portrait this morning, painted by a master's hand. It is worth at least six thousand francs." And at these words she patted Monsieur Guillaume on the arm. The old draper could not help making a grimace with his lips, which was peculiar to him.

"I know Monsieur de Sommervieux very well," the Dove ran on. "He has come to my evenings this fortnight past, and made them delightful. He has told me all his woes, and commissioned me to plead for him. I know since this morning that he adores Augustine, and he shall have her. Ah, cousin, do not shake your head in refusal. He will be created Baron, I can tell you, and has just been made Chevalier of the Legion of Honour, by the Emperor himself, at the Salon. Roquin is now his lawyer, and knows all his affairs. Well! Monsieur de Sommervieux has twelve thousand francs a year in good landed estate. Do you know that the father-in-law of such a man may get a rise in life—be mayor of his *arrondissement,* for instance. Have we not seen Monsieur Dupont become a Count of the Empire, and a senator, all because he went as mayor to congratulate the Emperor on his entry into Vienna? Oh, this marriage must take place! For my part, I adore the dear young man. His behaviour to Augustine is only met with in romances. Be easy, little one, you shall be happy, and every girl will wish she were in your place. Madame la Duchesse de Carigliano, who comes to my 'At Homes,' raves about Monsieur de Sommervieux. Some spiteful people say she only comes to me to meet him; as if a Duchess of yesterday was doing too much honour to a Chevrel, whose family have been respected citizens these hundred years!

"Augustine," Madame Roquin went on, after a short pause, "I have seen the portrait. Heavens! How lovely it is! Do you know that the Emperor wanted to have it? He laughed, and said to the Deputy High Constable that if there were many women like that at his court while all the kings visited it, he should have no difficulty about preserving the peace of Europe. Is not that a compliment?"

The tempests with which the day had begun were to resemble those of nature, by ending in clear and serene weather. Madame Roquin displayed so much address in her harangue, she was able to touch so many strings in the dry hearts of Monsieur and Guillaume, that at last she hit on one which she could work upon. At this strange period commerce and finance were more than ever possessed by the crazy mania for seeking alliance with rank; and the generals of the Empire took full advantage of this desire. Monsieur Guillaume, as a singular exception, opposed this deplorable craving. His favorite axioms were that, to secure happiness, a woman must marry a man of her own class; that every one was punished sooner or later for having climbed too high; that love could so little endure under the worries of a household, that both husband and wife needed sound good qualities to be happy; that it would not do for one to be far in advance of the other, because, above everything, they must understand each other; if a man spoke Greek and his wife Latin, they might come to die of hunger. He had himself invented this sort of adage. And he compared such marriages to old-fashioned materials of mixed silk and wool, in which the silk always at last wore through the wool. Still, there is so much vanity at the bottom of man's heart that the prudence of the pilot who steered the Cat and Racket so wisely gave way before Madame Roquin's aggressive volubility. Austere Madame Guillaume was the first to see in her daughter's affection a reason for abdicating her principles and for consenting to receive Monsieur de Sommervieux, whom she promised herself she would put under severe inquisition.

The old draper went to look for Joseph Lebas, and inform him of the state of affairs. At half-past six, the dining-room immortalised by the artist saw, united under its skylight, Monsieur and Madame Roquin, the young painter and his charming Augustine, Joseph Lebas, who found his happiness in patience, and Mademoiselle Virginie, convalescent from her headache. Monsieur and Madame Guillaume saw in perspective both their children married, and the fortunes of the Cat and Racket once more in skilful hands. Their satisfaction was at its height when, at dessert, Théodore made them a present of the wonderful picture which they had failed to see, representing the interior of the old shop, and to which they all owed so much happiness.

"Isn't it pretty!" cried Guillaume. "And to think that any one would pay thirty thousand francs for that!"

"Because you can see my lappets in it," said Madame Guillaume.

"And the cloth unrolled!" added Lebas; "you might take it up in your hand."

"Drapery always comes out well," replied the painter. "We should be only too happy, we modern artists, if we could touch the perfection of antique drapery."

"So you like drapery!" cried old Guillaume. "Well, then, by Gad! shake hands on that, my young friend. Since you can respect trade, we shall understand each other. And why should it be despised? The world began with trade, since Adam sold Paradise for an apple. He did not strike a good bargain though!" And the old man roared with honest laughter, encouraged by the champagne, which he sent round with a liberal hand. The band that covered the young artist's eyes was so thick that he thought his future parents amiable. He was not above enlivening them by a few jests in the best taste. So he too pleased every one. In the evening, when the drawing-room, furnished with what Madame Guillaume called "everything handsome," was deserted, and while she flitted from the table to the chimney-piece, from the candelabra to the tall candlesticks, hastily blowing out the wax-lights, the worthy draper, who was always clear-sighted when money was in question, called Augustine to him, and seating her on his knee, spoke as follows:— "My dear child, you shall marry your Sommervieux since you insist; you may, if you like, risk your capital in happiness. But I am not going to be hoodwinked by the thirty thousand francs to be made by spoiling good canvas. Money that is lightly earned is lightly spent. Did I not hear that hare-brained youngster declare this evening that money was made round that it might roll. If it is round for spend-thrifts, it is flat for saving folks who pile it up. Now, my child, that fine gentleman talks of giving you carriages and diamonds! He has money, let him spend it on you; so be it. It is no concern of mine. But as to what I can give you, I will not have the crown-pieces I have picked up with so much toil wasted in carriages and flippery. Those who spend too fast never grow rich. A hundred thousand crowns, which is your fortune, will not buy up Paris. It is all very well to look forward to a few hundred thousand francs to be yours some day; I shall keep you waiting for them as long as possible, by Gad! So I took your lover aside, and a man who managed the Lecocq bankruptcy had not much difficulty in persuading the artist to marry under a settlement of his wife's money on herself. I will keep an eye on the marriage contract to see that what he is to settle on you is safely tied up. So now my child, I hope to be a grandfather, by Gad! I will begin at once to lay up for my grandchildren; but swear to me, here and now, never to sign any papers relating to money without my advice; and if I go soon to join old father Chevrel, promise to consult young Lebas, your brother-in-law?"

"Yes, father, I swear it."

At these words, spoken in a gentle voice, the old man kissed his daughter on both cheeks. That night the lovers slept as soundly as Monsieur and Madame Guillaume.

Some few months after this memorable Sunday the high altar of Saint-Leu was the scene of two very different weddings. Augustine and Théodore appeared in all the radiance of happiness, their eyes beaming with love, dressed with elegance, while a fine carriage waited for them. Virginie, who had come in a good hired fly with the rest of the family, humbly followed her younger sister, dressed in the simplest fashion like a shadow necessary to the harmony of the picture. Monsieur Guillaume had exerted himself to the utmost in the church to get Virginie married before Augustine, but the priests, high and low, persisted in addressing the more elegant of the two brides. He heard some of his neighbours highly approving the good sense of Mademoiselle Virginie who was making, as they said, the more substantial match, and remaining faithful to the neighbourhood; while they fired a few taunts, prompted by envy of Augustine, who was marrying an artist and a man of rank; adding, with a sort of dismay, that if the Guillaumes were ambitious, there was an end to the business. An old fan-maker having remarked that such a prodigal would soon bring his wife to beggary, father Guillaume prided himself *in petto* for his prudence in the matter of marriage settlements. In the evening, after a splendid ball, followed by one of those substantial suppers of which the memory is dying out in the present generation, Monsieur and Madame Guillaume remained in a fine house belonging to them in the Rue du Colombier, where the wedding had been held; Monsieur and Madame Lebas returned in their fly to the old home in the Rue Saint-Denis, to steer the good ship Cat and Racket. The artist, intoxicated with happiness, carried off his beloved Augustine, and eagerly lifting her out of their carriage when it reached the Rue des Trois-Frères, led her to an apartment embellished by all the arts.

The fever of passion which possessed Théodore made a year fly over the young couple without a single cloud to dim the blue sky under which they lived. Life did not hang heavy on the lovers' hands. Théodore lavished on every day inexhaustible *fioriture* of enjoyment, and he delighted to vary the transports of passion by the soft languor of those hours of repose when souls soar so high that they seem to have for gotten all bodily union. Augustine was too happy for reflection; she floated on an undulating tide of rapture; she thought she could not do enough by abandoning herself to sanctioned and sacred married love; simple and artless, she had no coquetry, no reserves, none of the dominion which a worldly-minded girl acquires over her husband by ingenious caprice; she loved too well to calculate for the future, and never imagined that so exquisite a life could come to an end. Happy in being her husband's sole delight, she believed that her inextinguishable love would always be her greatest grace in his eyes, as her devotion and obedience would be a perennial charm. And, indeed, the ecstasy of love had made her so brilliantly lovely that her beauty filled her with pride, and gave her confidence that she could always reign over a man so easy to kindle as Monsieur de Sommervieux. Thus her position as a wife brought her no knowledge but the lessons of love.

In the midst of her happiness, she was still the simple child who had lived in obscurity in the Rue Saint-Denis, and she never thought of acquiring the manners, the information, the tone of the world she had to live in. Her words being the words of love, she revealed in them, no doubt, a certain pliancy of mind and a certain refinement of speech; but she used the language common to all women when they find themselves plunged in passion, which seems to be their element. When, by chance, Augustine expressed an idea that did not harmonise with Théodore's, the young artist laughed, as we laugh at the first mistakes of a foreigner, though they end by annoying us if they are not corrected.

In spite of all this love-making, by the end of this year, as delightful as it was swift, Sommervieux felt one morning the need for resuming his work and his old habits. His wife was expecting their first child. He saw some friends again. During the tedious discomforts of the year when a young wife is nursing an infant for the first time, he worked, no doubt, with zeal, but he occasionally sought diversion in the fashionable world. The house which he was best pleased to frequent was that of the Duchesse de Carigliano, who had at last attracted the celebrated artist to her parties. When Augustine was quite well again, and her boy no longer required the assiduous care which debars a mother from social pleasures, Théodore had come to the stage of wishing to know the joys of satisfied vanity to be found in society by a man who shows himself with a handsome woman, the object of envy and admiration.

To figure in drawing-rooms with the reflected lustre of her husband's fame, and to find other women envious of her, was to Augustine a new harvest of pleasures; but it was the last gleam of conjugal happiness. She first wounded her husband's vanity when, in spite of vain efforts, she betrayed her ignorance, the inelegance of her language, and the narrowness of her ideas. Sommervieux's nature, subjugated for nearly two years and a half by the first transports of love, now, in the calm of less new possession, recovered its bent and habits, for a while diverted from their channel. Poetry, painting, and the subtle joys of imagination have inalienable rights over a lofty spirit. These cravings of a powerful soul had not been starved in Théodore during these two years; they had only found fresh pasture. As soon as the meadows of love had been ransacked, and the artist had gathered roses and cornflowers as the children do, so greedily that he did not see that his hands could hold no more, the scene changed. When the painter showed his wife the sketches for his finest compositions he heard her exclaim, as her father had done, "How pretty!" This tepid admiration was not the outcome of conscientious feeling, but of her faith on the strength of love.

Augustine cared more for a look than for the finest picture. The only sublime she know was that of the heart. At last Théodore could not resist the evidence of the cruel fact— his wife was insensible to poetry, she did not dwell in his sphere, she could not follow him in all his vagaries, his inventions, his joys and his sorrows; she walked groveling in the world of reality, while his head was in the skies. Common minds cannot appreciate the perennial sufferings of a being who, while bound to another by the most intimate affections, is obliged constantly to suppress the dearest flights of his soul, and to thrust down into the void those images which a magic power compels him to create. To him the torture is all the more intolerable because his feeling towards his companion enjoins, as its first law, that they should have no concealments, but mingle the aspirations of their thought as perfectly as the effusions of their soul. The demands of nature are not to be cheated. She is as inexorable as necessity, which is, indeed, a sort of social nature. Sommervieux took refuge in the peace and silence of his studio, hoping that the habit of living with artists might mould his wife and develop in her the dormant germs of lofty intelligence which some superior minds suppose must exist in every being. But Augustine was too sincerely religious not to take fright at the tone of artists. At the first dinner Théodore gave, she heard a young painter say, with the childlike lightness, which to her was unintelligible, and which redeems a jest from the taint of profanity, "But, madame, your Paradise cannot be more beautiful than Raphael's Transfiguration!—Well, and I got tired of looking at that."

Thus Augustine came among this sparkling set in a spirit of distrust which no one could fail to see. She was a restraint on their freedom. Now an artist who feels restraint is pitiless; he stays away, or laughs it to scorn. Madame Guillaume, among other absurdities, had an excessive notion of the dignity she considered the prerogative of a married woman; and Augustine, though she had often made fun of it, could not help a slight imitation of her mother's primness. This extreme propriety, which virtuous wives do not always avoid, suggested a few epigrams in the form of sketches, in which the harmless jest was in such good taste that Sommervieux could not take offence; and even if they had been more severe, These pleasantries were after all only reprisals from his friends. Still, nothing could seem a trifle to a spirit so open as Théodore's to impressions from without. A coldness insensibly crept over him, and inevitably spread. To attain conjugal happiness we must climb a hill whose summit is a narrow ridge, close to a steep and slippery descent: the painter's love was falling down it. He regarded his wife as incapable of appreciating the moral considerations which justified him in his own eyes for his singular behavior to her, and believed himself quite innocent in hiding from her thoughts she could not enter into, and peccadilloes outside the jurisdiction of a *bourgeois* conscience. Augustine wrapped herself in sullen and silent grief. These unconfessed feelings placed a shroud between the husband and wife which could not fail to grow thicker day by day. Though her husband never failed in consideration for her, Augustine could not help trembling as she saw that he kept for the outer world those treasures of wit and grace that he formerly would lay at her feet. She soon began to find a sinister meaning in the jocular speeches that are current in the world as to the inconstancy of men. She made no complaints, but her demeanor conveyed reproach.

Three years after her marriage this pretty young woman, who dashed past in her handsome carriage, and lived in a sphere of glory and riches to the envy of heedless folk incapable of taking a just view of the situations of life, was a prey to intense grief. She lost her colour; she reflected; she made comparisons; then sorrow unfolded to her the first lessons of experience. She determined to restrict herself bravely within the round of duty, hoping that by this generous conduct she might sooner or later win back her husband's love. But it was not so. When Sommervieux, tired with work, came in from his studio, Augustine did not put away her work so quickly but that the painter might find his wife mending the household linen, and his own, with all the care of a good housewife. She supplied generously and without a murmur the money needed for his lavishness; but in her anxiety to husband her dear Théodore's fortune, she was strictly economical for herself and in certain details of domestic management. Such conduct is incompatible with the easy-going habits of artists, who, at the end of their life, have enjoyed it so keenly that they never inquire into the causes of their ruin.

It is useless to note every tint of shadow by which the brilliant hues of their honeymoon were overcast till they were lost in utter blackness. One evening poor Augustine, who had for some time heard her husband speak with enthusiasm of the Duchesse de Carigliano, received from a friend certain malignantly charitable warnings as to the nature of the attachment which Sommervieux had formed for this celebrated flirt of the Imperial Court. At one-and-twenty, in all the splendor of youth and beauty, Augustine saw herself deserted for a woman of six-and-thirty. Feeling herself so wretched in the midst of a world of festivity which to her was a blank, the poor little thing could no longer understand the admiration she excited, or the envy of which she was the object. Her face assumed a different expression. Melancholy tinged her features with the sweetness of resignation and the pallor of scorned love. Ere long she too was courted by the most fascinating men; but she remained lonely and virtuous. Some contemptuous words which escaped her husband filled her with incredible despair. A sinister flash showed her the breaches which, as a result of her sordid education, hindered the perfect union of her soul with Théodore's;

she loved him well enough to absolve him and condemn herself. She shed tears of blood, and perceived, too late, that there are *mésalliances* of the spirit as well as of rank and habits. As she recalled the early raptures of their union, she understood the full extent of that lost happiness, and accepted the conclusion that so rich a harvest of love was in itself a whole life, which only sorrow could pay for. At the same time, she loved too truly to lose all hope. At one-and-twenty she dared undertake to educate herself, and make her imagination, at least, worthy of that she admired. "If I am not a poet," thought she, "at any rate, I will understand poetry."

Then, with all the strength of will, all the energy which every woman can display when she loves, Madame de Sommervieux tried to alter her character, her manners, and her habits; but by dint of devouring books and learning undauntedly, she only succeeded in becoming less ignorant. Lightness of wit and the graces of conversation are a gift of nature, or the fruit of education begun in the cradle. She could appreciate music and enjoy it, but she could not sing with taste. She understood literature and the beauties of poetry, but it was too late to cultivate her refractory memory. She listened with pleasure to social conversation, but she could contribute nothing brilliant. Her religious notions and home-grown prejudices were antagonistic to the complete emancipation of her intelligence. Finally, a foregone conclusion against her had stolen into Théodore's mind, and this she could not conquer. The artist would laugh at those who flattered him about his wife, and his irony had some foundation; he so overawed the pathetic young creature that, in his presence, or alone with him, she trembled. Hampered by her too eager desire to please, her wits and her knowledge vanished in one absorbing feeling. Even her fidelity vexed the unfaithful husband, who seemed to bid her do wrong by stigmatising her virtue as insensibility. Augustine tried in vain to abdicate her reason, to yield to her husband's caprices and whims, to devote herself to the selfishness of his vanity. Her sacrifices bore no fruit. Perhaps they had both let the moment slip when souls may meet in comprehension. One day the young wife's too sensitive heart received one of those blows which so strain the bonds of feeling that they seem to be broken. She withdrew into solitude. But before long a fatal idea suggested to her to seek counsel and comfort in the bosom of her family.

So one morning she made her way towards the grotesque façade of the humble, silent home where she had spent her childhood. She sighed as she looked up at the sash-window, whence one day she had sent her first kiss to him who now shed as much sorrow as glory on her life. Nothing was changed in the cavern, where the drapery business had, however, started on a new life. Augustine's sister filled her mother's old place at the desk. The unhappy young woman met her brother-in-law with his pen behind his ear; he hardly listened to her, he was so full of business. The formidable symptoms of stock-taking were visible all round him; he begged her to excuse him. She was received coldly enough by her sister, who owed her a grudge. In fact, Augustine, in her finery, and stepping out of a handsome carriage, had never been to see her but when passing by. The wife of the prudent Lebas, imagining that want of money was the prime cause of this early call, tried to keep up a tone of reserve which more than once made Augustine smile. The painter's wife perceived that, apart from the cap and lappets, her mother had found in Virginie a successor who could uphold the ancient honour of the Cat and Racket. At breakfast she observed certain changes in the management of the house which did honour to Lebas' good sense; the assistants did not rise before dessert; they were allowed to talk, and the abundant meal spoke of ease without luxury. The fashionable woman found some tickets for a box at the Français, where she remembered having seen her sister from time to time. Madame Lebas had a cashmere shawl over her shoulders, of which the value bore witness to her husband's generosity to her. In short, the couple were keeping pace with the times. During the two-thirds of the day she spent there, Augustine was touched to the heart by the equable happiness, devoid, to be sure, of all emotion, but equally free from storms, enjoyed by this well-matched couple. They had accepted life as a commercial enterprise, in which, above all, they must do credit to the business. Not finding any great love in her husband, Virginie had set to work to create it. Having by degrees learned to esteem and care for his wife, the time that his happiness had taken to germinate was to Joseph Lebas a guarantee of its durability. Hence, when Augustine plaintively set forth her painful position, she had to face the deluge of commonplace morality which the traditions of the Rue Saint-Denis furnished to her sister.

"The mischief is done, wife," said Joseph Lebas; "we must try to give our sister good advice." Then the clever tradesman ponderously analysed the resources which law and custom might offer Augustine as a means of escape at this crisis; he ticketed every argument, so to speak, and arranged them in their degrees of weight under various categories, as though they were articles of merchandise of different qualities; then he put them in the scale, weighed them, and ended by showing the necessity for his sister-in-law's taking violent steps which could not satisfy the love she still had for her husband; and, indeed, the feeling had revived in all its strength when she heard Joseph Lebas speak of legal proceedings. Augustine thanked them, and returned home even more undecided than she had been before consulting them. She now ventured to go to the house in the Rue du Colombier, intending to confide her troubles to her father and mother; for she was like a sick man who, in his desperate plight, tries every prescription, and even puts faith in old wives' remedies.

The old people received their daughter with an effusiveness that touched her deeply. Her visit brought them some little change, and that to them was worth a fortune. For the last four years they had gone their way in life like navigators without a goal or a compass. Sitting by the chimney corner, they would talk over their disasters under the old law of *maximum*, of their great investments in cloth, of the way they had weathered bankruptcies, and, above all, the famous failure of Lecocq, Monsieur Guillaume's battle of Marengo. Then, when they had exhausted the tale of lawsuits, they recapitulated the sum total of their most profitable stock-takings, and told each other old stories of the Saint-Denis quarter. At two o'clock old Guillaume went to cast an eye on the business at the Cat and Racket; on his way back he called at all the shops, formerly the rivals of his own, where the young proprietors hoped to inveigle the old draper into some risky discount, which, as was his wont, he never refused point-blank. Two good Normandy horses were dying of their own fat in the stables of this big house; Madame Guillaume never used them but to drag her on Sundays to high mass at the parish church. Three times a week the worthy couple kept open house. By the influence of his son-in-law Sommervieux, Monsieur Guillaume had been named a member of the consulting board for the clothing of the Army. Since her husband had stood so high in office, Madame Guillaume had decided that she must receive; her rooms were so crammed with gold and silver ornaments, and furniture, tasteless but of undoubted value, that the simplest room in the house looked like a chapel. Economy and expense seemed to be struggling for the upper hand in every accessory. It was as though Monsieur Guillaume had looked to a good investment, even, in the purchase of a candlestick. In the midst of this bazaar, where splendour revealed the owner's want of occupation, Sommervieux's famous picture filled the place of honour, and in it Monsieur and Madame Guillaume found their chief consolation, tuning their eyes, harnessed with eye-glasses, twenty times a day on this presentment of their past life, to them so active and amusing. The appearance of this mansion and these rooms, where everything had an aroma of staleness and mediocrity, the spectacle offered by these two beings, cast away, as it were, on a rock far from the world and the ideas which are life, startled Augustine; she could here contemplate the sequel of the scene of which the first part had struck her at the house of Lebas—a life of stir without movement, a mechanical and instinctive existence like that of the beaver; and then she felt an indefinable pride in her troubles, as she reflected that they had their source in eighteen months of such happiness as, in her eyes, was worth a thousand lives like this; its vacuity seemed to her horrible. However, she concealed this not very charitable feeling, and displayed for her parents her newly-acquired accomplishments of mind, and the ingratiating tenderness that love had revealed to her, disposing them to listen to her matrimonial grievances. Old people have a weakness for this kind of confidences. Madame Guillaume wanted to know the most trivial details of that alien life, which to her seemed almost fabulous. The travels of Baron de la Houtan, which she began again and again and never finished, told her nothing more unheard-of concerning the Canadian savages.

"What, child, your husband shuts himself into a room with naked women! And you are so simple as to believe that he draws them?"

As she uttered this exclamation, the grandmother laid her spectacles on little work-table, shook her skirts, and clasped her hands on her knees, raised by a foot-warmer, her favorite pedestal.

"But, mother, all artists are obliged to have models."

"He took good care not to tell us that when he asked leave to marry you. If I had known it, I would never have given my daughter to a man who followed such a trade. Religion forbids such horrors; they are immoral. And at what time of night do you say he comes home?"

"At one o'clock—two—"

The old folks looked at each other in utter amazement.

"Then he gambles?" said Monsieur Guillaume. "In my day only gamblers stayed out so late."

Augustine made a face that scorned the accusation.

"He must keep you up through dreadful nights waiting for him," said Madame Guillaume. "But you go to bed, don't you? And when he has lost, the wretch wakes you."

"No, mama, on the contrary, he is sometimes in very good spirits. Not unfrequently, indeed, when it is fine, he suggests that I should get up and go into the woods."

"The woods! At that hour? Then have you such a small set of rooms that his bedroom and his sitting-rooms are not enough, and that he must run about? But it is just to give you cold that the wretch proposes such expeditions. He wants to get rid of you. Did one ever hear of a man settled in life, a well-behaved, quiet man galloping about like a warlock?"

"But, my dear mother, you do not understand that he must have excitement to fire his genius. He is fond of scenes which—"

"I would makes scenes for him, fine scenes!" cried Madame Guillaume, interrupting her daughter. "How can you show any consideration to such a man? In the first place, I don't like his drinking water only; it is not wholesome. Why does he object to see a woman eating? What queer notion is that! But he is mad. All you tell us about him is impossible. A man cannot leave his home without a word, and never come back for ten days. And then he tells you he has been to Dieppe to paint the sea. As if any one painted the sea! He crams you with a pack of tales that are too absurd."

Augustine opened her lips to defend her husband; but Madame Guillaume enjoined silence with a wave of her hand, which she obeyed by a survival of habit, and her mother went on in harsh tones: "Don't talk to me about the man! He never set foot in a church excepting to see you and to be married. People without religion are capable of anything. Did Guillaume ever dream of hiding anything from me, of spending three days without saying a word to me, and of chattering afterwards like a blind magpie?"

"My dear mother, you judge superior people too severely. If their ideas were the same as other folks', they would not be men of genius."

"Very well, then let men of genius stop at home and not get married. What! A man of genius is to make his wife miserable? And because he is a genius it is all right! Genius, genius! It is not so very clever to say black one minute and white the next, as he does, to interrupt other people, to dance such rigs at home, never to let you know which foot you are to stand on, to compel his wife never to be amused unless my lord is in gay spirits, and to be dull when he is dull."

"But, mother, the very nature of such imaginations—"

"What are such 'imaginations'?" Madame Guillaume went on, interrupting her daughter again. "Fine ones his are, my word! What possesses a man that all on a sudden, without consulting a doctor, he takes it into his head to eat nothing but vegetables? If indeed it were from religious motives, it might do him some good—but he has no more religion than a Huguenot. Was there ever a man known who, like him, loved horses better than his fellow-creatures, had his hair curled like a heathen, laid statues under muslin coverlets, shut his shutters in broad day to work by lamp-light? There, get along; if he were not so grossly immoral, he would be fit to shut up in a lunatic asylum. Consult Monsieur Loraux, the priest at Saint Sulpice, ask his opinion about it all, and he will tell you that your husband does not behave like a Christian."

"Oh, mother, can you believe—?"

"Yes, I do believe. You loved him, and you can see none of these things. But I can remember in the early days after your marriage. I met him in the Champs-Elysées. He was on horseback. Well, at one minute he was galloping as hard as he could tear, and then pulled up to a walk. I said to myself at that moment, 'There is a man devoid of judgment.'"

"Ah, ha!" cried Monsieur Guillaume, "how wise I was to have your money settled on yourself with such a queer fellow for a husband!"

When Augustine was so imprudent as to set forth her serious grievances against her husband, the two old people were speechless with indignation. But the word "divorce" was ere long spoken by Madame Guillaume. At the sound of the word divorce the apathetic old draper seemed to wake up. Prompted by his love for his daughter and also by the excitement which the proceedings would bring into his uneventful life, father Guillaume took up the matter. He made himself the leader of the application for a divorce, laid down the lines of it, almost argued the case; he offered to be at all the charges, to see the lawyers, the pleaders, the judges, to move heaven and earth. Madame de Sommervieux was frightened, she refused her father's services, said she would not be separated from her husband even if she were ten times as unhappy, and talked no more about her sorrows. After being overwhelmed by her parents with all the little wordless and consoling kindnesses by which the old couple tried in vain to make up to her for her distress of heart, Augustine went away, feeling the impossibility of making a superior mind intelligible to weak intellects. She had leaned that a wife must hide from every one, even from her parents, woes for which it is so difficult to find sympathy. The storms and sufferings of the upper spheres are appreciated only by the lofty spirits who inhabit there. In every circumstance we can only be judged by our equals.

Thus poor Augustine found herself thrown back on the horror of her meditations, in the cold atmosphere of her home. Study was indifferent to her, since study had not brought her back her husband's heart. Initiated into the secret of these souls of fire, but bereft of their resources, she was compelled to share their sorrows without sharing their pleasures. She was disgusted with the world, which to her seemed mean and small as compared with the incidents of passion. In short, her life was a failure.

One evening an idea flashed upon her that lighted up her dark grief like a beam from heaven. Such an idea could never have smiled on a heart less pure, less virtuous than hers. She determined to go to the Duchesse de Carigliano, not to ask her to give her back her husband's heart, but to learn the arts by which it had been captured; to engage the interest of this haughty fine lady for the mother of her lover's children; to appeal to her and make her the instrument of her future happiness, since she was the cause of her present wretchedness.

So one day Augustine, timid as she was, but armed with supernatural courage, got into her carriage at two in the afternoon to try for admittance to the boudoir of the famous coquette, who was never visible till that hour. Madame de Sommervieux had not yet seen any of the ancient and magnificent mansions of the Faubourg Saint-Germain. As she made her way through the stately corridors, the handsome staircases, the vast drawing-rooms—full of flowers, though it was in the depth of winter, and decorated with the taste peculiar to women born to opulence or to the elegant habits of the aristocracy, Augustine felt a terrible clutch at her heart; she coveted the secrets of an elegance of which she had never had an idea; she breathed an air of grandeur which explained the attraction of the house for her husband. When she reached the private rooms of the Duchess she was filled with jealousy and a sort of despair, as she admired the luxurious arrangement of the furniture, the draperies and the hangings. Here disorder was a grace, here luxury affected a certain contempt of splendour. The fragrance that floated in the warm air flattered the sense of smell without offending it. The accessories of the rooms were in harmony with a view, through plate-glass windows, of the lawns in a garden planted with evergreen trees. It was all bewitching, and the art of it was not perceptible. The whole spirit of the mistress of these rooms pervaded the drawing-room where Augustine awaited her. She tried to divine her rival's character from the aspect of the scattered objects; but there was here something as impenetrable in the disorder as in the symmetry, and to the simple-minded young wife all was a sealed letter. All that she could discern was that, as a woman, the Duchess was a superior person. Then a painful thought came over her.

"Alas! And is it true," she wondered, "that a simple and loving heart is not all-sufficient to an artist; that to balance the weight of these powerful souls they need a union with feminine souls of a strength equal to their own? If I had been brought up like this siren, our weapons at least might have been equal in the hour of struggle."

"But I am not at home!" The sharp, harsh words, though spoken in an undertone in the adjoining boudoir, were heard by Augustine, and her heart beat violently.

"The lady is in there," replied the maid.

"You are an idiot! Show her in," replied the Duchess, whose voice was sweeter, and had assumed the dulcet tones of politeness. She evidently now meant to be heard.

Augustine shyly entered the room. At the end of the dainty boudoir she saw the Duchess lounging luxuriously on an ottoman covered with brown velvet and placed in the centre of a sort of apse outlined by soft folds of white muslin over a yellow lining. Ornaments of gilt bronze, arranged with exquisite taste, enhanced this sort of dais, under which the Duchess reclined like a Greek statue. The dark hue of the velvet gave relief to every fascinating charm. A subdued light, friendly to her beauty, fell like a reflection rather than a direct illumination. A few rare flowers raised their perfumed heads from costly Sèvres vases. At the moment when this picture was presented to Augustine astonished eyes, she was approaching so noiselessly that she caught a glance from those of the enchantress. This look seemed to say to some one whom Augustine did not at first perceive, "Stay; you will see a pretty woman, and make her visit less of a bore."

On seeing Augustine, the Duchess rose and made her sit down by her.

"And to what do I owe the pleasure of this visit, madame?" she said with a most gracious smile.

"Why all this falseness?" thought Augustine, replying only with a bow.

Her silence was compulsory. The young woman saw before her a superfluous witness of the scene. This personage was, of all the Colonels in the army, the youngest, the most fashionable, and the finest man. His face, full of life and youth, but already expressive, was further enhanced by a small moustache twirled up into points, and as black as jet, by a full imperial, by whiskers carefully combed, and a forest of black hair in some disorder. He was whisking a riding whip with an air of ease and freedom which suited his self-satisfied expression and the elegance of his dress; the ribbons attached to his button-hole were carelessly tied, and he seemed to pride himself much more on his smart appearance than on his courage. Augustine looked at the Duchesse de Carigliano, and indicated the Colonel by a sidelong glance. All its mute appeal was understood.

"Good-bye, then, Monsieur d'Aiglemont, we shall meet in the Bois de Boulogne."

These words were spoken by the siren as though they were the result of an agreement made before Augustine's arrival, and she winged them with a threatening look that the officer deserved perhaps for the admiration he showed in gazing at the modest flower, which contrasted so well with the haughty Duchess. The young fop bowed in silence, turned on the heels of his boots, and gracefully quitted the boudoir. At this instant, Augustine, watching her rival, whose eyes seemed to follow the brilliant officer, detected in that glance a sentiment of which the transient expression is known to every woman. She perceived with the deepest anguish that her visit would be useless; this lady, full of artifice, was too greedy of homage not to have a ruthless heart.

"Madame," said Augustine in a broken voice, "the step I am about to take will seem to you very strange; but there is a madness of despair which ought to excuse anything. I understand only too well why Théodore prefers your house to any other, and why your mind has so much power over his. Alas! I have only to look into myself to find more than ample reasons. But I am devoted to my husband, madame. Two years of tears have not effaced his image from my heart, though I have lost his. In my folly I dared to dream of a contest with you; and I have come to you to ask you by what means I may triumph over yourself. Oh, madame," cried the young wife, ardently seizing the hand which her rival allowed her to hold, "I will never pray to God for my own happiness with so much fervour as I will beseech Him for yours, if you will help me to win back Sommervieux's regard—I will not say his love. I have no hope but in you. Ah! tell me how you could please him, and make him forget the first days—" At these words Augustine broke down, suffocated with sobs she could not suppress. Ashamed of her weakness, she hid her face in her handkerchief, which she bathed with tears.

"What a child you are, my dear little beauty!" said the Duchess, carried away by the novelty of such a scene, and touched, in spite of herself, at receiving such homage from the most perfect virtue perhaps in Paris. She took the young wife's handkerchief, and herself wiped the tears from her eyes, soothing her by a few monosyllables murmured with gracious compassion. After a moment's silence the Duchess, grasping poor Augustine's hands in both her own—hands that had a rare character of dignity and powerful beauty—said in a gentle and friendly voice: "My first warning is to advise you not to weep so bitterly; tears are disfiguring. We must learn to deal firmly with the sorrows that make us ill, for love does not linger long by a sick-bed. Melancholy, at first, no doubt, lends a certain attractive grace, but it ends by dragging the features and blighting the loveliest face. And besides, our tyrants are so vain as to insist that their slaves should be always cheerful."

"But, madame, it is not in my power not to feel. How is it possible, without suffering a thousand deaths, to see the face which once beamed with love and gladness turn chill, colourless, and indifferent? I cannot control my heart!"

"So much the worse, sweet child. But I fancy I know all your story. In the first place, if your husband is unfaithful to you, understand clearly that I am not his accomplice. If I was anxious to have him in my drawing-room, it was, I own, out of vanity; he was famous, and he went nowhere. I like you too much already to tell you all the mad things he has done for my sake. I will only reveal one, because it may perhaps help us to bring him back to you, and to punish him for the audacity of his behaviour to me. He will end by compromising me. I know the world too well, my dear, to abandon myself to the discretion of a too superior man. You should know that one may allow them to court one, but marry them—that is a mistake! We women ought to admire men of genius, and delight in them as a spectacle, but as to living with them? Never.—No, no. It is like wanting to find pleasure in inspecting the machinery of the opera instead of sitting in a box to enjoy its brilliant illusions. But this misfortune has fallen on you, my poor child, has it not? Well, then, you must try to arm yourself against tyranny."

"Ah, madame, before coming in here, only seeing you as I came in, I already detected some arts of which I had no suspicion."

"Well, come and see me sometimes, and it will not be long before you have mastered the knowledge of these trifles, important, too, in their way. Outward things are, to fools, half of life; and in that matter more than one clever man is a fool, in spite of all his talent. But I dare wager you never could refuse your Théodore anything!"

"How refuse anything, madame, if one loves a man?"

"Poor innocent, I could adore you for your simplicity. You should know that the more we love the less we should allow a man, above all, a husband, to see the whole extent of our passion. The one who loves most is tyrannized over, and, which is worse, is sooner or later neglected. The one who wishes to rule should—"

"What, madame, must I then dissimulate, calculate, become false, form an artificial character, and live in it? How is it possible to live in such a way? Can you—" she hesitated; the Duchess smiled.

"My dear child," the great lady went on in a serious tone, "conjugal happiness has in all times been a speculation, a business demanding particular attention. If you persist in talking passion while I am talking marriage, we shall soon cease to understand each other. Listen to me," she went on, assuming a confidential tone. "I have been in the way of seeing some of the superior men of our day. Those who have married have for the most part chosen quite insignificant wives. Well, those wives governed them, as the Emperor governs us; and if they were not loved, they were at least respected. I like secrets—especially those which concern women—well enough to have amused myself by seeking the clue to the riddle. Well, my sweet child, those worthy women had the gift of analysing their husbands' nature; instead of taking fright, like you, at their superiority, they very acutely noted the qualities they lacked, and either by possessing those qualities, or by feigning to possess them, they found means of making such a handsome display of them in their husbands' eyes that in the end they impressed them. Also, I must tell you, all these souls which appear so lofty have just a speck of madness in them, which we ought to know how to take advantage of. By firmly resolving to have the upper hand and never deviating from that aim, by bringing all our actions to bear on it, all our ideas, our cajolery, we subjugate these eminently capricious natures, which, by the very mutability of their thoughts, lend us the means of influencing them."

"Good heavens!" cried the young wife in dismay. "And this is life. It is a warfare—"

"In which we must always threaten," said the Duchess, laughing. "Our power is wholly factitious. And we must never allow a man to despise us; it is impossible to recover from such a descent but by odious manœuvring. Come," she added, "I will give you a means of bringing your husband to his senses."

She rose with a smile to guide the young and guileless apprentice to conjugal arts through the labyrinth of her palace.

They came to a back-staircase, which led up to the reception rooms. As Madame de Carigliano pressed the secret spring-lock of the door she stopped, looking at Augustine with an inimitable gleam of shrewdness and grace. "The Duc de Carigliano adores me," said she. "Well, he dare not enter by this door without my leave. And he is a man in the habit of commanding thousands of soldiers. He knows how to face a battery, but before me—he is afraid!"

Augustine sighed. They entered a sumptuous gallery, where the painter's wife was led by the Duchess up to the portrait painted by Théodore of Mademoiselle Guillaume. On seeing it, Augustine uttered a cry.

"I knew it was no longer in my house," she said, "but—here I—"

"My dear child, I asked for it merely to see what pitch of idiocy a man of genius may attain to. Sooner or later I should have returned it to you, for I never expected the pleasure of seeing the original here face to face with the copy. While we finish our conversation I will have it carried down to your carriage. And if, armed with such a talisman, you are not your husband's mistress for a hundred years, you are not a woman, and you deserve your fate."

Augustine kissed the Duchess' hand, and the lady clasped her to her heart, with all the more tenderness because she would forget her by the morrow. This scene might perhaps have destroyed for ever the candor and purity of a less virtuous woman than Augustine, for the astute politics of the higher social spheres were no more consonant to Augustine than the narrow reasoning of Joseph Lebas, or Madame Guillaume's vapid morality. Strange are the results of the false positions into which we may be brought by the slightest mistake in the conduct of life! Augustine was like an Alpine cowherd surprised by an avalanche; if he hesitates, if he listens to the shouts of his comrades, he is almost certainly lost. In such a crisis the heart steels itself or breaks.

Madame de Sommervieux returned home a prey to such agitation as it is difficult to describe. Her conversation with the Duchesse de Carigliano had roused in her mind a crowd of contradictory thoughts. Like the sheep in the fable, full of courage in the wolf's absence, she preached to herself, and laid down admirable plans of conduct; she devised a thousand coquettish strategies; she even talked to her husband, finding, away from him, all the springs of true eloquence which never desert a woman; then, as she pictured to herself Théodore's clear and steadfast gaze, she began to quake. When she asked whether monsieur were at home her voice shook. On learning that he would not be in to dinner, she felt an unaccountable thrill of joy. Like a criminal who has appealed against sentence of death, a respite, however short, seemed to her a lifetime. She placed the portrait in her room, and waited for her husband in all the agonies of hope. That this venture must decide her future life, she felt too keenly not to shiver at every sound, even the low ticking of the clock, which seemed to aggravate her terrors by doling them out to her. She tried to cheat time by various devices. The idea struck her of dressing in a way which would make her exactly like the portrait. Then, knowing her husband's restless temper, she had her room lighted up with unusual brightness, feeling sure that when he came in curiosity would bring him there at once. Midnight had struck when, at the call of the groom, the street gate was opened, and the artist's carriage rumbled in over the stones of the silent courtyard.

"What is the meaning of this illumination?" asked Théodore in glad tones, as he came into her room.

Augustine skilfully seized the auspicious moment; she threw herself into her husband's arms, and pointed to the portrait. The artist stood rigid as a rock, an his eyes turned alternately on Augustine, on the accusing dress. The frightened wife, half-dead, as she watched her husband's changeful brow—that terrible brow—saw the expressive furrows gathering like clouds; then she felt her blood curdling in her veins when, with a glaring look, and in a deep hollow voice, he began to question her:

"Where did you find that picture?"

"The Duchesse de Carigliano returned it to me."

"You asked her for it?"

"I did not know that she had it."

The gentleness, or rather the exquisite sweetness of this angel's voice, might have touched a cannibal, but not an artist in the clutches of wounded vanity.

"It is worthy of her!" exclaimed the painter in a voice of thunder. "I will be revenged!" he cried, striding up and down the room. "She shall die of shame; I will paint her! Yes, I will paint her as Messalina stealing out at night from the palace of Claudius."

"Théodore!" said a faint voice.

"I will kill her!"

"My dear—"

"She is in love with that little cavalry colonel, because he rides well—"

"Théodore!"

"Let me be!" said the painter in a tone almost like a roar.

It would be odious to describe the whole scene. In the end the frenzy of passion prompted the artist to acts and words which any woman not so young as Augustine would have ascribed to madness.

At eight o'clock next morning Madame Guillaume, surprising her daughter, found her pale, with red eyes, her hair in disorder, holding a handkerchief soaked with tears, while she gazed at the floor strewn with the torn fragments of a dress and the broken pieces of a large gilt picture-frame. Augustine, almost senseless with grief, pointed to the wreck with a gesture of deep despair.

"I don't know that the loss is very great!" cried the old mistress of the Cat and Racket. "It was like you, no doubt; but I am told that there is a man on the boulevard who paints lovely portraits for fifty crowns."

"Oh, mother!"

"Poor child, you are quite right," replied Madame Guillaume, who misinterpreted the expression of her daughter's glance at her. "True, my child, no one ever can love you as fondly as a mother. My darling, I guess it all; but confide your sorrows to me, and I will comfort you. Did I not tell you long ago that the man was mad! Your maid has told me pretty stories. Why, he must be a perfect monster!"

Augustine laid a finger on her white lips, as if to implore a moment's silence. During this dreadful night misery had led her to that patient resignation which in mothers and loving wives transcends in its effects all human energy, and perhaps reveals in the heart of women the existence of certain chords which God has withheld from men.

An inscription engraved on a broken column in the cemetery at Montmartre states that Madame de Sommervieux died at the age of twenty-seven. In the simple words of this epitaph one of the timid creature's friends can read the last scene of a tragedy. Every year, on the second of November, the solemn day of the dead, he never passes this youthful monument without wondering whether it does not need a stronger woman than Augustine to endure the violent embrace of genius?

"The humble and modest flowers that bloom in the valley," he reflects, "perish perhaps when they are transplanted too near the skies to the region where storms gather and the sun is scorching."

1. *Fenêtre à la Guillotine.*

THE BALL AT SCEAUX

To Henri de Balzac, his brother Honoré.

THE Comte de Fontaine, head of one of the oldest families in Poitou, had served the Bourbon cause with intelligence and bravery during the war in La Vendée against the Republic. After having escaped all the dangers which threatened the royalist leaders during this stormy period of modem history, he was wont to say in jest, "I am one of the men who gave themselves to be killed on the steps of the throne." And the pleasantry had some truth in it, as spoken by a man left for dead at the bloody battle of Les Quatre Chemins. Though ruined by confiscation, the staunch Vendéen steadily refused the lucrative posts offered to him by the Emperor Napoleon. Immovable in his aristocratic faith, he had blindly obeyed its precepts when he thought it fitting to choose a companion for life. In spite of the blandishments of a rich but revolutionary parvenu, who valued the alliance at a high figure, he married Mademoiselle de Kergarouët, without a fortune, but belonging to one of the oldest families in Brittany.

When the second revolution burst on Monsieur de Fontaine he was encumbered with a large family. Though it was no part of the noble gentleman's views to solicit favours, he yielded to his wife's wish, left his country estate, of which the income barely sufficed to maintain his children, and came to Paris. Saddened by seeing the greediness of his former comrades in the rush for places and dignities under the new Constitution, he was about to return to his property when he received a ministerial despatch, in which a well-known magnate announced to him his nomination as *maréchal de camp*, or brigadier-general, under a rule which allowed the officers of the Catholic armies to count the twenty submerged years of Louis XVIII's reign as years of service. Some days later he further received, without any solicitation, *ex officio*, the crosses of the Legion of Honour and of Saint-Louis.

Shaken in his determination by these successive favours, due, as he supposed, to the monarch's remembrance, he was no longer satisfied with taking his family, as he had piously done every Sunday, to cry "Vive le Roi" in the hall of the Tuileries when the royal family passed through on their way to chapel; he craved the favour of a private audience. The audience, at once granted, was in no sense private. The royal drawing-room was full of old adherents, whose powdered heads, seen from above, suggested a carpet of snow. There the Count met some old friends, who received him somewhat coldly; but the princes he thought *adorable,* an enthusiastic expression which escaped him when the most gracious of his masters, to whom the Count had supposed himself to be known only by name, came to shake hands with him, and spoke of him as the most thorough Vendéen of them all. Notwithstanding this ovation, none of these august persons thought of inquiring as to the sum of his losses, or of the money he had poured so generously into the chests of the Catholic regiments. He discovered, a little late, that he had made war at his own cost. Towards the end of the evening he thought he might venture on a witty allusion to the state of his affairs, similar, as it was, to that of many other gentlemen. His Majesty laughed heartily enough; any speech that bore the hall-mark of wit was certain to please him; but he nevertheless replied with one of those royal pleasantries whose sweetness is more formidable than the anger of a rebuke. One of the King's most intimate advisers took an opportunity of going up to the fortune-seeking Vendéen, and made him understand by a keen and polite hint that the time had not yet come for settling accounts with the sovereign; that there were bills of much longer standing than his on the books, and there, no doubt, they would remain, as part of the history of the Revolution. The Count prudently withdrew from the venerable group, which formed a respectful semi-circle before the august family; then, having extricated his sword, not without some difficulty, from among the lean legs which had got mixed up with it, he crossed the courtyard of the Tuileries and got into the hackney cab he had left on the quay. With the restive spirit, which is peculiar to the nobility of the old school, in whom still survives the memory of the League and the day of the Barricades (in 1588), he bewailed himself in his cab, loudly enough to compromise him, over the change that had come over the Court. "Formerly," he said to himself, "every one could speak freely to the King of his own little affairs; the nobles could ask him a favour, or for money, when it suited them, and nowadays one cannot recover the money advanced for his service without raising a scandal! By Heaven! the cross of Saint-Louis and the rank of brigadier-general will not make good the three hundred thousand livres I have spent, out and out, on the royal cause. I must speak to the King, face to face, in his own room."

This scene cooled Monsieur de Fontaine's ardour all the more effectually because his requests for an interview were never answered. And, indeed, he saw the upstarts of the Empire obtaining some of the offices reserved, under the old monarchy, for the highest families.

"All is lost!" he exclaimed one morning. "The King has certainly never been other than a revolutionary. But for Monsieur, who never derogates, and is some comfort to his faithful adherents, I do not know what hands the crown of France might not fall into if things are to go on like this. Their cursed constitutional system is the worst possible government, and can never suit France. Louis XVIII and Monsieur Beugnot spoiled everything at Saint Ouen."

The Count, in despair, was preparing to retire to his estate, abandoning, with dignity, all claims his to repayment. At this moment the events of the 20th March (1815) gave warning of a fresh storm, threatening to overwhelm the legitimate monarch and his defenders. Monsieur de Fontaine, like one of those generous souls who do not dismiss a servant in a torrent of rain, borrowed on his lands to follow the routed monarchy, without knowing whether this complicity in emigration would prove more propitious to him than his past devotion. But when he perceived that the companions of the King's exile were in higher favour than the brave men who had protested, sword in hand, against the establishment of the republic, he may perhaps have hoped to derive greater profit from this journey into a foreign land than from active and dangerous service in the heart of his own country. Nor was his courtier-like calculation one of these rash speculations which promise splendid results on paper, and are ruinous in effect. He was—to quote the wittiest and most successful of our diplomates—one of the faithful five hundred who shared the exile of the Court at Ghent, and one of the fifty thousand who returned with it. During the short banishment of royalty, Monsieur de Fontaine was so happy as to be employed by Louis XVIII, and found more than one opportunity of giving him proofs of great political honesty and sincere attachment. One evening, when the King had nothing better to do, he recalled Monsieur de Fontaine's witticism at the Tuileries. The old Vendéen did not let such a happy chance slip; he told his history with so much vivacity that a king, who never forgot anything, might remember it at a convenient season. The royal amateur of literature also observed the elegant style given to some notes which the discreet gentleman had been invited to recast. This little success stamped Monsieur de Fontaine on the King's memory as one of the loyal servants of the Crown.

At the second restoration the Count was one of those special envoys who were sent throughout the departments charged with absolute jurisdiction over the leaders of revolt; but he used his terrible powers with moderation. As soon as this temporary commission was ended, the High Provost found a seat in the Privy Council, became a deputy, spoke little, listened much, and changed his opinions very considerably. Certain circumstances, unknown to historians, brought him into such intimate relations with the Sovereign, that one day, as he came in, the shrewd monarch addressed him thus: "My friend Fontaine, I shall take care never to appoint you to be director-general, or minister. Neither you nor I, as employés, could keep our place on account of our opinions. Representative government has this advantage: it saves Us the trouble We used to have, of dismissing Our Secretaries of State. Our Council is a perfect inn-parlour, whither public opinion sometimes sends strange travellers; however, We can always find a place for Our faithful adherents."

This ironical speech was introductory to a rescript giving Monsieur de Fontaine an appointment as administrator in the office of Crown lands. As a consequence of the intelligent attention with which he listened to his royal Friend's sarcasms, his name always rose to His Majesty's lips when a commission was to be appointed of which the members were to receive a handsome salary. He had the good sense to hold his tongue about the favour with which he was honoured, and knew how to entertain the monarch in those familiar chats in which Louis XVIII delighted as much as in a well-written note, by his brilliant manner of repeating political anecdotes, and the political or Parliamentary tittle-tattle—if the expression may pass—which at that time was rife. It is well known that he was immensely amused by every detail of his *Gouvernementabilité*—a word adopted by his facetious Majesty.

Thanks to the Comte do Fontaine's good sense, wit, and tact, every member of his numerous family, however young, ended, as he jestingly told his Sovereign, in attaching himself like a silkworm to the leaves of the Pay-List. Thus, by the King's intervention, his eldest son found a high and fixed position as a lawyer. The second, before the restoration a mere captain, was appointed to the command of a legion on the return from Ghent; then, thanks to the confusion of 1815, when the regulations were evaded, he passed into the bodyguard, returned to a line regiment, and found himself after the affair of the Trocadéro a lieutenant-general with a commission in the Guards. The youngest, appointed sous-préfet, ere long became a legal official and director of a municipal board of the city of Paris, where he was safe from changes in the Legislature. These bounties, bestowed without parade, and as secret as the favour enjoyed by the Count, fell unperceived. Though the father and his three sons each had sinecures enough to enjoy an income in salaries almost equal to that of a chief of department, their political good fortune excited no envy. In those early days of the constitutional system, few persons had very precise ideas of the peaceful domain of the civil service, where astute favourites managed to find an equivalent for the demolished abbeys. Monsieur le Comte de Fontaine, who till lately boasted that he had not read the Charter, and displayed such indignation at the greed of courtiers, had, before long, proved to his august master that he understood, as well as the King himself, the spirit and resources of the representative system. At the same time, notwithstanding the established careers open to his three sons, and the pecuniary advantages derived from four official appointments, Monsieur de Fontaine was the head of too large a family to be able to re-establish his fortune easily and rapidly.

His three sons were rich in prospects, in favour, and in talent; but he had three daughters, and was afraid of wearying the monarch's benevolence. It occurred to him to mention only one by one, these virgins eager to light their torches. The King had too much good taste to leave his work incomplete. The marriage of the eldest with a Receiver-General, Planat de Baudry, was arranged by one of those royal speeches which cost nothing and are worth millions. One evening, when the Sovereign was out of spirits, he smiled on hearing of the existence of another Demoiselle de Fontaine, for whom he found a husband in the person of a young magistrate, of inferior birth, no doubt, but wealthy, and whom he created Baron. When, the year after, the Vendéen spoke of Mademoiselle Emilie de Fontaine, the King replied in his thin, sharp tones, "*Amicus Plato sed magis amica Natio.*" Then, a few days later, he treated his "friend Fontaine" to a quatrain, harmless enough, which he styled an epigram, in which he made fun of these three daughters so skilfully introduced, under the form of a trinity. Nay, if report is to be believed, the monarch had found the point of the jest in the Unity of the three Divine Persons.

"If your Majesty would only condescend to turn the epigram into an epithalamium?" said the Count, trying to turn the sally to good account.

"Though I see the rhyme of it, I fail to see the reason," retorted the King, who did not relish any pleasantry, however mild, on the subject of his poetry.

From that day his intercourse with Monsieur de Fontaine showed less amenity. Kings enjoy contradicting more than people think. Like most youngest children, Emilie de Fontaine was a Benjamin spoilt by almost everybody. The King's coolness, therefore, caused the Count all the more regret, because no marriage was ever so difficult to arrange as that of this darling daughter. To understand all the obstacles we must make our way into the fine residence where the official was housed at the expense of the nation. Emilie had spent her childhood on the family estate, enjoying the abundance which suffices for the joys of early youth; her lightest wishes had been law to her sisters, her brothers, her mother, and even her father. All her relations doted on her. Having come to years of discretion just when her family was loaded with the favours of fortune, the enchantment of life continued. The luxury of Paris seemed to her just as natural as a wealth of flowers or fruit, or as the rural plenty which bad been the joy of her first years. Just as in her childhood she had never been thwarted in the satisfaction of her playful desires, so now, at fourteen, she was still obeyed when she rushed into the whirl of fashion.

Thus, accustomed by degrees to the enjoyment of money, elegance of dress, of gilded drawing-rooms and fine carriages, became as necessary to her as the compliments of flattery, sincere or false, and the festivities and vanities of court life. Like most spoiled children, she tyrannized over those who loved her, and kept her blandishments for those who were indifferent. Her faults grew with her growth, and her parents were to gather the bitter fruits of this disastrous education. At the age of nineteen Emilie de Fontaine had not yet been pleased to make a choice from among the many young men whom her father's politics brought to his entertainments. Though so young, she asserted in society all the freedom of mind that a married woman can enjoy. Her beauty was so remarkable that, for her, to appear in a room was to be its queen; but, like sovereigns, she had no friends, though she was everywhere the object of attentions to which a finer nature than hers might perhaps have succumbed. Not a man, not even an old man, had it in him to contradict the opinions of a young girl whose lightest look could rekindle love in the coldest heart.

She had been educated with a care which her sisters had not enjoyed; painted pretty well, spoke Italian and English, and played the piano brilliantly; her voice, trained by the best masters, had a ring in it which made her singing irresistibly charming. Clever, and intimate with every branch of literature, she might have made folks believe that, as Mascarille says, people of quality come into the world knowing everything. She could argue fluently on Italian or Flemish painting, on the Middle Ages or the Renaissance; pronounced at haphazard on books new or old, and could expose the defects of a work with a cruelly graceful wit. The simplest thing she said was accepted by an admiring crowd as a *fetfah* of the Sultan by the Turks. She thus dazzled shallow persons; as to deeper minds, her natural tact enabled her to discern them, and for them she put forth so much fascination that, under cover of her charms, she escaped their scrutiny. This enchanting veneer covered a careless heart; the opinion—common to many young girls—that no one else dwelt in a sphere so lofty as to be able to understand the merits of her soul; and a pride based no less on her birth than on her beauty. In the absence of the overwhelming sentiment which, sooner or later, works havoc in a woman's heart, she spent her young ardour in an immoderate love of distinctions, and expressed the deepest contempt for persons of inferior birth. Supremely impertinent to all newly-created nobility, she made every effort to get her parents recognised as equals by the most illustrious families of the Saint-Germain quarter.

These sentiments had not escaped the observing eye of Monsieur de Fontaine, who more than once, when his two elder girls were married, had smarted under Emilie's sarcasm. Logical readers will be surprised to see the old Royalist bestowing his eldest daughter on a Receiver-General, possessed, indeed, of some old hereditary estates, but whose name was not preceded by the little word to which the throne owed so many partisans, and his second to a magistrate too lately Baronified to obscure the fact that his father had sold firewood. This noteworthy change in the ideas of a noble on the verge of his sixtieth year—an age when men rarely renounce their convictions due not merely to his unfortunate residence in the modern Babylon, where, sooner or later, country folks all get their corners rubbed down; the Comte de Fontaine's new political conscience was also a result of the King's advice and friendship. The philosophical prince had taken pleasure in converting the Vendéen to the ideas required by the advance of the nineteenth century, and the new aspect of the Monarchy. Louis XVIII aimed at fusing parties as Napoleon had fused things and men. The legitimate King, who was not less clever perhaps than his rival, acted in a contrary direction. The last head of the House of Bourbon was just as eager to satisfy the third estate and the creations of the Empire, by curbing the clergy, as the first of the Napoleons had been to attract the grand old nobility, or to endow the Church. The Privy Councillor, being in the secret of these royal projects, had insensibly become one of the most prudent and influential leaders of that moderate party which most desired a fusion of opinion in the interests of the nation. He preached the expensive doctrines of constitutional government, and lent all his weight to encourage the political see-saw which enabled his master to rule France in the midst of storms. Perhaps Monsieur de Fontaine hoped that one of the sudden gusts of legislation, whose unexpected efforts then startled the oldest politicians, might carry him up to the rank of peer. One of his most rigid principles was to recognise no nobility in France but that of the peerage—the only families that might enjoy any privileges.

"A nobility bereft of privileges," he would say, "is a tool without a handle."

As far from Lafayette's party as he was from La Bourdonnaye's, he ardently engaged in the task of general reconciliation, which was to result in a new era and, splendid fortunes for France. He strove to convince the families who frequented his drawing-room, or those whom he visited, how few favourable openings would henceforth be offered by a civil or military career. He urged mothers to give their boys a start in independent and industrial professions, explaining that military posts and high Government appointments must at last pertain, in a quite constitutional order, to the younger sons of members of the peerage. According to him, the people had conquered a sufficiently large share in practical government by its elective assembly, its appointments to law-offices, and those of the exchequer, which, said he, would always, as heretofore, be the natural right of the distinguished men of the third estate.

These new notions of the head of the Fontaines, and the prudent matches for his eldest girls to which they had led, met with strong resistance in the bosom of his family. The Comtesse de Fontaine remained faithful to the ancient beliefs which no woman could disown, who, through her mother, belonged to the Rohans. Although she had for a while opposed the happiness and fortune awaiting her two eldest girls, she yielded to those private considerations which husband and wife confide to each other when their heads are resting on the same pillow. Monsieur de Fontaine calmly pointed out to his wife, by exact arithmetic, that their residence in Paris, the necessity for entertaining, the magnificence of the house which made up to them now for the privations so bravely shared in La Vendée, and the expenses of their sons, swallowed up the chief part of their income from salaries. They must therefore seize, as a boon from heaven, the opportunities which offered for settling their girls with such wealth. Would they not some day enjoy sixty—eighty—a hundred thousand francs a year? Such advantageous matches were not to be met with every day for girls without a portion. Again, it was time that they should begin to think of economising, to add to the estate of Fontaine, and re-establish the old territorial fortune of the family. The Countess yielded to such cogent arguments, as every mother would have done in her place, though perhaps with a better grace; but she declared that Emilie, at any rate, should marry in such a way as to satisfy the pride she had unfortunately contributed to foster in the girl's young soul.

Thus events, which ought to have brought joy into the family, had introduced a small leaven of discord. The Receiver-General and the young lawyer were the objects of a ceremonious formality which the Countess and Emilie contrived to create. This etiquette soon found even ampler opportunity for the display of domestic tyranny; for Lieutenant-General de Fontaine married Mademoiselle Mongenod, the daughter of a rich banker; the Président very sensibly found a wife in a young lady whose father, twice or thrice a millionaire, had traded in salt; and the third brother, faithful to his plebeian doctrines, married Mademoiselle Grossetête the only daughter of the Receiver-General at Bourges. The three sisters-in-law and the two brothers-in-law found the high sphere of political bigwigs, and the drawing-rooms of the Faubourg Saint-Germain, so full of charm and of personal advantages, that they united in forming a little court round the overbearing Emilie. This treaty between interest and pride was not, however, so firmly cemented but that the young despot was, not unfrequently, the cause of revolts in her little realm. Scenes, which the highest circles would not have disowned, kept up a sarcastic temper among all the members of this powerful family; and this, without seriously diminishing the regard they professed in public, degenerated sometimes in private into sentiments far from charitable. Thus the Lieutenant-General's wife, having become a Baronne, thought herself quite as noble as a Kergarouët, and imagined that her good hundred thousand francs a year gave her the right to be as impertinent as her sister-in-law Emilie, whom she would sometimes wish to see happily married, as she announced that the daughter of some peer of France had married Monsieur So-and-So with no title to his name. The Vicomtesse do Fontaine amused herself by eclipsing Emilie in the taste and magnificence that were conspicuous in her dress, her furniture, and her carriages. The satirical spirit in which her brothers and sisters sometimes received the claims avowed by Mademoiselle de Fontaine roused her to wrath that a perfect hailstorm of sharp sayings could hardly mitigate. So when the head of the family felt a slight chill in the King's tacit and precarious friendship, he trembled all the more because, as a result of her sisters' defiant mockery, his favourite daughter had never looked so high.

In the midst of these circumstances, and at a moment when this petty domestic warfare had become serious, the monarch, whose favour Monsieur de Fontaine still hoped to regain, was attacked by the malady of which he was to die. The great political chief, who knew so well how to steer his bark in the midst of tempests, soon succumbed. Certain then of favours to come, the Comte de Fontaine made every effort to collect the élite of marrying men about his youngest daughter. Those who may have tried to solve the difficult problem of settling a haughty and capricious girl, will understand the trouble taken by the unlucky father. Such an affair, carried out to the liking of his beloved child, would worthily crown the career the Count had followed for these ten years at Paris. From the way in which his family claimed salaries under every department, it might be compared with the House of Austria, which, by intermarriage, threatens to pervade Europe. The old Vendéen was not to be discouraged in bringing forward suitors, so much had he his daughter's happiness at heart, but nothing could be more absurd than the way in which the impertinent young thing pronounced her verdicts and judged the merits of her adorers. It might have been supposed that, like a princess in the *Arabian Nights,* Emilie was rich enough and beautiful enough to choose from among all the princes in the world. Her objections were each more preposterous than the last: one had too thick knees and was bow-legged, another was short-sighted, this one's name was Durand, that one limped, and almost all were too fat. Livelier, more attractive, and gayer than ever after dismissing two or three suitors, she rushed into the festivities of the winter season, and to balls, where her keen eyes criticised the celebrities of the day, delighted in encouraging proposals which she invariably rejected.

Nature had bestowed on her all the advantages needed for playing the part of Célimène. Tall and slight, Emilie de Fontaine could assume a dignified or a frolicsome mien at her will. Her neck was rather long, allowing her to affect beautiful attitudes of scorn and impertinence She had cultivated a large variety of those turns of the head and feminine gestures, which emphasize so cruelly or so happily a hint or a smile. Fine black hair, thick and strongly-arched eyebrows, lent her countenance an expression of pride, to which her coquettish instincts and her mirror had taught her to add terror by a stare, or gentleness by the softness of her gaze, by the set or the gracious curve of her lips, by the coldness or the sweetness of her smile. When Emilie meant to conquer a heart, her pure voice did not lack melody; but she could also give it a sort of curt clearness when she was minded to paralyse a partner's indiscreet tongue. Her colourless face and alabaster brow were like the limpid surface of a lake, which by turns is rippled by the impulse of a breeze and recovers its glad serenity when the air is still. More than one young man, a victim to her scorn, accused her of acting a part; but she justified herself by inspiring her detractors with the desire to please her, and then subjecting them to all her most contemptuous caprice. Among the young girls of fashion, not one knew better than she how to assume an air of reserve when a man of talent was introduced to her, or how to display the insulting politeness which treats an equal as an inferior, and to pour out her impertinence on all who tried to hold their heads on a level with hers.. Wherever she went she seemed to be accepting homage rather than compliments, and even in a princess her airs and manner would have transformed the chair on which she sat into an imperial throne.

Monsieur de Fontaine discovered too late how utterly the education of the daughter he loved had been ruined by the tender devotion of the whole family. The admiration which the world is at first ready to bestow on a young girl, but for which, sooner or later, it takes its revenge, had added to Emilie's pride, and increased her self-confidence. Universal subservience had developed in her the selfishness natural to spoilt children, who, like kings, make a plaything of every thing that comes to hand. As yet the graces of youth and the charms of talent hid these faults from every eye; faults all the more odious in a woman, since she can only please by self-sacrifice and unselfishness; but nothing escapes the eye of a good father, and Monsieur de Fontaine often tried to explain to his daughter the more important pages of the mysterious book of life. Vain effort! He had to lament his daughter's capricious indocility and ironical shrewdness too often to persevere in a task so difficult as that of correcting an ill-disposed nature. He contented himself with giving her from time to time some gentle and kind advice; but he had the sorrow of seeing his tenderest words slide from his daughter's heart as if it were of marble. A father's eyes are slow to be unsealed, and it needed more than one experience before the old Royalist perceived that his daughter's rare caresses were bestowed on him with an air of condescension. She was like young children, who seem to say to their mother, "Make haste to kiss me, that I may go to play." In short, Emilie vouchsafed to be fond of her parents. But, often, by those sudden whims, which seem inexplicable in young girls, she kept aloof and scarcely ever appeared; she complained of having to share her father's and mother's heart with too many people; she was jealous of every one, even of her brothers and sisters. Then, after creating a desert about her, the strange girl accused all nature of her unreal solitude and her wilful griefs. Strong in the experience of her twenty years, she blamed fate, because, not knowing that the mainspring of happiness is in ourselves, she demanded it of the circumstances of life. She would have fled to the ends of the earth to escape a marriage such as those of her two sisters, and nevertheless her heart was full of horrible jealousy at seeing them married, rich, and happy. In short, she sometimes led her mother—who was as much a victim to her vagaries as Monsieur de Fontaine—to suspect that she had a touch of madness.

But such aberrations are quite inexplicable; nothing is commoner than this unconfessed pride developed in the heart of young girls belonging to families high in the social scale, and gifted by nature with great beauty. They are almost all convinced that their mothers, now forty or fifty years of age, can neither sympathise with their young souls, nor conceive of their imaginings. They fancy that most mothers, jealous of their girls, want to dress them in their own way with the premeditated purpose of eclipsing them or robbing them of admiration. Hence, often, secret tears and dumb revolt against supposed tyranny. In the midst of these woes, which become very real though built on an imaginary basis, they have also a mania for composing a scheme of life, while casting for themselves a brilliant horoscope; their magic consists in taking their dreams for reality; secretly, in their long meditations; they resolve to give their heart and hand to none but a man possessing this or the other qualification; and they paint in fancy a model to which, whether or no, the future lover must correspond. After some little experience of life, and, the serious reflections that come with years, by dint of seeing the world and its prosaic round, by dint of observing unhappy examples, the brilliant hues of their ideal are extinguished. Then, one fine day, in the course of events, they are quite astonished to find themselves happy without the nuptial poetry of their day-dreams. It was on the strength of that poetry that Mademoiselle Emilie de Fontaine, in her slender wisdom, had drawn up a programme to which a suitor must conform to be accepted. Hence her disdain and sarcasm.

"Though young and of an ancient family, he must be a peer of France," said she to herself. "I could not bear not to see my coat-of-arms on the panels of my carriage among the folds of azure mantling, not to drive like the princes down the broad walk of the Champs-Elysées on the days of Longchamps in Holy Week. Besides, my father says that it will some day be the highest dignity in France. He must be a soldier—but I reserve the right of making him retire; and he must bear an Order, that the sentries may present arms to us."

And these rare qualifications would count for nothing if this creature of fancy had not a most amiable temper, a fine figure, intelligence, and, above all, if he were not slender. To be lean, a personal grace which is but fugitive, especially under a representative government, was an indispensable condition. Mademoiselle de Fontaine had an ideal standard which was to be the model. A young man who at the first glance did not fulfil the requisite conditions did not even get a second look.

"Good Heavens! see how fat he is!" was with her the utmost expression of contempt.

To hear her, people of respectable corpulence were incapable of sentiment, bad husbands, and unfit for civilized society. Though it is esteemed a beauty in the East, to be fat seemed to her a misfortune for a woman; but in a man it was a crime. These paradoxical views were amusing, thanks to a certain liveliness of rhetoric. The Count felt nevertheless that by-and-by his daughter's affections, of which the absurdity would be evident to some women who were not less clear-sighted than merciless, would inevitably become a subject of constant ridicule. He feared lest her eccentric notions should deviate into bad style. He trembled to think that the pitiless world might already be laughing at a young woman who remained so long on the stage without arriving at any conclusion of the drama she was playing. More than one actor in it, disgusted by a refusal, seemed to be waiting for the slightest turn of ill-luck to take his revenge. The indifferent, the lookers-on were beginning to weary of it; admiration is always exhausting to human beings. The old Vendéen knew better than any one that if there is an art in choosing the right moment for coming forward on the boards of the world, on those of the Court, in a drawing-room or on the stage, it is still more difficult to quit them in the nick of time. So during the first winter after the accession of Charles X, he redoubled his efforts, seconded by his three sons and his sons-in-law, to assemble in the rooms of his official residence the best matches which Paris and the various deputations from departments could offer. The splendour of his entertainments, the luxury of his dining-room, and his dinners, fragrant with truffles, rivaled the famous banquets by which the ministers of that time secured the vote of their parliamentary recruits.

The Honourable Deputy was consequently pointed at as a most influential corrupter of the legislative honesty of the illustrious Chamber that was dying as it would seem of indigestion. A whimsical result! his efforts to get his daughter married secured him a splendid popularity. He perhaps found some covert advantage in selling his truffles twice over. This accusation, started by certain mocking Liberals, who made up by their flow of words for their small following in the Chamber, was not a success. The Poitevin gentleman had always been so noble and so honourable, that he was not once the object of those epigrams which the malicious journalism of the day hurled at the three hundred votes of the centre, at the Ministers, the cooks, the Directors-General, the princely Amphitryons, and the official supporters of the Villèle Ministry.

At the close of this campaign, during which Monsieur de Fontaine had on several occasions brought out all his forces, he believed that this time the procession of suitors would not be a mere dissolving view in his daughter's eyes; that it was time she should make up her mind. He felt a certain inward satisfaction at having well fulfilled his duty as a father. And having left no stone unturned, he hoped that, among so many hearts laid at Emilie's feet, there might be one to which her caprice might give a preference. Incapable of repeating such an effort; and tired, too, of his daughter's conduct, one morning, towards the end of Lent, when the business at the Chamber did not demand his vote, he determined to ask what her views were. While his valet was artistically decorating his bald yellow head with the delta of powder which, with the hanging "*ailes de pigeon*," completed his venerable style of hairdressing, Emilie's father, not without some secret misgivings, told his old servant to go and desire the haughty damsel to appear in the presence of the head of the family.

"Joseph," he added, when his hair was dressed, "take away that towel, draw back the curtains, put those chairs square, shake the rug, and lay it quite straight. Dust every thing.—Now, air the room a little by opening the window."

The Count multiplied his orders, putting Joseph out of breath, and the old servant, understanding his master's intentions, aired and tidied the room, of course the least cared for of any in the house, and succeeded in giving a look of harmony to the files of bills, the letter-boxes, the books and furniture of this sanctum, where the interests of the royal demesnes were debated over. When Joseph had reduced this chaos to some sort of order, and brought to the front such things as might be most pleasing to the eye, as if it were a shop front, or such as by their colour might give the effect of a kind of official poetry, he stood for a minute in the midst of the labyrinth of papers piled in some places even on the floor, admired his handiwork, jerked his head, and went.

The anxious sinecure-holder did not share his retainer's favourable opinion. Before seating himself in his deep chair, whose rounded back screened him from draughts, he looked round him doubtfully, examined his dressing-gown with a hostile expression, shook off a few grains of snuff, carefully wiped his nose, arranged the tongs and shovel, made the fire, pulled up the heels of his slippers, pulled out his little queue of hair which had lodged horizontally between the collar of his waistcoat and that of his dressing-gown, restoring it to its perpendicular position; then he swept up the ashes of the hearth, which bore witness to a persistent catarrh. Finally, the old man did not settle himself till he had once more looked all over the room, hoping that nothing could give occasion to the saucy and impertinent remarks with which his daughter was apt to answer his good advice. On this occasion he was anxious not to compromise his dignity as a father. He daintily took a pinch of snuff, cleared his throat two or three times, as if he were about to demand a count out of the House; then he heard his daughter's light step, and she came in humming an air from *Il Barbiere.*

"Good-morning, papa. What do you want with me so early?" Having sung these words, as though they were the refrain of the melody, she kissed the Count, not with the familiar tenderness which makes a daughter's love so sweet a thing, but with the light carelessness of a mistress confident of pleasing, whatever she may do.

"My dear child," said Monsieur de Fontaine, gravely, "I sent for you to talk to you very seriously about your future prospects. You are at this moment under the necessity of making such a choice of a husband as may secure you durable happiness—"

"My good father," replied Emilie, assuming her most coaxing tone of voice to interrupt him, "it strikes me that the armistice on which we agreed as to my suitors is not yet expired."

"Emilie, we must to-day forbear from jesting on so important a matter. For some time past the efforts of those who most truly love you, my dear child, have been concentrated on the endeavour to settle you suitably; and you would be guilty of ingratitude in meeting with levity those proofs of kindness which I am not alone in lavishing on you."

As she heard these words, after flashing a mischievously inquisitive look at the furniture of her father's study, the young girl brought forward the armchair which looked as if it had been least used by petitioners, set it at the side of the fireplace so as to sit facing her father, and settled herself in so solemn an attitude that it was impossible not to read in it a mocking intention, crossing her arms over the dainty trimmings of a pelerine *à la neige,* and ruthlessly crushing its endless frills of white tulle. After a laughing side glance at her old father's troubled face, she broke silence.

"I never heard you say, my dear father, that the Government issued its instructions in its dressing-gown. However," and she smiled, "that does not, matter; the mob are probably not particular. Now, what are your proposals for legislation, and your official introductions?"

"I shall not always be able to make them, headstrong girl!—Listen, Emilie. It is my intention no longer to compromise my reputation, which is part of my children's fortune, by recruiting the regiment of dancers which, spring after spring, you put to rout. You have already been the cause of many dangerous misunderstandings with certain families. I hope to make you perceive more truly the difficulties of your position and of ours. You are two-and-twenty, my dear child, and you ought to have been married nearly three years since. Your brothers and your two sisters are richly and happily provided for. But, my dear, the expenses occasioned by these marriages, and the style of housekeeping you require of your mother, have made such inroads on our income that I can hardly promise you a hundred thousand francs as a marriage portion. From this day forth I shall think only of providing for your mother, who must not be sacrificed to her children. Emilie, if I were to be taken from my family, Madame de Fontaine could not be left at anybody's mercy, and ought to enjoy the affluence which I have given her too late as the reward of her devotion in my misfortunes. You see, my child, that the amount of your fortune bears no relation to your notions of grandeur. Even that would be such a sacrifice as I have not hitherto made for either of my children; but they have generously agreed not to expect in the future any compensation for the advantage thus given to a too favoured child."

"In their position!" said Emilie, with an ironical toss of her head.

"My dear, do not so depreciate those who love you. Only the poor are generous as a rule; the rich have always excellent reasons for not handing over twenty thousand francs to a relation. Come, my child, do not pout, let us talk rationally.—Among the young marrying men have you noticed Monsieur de Manerville?"

"Oh, he minces his words—he says Zules instead of Jules; he is always looking at his feet, because he thinks them small, and he gazes at himself in the glass! Besides, he is fair. I don't like fair men."

"Well, then, Monsieur de Beaudenord?"

"He is not noble! he is ill made and stout. He is dark, it is true.—If the two gentlemen could agree to combine their fortunes, and the first would give his name and his figure to the second, who should keep his dark hair, then—perhaps—"

'What can you say against Monsieur de Rastignac?"

"Madame de Nucingen has made a banker of him," she said with meaning.

"And our cousin, the Vicomte de Portenduère?"

"A mere boy, who dances badly; besides, he has no fortune. And, after all, papa, none of these people have titles. I want, at least, to be a countess like my mother."

"Have you seen no one, then, this winter—?"

"No, papa."

"What then do you want?"

"The son of a peer of France."

"My dear girl, you are mad!" said Monsieur de Fontaine, rising.

But he suddenly lifted his eyes to heaven, and seemed to find a fresh fount of resignation in some religious thought; then, with a look of fatherly pity at his daughter, who herself was moved, he took her hand, pressed it, and said with deep feeling: "God is my witness, poor mistaken child, I have conscientiously discharged my duty to you as a father—conscientiously, do I say? Most lovingly, my Emilie. Yes, God knows! This winter I have brought before you more than one good man, whose character, whose habits, and whose temper were known to me, and all seemed worthy of you. My child, my task is done. From this day forth you are the arbiter of your fate, and I consider myself both happy and unhappy at finding myself relieved of the heaviest of paternal functions. I know not whether you will for any long time, now, hear a voice which, to you, has never been stern; but remember that conjugal happiness does not rest so much on brilliant qualities and ample fortune as on reciprocal esteem. This happiness is, in its nature, modest, and devoid of show. So now, my dear, my consent is given beforehand, whoever the son-in-law may be whom you introduce to me; but if you should be unhappy, remember you will have no right to accuse your father. I shall not refuse to take proper steps and help you, only your choice must be serious and final. I will never twice compromise the respect due to my white hairs."

The affection thus expressed by her father, the solemn tones of his urgent address, deeply touched Mademoiselle de Fontaine; but she concealed her emotion, seated herself on her father's knees—for he had dropped all tremulous into his chair again—caressed him fondly, and coaxed him so engagingly that the old man's brow cleared. As soon as Emilie thought that her father had got over his painful agitation, she said in a gentle voice: "I have to thank you for your graceful attention, my dear father. You have had your room set in order to receive your beloved daughter. You did not perhaps know that you would find her so foolish and so headstrong. But, papa, is it so difficult to get married to a peer of France? You declared that they were manufactured by dozens. At least, you will not refuse to advise me."

"No, my poor child, no;—and more than once I may have occasion to cry, 'Beware!' Remember that the making of peers is so recent a force in our government machinery that they have no great fortunes. Those who are rich look to becoming richer. The wealthiest member of our peerage has not half the income of the least rich lord in the English Upper Chamber. Thus all the French peers are on the lookout for great heiresses for their sons, wherever they may meet with them. The necessity in which they find themselves of marrying for money will certainly exist for at least two centuries.

"Pending such a fortunate accident as you long for—and this fastidiousness may cost you the best years of your life—your attractions might work a miracle, for men often marry for love in these days. When experience lurks behind so sweet a face as yours it may achieve wonders. In the first place, have you not the gift of recognising virtue in the greater or smaller dimensions of a man's body? This is no small matter! To so wise a young person as you are, I need not enlarge on all the difficulties of the enterprise. I am sure that you would never attribute good sense to a stranger because he had a handsome face, or all the virtues because he had a fine figure. And I am quite of your mind in thinking that the sons of peers ought to have an air peculiar to themselves, and perfectly distinctive manners. Though nowadays no external sign stamps a man of rank, those young men will have, perhaps, to you the indefinable something that will reveal it. Then, again, you have your heart well in hand, like a good horseman who is sure his steed cannot bolt. Luck be with you, my dear!"

"You are making game of me, papa. Well, I assure you that I would rather die in Mademoiselle de Condé's convent than not be the wife of a peer of France."

She slipped out of her father's arms, and, proud of being her own mistress, went off singing the air of *Cara non dubitare*, in the "Matrimonio Segreto."

As it happened, the family were that day keeping the anniversary of a family fête. At dessert, Madame Planat, the Receiver-General's wife, spoke with some enthusiasm of a young American owning an immense fortune, who had fallen passionately in love with her sister, and made through her the most splendid proposals.

"A banker, I rather think," observed Emilie carelessly. "I do not like money dealers."

"But, Emilie," replied the Baron de Villaine, the husband of the Count's second daughter, "you do not like lawyers either; so that if you refuse men of wealth who have not titles, I do not quite see in what class you are to choose a husband."

"Especially, Emilie, with your standard of slimness," added the Lieutenant-General.

"I know what I want," replied the young lady.

"My sister wants a fine name, a fine young man, fine prospects, and a hundred thousand francs a year," said the Baronne de Fontaine. "Monsieur de Marsay, for instance."

"I know, my dear," retorted Emilie, "that I do not mean to make such a foolish marriage as some I have seen. Moreover, to put an end to these matrimonial discussions, I hereby declare that I shall look on anyone who talks to me of marriage as a foe to my peace of mind."

An uncle of Emilie's, a vice-admiral, whose fortune had just been increased by twenty thousand francs a year in consequence of the Act of Indemnity, and a man of seventy, feeling himself privileged to say hard things to his grand-niece, on whom he doted, in order to mollify the bitter tone of the discussion now exclaimed:

"Do not tease my poor little Emilie; don't you see she is waiting till the Duc de Bordeaux comes of age!"

The old man's pleasantry was received with general laughter.

"Take care I don't marry you, old fool!" replied the young girl, whose last words were happily droned in the noise.

"My dear children," said Madame de Fontaine, to soften this saucy retort, "Emilie, like you, will take no advice but her mother's."

"Bless me! I shall take no advice but my own in a matter which concerns no one but myself," said Mademoiselle de Fontaine very distinctly.

At this all eyes were turned to the head of the family. Every one seemed anxious as to what he would do to assert his dignity. The venerable gentleman enjoyed much consideration, not only in the world; happier than many fathers, he was also appreciated by his family, all its members having a just esteem for the solid qualities by which he had been able to make their fortunes. Hence he was treated with the deep respect which is shown by English families, and some aristocratic houses on the continent, to the living representative of an ancient pedigree. Deep silence had fallen; and the guests looked alternately from the spoilt girl's proud and sulky pout to the severe faces of Monsieur and Madame de Fontaine.

"I have made my daughter Emilie mistress of her own fate," was the reply spoken by the Count in a deep voice.

Relations and guests gazed at Mademoiselle de Fontaine with mingled curiosity and pity. The words seemed to declare that fatherly affection was weary of the contest with a character that the whole family knew to be incorrigible. The sons-in-law muttered, and the brothers glanced at their wives with mocking smiles. From that moment every one ceased to take any interest in the haughty girl's prospects of marriage. Her old uncle was the only person who, as an old sailor, ventured to stand on her tack, and take her broadsides, without ever troubling himself to return her fire.

When the fine weather was settled, and after the budget was voted, the whole family—a perfect example of the parliamentary families on the northern side of the Channel who have a footing in every government department, and ten votes in the House of Commons—flew away like a brood of young birds to the charming neighbourhoods of Aulnay, Antony, and Châtenay. The wealthy Receiver-General had lately purchased in this part of the world a country-house for his wife, who remained in Paris only during the session. Though the fair Emilie despised the commonalty, her feeling was not carried so far as to scorn the advantages of a fortune acquired in a profession; so she accompanied her sister to the sumptuous villa, less out of affection for the members of her family who were visiting there, than because fashion has ordained that every woman who has any self-respect must leave Paris in the summer. The green seclusion of Sceaux answered to perfection the requirements of good style and of the duties of an official position.

As it is extremely doubtful that the fame of the "Bal de Sceaux" should ever have extended beyond the borders of the Department of the Seine, it will be necessary to give some account of this weekly festivity, which at that time was important enough to threaten to become an institution. The environs of the little town of Sceaux enjoy a reputation due to the scenery, which is considered enchanting. Perhaps it is quite ordinary, and owes its fame only to the stupidity of the Paris townsfolk, who, emerging from the stony abyss in which they are buried, would find something to admire in the flats of La Beauce. However, as the poetic shades of Aulnay, the hillsides of Antony, and the valley of the Biève are peopled with artists who have traveled far, by foreigners who are very hard to please, and by a great many pretty women not devoid of taste, it is to be supposed that the Parisians are right. But Sceaux possesses another attraction not less powerful to the Parisian. In the midst of a garden whence there are delightful views, stands a large rotunda open on all sides, with a light, spreading roof supported on elegant pillars. This rural baldachino shelters a dancing-floor. The most stuck-up landowners of the neighborhood rarely fail to make an excursion thither once or twice during the season, arriving at this rustic palace of Terpsichore either in dashing parties on horseback, or in the light and elegant carriages which powder the philosophical pedestrian with dust. The hope of meeting some women of fashion, and of being seen by them—and the hope, less often disappointed, of seeing young peasant girls, as wily as judges—crowds the ballroom at Sceaux with numerous swarm of lawyers' clerks, of the disciples of Æsculapius, and other youths whose complexions are kept pale and moist by the damp atmosphere of Paris back-shops. And a good many bourgeois marriages have had their beginning to the sound of the band occupying the centre of this circular ball room. If that roof could speak, what love-stories could it not tell!

This interesting medley gave the Sceaux balls at that time a spice of more amusement than those of two or three places of the same kind near Paris; and it had incontestable advantages in its rotunda, and the beauty of its situation and its garden. Emilie was the first to express a wish to play at being *common folk* at this gleeful suburban entertainment, and promised herself immense pleasure in mingling with the crowd. Everybody wondered at her desire to wander through such a mob; but is there not a keen pleasure to grand people in an *incognito*? Mademoiselle de Fontaine amused herself with imagining all these town-bred figures; she fancied herself leaving the memory of a bewitching glance and smile stamped on more than one shopkeeper's heart, laughed beforehand at the damsels' airs, and sharpened her pencils for the scenes he proposed to sketch in her satirical album. Sunday could not come soon enough to satisfy her impatience.

The party from the Villa Planat set out on foot, so as not to betray the rank of the personages who were about to honour the ball with their presence. They dined early. And the month of May humoured this aristocratic escapade by one of its finest evenings. Mademoiselle de Fontaine was quite surprised to find in the rotunda some quadrilles made up of persons who seemed to belong to the upper classes. Here and there, indeed, were some young men who look as though they must have saved for a month to shine for a day; and she perceived several couples whose too hearty glee suggested nothing conjugal; still, she could only glean instead of gathering a harvest. She was amazed to see that pleasure in a cotton dress was so very like pleasure robed in satin, and that the girls of the middle class danced quite as well as ladies—nay, sometimes better. Most of the women were simply and suitably dressed. Those who in this assembly represented the ruling power, that is to say, the country-folk, kept apart with wonderful politeness. In fact, Mademoiselle Emilie had to study the various elements that composed the mixture before she could find any subject for pleasantry. But she had not time to give herself up to malicious criticism, nor opportunity for hearing many of the startling speeches which caricaturists so gladly pick up. The haughty young lady suddenly found a flower in this wide field—the metaphor is reasonable—whose splendour and colouring worked on her imagination with all the fascination of novelty. It often happens that we look at a dress, a hanging, a blank sheet of paper, with so little heed that we do not at first detect a stain or a bright spot which afterwards strikes the eye as though it had come there at the very instant when we see it; and by a sort of moral phenomenon somewhat resembling this, Mademoiselle de Fontaine discovered in a young man the external perfections of which she had so long dreamed.

Seated on one of the clumsy chairs which marked the boundary line of the circular floor, she had placed herself at the end of the row formed by the family party, so as to be able to stand up or push forward as her fancy moved her, treating the living pictures and groups in the hall as if she were in a picture gallery; impertinently turning her eye glass on persons not two yards away, and making her remarks as though she were criticising or praising a study of a head, a painting of *genre*. Her eyes, after wandering over the vast moving picture, were suddenly caught by this figure, which seemed to have been placed on purpose in one corner of the canvas, and in the best light, like a person out of all proportion with the rest.

The stranger, alone and absorbed in thought, leaned lightly against one of the columns that supported the roof; his arms were folded, and he leaned slightly on one side as though he had placed himself there to have his portrait taken by a painter. His attitude, though full of elegance and dignity, was devoid of affectation. Nothing suggested that he had half turned his head, and bent it a little to the right like Alexander, or Lord Byron, and some other great men, for the sole purpose of attracting attention. His fixed gaze followed a girl who was dancing, and betrayed some strong feeling. His slender, easy frame recalled the noble proportions of the Apollo. Fine black hair curled naturally over a high forehead. At a glance Mademoiselle de Fontaine observed that his linen was fine, his gloves fresh, and evidently bought of a good maker, and his feet small and well shod in boots of Irish kid. He had none of the vulgar trinkets displayed by the dandies of the National Guard or the Love-laces of the counting-house. A black ribbon, to which an eye-glass was attached, hung over a waistcoat of the most fashionable cut. Never had the fastidious Emilie seen a man's eyes shaded by such long, curled lashes. Melancholy and passion were expressed in this face, and the complexion was of a manly olive hue. His mouth seemed ready to smile, unbending the corners of eloquent lips; but this, far from hinting at gaiety, revealed on the contrary a sort of pathetic grace. There was too much promise in that head, too much distinction in his whole person, to allow of one's saying, "What a handsome man!" or "What a fine man!" One wanted to know him. The most clear-sighted observer, on seeing this stranger, could not have helped taking him for a clever man attracted to this rural festivity by some powerful motive.

All these observations cost Emilie only a minute's attention, during which the privileged gentleman under her severe scrutiny became the object of her secret admiration. She did not say to herself, "He must be a peer of France!" but, "Oh, if only he is noble, and he surely must be—" Without finishing her thought, she suddenly rose, and followed by her brother the General, she made her way towards the column, affecting to watch the merry quadrille; but by a stratagem of the eye, familiar to women, she lost not a gesture of the young man as she went towards him. The stranger politely moved to make way for the newcomers, and went to lean against another pillar. Emilie, as much nettled by his politeness as she might have been by an impertinence, began talking to her brother in a louder voice than good taste enjoined; she turned and tossed her head, gesticulated eagerly, and laughed for no particular reason, less to amuse her brother than to attract the attention of the imperturbable stranger. None of her little arts succeeded. Mademoiselle de Fontaine then followed the direction in which his eyes were fixed, and discovered the cause of his indifference.

In the midst of the quadrille, close in front of them, a pale girl was dancing; her face was like one of the divinities which Girodet has introduced into his immense composition of French Warriors received by Ossian. Emilie fancied that she recognized her as a distinguished *milady* who for some months had been living on a neighbouring estate. Her partner was a lad of about fifteen, with red hands, and dressed in nankeen trousers, a blue coat, and white shoes, which showed that the damsel's love of dancing made her easy to please in the matter of partners. Her movements did not betray her apparent delicacy, but a faint flush already tinged her white cheeks, and her complexion was gaining colour. Mademoiselle de Fontaine went nearer, to be able to examine the young lady at the moment when she returned to her place, while the side couples in their turn danced the figure. But the stranger went up to the pretty dancer, and leaning over, said in a gentle but commanding tone:

"Clara, my child, do not dance any more."

Clara made a little pouting face, bent her head, and finally smiled. When the dance was over, the young man wrapped her in a cashmere shawl with a lover's care, and seated her in a place sheltered from the wind. Very soon Mademoiselle de Fontaine, seeing them rise and walk round the place as if preparing to leave, found means to follow them under pretence of admiring the views from the garden. Her brother lent himself with malicious good-humour to the divagations of her rather eccentric wanderings. Emilie then saw the attractive couple get into an elegant tilbury, by which stood a mounted groom in livery. At the moment when, from his high seat, the young man was drawing the reins even, she caught a glance from his eye such as a man casts aimlessly at the crowd; and then she enjoyed the feeble satisfaction of seeing him twice turn his head to look at her. The young lady did the same. Was it from jealousy?

"I imagine you have now seen enough of the garden," said her brother. "We may go back to the dancing."

"I am ready," said she. "Do you think the girl can be a relation of Lady Dudley's?"

"Lady Dudley may have some male relation staying with her," said the Baron de Fontaine; "but a young girl!—No!"

Next day Mademoiselle de Fontaine expressed a wish to take a ride. Then she gradually accustomed her old uncle and her brothers to escorting her in very early rides, excellent, she declared, for her health. She had a particular fancy for the environs of the hamlet where Lady Dudley was living. Notwithstanding her cavalry manuvres, she did not meet the stranger so soon as the eager search she pursued might have allowed her to hope. She went several times to the "Bal de Sceaux" without seeing the young Englishman who had dropped from the skies to pervade and beautify her dreams. Though nothing spurs on a young girl's infant passion so effectually as an obstacle, there was a time when Mademoiselle de Fontaine was on the point of giving up her strange and secret search, almost despairing of the success of an enterprise whose singularity may give some idea of the boldness of her temper. In point of fact, she might have wandered long about the village of Châtenay without meeting her Unknown. The fair Clara—since that was the name Emilie had overheard—was not English, and the stranger who escorted her did not dwell among the flowery and fragrant bowers of Châtenay.

One evening Emilie, out riding with her uncle, who, during the fine weather, had gained a fairly long truce from the gout, met Lady Dudley. The distinguished foreigner had with her in her open carriage Monsieur Vandenesse. Emilie recognized the handsome couple, and her suppositions were at once dissipated like a dream. Annoyed, as any woman must be whose expectations are frustrated, she touched up her horse so suddenly that her uncle had the greatest difficulty in following her, she had set off at such a pace.

"I am too old, it would seem, to understand these youthful spirits," said the old sailor to himself as he put his horse to a canter; "or perhaps young people are not what they used to be. But what ails my niece? Now she is walking at a foot-pace like a gendarme on patrol in the Paris streets. One might fancy she wanted to outflank that worthy man, who looks to me like an author dreaming over his poetry, for he has, I think, a notebook in his hand. My word, I am a great simpleton! Is not that the very young man we are in search of!"

At this idea the old admiral moderated his horse's pace so as to follow his niece without making any noise. He had played too many pranks in the years

1771 and soon after, a time of our history when gallantry was held in honour, not to guess at once that by the merest chance Emilie had met the Unknown of the Sceaux gardens. In spite of the film which age had drawn over his grey eyes, the Comte de Kergarouët could recognize the signs of extreme agitation in his niece, under the unmoved expression she tried to give to her features. The girl's piercing eyes were fixed in a sort of dull amazement on the stranger, who quietly walked on in front of her.

"Ay, that's it," thought the sailor. "She is following him as a pirate follows a merchantman. Then, when she has lost sight of him, she will be in despair at not knowing who it is she is in love with, and whether he is a marquis or a shopkeeper. Really these young heads need an old fogy like me always by their side …"

He unexpectedly spurred his horse in such a way as to make his niece's bolt, and rode so hastily between her and the young man on foot that he obliged him to fall back on to the grassy bank which rose from the roadside. Then, abruptly drawing up, the Count exclaimed:

"Couldn't you get out of the way?"

"I beg your pardon, monsieur. But I did not know that it lay with me to apologise to you because you almost rode me down."

"There, enough of that, my good fellow!" replied the sailor harshly, in a sneering tone that was nothing less than insulting. At the same time the Count raised his hunting-crop as if to strike his horse, and touched the young fellow's shoulder, saying, "A liberal citizen is a reasoner; every reasoner should be prudent."

The young man went up the bankside as he heard the sarcasm; then he crossed his arms, and said in an excited tone of voice, "I cannot suppose, monsieur, as I look at your white hairs, that you still amuse yourself by provoking duels—"

"White hairs!" cried the sailor, interrupting him. "You lie in your throat. They are only grey."

A quarrel thus begun had in a few seconds become so fierce that the younger man forgot the moderation he had tried to preserve. Just as the Comte de Kergarouët saw his niece coming back to them with every sign of the greatest uneasiness, he told his antagonist his name, bidding him keep silence before the young lady entrusted to his care. The stranger could not help smiling as he gave a visiting card to the old man, desiring him to observe that he was living in a country-house at Chevreuse; and, after pointing this out to him, he hurried away.

"You very nearly damaged that poor young counter-jumper, my dear," said the Count, advancing hastily to meet Emilie. "Do you not know how to hold your horse in?—And there you leave me to compromise my dignity in order to screen your folly; whereas if you had but stopped, one of your looks, or one of your pretty speeches—one of those you can make so prettily when you are not pert—would have set everything right, even if you had broken his arm."

"But, my dear uncle, it was your horse, not mine, that caused the accident. I really think you can no longer ride; you are not so good a horseman as you were last year.—But instead of talking nonsense—"

"Nonsense, by Gad! Is it nothing to be so impertinent to your uncle?"

"Ought we not to go on and inquire if the young man is hurt? He is limping, uncle, only look!"

"No, he is running; I rated him soundly."

"Oh, yes, uncle; I know you there!"

"Stop," said the Count, pulling Emilie's horse by the bridle, "I do not see the necessity of making advances to some shopkeeper who is only too lucky to have been thrown down by a charming young lady, or the commander of *La Belle-Poule*."

"Why do you think he is anything so common, my dear uncle? He seems to me to have very fine manners."

"Every one has manners nowadays, my dear."

"No, uncle, not every one has the air and style which come of the habit of frequenting drawing-rooms, and I am ready to lay a bet with you that the young man is of noble birth."

"You had not long to study him."

"No, but it is not the first time I have seen him."

"Nor is it the first time you have looked for him," replied the admiral with a laugh.

Emilie coloured. Her uncle amused himself for some time with her embarrassment; then he said: "Emilie, you know that I love you as my own child, precisely because you are the only member of the family who has the legitimate pride of high birth. Devil take it, child, who could have believed that sound principles would become so rare? Well, I will be your confidant. My dear child, I see that this young gentleman is not indifferent to you. Hush! All the family would laugh at us if we sailed under the wrong flag. You know what that means. We two will keep our secret, and I promise to bring him straight into the drawing-room."

"When, uncle?"

"To-morrow."

"But, my dear uncle, I am not committed to anything?"

"Nothing whatever, and you may bombard him, set fire to him, and leave him to founder like an old hulk if you choose. He won't be the first, I fancy?"

"You *are* kind, uncle!"

As soon as the Count got home he put on his glasses, quietly took the card out of his pocket, and read, "Maximilien Longueville, Rue du Sentier."

"Make yourself happy, my dear niece," he said to Emilie, "you may hook him with an easy conscience; he belongs to one of our historical families, and if he is not a peer of France, he infallibly will be."

"How do you know so much?"

"That is my secret."

"Then do you know his name?"

The old man bowed his grey head, which was not unlike a gnarled oak-stump, with a few leaves fluttering about it, withered by autumnal frosts; and his niece immediately began to try the ever-new power of her coquettish arts. Long familiar with the secret of cajoling the old man, she lavished on him the most childlike caresses, the tenderest names; she even went so far as to kiss him to induce him to divulge so important a secret. The old man, who spent his life in playing off these scenes on his niece, often paying for them with a present of jewelry, or by giving her his box at the opera, this time amused himself with her entreaties, and, above all, her caresses. But as he spun out this pleasure too long, Emilie grew angry, passed from coaxing to sarcasm and sulks; then, urged by curiosity, she recovered herself. The diplomatic admiral extracted a solemn promise from his niece that she would for the future be gentler, less noisy and less wilful, that she would spend less, and, above all, tell him everything. The treaty being concluded, and signed by a kiss impressed on Emilie's white brow, he led her into a corner of the room, drew her on to his knee, held the card under the thumbs so as to hide it, and then uncovered the letters one by one, spelling the name of Longueville; but he firmly refused to show her anything more.

This incident added to the intensity of Mademoiselle le Fontaine's secret sentiment, and during chief part of the night she evolved the most brilliant pictures from the dreams with which she had fed her hopes. At last, thanks to chance, to which she had so often appealed, Emilie could now see something very unlike a chimera at the fountain-head of the imaginary wealth with which she gilded her married life. Ignorant, as all young girls are, of the perils of love and marriage, she was passionately captivated by the externals of marriage and love. Is not this as much as to say that her feeling had birth like all the feelings of extreme youth—sweet but cruel mistakes, which exert a fatal influence on the lives of young girls so inexperienced as to trust their own judgment to take care of their future happiness?

Next morning, before Emilie was awake, her uncle had hastened to Chevreuse. On recognizing, in the courtyard of an elegant little villa, the young man he had so determinedly insulted the day before, he went up to him with the pressing politeness of men of the old court.

"Why, my dear sir, who could have guessed that I should have a brush, at the age of seventy-three, with the son, or the grandson, of one of my best friends. I am a vice-admiral, monsieur; is not that as much as to say that I think no more of fighting a duel than of smoking a cigar? Why, in my time, no two young men could be intimate till they had seen the colour of their blood! But 'sdeath, sir, last evening, sailor-like, I had taken a drop too much grog on board, and I ran you down. Shake hands; I would rather take a hundred rebuffs from a Longueville than cause his family the smallest regret."

However coldly the young man tried to behave to the Comte de Kergarouët, he could not long resist the frank cordiality of his manner, and presently gave him his hand.

"You were going out riding," said the Count. "Do not let me detain you. But, unless you have other plans, I beg you will come to dinner to-day at the Villa Planat. My nephew, the Comte de Fontaine, is a man it is essential that you should know. Ah, ha! And I propose to make up to you for my clumsiness by introducing you to five of the prettiest women in Paris. So, so, young man, your brow is clearing! I am fond of young people, and I like to see them happy. Their happiness reminds me of the good times of my youth, when adventures were not lacking, any more than duels. We were gay dogs then! Nowadays you think and worry over everything, as though there had never been a fifteenth and a sixteenth century."

"But, monsieur, are we not in the right? The sixteenth century only gave religious liberty to Europe, and the nineteenth will give it political lib—"

"Oh, we will not talk politics. I am a perfect old woman—*ultra* you see. But I do not hinder young men from being revolutionary, so long as they leave the King at liberty to disperse their assemblies."

When they had gone a little way, and the Count and his companion were in the heart of the woods, the old sailor pointed out a slender young birch sapling, pulled up his horse, took out one of his pistols, and the bullet was lodged in the heart of the tree, fifteen paces away.

"You see, my dear fellow, that I am not afraid of a duel," he said with comical gravity, as he looked at Monsieur Longueville

"Nor am I," replied the young man, promptly cocking his pistol; he aimed at the hole made by the Comte's bullet, and sent his own in close to it.

"That is what I call a well-educated man," cried the admiral with enthusiasm.

During this ride with the youth, whom he already regarded as his nephew, he found endless opportunities of catechizing him on all the trifles of which a perfect knowledge constituted, according to his private code, an accomplished gentleman.

"Have you any debts?" he at last asked of his companion, after many other inquiries.

"No, monsieur."

'What, you pay for all you have?"

"Punctually; otherwise we should lose our credit, and every sort of respect."

"But at least you have more than one mistress? Ah, you blush, comrade! Well, manners have changed. All these notions of lawful order, Kantism, and liberty have spoilt the young men. You have no Guimard now, no Duthé, no creditors—and you know nothing of heraldry; why, my dear young friend, you are not fully fledged. The man who does not sow his wild oats in the spring sows them in the winter. If I have but eighty thousand francs a year at the age of seventy, it is because I ran through the capital at thirty. Oh! with my wife—in decency and honour. However, your imperfections will not interfere with my introducing you at the Pavillon Planat. Remember, you have promised to come, and I shall expect you."

"What an odd little old man!" said Longueville to himself. "He is so jolly and hale; but though he wishes to seem a good fellow, I will not trust him too far."

Next day, at about four o'clock, when the house party were dispersed in the drawing-rooms and billiard-room, a servant announced to the inhabitants of the Villa Planat, "Monsieur *de* Longueville." On hearing the name of the old admiral's protégé, every one, down to the player who was about to miss his stroke, rushed in, as much to study Mademoiselle de Fontaine's countenance as to judge of this phœnix of men, who had earned honourable mention to the detriment of so many rivals. A simple but elegant style of dress, an air of perfect ease, polite manners, a pleasant voice with a ring in it which found a response in the hearer's heart strings, won the good-will of the family for Monsieur

Longueville. He did not seem unaccustomed to the luxury of the Receiver-General's ostentatious mansion. Though his conversation was that of a man of the world, it was easy to discern that he had had a brilliant education, and that his knowledge was as thorough as it was extensive. He knew so well the right thing to say in a discussion on naval architecture, trivial, it is true, started by the old admiral, that one of the ladies remarked that he must have passed through the École Polytechnique.

"And I think, madame," he replied, "that I may regard it as an honour to have got in."

In spite of urgent pressing, he refused politely but firmly to be kept to dinner, and put an end to the persistency of the ladies by saying that he was the Hippocrates of his young sister, whose delicate health required great care.

"Monsieur is perhaps a medical man?" asked one of Emilie's sisters-in-law with ironical meaning.

"Monsieur has left the École Polytechnique," Mademoiselle de Fontaine kindly put in; her face had flushed with richer colour, as she learned that the young lady of the ball was Monsieur Longueville's sister.

"But, my dear, he may be a doctor and yet have been to the École Polytechnique—is it not so, monsieur?"

"There is nothing to prevent it, madame," replied the young man.

Every eye was on Emilie, who was gazing with uneasy curiosity at the fascinating stranger. She breathed more freely when he added, not without a smile, "I have not the honour of belonging to the medical profession; and I even gave up going into the Engineers in order to preserve my independence."

"And you did well," said the Count. "But how can you regard it as an honour to be a doctor?" added the Breton nobleman. "Ah, my young friend, such a man as you—"

"Monsieur le Comte, I respect every profession that has a useful purpose."

"Well, in that we agree. You respect those professions, I imagine, as a young man respects a dowager."

Monsieur Longueville made his visit neither too long nor too short. He left at the moment when he saw that he had pleased everybody, and that each one's curiosity about him had been roused.

"He is a cunning rascal!" said the Count, coming into the drawing-room after seeing him to the door.

Mademoiselle de Fontaine, who had been in the secret of this call, had dressed with some care to attract the young man's eye; but she had the little disappointment of finding that he did not bestow on her so much attention as she thought she deserved. The family were a good deal surprised at the silence into which she had retired. Emilie generally displayed all her arts for the benefit of newcomers, her witty prattle, and the inexhaustible eloquence of her eyes and attitudes. Whether it was that the young man's pleasing voice and attractive manners had charmed her; that she was seriously in love, and that this feeling had worked a change in her, her demeanor had lost all its affectations. Being simple and natural, she must, no doubt, have seemed more beautiful. Some of her sisters, and an old lady, a friend of the family, saw in this behaviour a refinement of art. They supposed that Emilie, judging the man worthy of her, intended to delay revealing her merits, so as to dazzle him suddenly when she found that she pleased him. Every member of the family was curious to know what this capricious creature thought of the stranger; but when, during dinner, every one chose to endow Monsieur Longueville with some fresh quality which no one else had discovered, Mademoiselle de Fontaine sat for some time in silence. A sarcastic remark of her uncle's suddenly roused her from her apathy; she said, somewhat epigrammatically, that such heavenly perfection must cover some great defect, and that she would take good care how she judged so gifted a man at first sight.

"Those who please everybody, please nobody," she added; "and the worst of all faults is to have none."

Like all girls who are in love, Emilie cherished the hope of being able to hide her feelings at the bottom of her heart by putting the Argus-eyes that watched on the wrong tack; but by the end of a fortnight there was not a member of the large family party who was not in this little domestic secret. When Monsieur Longueville called for the third time, Emilie believed it was chiefly for her sake. This discovery gave her such intoxicating pleasure that she was startled as she reflected on it. There was something in it very painful to her pride. Accustomed as she was to be the centre of her world, she was obliged to recognise a force that attracted her outside herself; she tried to resist, but she could not chase from her heart the fascinating image of the young man.

Then came some anxiety. Two of Monsieur Longueville's qualities, very adverse to general curiosity, and especially to Mademoiselle de Fontaine's, were unexpected modesty and discretion. He never spoke of himself, of his pursuits, or of his family. The hints Emilie threw out in conversation, and the traps she laid to extract from the young fellow some facts concerning himself, he could evade with the adroitness of a diplomatist concealing a secret. If she talked of painting, he responded as a connoisseur; if she sat down to play, he showed without conceit that he was a very good pianist; one evening he delighted all the party by joining his delightful voice to Emilie's in one of Cimarosa's charming duets. But when they tried to find out whether he were a professional singer, he baffled them so pleasantly that he did not afford these women, practised as they were in the art of reading feelings, the least chance of discovering to what social sphere he belonged. However boldly the old uncle cast the boarding-hooks over the vessel, Longueville slipped away cleverly, so as to preserve the charm of mystery; and it was easy to him to remain the "handsome Stranger" at the Villa, because curiosity never overstepped the bounds of good breeding.

Emilie, distracted by this reserve, hoped to get more out of the sister than the brother, in the form of confidences. Aided by her uncle, who was as skilful in such manœuvres as in handling a ship, she endeavoured to bring upon the scene the hitherto unseen figure of Mademoiselle Clara Longueville. The family party at the Villa Planat soon expressed the greatest desire to make the acquaintance of so amiable a young lady, and to give her some amusement. An informal dance was proposed and accepted. The ladies did not despair of making a young girl of sixteen talk.

Notwithstanding the little clouds piled up by suspicion and created by curiosity, a light of joy shone in Emilie's soul, for she found life delicious when thus intimately connected with another than herself. She began to understand the relations of life. Whether it is that happiness makes us better, or that she was too fully occupied to torment other people, she became less caustic, more gentle, and indulgent. This change in her temper enchanted and amazed her family. Perhaps, at last, her selfishness was being transformed to love. It was a deep delight to her to look for the arrival of her bashful and unconfessed adorer. Though they had not uttered a word of passion, she knew that she was loved, and with what art did she not lead the stranger to unlock the stores of his information, which proved to be varied! She perceived that she, too, was being studied, and that made her endeavour to remedy the defects her education had encouraged. Was not this her first homage to love, and a bitter reproach to herself? She desired to please, and she was enchanting; she loved, and she was idolised. Her family, knowing that her pride would sufficiently protect her, gave her enough freedom to enjoy the little childish delights which give to first love its charm and its violence. More than once the young man and Mademoiselle de Fontaine walked, *tête-à-tête*, in the avenues of the garden, where nature was dressed like a woman going to a ball. More than once they had those conversations, aimless and meaningless, in which the emptiest phrases are those which cover the deepest feelings. They often admired together the setting sun and its gorgeous colouring. They gathered daisies to pull the petals off, and sang the most impassioned duets, using the notes set down by Pergolesi or Rossini as faithful interpreters to express their secrets.

The day of the dance came. Clara Longueville and her brother, whom the servants persisted in honouring with the noble *de*, were the principal guests. For the first time in her life Mademoiselle de Fontaine felt pleasure in a young girl's triumph. She lavished on Clara in all sincerity the gracious petting and little attentions which women generally give each other only to excite the jealousy of men. Emilie had, indeed, an object in view; she wanted to discover some secrets. But, being a girl, Mademoiselle Longueville showed even more mother-wit than her brother, for she did not even look as if she were hiding a secret, and kept the conversation to subjects unconnected with personal interests, while, at the same time, she gave it so much charm that Mademoiselle de Fontaine was almost envious, and called her "the Siren." Though Emilie had intended to make Clara talk, it was Clara, in fact, who questioned Emilie; she had meant to judge her, and she was judged by her; she was constantly provoked to find that she had betrayed her own character in some reply which Clara had extracted from her, while her modest and candid manner prohibited any suspicion of perfidy. There was a moment when Mademoiselle de Fontaine seemed sorry for an ill-judged sally against the commonalty to which Clara had led her.

"Mademoiselle," said the sweet child, "I have heard so much of you from Maximilien that I had the keenest desire to know you, out of affection for him; but is not a wish to know you a wish to love you?"

"My dear Clara, I feared I might have displeased you by speaking thus of people who are not of noble birth."

"Oh, be quite easy. That sort of discussion is pointless in these days. As for me, it does not affect me. I am beside the question."

Ambitious as the answer might seem, it filled Mademoiselle de Fontaine with the deepest joy; for, like all infatuated people, she explained it, as oracles are explained, in the sense that harmonised with her wishes; she began dancing again in higher spirits than ever, as she watched Longueville, whose figure and grace almost surpassed those of her imaginary ideal. She felt added satisfaction in believing him to be well born, her black eyes sparkled, and she danced with all the pleasure that comes of dancing in the presence of the being we love. The couple had never understood each other so well as at this moment; more than once they felt their finger tips thrill and tremble as they were married in the figures of the dance.

The early autumn had come to the handsome pair, in the midst of country festivities and pleasures; they had abandoned themselves softly to the tide of the sweetest sentiment in life, strengthening it by a thousand little incidents which any one can imagine; for love is in some respects always the same. They studied each other through it all, as much as lovers can.

"Well, well; a flirtation never turned so quickly into a love match," said the old uncle, who kept an eye on the two young people as a naturalist watches an insect in the microscope.

This speech alarmed Monsieur and Madame Fontaine. The old Vendéen had ceased to be so indifferent to his daughter's prospects as he had promised to be. He went to Paris to seek information, and found none. Uneasy at this mystery, and not yet knowing what might be the outcome of the inquiry which he had begged a Paris friend to institute with reference to the family of Longueville, he thought it his duty to warn his daughter to behave prudently. The fatherly admonition was received with mock submission spiced with irony.

"At least, my dear Emilie, if you love him, do not own it to him."

"My dear father, I certainly do love him; but I will await your permission before I tell him so."

"But remember, Emilie, you know nothing of his family or his pursuits."

"I may be ignorant, but I am content to be. But, father, you wished to see me married; you left me at liberty to make my choice; my choice is irrevocably made—what more is needful?"

"It is needful to ascertain, my dear, whether the man of your choice is the son of a peer of France," the venerable gentleman retorted sarcastically.

Emilie was silent for a moment. She presently raised her head, looked at her father, and said somewhat anxiously, "Are not the Longuevilles—?"

"They became extinct in the person of the old Duc de Rostein-Limbourg, who perished on the scaffold in 1793. He was the last representative of the last and younger branch."

"But, papa, there are some very good families descended from bastards. The history of France swarms with princes bearing the bar sinister on their shields."

"Your ideas are much changed," said the old man, with a smile.

The following day was the last that the Fontaine family were to spend at the Pavilion Planat. Emilie, greatly disturbed by her father's warning, awaited with extreme impatience the hour at which young Longueville was in the habit of coming, to wring some explanation from him. She went out after dinner, and walked alone across the shrubbery towards an arbour fit for lovers, where she knew that the eager youth would seek her; and as she hastened thither she considered of the best way to discover so important a matter without compromising herself—a rather difficult thing! Hitherto no direct avowal had sanctioned the feelings which bound her to this stranger. Like Maximilien, she had secretly enjoyed the sweetness of first love; but both were equally proud, and each feared to confess that love.

Maximilien Longueville, to whom Clara had communicated her not unfounded suspicions as to Emilie's character, was by turns carried away by the violence of a young man's passion, and held back by a wish to know and test the woman to whom he would be entrusting his happiness. His love had not hindered him from perceiving in Emilie the prejudices which marred her young nature; but before attempting to counteract them, he wished to be sure that she loved him, for he would no sooner risk the fate of his love than of his life. He had, therefore, persistently kept a silence to which his looks, his behaviour, and his smallest actions gave the lie.

On her side, the self-respect natural to a young girl, augmented in Mademoiselle de Fontaine by the monstrous vanity founded on her birth and beauty, kept her from meeting the declaration half-way, which her growing passion sometimes urged her to invite. Thus the lovers had instinctively understood the situation without explaining to each other their secret motives. There are times in life when such vagueness pleases youthful minds. Just because each had postponed speaking too long, they seemed to be playing a cruel game of suspense. He was trying to discover whether he was beloved, by the effort any confession would cost his haughty mistress; she every minute hoped that he would break a too respectful silence.

Emilie, seated on a rustic bench, was reflecting on all that had happened in these three months full of enchantment. Her father's suspicions were the last that could appeal to her; she even disposed of them at once by two or three of those reflections natural to an inexperienced girl, which, to her, seemed conclusive. Above all, she was convinced that it was impossible that she should deceive herself. All the summer through she had not been able to detect in Maximilien a single gesture, or a single word, which could indicate a vulgar origin or vulgar occupations; nay more, his manner of discussing things revealed a man devoted to the highest interests of the nation. "Besides," she reflected, "an office clerk, a banker, or a merchant, would not be at leisure to spend a whole season in paying his addresses to me in the midst of woods and fields; wasting his time as freely as a nobleman who has life before him free of all care."

She had given herself up to meditations far more interesting to her than these preliminary thoughts, when a slight rustling in the leaves announced to her that Maximilien had been watching her for a minute, not probably without admiration.

"Do you know that it is very wrong to take a young girl thus unawares?" she asked him, smiling.

"Especially when they are busy with their secrets," replied Maximilian archly.

"Why should I not have my secrets? You certainly have yours."

"Then you really were thinking of your secrets?" he went on, laughing.

"No, I was thinking of yours. My own, I know."

"But perhaps my secrets are yours, and yours mine," cried the young man, softly seizing Mademoiselle de Fontaine's hand and drawing it through his arm.

After walking a few steps they found themselves under a clump of trees which the hues of the sinking sun wrapped in a haze of red and brown. This touch of natural magic lent a certain solemnity to the moment. The young man's free and eager action, and, above all, the throbbing of his surging heart, whose hurried beating spoke to Emilie's arm, stirred her to an emotion that was all the more disturbing because it was produced by the simplest and most innocent circumstances. The restraint under which young girls of the upper class live gives incredible force to any explosion of feeling, and to meet an impassioned lover is one of the greatest dangers they can encounter. Never had Emilie and Maximilien allowed their eyes to say so much that they dared never speak. Carried away by this intoxication, they easily forgot the petty stipulations of pride, and the cold hesitancies of suspicion. At first, indeed, they could only express themselves by a pressure of hands which interpreted their happy thoughts. After slowly pacing a few steps in long silence, Mademoiselle de Fontaine spoke. "Monsieur, I have a question to ask you," she said, trembling, and in an agitated voice. "But, remember, I beg, that it is in a manner compulsory on me, from the rather singular position I am in with regard to my family."

A pause, terrible to Emilie, followed these sentences, which she had almost stammered out. During the minute while it lasted, the girl, haughty as she was, dared not meet the flashing eye of the man she loved, for she was secretly conscious of the meanness of the next words she added: "Are you of noble birth?"

As soon as the words were spoken she wished herself at the bottom of a lake.

"Mademoiselle," Longueville gravely replied, and his face assumed a sort of stern dignity, "I promise to answer you truly as soon as you shall have answered in all sincerity a question I will put to you!"—He released her arm, and the girl suddenly felt alone in the world, as he said: 'What is your object in questioning me as to my birth?"

She stood motionless, cold, and speechless.

"Mademoiselle," Maximilien went on, "let us go no further if we do not understand each other. I love you," he said, in a voice of deep emotion. 'Well, then," he added, as he heard the joyful exclamation she could not suppress, "why ask me if I am of noble birth?"

"Could he speak so if he were not?" cried a voice within her, which Emilie believed came from the depths of her heart. She gracefully raised her head, seemed to find new life in the young man's gaze, and held out her hand as if to renew the alliance.

"You thought I cared very much for dignities?" said she with keen archness.

"I have no titles to offer my wife," he replied, in a half-sportive, half-serious tone. "But if I choose one of high rank, and among women whom a wealthy home has accustomed to the luxury and pleasures of a fine fortune, I know what such a choice requires of me. Love gives everything," he added lightly, "but only to lovers. Once married, they need something more than the vault of heaven and the carpet of a meadow."

"He is rich;" she reflected. "As to titles, perhaps he only wants to try me. He has been told that I am mad about titles, and bent on marrying none but a peer's son. My priggish sisters have played me that trick."—"I assure you, monsieur," she said aloud, "that I have had very extravagant ideas about life and the world; but now," she added pointedly, looking at him in a perfectly distracting way, "I know where true riches are to be found for a wife."

"I must believe that you are speaking from the depths of your heart," he said, with gentle gravity. "But this winter, my dear Emilie, in less than two months perhaps, I may be proud of what I shall have to offer you if you care for the pleasures of wealth. This is the only secret I shall keep locked here," and he laid his hand on his heart, "for on its success my happiness depends. I dare not say ours."

"Yes, yes, ours!"

Exchanging such sweet nothings, they slowly made their way back to rejoin the company. Mademoiselle de Fontaine had never found her lover more amiable or wittier; his light figure, his engaging manners, seemed to her more charming than ever, since the conversation which had made her to some extent the possessor of a heart worthy to be the envy of every woman. They sang an Italian duet with so much expression that the audience applauded enthusiastically. Their adieux were in a conventional tone, which concealed their happiness. In short, this day had been to Emilie like a chain binding her more closely than ever to the Stranger's fate. The strength and dignity he had displayed in the scene when they had confessed their feelings had perhaps impressed Mademoiselle de Fontaine with the respect without which there is no true love.

When she was left alone in the drawing-room with her father, the old man went up to her affectionately, held her hands, and asked, her whether she had gained any light as to Monsieur Longueville's family and fortune.

"Yes, my dear father," she replied, "and I am happier than I could have hoped. In short, Monsieur de Longueville is the only man I could ever marry."

"Very well, Emilie," said the Count, "then I know what remains for me to do."

"Do you know of any impediment?" she asked, in sincere alarm.

"My dear child, the young man is totally unknown to me; but unless he is not a man of honour, so long as you love him, he is as dear to me as a son."

"Not a man of honour!" exclaimed Emilie. "As to that, I am quite easy. My uncle, who introduced him to us, will answer for him. Say, my dear uncle, has he been a filibuster, an outlaw, a pirate?"

"I knew I should find myself in this fix!" cried the old sailor, waking up. He looked round the room, but his niece had vanished "like Saint-Elmo's fires," to use his favourite expression.

"Well, uncle, " Monsieur de Fontaine went on, "how could you hide from us all you knew about this young man? You must have seen how anxious we have been. Is Monsieur de Longueville a man of family?"

"I don't know him from Adam or Eve," said the Comte de Kergarouët. "Trusting to that crazy child's tact, I got him here by a method of my own. I know that the boy shoots with a pistol to admiration, hunts well, plays wonderfully at billiards, at chess, and at backgammon; he handles the foils, and rides a horse like the late Chevalier de Saint-Georges. He has a thorough knowledge of all our vintages. He is as good an arithmetician as Barême, draws, dances, and sings well. The devil's in it! what more do you want? If that is not a perfect gentleman, find me a *bourgeois* who knows all this, or any man who lives more nobly than he does. Does he do anything, I ask you? Does he compromise his dignity by hanging about an office, bowing down before the upstarts you call Directors-General? He walks upright. He is a man.—However, I have just found in my waistcoat pocket the card he gave me when he fancied I wanted to cut his throat, poor innocent. Young men are very simple-minded nowadays! Here it is."

"Rue du Sentier, No. 5," said Monsieur de Fontaine, trying to recall among all the information he had received, something which might concern the stranger. "What the devil can it mean? Messrs. Palma, Werbrust & Co., wholesale dealers in muslins, calicoes, and printed cotton goods, live there.—Stay, I have it: Longueville the deputy has an interest in their house. Well, but so far as I know, Longueville has but one son of two-and-thirty, who is not at all like our man, and to whom he gave fifty thousand francs a year that he might marry a minister's daughter; he wants to be made a peer like the rest of 'em.—I never heard him mention this Maximilien. Has he a daughter? What is this girl Clara? Besides, it is open to any adventurer to call himself Longueville. But is not the house of Palma, Werbrust & Co. half ruined by some speculation in Mexico or the Indies? I will clear all this up."

"You speak a soliloquy as if you were on the stage, and seem to account me a cipher," said the old admiral suddenly. "Don't you know that if he is a gentleman, I have more than one bag in my hold that will stop any leak in his fortune?"

"As to that, if he is a son of Longueville's, he will want nothing; but," said Monsieur de Fontaine, shaking his head from side to side, "his father has not even washed off the stains of his origin. Before the Revolution he was an attorney, and the *de* he has since assumed no more belongs to him than half of his fortune."

"Pooh! pooh! happy those whose fathers were hanged!" cried the admiral gaily.

Three or four days after this memorable day, on one of those fine mornings in the month of November, which show the boulevards cleaned by the sharp cold of an early frost, Mademoiselle de Fontaine, wrapped in a new style of fur cape, of which she wished to set the fashion, went out with two of her sisters-in-law, on whom she had been wont to discharge her most cutting remarks. The three women were tempted to the drive, less by their desire to try a very elegant carriage, and wear gowns which were to set the fashions for the winter, than by their wish to see a cape which a friend had observed in a handsome lace and linen shop at the corner of the Rue de la Paix. As soon as they were in the shop the Baronne de Fontaine pulled Emilie by the sleeve, and pointed out to her Maximilien Longueville seated behind the desk, and engaged in paying out the change for a gold piece to one of the workwomen with whom he seemed to be in consultation. The "handsome stranger" held in his hand a parcel of patterns, which left no doubt as to his honourable profession.

Emilie felt an icy shudder, though no one perceived it. Thanks to the good breeding of the best society, she completely concealed the rage in her heart, and answered her sister-in-law with the words, "I knew it," with a fullness of intonation and inimitable decision which the most famous actress of the time might have envied her. She went straight up to the desk. Longueville looked up, put the patterns in his pocket with distracting coolness, bowed to Mademoiselle de Fontaine, and came forward, looking at her keenly.

"Mademoiselle," he said to the shopgirl, who followed him, looking very much disturbed, "I will send to settle that account; my house deals in that way. But here," he whispered into her ear, as he gave her a thousand-franc note, "take this—it is between ourselves.—You will forgive me, I trust, mademoiselle," he added, turning to Emilie. "You will kindly excuse the tyranny of business matters."

"Indeed, monsieur, it seems to me that it is no concern of mine," replied Mademoiselle de Fontaine, looking at him with a bold expression of sarcastic indifference which might have made any one believe that she now saw him for the first time.

"Do you really mean it?" asked Maximilien in a broken voice.

Emilie turned her back upon him with amazing insolence. These words, spoken in an undertone, had escaped the ears of her two sisters-in-law. When, after buying the cape, the three ladies got into the carriage again, Emilie, seated with her back to the horses, could not resist one last comprehensive glance into the depths of the odious shop, where she saw Maximilien standing with his arms folded, in the attitude of a man superior to the disaster that had so suddenly fallen on him. Their eyes met and flashed implacable looks. Each hoped to inflict a cruel wound on the heart of a lover. In one instant they were as far apart as if one had been in China and the other in Greenland.

Does not the breath of vanity wither everything? Mademoiselle de Fontaine, a prey to the most violent struggle that can torture the heart of a young girl, reaped the richest harvest of anguish that prejudice and narrow-mindedness ever sowed in a human soul. Her face, but just now fresh and velvety, was streaked with yellow lines and red patches; the paleness of her cheeks seemed every now and then to turn green. Hoping to hide her despair from her sisters, she would laugh as she pointed out some ridiculous dress or passer-by; but her laughter was spasmodic. She was more deeply hurt by their unspoken compassion than by any satirical comments for which she might have revenged herself. She exhausted her wit in trying to engage them in a conversation, in which she tried to expend her fury in senseless paradoxes, heaping on all men engaged in trade the bitterest insults and witticisms in the worst taste.

On getting home, she had an attack of fever, which at first assumed a somewhat serious character. By the end of a month the care of her parents and of the physician restored her to her family.

Every one hoped that this lesson would be severe enough to subdue Emilie's nature; but she insensibly fell into her old habits and threw herself again into the world of fashion. She declared that there was no disgrace in making a mistake. If she, like her father, had a vote in the Chamber, she would move for an edict, she said, by which all merchants, and especially dealers in calico, should be branded on the forehead, like Berri sheep, down to the third generation. She wished that none but nobles should have a right to wear the antique French costume, which was so becoming to the courtiers of Louis XV. To hear her, it was a misfortune for France, perhaps, that there was no outward and visible difference between a merchant and a peer of France. And a hundred more such pleasantries, easy to imagine, were rapidly poured out when any accident brought up the subject.

But those who loved Emilie could see through all her banter a tinge of melancholy. It was clear that Maximilien Longueville still reigned over that inexorable heart. Sometimes she would be as gentle as she had been during the brief summer that had seen the birth of her love; sometimes, again, she was unendurable. Every one made excuses for her inequality of temper, which had its source in sufferings at once secret and known to all. The Comte de Kergarouët had some influence over her, thanks to his increased prodigality, a kind of consolation which rarely fails of its effect on a Parisian girl.

The first ball at which Mademoiselle de Fontaine appeared was at the Neapolitan ambassador's. As she took her place in the first quadrille she saw, a few yards away from her, Maximilien Longueville, who nodded slightly to her partner.

"Is that young man a friend of yours?" she asked, with a scornful air.

"Only my brother," he replied.

Emilie could not help starting. "Ah!" he continued, "and he is the noblest soul living—"

"Do you know my name?" asked Emilie, eagerly interrupting him.

"No, mademoiselle. It is a crime, I confess, not to remember a name which is on every lip—I ought to say in every heart. But I have a valid excuse. I have but just arrived from Germany. My ambassador, who is in Paris on leave, sent me here this evening to take care of his amiable wife, whom you may see yonder in that corner."

"A perfect tragic mask!" said Emilie, after looking at the ambassadress.

"And yet that is her ballroom face!" said the young man, laughing. "I shall have to dance with her! So I thought I might have some compensation." Mademoiselle de Fontaine curtsied. "I was very much surprised," the voluble young secretary went on, "to find my brother here. On arriving from Vienna I heard that the poor boy was ill in bed, and I counted on seeing him before coming to this ball; but good policy will not always allow us to indulge family affection. The *Padrona della casa* would not give me time to call on my poor Maximilian."

"Then, monsieur, your brother is not, like you, in diplomatic employment."

"No," said the attaché, with a sigh, "the poor fellow sacrificed himself for me. He and my sister Clara have renounced their share of my father's fortune to make an eldest son of me. My father dreams of a peerage, like all who vote for the ministry. Indeed, it is promised him," he added in an undertone. "After saving up a little capital my brother joined a banking firm, and I hear he has just effected a speculation in Brazil which may make him a millionaire. You see me in the highest spirits at having been able, by my diplomatic connections, to contribute to his success. I am impatiently expecting a dispatch from the Brazilian Legation, which will help to lift the cloud from his brow. What do you think of him?"

'Well, your brother's face does not look to me like that of a man busied with money matters."

The young attaché shot a scrutinizing glance at the apparently calm face of his partner.

"What!" he exclaimed, with a smile, "can young ladies read the thoughts of love behind a silent brow?"

"Your brother is in love, then?" she asked, betrayed into a movement of curiosity.

"Yes; my sister Clara, to whom he is as devoted as a mother, wrote to me that he had fallen in love this summer with a very pretty girl; but I have had no further news of the affair. Would you believe that the poor boy used to get up at five in the morning, and went off to settle his business that he might be back by four o'clock in the country where the lady was? In fact, he ruined a very nice thoroughbred that I had given him. Forgive my chatter, mademoiselle; I have but just come home from Germany. For a year I have heard no decent French, I have been weaned from French faces, and satiated with Germans, to such a degree that, I believe, in my patriotic mania, I could talk to the chimeras on a French candlestick. And if I talk with a lack of reserve unbecoming in a diplomatist, the fault is yours, mademoiselle. Was it not you who pointed out my brother? When he is the theme I become inexhaustible. I should like to proclaim to all the world how good and generous he is. He gave up no less than a hundred thousand francs a year, the income from the Longueville property."

If Mademoiselle de Fontaine had the benefit of these important revelations, it was partly due to the skill with which she continued to question her confiding partner from the moment when she found that he was the brother of her scorned lover.

"And could you, without being grieved, see your brother selling muslin and calico?" asked Emilie, at the end of the third figure of the quadrille.

"How do you know that?" asked the attaché. "Thank God, though I pour out a flood of words, I have already acquired the art of not telling more than I intend, like all the other diplomatic apprentices I know."

"You told me, I assure you."

Monsieur de Longueville looked at Mademoiselle de Fontaine with a surprise that was full of perspicacity. A suspicion flashed upon him. He glanced inquiringly from, his brother to his partner, guessed everything, clasped his hands, fixed his eyes on the ceiling, and began to laugh, saying, "I am an idiot! You are the handsomest person here; my brother keeps stealing glances at you; he is dancing in spite of his illness, and you pretend not to see him. Make him happy," he added, as he led her back to her old uncle. "I shall not be jealous, but I shall always shiver a little at calling you my sister—"

The lovers, however, were to prove as inexorable to each other as they were to themselves. At about two in the morning, refreshments were served in an immense corridor, where, to leave persons of the same coterie free to meet each other, the tables were arranged as in a restaurant. By one of those accidents which always happen to lovers, Mademoiselle de Fontaine found herself at a table next to that at which the more important guests were seated. Maximilien was one of the group. Emilie, who lent an attentive ear to her neighbours' conversation, overheard one of those dialogues into which a young woman so easily falls with a young man who has the grace and style of Maximilien Longueville. The lady talking to the young banker was a Neapolitan Duchess, whose eyes shot lightning flashes, and whose skin had the sheen of satin. The intimate terms on which Longueville affected to be with her stung Mademoiselle de Fontaine all the more because she had just given her lover back twenty times as much tenderness as she had ever felt for him before.

"Yes, monsieur, in my country true love can make every kind of sacrifice," the Duchess was saying, with a simper.

"You have more passion than Frenchwomen," said Maximilien, whose burning gaze fell on Emilie. "They are all vanity."

"Monsieur," Emilie eagerly interposed, "is it not very wrong to calumniate your own country. Devotion is to be found in every nation."

"Do you imagine, mademoiselle," retorted the Italian, with a sardonic smile, "that a Parisian would be capable of following her lover all over the world?"

"Oh, madame, let us understand each other. She would follow him to a desert and live in a tent, but not to sit in a shop."

A disdainful gesture completed her meaning. Thus, under the influence of her disastrous education, Emilie for the second time killed her budding happiness, and destroyed its prospects of life. Maximilien's apparent indifference, and a woman's smile, had wrung from her one of those sarcasms whose treacherous zest always led her astray.

"Mademoiselle," said Longueville, in a low voice, under cover of the noise made by the ladies as they rose from the table, "no one will ever more ardently desire your happiness than I; permit me to assure you of this, as I am taking leave of you. I am starting for Italy in a few days."

"With a Duchess, no doubt?"

"No, but perhaps with a mortal blow."

"Is not that pure fancy?" asked Emilie, with an anxious glance.

"No," he replied. "There are wounds which never heal."

"You are not to go," said the girl, imperiously, and she smiled.

"I shall go," replied Maximilien, gravely.

"You will find me married on your return, I warn you," she said coquettishly.

"I hope so."

"Impertinent wretch!" she exclaimed. "How cruel a revenge!"

A fortnight later Maximilien set out with his sister Clara for the warm and poetic scenes of beautiful Italy, leaving Mademoiselle de Fontaine a prey to the most vehement regret. The young Secretary to the Embassy took up his brother's quarrel, and contrived to take signal vengeance on Emilie's disdain by making known the occasion of the lovers' separation. He repaid his fair partner with interest all the sarcasm with which she had formerly attacked Maximilien, and often made more than one Excellency smile by describing the fair foe of the counting-house, the amazon who preached a crusade against bankers, the young girl whose love had evaporated before a bale of muslin. The Comte de Fontaine was obliged to use his influence to procure an appointment to Russia for Auguste Longueville in order to protect his daughter from the ridicule heaped upon her by this dangerous young persecutor.

Not long after, the Ministry being compelled to raise a levy of peers to support the aristocratic party, trembling in the Upper Chamber under the lash of an illustrious writer, gave Monsieur Guiraudin de Longueville a peerage, with the title of Vicomte. Monsieur de Fontaine also obtained a peerage, the reward due as much to his fidelity in evil days as to his name, which claimed a place in the hereditary Chamber.

About this time Emilie, now of age, made, no doubt, some serious reflections on life, for her tone and manners changed perceptibly. Instead of amusing herself by saying spiteful things to her uncle, she lavished on him the most affectionate attentions; she brought him his stick with a persevering devotion that made the cynical smile, she gave him her arm, rode in his carriage, and accompanied him in all his drives; she even persuaded him that she liked the smell of tobacco, and read him his favourite paper *La Quotidienne* in the midst of clouds of smoke, which the malicious old sailor intentionally blew over her; she learned piquet to be a match for the old Count; and this fantastic damsel even listened without impatience to his periodical narratives of the battles of the *Belle-Poule*, the manœuvres of the *Ville de Paris,* M. de Suffren's first expedition, or the battle of Aboukir.

Though the old sailor had often said that he knew his longitude and latitude too well to allow himself to be captured by a young corvette, one fine morning Paris drawing-rooms heard the news of the marriage of Mademoiselle de Fontaine to the Comte de Kergarouët. The young Countess gave splendid entertainments to drown thought; but she, no doubt, found a void at the bottom of the whirlpool; luxury was ineffectual to disguise the emptiness and grief of her sorrowing soul; for the most part, in spite of the flashes of assumed gaiety, her beautiful face expressed unspoken melancholy. Emilie appeared, however, full of attentions and consideration for her old husband, who, on retiring to his rooms at night, to the sounds of a lively band, would often say, "I do not know myself. Was I to wait till the age of seventy-two to embark as pilot on board the *Belle Emilie* after twenty years of matrimonial galleys?"

The conduct of the young Countess was marked by such strictness that the most clear-sighted criticism had no fault to find with her. Lookers on chose to think that the vice-admiral had reserved the right of disposing of his fortune to keep his wife more tightly in hand; but this was a notion as insulting to the uncle as to the niece. Their conduct was indeed so delicately judicious that the men who were most interested in guessing the secrets of the couple could never decide whether the old Count regarded her as a wife or as a daughter. He was often heard to say that he had rescued his niece as a castaway after shipwreck; and that, for his part, he had never taken a mean advantage of hospitality when he had saved an enemy from the fury of the storm. Though the Countess aspired to reign in Paris and tried to keep pace with Mesdames the Duchesses de Maufrigneuse and de Chaulieu, the Marquises d'Espard and d'Aiglemont, the Comtesses Féraud, de Montcornet, and de Restaud, Madame de Camps, and Mademoiselle des Touches, she did not yield to the addresses of the young Vicomte de Portenduère, who made her his idol.

Two years after her marriage, in one of the old drawing-rooms in the Faubourg Saint-Germain, where she was admired for her character, worthy of the old school, Emilie heard the Vicomte de Longueville announced. In the corner of the room where she was sitting, playing piquet with the Bishop of Persepolis, her agitation was not observed; she turned her head and saw her former lover come in, in all the freshness of youth. His father's death, and then that of his brother, killed by the severe climate of Saint-Petersburg, had placed on Maximilien's head the hereditary plumes of the French peer's hat. His fortune matched his learning and his merits; only the day before his youthful and fervid eloquence had dazzled the Assembly. At this moment he stood before the Countess, free, and graced with all the advantages she had formerly required of her ideal. Every mother with a daughter to marry made amiable advances to a man gifted with the virtues which they attributed to him, as they admired his attractive person; but Emilie knew, better than any one, that the Vicomte de Longueville had the steadfast nature in which a wise woman sees a guarantee of happiness. She looked at the admiral who, to use his favourite expression, seemed likely to hold his course for a long time yet, and cursed the follies of her youth.

At this moment Monsieur de Persepolis said with Episcopal grace: "Fair lady, you have thrown away the king of hearts—I have won. But do not regret your money. I keep it for my little seminaries."

PARIS, *December* 1829.

THE PURSE

To Sofka

Have you observed, mademoiselle, that the painters and sculptors of the Middle Ages, when they placed two figures in adoration, one on each side of a fair Saint, never failed to give them a family likeness? When you here see your name among those that are dear to me, and under whose auspices I place my works, remember that touching harmony, and you will see in this not so much an act of homage as an expression of the brotherly affection of your devoted servant,

DE BALZAC.

FOR souls to whom effusiveness is easy there is a delicious hour that falls when it is not yet night, but is no longer day; the twilight gleam throws softened lights or tricksy reflections on every object, and favours a dreamy mood which vaguely weds itself to the play of light and shade. The silence which generally prevails at that time makes it particularly dear to artists, who grow contemplative, stand a few paces back from the pictures on which they can no longer work, and pass judgment on them, rapt by the subject whose most recondite meaning then flashes on the inner eye of genius. He who has never stood pensive by a friend's side in such an hour of poetic dreaming can hardly understand its in expressible soothingness. Favoured by the clear-obscure, the material skill employed by art to produce illusion entirely disappears. If the work is a picture, the figures represented seem to speak and walk; the shade is shadow, the light is day; the flesh lives, eyes move, blood flows in their veins, and stuffs have a changing sheen. Imagination helps the realism of every detail, and only sees the beauties of the work. At that hour illusion reigns despotically; perhaps it wakes at nightfall! Is not illusion a sort of night to the mind, which we people with dreams? Illusion then unfolds its wings, it bears the soul aloft to the world of fancies, a world full of voluptuous imaginings, where the artist forgets the real world, yesterday and the morrow, the future—everything down to its miseries, the good and the evil alike.

At this magic hour a young painter, a man of talent, who saw in art nothing but Art itself, was perched on a step ladder which helped him to work at a large high painting, now nearly finished. Criticising himself, honestly admiring himself, floating on the current of his thoughts, he then lost himself in one of those meditative moods which ravish and elevate the soul, soothe it, and comfort it. His reverie had no doubt lasted a long time. Night fell. Whether he meant to come down from his perch, or whether he made some ill-judged movement, believing himself to be on the floor—the event did not allow of his remembering exactly the cause of his accident—he fell, his head struck a footstool, he lost consciousness and lay motionless during a space of time of which he knew not the length.

A sweet voice roused him from the stunned condition into which he had sunk. When he opened his eyes the flash of a bright light made him close them again immediately; but through the mist that veiled his senses he heard the whispering of two women, and felt two young, two timid hands on which his head was resting. He soon recovered consciousness, and by the light of an old-fashioned Argand lamp he could make out the most charming girl's face he had ever seen, one of those heads which are often supposed to be a freak of the brush, but which to him suddenly realised the theories of the ideal beauty which every artist creates for himself and whence his art proceeds. The features of the unknown belonged, so to say, to the refined and delicate type of Prudhon's school, but had also the poetic sentiment which Girodet gave to the inventions of his phantasy. The freshness of the temples, the regular arch of the eyebrows, the purity of outline, the virginal innocence so plainly stamped on every feature of her countenance, made the girl a perfect creature. Her figure was slight and graceful, and frail in form. Her dress, though simple and neat, revealed neither wealth nor penury.

As he recovered his senses, the painter gave expression to his admiration by a look of surprise, and stammered some confused thanks. He found a handkerchief pressed to his forehead, and above the smell peculiar to a studio, he recognized the strong odour of ether, applied no doubt to revive him from his fainting fit. Finally he saw an old woman, looking like a marquise of the old school, who held the lamp and was advising the young girl.

"Monsieur," said the younger woman in reply to one of the, questions put by the painter during the few minutes when he was still under the influence of the vagueness that the shock had produced in his ideas, "my mother and I heard the noise of your fall on the floor, and we fancied we heard a groan. The silence following on the crash alarmed us, and we hurried up. Finding the key in the latch, we happily took the liberty of entering, and we found you lying motionless on the ground. My mother went to fetch what was needed to bathe your head and revive you. You have cut your forehead—there. Do you feel it?"

"Yes, I do now," he replied.

"Oh, it will be nothing," said the old mother. "Happily your head rested against this lay-figure."

"I feel infinitely better," replied the painter. "I need nothing further but a hackney cab to take me home. The porter's wife will go for one."

He tried to repeat his thanks to the two strangers; but at each sentence the elder lady interrupted him, saying, "To-morrow, monsieur, pray be careful to put on leeches, or to be bled, and drink a few cups of something healing. A fall may be dangerous."

The young girl stole a look at the painter and at the pictures in the studio. Her expression and her glances revealed perfect propriety; her curiosity seemed rather absence of mind, and her eyes seemed to speak the interest which women feel, with the most engaging spontaneity, in everything which causes us suffering. The two strangers seemed to forget the painter's works in the painter's mishap. When he had reassured them as to his condition they left, looking at him with an anxiety that was equally free from insistence and from familiarity, without asking any indiscreet questions, or trying to incite him to any wish to visit them. Their proceedings all bore the hall-mark of natural refinement and good taste. Their noble and simple manners at first made no great impression on the painter, but subsequently, as he recalled all the details of the incident, he was greatly struck by them.

When they reached the floor beneath that occupied by the painter's studio, the old lady gently observed, "Adélaïde, you left the door open."

"That was to come to my assistance," said the painter, with a grateful smile.

"You came down just now, mother," replied the young girl, with a blush.

'Would you like us to accompany you all the way down stairs?" asked the mother. "The stairs are dark."

"No, thank you, indeed, madame; I am much better."

"Hold tightly by the rail."

The two women remained on the landing to light the young man, listening to the sound of his steps.

In order to set forth clearly all the exciting and unexpected interest this scene might have for the young painter, it must be told that he had only a few days since established his studio in the attics of this house, situated in the darkest and, therefore, the most muddy part of the Rue de Suresnes, almost opposite the Church of the Madeleine, and quite close to his rooms in the Rue des Champs-Elysées. The fame his talent had won him having made him one of the artists most dear to his country, he was beginning to feel free from want, and, to use his own expression, was enjoying his last privations. Instead of going to his work in one of the studios near the city gates, where the moderate rents had hitherto been in proportion to his humble earnings, he had gratified a wish that was new every morning, by sparing himself a long walk, and the loss of much time, now more valuable than ever.

No man in the world would have inspired feelings of greater interest than Hippolyte Schinner if he would ever have consented to make acquaintance; but he did not lightly entrust to others the secrets of his life. He was the idol of a necessitous mother, who had brought him up at the cost of the severest privations. Mademoiselle Schinner, the daughter of an Alsatian farmer, had never been married. Her tender soul had been cruelly crushed, long ago, by a rich man, who did not pride himself on any great delicacy in his love affairs. The day when, as a young girl, in all the radiance of her beauty and all the triumph of her life, she suffered, at the cost of her heart and her sweet illusions, the disenchantment which falls on us so slowly and yet so quickly—for we try to postpone as long as possible our belief in evil, and it seems to come too soon—that day was a whole age of reflection, and it was also a day of religious thought and resignation. She refused the alms of the man who had betrayed her, renounced the world, and made a glory of her shame. She gave herself up entirely to her motherly love, seeking in it all her joys in exchange for the social pleasures to which she bid farewell. She lived by work, saving up a treasure in her son. And, in after years, a day, an hour repaid her amply for the long and weary sacrifices of her indigence.

At the last exhibition her son had received the Cross of the Legion of Honour. The newspapers, unanimous in hailing an unknown genius, still rang with sincere praises. Artists themselves acknowledged Schinner as a master, and dealers covered his canvases with gold pieces. At five-and-twenty Hippolyte Schinner, to whom his mother had transmitted her woman's soul, understood more clearly than ever his position in the world. Anxious to restore to his mother the pleasures of which society had so long robbed her, he lived for her, hoping by the aid of fame and fortune to see her one day happy, rich, respected, and surrounded by men of mark. Schinner had therefore chosen his friends among the most honourable and distinguished men. Fastidious in the selection of his intimates, he desired to raise still further a position which his talent had placed high. The work to which he had devoted himself from boyhood, by compelling him to dwell in solitude—the mother of great thoughts— had left him the beautiful beliefs which grace the early days of life. His adolescent soul was not closed to any of the thousand bashful emotions by which a young man is a being apart, whose heart abounds in joys, in poetry, in virginal hopes, puerile in the eyes of men of the world, but deep because they are single-hearted.

He was endowed with the gentle and polite manners which speak to the soul, and fascinate even those who do not understand them. He was well made. His voice, coming from his heart, stirred that of others to noble sentiments, and bore witness to his true modesty by a certain ingenuousness of tone. Those who saw him felt drawn to him by that attraction of the moral nature which men of science are happily unable to analyse; they would detect in it some phenomenon of galvanism, or the current of I know not what fluid, and express our sentiments in a formula of ratios of oxygen and electricity.

These details will perhaps explain to strong-minded persons and to men of fashion why, in the absence of the porter whom he had sent to the end of the Rue de la Madeleine to call him a coach, Hippolyte Schinner did not ask the man's wife any questions concerning the two women whose kindness of heart had shown itself in his behalf. But though he replied Yes or No to the inquiries, natural under the circumstances, which the good woman made as to his accident, and the friendly intervention of the tenants occupying the fourth floor, he could not hinder her from following the instinct of her kind; she mentioned the two strangers, speaking of them as prompted by the interests of her policy and the subterranean opinions of the porter's lodge.

"Ah," said she, "they were, no doubt, Mademoiselle Leseigneur and her mother, who have lived here these four years. We do not yet know exactly what these ladies do; in the morning, only till the hour of noon, an old woman who is half deaf, and who never speaks any more than a wail, comes in to help them; in the evening, two or three old gentlemen, with loops of ribbon, like you, monsieur, come to see them, and often stay very late. One of them comes in a carriage with servants, and is said to have sixty thousand francs a year. However, they are very quiet tenants, as you are, monsieur; and economical! they live on nothing, and as soon as a letter is brought they pay for it. It is a queer thing, monsieur, the mother's name is not the same as the daughter's. Ah, but when they go for a walk in the Tuileries, mademoiselle is very smart, and she never goes out but she is followed by a lot of young men; but she shuts the door in their face, and she is quite right. The proprietor would never allow—"

The coach having come, Hippolyte heard no more, and went home. His mother, to whom he related his adventure, dressed his wound afresh, and would not allow him to go to the studio next day. After taking advice, various treatments were prescribed, and Hippolyte remained at home three days. During this retirement his idle fancy recalled vividly, bit by bit, the details of the scene that had ensued on his fainting fit. The young girl's profile was clearly projected against the darkness of his inward vision; he saw once more the mother's faded features, or he felt the touch of Adélaïde's hands. He remembered some gesture which at first had not greatly struck him, but whose exquisite grace was thrown into relief by memory; then an attitude, or the tones of a melodious voice, enhanced by the distance of remembrance, suddenly rose before him, as objects plunging to the bottom of deep waters come back to the surface.

So, on the day when he could resume work, he went early to his studio; but the visit he undoubtedly had a right to pay to his neighbours was the true cause of his haste; he had already forgotten the pictures he had begun. At the moment when a passion throws off its swaddling clothes, inexplicable pleasures are felt, known to those who have loved. So some readers will understand why the painter mounted the stairs to the fourth floor but slowly, and will be in the secret of the throbs that followed each other so rapidly in his heart at the moment when he saw the humble brown door of the rooms inhabited by Mademoiselle Leseigneur. This girl, whose name was not the same as her mother's, had aroused the young painter's deepest sympathies; he chose to fancy some similarity between himself and her as to their position, and attributed to her misfortunes of birth akin to his own. All the time he worked Hippolyte gave himself very willingly to thoughts of love, and made a great deal of noise to compel the two ladies to think of him, as he was thinking of them. He stayed late at the studio and dined there; then, at about seven o'clock, he went down to call on his neighbours.

No painter of manners has ventured to initiate us—perhaps out of modesty—into the really curious privacy of certain Parisian existences, into the secret of the dwellings whence emerge such fresh and elegant toilets, such brilliant women, who, rich on the surface, allow the signs of very doubtful comfort to peep out in every part of their home. If, here, the picture is too boldly drawn, if you find it tedious in places, do not blame the description, which is, indeed, part and parcel of my story; for the appearance of the rooms inhabited by his two neighbours had a great influence on the feelings and hopes of Hippolyte Schinner.

The house belonged to one of those proprietors in whom there is a foregone and profound horror of repairs and decoration, one of the men who regard their position as Paris house-owners as a business. In the vast chain of moral species, these people hold a middle place between the miser and the usurer. Optimists in their own interests, they are all faithful to the Austrian *status quo.* If you speak of moving a cupboard or a door, of opening the most indispensable air-hole, their eyes flash, their bile rises, they rear like a frightened horse. When the wind blows down a few chimney-pots they are quite ill, and deprive themselves of an evening at the Gymnase or the Porte-Saint-Martin Theatre, "on account of repairs." Hippolyte, had seen the performance gratis of a comical scene with Monsieur Molineux as concerning certain decorative repairs in his studio, was not surprised to see the dark greasy paint, the oily stains, spots, and other disagreeable accessories that varied the woodwork. And these stigmata of poverty are not altogether devoid of poetry in an artist's eyes.

Mademoiselle Leseigneur herself opened the door. On recognizing the young artist she bowed, and at the same time, with Parisian adroitness, and with the presence of mind that pride can lend, she turned round to shut a door in a glass partition through which Hippolyte might have caught sight of some linen hung by lines over patent ironing stoves, an old camp-bed, some wood-embers charcoal, irons, a filter, the household crockery, and all the utensils familiar to a small household. Muslin curtains, fairly white, carefully screened this lumber-room—a *capharnaûm*, as the French call such a domestic laboratory,—which was lighted by windows looking out on a neighbouring yard.

Hippolyte, with the quick eye of an artist, saw the uses, the furniture, the general effect and condition of this first room, thus cut in half. The more honourable half, which served both as ante-room and dining-room, was hung with an old salmon-rose-coloured paper, with a flock border, the manufacture of Reveillon, no doubt; the holes and spots had been carefully touched over with wafers. Prints representing the battles of Alexander, by Lebrun, in frames with the gilding rubbed off, were symmetrically arranged on the walls. In the middle stood a massive mahogany table, old-fashioned in shape, and worn at the edges. A small stove, whose thin straight pipe was scarcely visible, stood in front of the chimney-place, but the hearth was occupied by a cupboard. By a strange contrast the chairs showed some remains of former splendour; they were of carved mahogany, but the red morocco seats, the gilt nails and reeded backs, showed as many scars as an old sergeant of the Imperial Guard.

This room did duty as a museum of certain objects, such as are never seen but in this kind of amphibious household; nameless objects with the stamp at once of luxury and penury. Among other curiosities Hippolyte noticed a splendidly finished telescope, hanging over the small discolored glass that decorated the chimney. To harmonise with this strange collection of furniture, there was, between the chimney and the partition, a wretched sideboard of painted wood, pretending to be mahogany, of all woods the most impossible to imitate. But the slippery red quarries, the shabby little rugs in front of the chairs, and all the furniture, shone with the hard rubbing cleanliness which lends a treacherous lustre to old things by making their defects, their age, and their long service still more conspicuous. An indescribable odour pervaded the room, a mingled smell of the exhalations from the lumber room, and the vapors of the dining-room, with those from the stairs, though the window was partly open. The air from the street fluttered the dusty curtains, which were carefully drawn so as to hide the window bay, where former tenants had testified to their presence by various ornamental additions—a sort of domestic fresco.

Adélaïde hastened to open the door of the inner room, where she announced the painter with evident pleasure. Hippolyte, who, of yore, had seen the same signs of poverty in his mother's home, noted them with the singular vividness of impression which characterises the earliest acquisitions of memory, and entered into the details of this existence better than any one else would have done. As he recognized the facts of his life as a child, the kind young fellow felt neither scorn for disguised misfortune nor pride in the luxury he had lately conquered for his mother.

"Well, monsieur, I hope you no longer feel the effects of your fall," said the old lady, rising from an antique armchair that stood by the chimney, and offering him a seat.

"No, madame. I have come to thank you for the kind care you gave me, and above all mademoiselle, who heard me fall."

As he uttered this speech, stamped with the exquisite stupidity given to the mind by the first disturbing symptoms of true love, Hippolyte looked at the young girl. Adélaïde was lighting the Argand lamp, no doubt that she might get rid of a tallow candle fixed in a large copper flat-candlestick, and graced with a heavy fluting of grease from its guttering. She answered with a slight bow, carried the flat candlestick into the ante-room, came back, and after placing the lamp on the chimney shelf, seated herself by her mother, a little behind the painter, so as to be able to look at him at her ease, while apparently much interested in the burning of the lamp; the flame, checked by the damp in a dingy chimney, sputtered as it struggled with a charred and badly-trimmed wick. Hippolyte, seeing the large mirror that decorated the chimney-piece, immediately fixed his eyes on it to admire Adélaïde. Thus the girl's little stratagem only served to embarrass them both.

While talking with Madame Leseigneur, for Hippolyte called her so, on the chance of being right, he examined the room, but unobtrusively and by stealth.

The Egyptian figures on the iron fire-dogs were scarcely visible, the hearth was so heaped with cinders; two brands tried to meet in front of a sham log of fire-brick, as carefully buried as a miser's treasure could ever be. An old Aubusson carpet, very much faded, very much mended, and as worn as a pensioner's coat, did not cover the whole of the tiled floor, and the cold struck to his feet. The walls were hung with a reddish paper, imitating figured silk with a yellow pattern. In the middle of the wall opposite the windows the painter saw a crack, and the outline marked on the paper of double-doors, shutting off a recess where Madame Leseigneur slept no doubt, a fact ill disguised by a sofa in front of the door. Facing the chimney, above a mahogany chest of drawers of handsome and tasteful design, was the portrait of an officer of rank, which the dim light did not allow him to see well; but from what he could make out he thought that the fearful daub must have been painted in China. The window-curtains of red silk were as much faded as the furniture, in red and yellow worsted work, if this room "contrived a double debt to pay." On the marble top of the chest of drawers was a costly malachite tray, with a dozen coffee cups magnificently painted, and made, no doubt, at Sèvres. On the chimney shelf stood the omnipresent Empire clock: a warrior driving the four horses of a chariot, whose wheel bore the numbers of the hours on its spokes. The tapers in the tall candlesticks were yellow with smoke, and at each corner of the shelf stood a porcelain vase crowned with artificial flowers full of dust and stuck into moss.

In the middle of the room Hippolyte remarked a card-table ready for play, with new packs of cards. For an observer there was something heartrending in the sight of this misery painted up like an old woman who wants to falsify her face. At such a sight every man of sense must at once have stated to himself this obvious dilemma these two women are honesty itself, or they live by intrigue and gambling. But on looking at Adélaïde, a man so pure-minded as Schinner could not but believe in her perfect innocence, and ascribe the incoherence of the furniture to honourable causes.

"My dear," said the old lady to the young one, "I am cold; make a little fire, and give me my shawl."

Adélaïde went into a room next the drawing-room, where she no doubt slept, and returned bringing her mother a cashmere shawl, which when new must have been very costly; the pattern was Indian; but it was old, faded, and full of darns, and matched the furniture. Madame Leseigneur wrapped herself in it very artistically, and with the readiness of an old woman who wishes to make her words seem truth. The young girl ran lightly off to the lumber-room and reappeared with a bundle of small wood, which she gallantly threw on the fire to revive it.

It would be rather difficult to reproduce the conversation which followed among these three persons. Hippolyte, guided by the tact which is almost always the outcome of misfortune suffered in early youth, dared not allow himself to make the least remark as to his neighbours' situation, as he saw all about him the signs of ill-disguised poverty. The simplest question would have been an indiscretion, and could only be ventured on by old friendship. The painter was nevertheless absorbed in the thought of this concealed penury, it pained his generous soul; but knowing how offensive every kind of pity may be, even the friendliest, the disparity between his thoughts and his words made him feel uncomfortable.

The two ladies at first talked of painting, for women easily guess the secret embarrassment of a first call; they themselves feel it perhaps, and the nature of their mind supplies them with a thousand devices to put an end to it. By questioning the young man as to the material exercise of his art, and as to his studies, Adélaïde and her mother emboldened him to talk. The indefinable nothings of their chat, animated by kind feeling, naturally led Hippolyte to flash forth remarks or reflections which showed the character of his habits and of his mind. Trouble had prematurely faded the old lady's face, formerly handsome, no doubt; nothing was left but the more prominent features, the outline, in a word, the skeleton of a countenance of which the whole effect indicated great shrewdness with much grace in the play of the eyes, in which could be discerned the expression peculiar to women of the old Court; an expression that cannot be defined in words. Those fine and mobile features might quite as well indicate bad feelings, and suggest astuteness and womanly artifice carried to a high pitch of wickedness, as reveal the refined delicacy of a beautiful soul.

Indeed, the face of a woman has this element of mystery to puzzle the ordinary observer, that the difference between frankness and duplicity, the genius for intrigue and the genius of the heart, is there inscrutable. A man gifted with a penetrating eye can read the intangible shade of difference produced by a more or less curved line, a more or less deep dimple, a more or less prominent feature. The appreciation of these indications he is entirely in the domain of intuition; this alone can lead to the discovery of what every one is interested in concealing. The old lady's face was like the room she inhabited; it seemed as difficult to detect whether this squalor covered vice or the highest virtue, as to decide whether Adélaïde's mother was an old coquette accustomed to weigh, to calculate, to sell everything, or a loving woman, full of noble feeling and amiable qualities. But at Schinner's age the first impulse of the heart is to believe in goodness. And indeed, as he studied Adélaïde's noble and almost haughty brow, as he looked into her eyes full of soul and thought, he breathed, so to speak, the sweet and modest fragrance of virtue. In the course of the conversation he seized an opportunity of discussing portraits in general, to give himself a pretext for examining the frightful pastel, of which the colour had flown, and the chalk in many places fallen away.

"You are attached to that picture for the sake of the likeness, no doubt, mesdames, for the drawing is dreadful?" he said, looking at Adélaïde .

"It was done at Calcutta, in great haste," replied the mother, in an agitated voice.

She gazed at the formless sketch with the deep absorption which memories of happiness produce when they are roused and fall on the heart like a beneficent dew to whose refreshing touch we love to yield ourselves up; but in the expression of the old lady's face there were traces too of perennial regret. At least, it was thus that the painter chose to interpret her attitude and countenance, and he presently sat down again by her side.

"Madame," he said, "in a very short time the colours of that pastel will have disappeared. The portrait will only survive in your memory. Where you will still see the face that is dear to you, others will see nothing at all. Will you allow me to reproduce the likeness on canvas? It will be more permanently recorded then than on that sheet of paper. Grant me, I beg, as a neighborly favour, the pleasure of doing you this service. There are times when an artist is glad of a respite from his greater undertakings by doing work of less lofty pretensions, so it will be a recreation for me to paint that head."

The old lady flushed as she heard the painter's words, and Adélaïde shot one of those glances of deep feeling which seem to flash from the soul. Hippolyte wanted to feel some tie linking him with his two neighbours, to conquer a right to mingle in their life. His offer, appealing as it did to the liveliest affections of the heart, was the only one he could possibly make; it gratified his pride as an artist, and could not hurt the feelings of the ladies. Madame Leseigneur accepted, without eagerness or reluctance, but with the self-possession of a noble soul, fully aware of the character of bonds formed by such an obligation, while, at the same time, they are its highest glory as a proof of esteem.

"I fancy," said the painter, "that the uniform is that of a naval officer"

"Yes," she said, "that of a captain in command of a vessel. Monsieur de Rouville—my husband—died at Batavia in consequence of a wound received in a fight with an English ship they fell in with off the Asiatic coast. He commanded a frigate of fifty-six guns, and the *Revenge* carried ninety-six. The struggle was very unequal, but he defended his ship so bravely that he held out till nightfall and got away. When I came back to France Bonaparte was not yet in power, and I was refused a pension. When I applied again for it, quite lately, I was sternly informed that if the Baron de Rouville had emigrated I should not have lost him; that by this time he would have been rear-admiral; finally, his Excellency quoted I know not what degree of forfeiture. I took this step, to which I was urged by my friends, only for the sake of my poor Adélaïde. I have always hated the idea of holding out my hand as a beggar in the name of a grief which deprives a woman of voice and strength. I do not like this money valuation for blood irreparably spilt—"

"Dear mother, this subject always does you harm."

In response to this remark from Adélaïde, the Baronne Leseigneur bowed, and was silent.

"Monsieur," said the young girl to Hippolyte, "I had supposed that a painter's work was generally fairly quiet?"

At this question Schinner coloured, remembering the noise he had made. Adélaïde said no more, and spared him a falsehood by rising at the sound of a carriage stopping at the door. She went into her own room, and returned carrying a pair of tall gilt candlesticks with partly burnt wax candles, which she quickly lighted, and without waiting for the bell to ring, she opened the door of the outer room, where she set the lamp down. The sound of a kiss given and received found an echo in Hippolyte's heart. The young man's impatience to see the man who treated Adélaïde with so much familiarity, was not immediately gratified; the newcomers had a conversation, which he thought very long, in an under tone, with the young girl.

At last Mademoiselle de Rouville returned, followed by two men, whose costume, countenance, and appearance are a long story.

The first, a man of about sixty, wore one of the coats invented, I believe, for Louis XVIII, then on the throne, in which the most difficult problem of the sartorial art had been solved by a tailor who ought to be immortal. That artist certainly understood the art of compromise, which was the moving genius of that period of shifting politics. Is it not a rare merit to be able to take the measure of the time? This coat, which the young men of the present day may conceive to be fabulous, was neither civil nor military, and might pass for civil or military by turns. *Fleurs-de-lis* were embroidered on the lapels of the back skirts. The gilt buttons also bore *fleurs-de-lis*; on the shoulders a pair of straps cried out for useless epaulettes; these military appendages were there like a petition without a recommendation. This old gentleman's coat was of dark blue cloth, and the buttonhole had blossomed into many coloured ribbons. He, no doubt, always carried his hat in his hand—a three-cornered cocked hat, with a gold cord—for the snowy wings of his powdered hair showed not a trace of its pressure. He might have been taken for not more than fifty years of age, and seemed to enjoy robust health. While wearing the frank and loyal expression of the old émigrés, his countenance also hinted at the easy habits of a libertine, at the light and reckless passions of the Musketeers formerly so famous in the annals of gallantry. His gestures, his attitude, and his manner proclaimed that he had no intention of correcting himself of his royalism, of his religion, or of his love affairs.

A really fantastic figure came in behind this specimen of "Louis XIV's light infantry"—a nickname given by the Bonapartists to these venerable survivors of the Monarchy. To do it justice it ought to be made the principal object in the picture, and it is but an accessory. Imagine a lean, dry man, dressed like the former, but seeming to be only his reflection, or his shadow, if you will. The coat, new on the first, on the second was old; the powder in his hair looked less white, the gold of the *fleurs-de-lis* less bright, the shoulder straps more hopeless and dog's eared; his intellect seemed more feeble, his life nearer the fatal term than in the former. In short, he realized Rivarol's witticism on Champcenetz, "He is the moonlight of me." He was simply his double, a paler and poorer double, for there was between them all the difference that lies between the first and last impressions of a lithograph.

This speechless old man was a mystery to the painter, and always remained a mystery. The *Chevalier,* for he was a *Chevalier*, did not speak, nobody spoke to him. Was he a friend, a poor relation, a man who followed at the old gallant's heels as a lady companion does at an old lady's? Did he fill a place midway between a dog, a parrot, and a friend? Had he saved his patron's fortune, or only his life? Was he the Trim to another Captain Toby? Elsewhere, as at the Baronne de Rouville's, he always piqued curiosity without satisfying it. Who, after the Restoration, could remember the attachment which, before the Revolution, had bound this man to his friend's wife, dead now these twenty years?

The leader, who appeared the least dilapidated of these wrecks, came gallantly up to Madame de Rouville, kissed her hand, and sat down by her. The other bowed and placed himself not far from his model, at a distance represented by two chairs. Adélaïde came behind the old gentleman's arm chair and leaned her elbows on the back, unconsciously imitating the attitude given to Dido's sister by Guérin in his famous picture.

Though the gentleman's familiarity was that of a father, his freedom seemed at the moment to annoy the young girl.

'What, are you sulky with me?" he said.

Then he shot at Schinner one of those side-looks full of shrewdness and cunning, diplomatic looks, whose expression betrays the discreet uneasiness, the polite curiosity of well-bred people, and seems to ask, when they see a stranger, "Is he one of us?"

"This is our neighbour," said the old lady, pointing to Hippolyte. "Monsieur is a celebrated painter, whose name must be known to you in spite of your indifference to the arts."

The old man saw his friend's mischievous intent in suppressing the name, and bowed to the young man.

"Certainly," said he. "I heard a great deal about his pictures at the last Salon. Talent has immense privileges," he added, observing the artist's red ribbon. "That distinction, which we must earn at the cost of our blood and long service, you win in your youth; but all glory is of the same kindred," he said, laying his hand on his Cross of Saint-Louis.

Hippolyte murmured a few words of acknowledgment, and was silent again, satisfied to admire with growing enthusiasm the beautiful girl's head that charmed him so much. He was soon lost in contemplation, completely forgetting the extreme misery of the dwelling. To him Adélaïde's face stood out against a luminous atmosphere. He replied briefly to the questions addressed to him, which, by good luck, he heard, thanks to a singular faculty of the soul which some times seems to have a double consciousness. Who has not known what it is to sit lost in sad or delicious meditation, listening to its voice within, while attending to a conversation or to reading? An admirable duality which often helps us to tolerate a bore! Hope, prolific and smiling, poured out before him a thousand visions of happiness; and he refused to consider what was going on around him. As confiding as a child, it seemed to him base to analyse a pleasure.

After a short lapse of time he perceived that the old lady and her daughter were playing cards with the old gentleman. As to the satellite, faithful to his function as a shadow, he stood behind his friend's chair watching his game, and answering the player's mute inquiries by little approving nods, repeating the questioning gestures of the other countenance.

"Du Halga, I always lose," said the gentleman.

"You discard badly," replied the Baronne de Rouville.

"For three months now I have never won a single game," said he.

"Have you the aces?" asked the old lady.

"Yes, one more to mark," said he.

"Shall I come and advise you?" said Adélaïde .

"No, no. Stay where I can see you. By Gad, it would be losing too much not to have you to look at!"

At last the game was over. The gentleman pulled out his purse, and, throwing two louis d'or on the table, not without temper— "Forty francs," he exclaimed, "the exact sum.—Deuce take it! It is eleven o'clock."

"It is eleven o'clock," repeated the silent figure, looking at the painter.

The young man, hearing these words rather more distinctly than all the others, thought it time to retire. Coming back to the world of ordinary ideas, he found a few commonplace remarks to make, took leave of the Baroness, her daughter, and the two strangers, and went away, wholly possessed by the first raptures of true love, without attempting to analyze the little incidents of the evening.

On the morrow the young painter felt the most ardent desire to see Adélaïde once more. If he had followed the call of his passion, he would have gone to his neighbour's door at six in the morning, when he went to his studio. However, he still was reasonable enough to wait till the afternoon. But as soon as he thought he could present himself to Madame de Rouville, he went downstairs, rang, blushing like a girl, shyly asked Mademoiselle Leseigneur, who came to let him in, to let him have the portrait of the Baron.

"But come in," said Adélaïde, who had no doubt heard him come down from the studio.

The painter followed, bashful and out of countenance, not knowing what to say, happiness had so dulled his wit. To see Adélaïde, to hear the rustle of her skirt, after longing for a whole morning to be near her, after starting up a hundred time—"I will go down now"—and not to have gone; this was to him life so rich that such sensations, too greatly prolonged, would have worn out his spirit. The heart has the singular power of giving extraordinary value to mere nothings. What joy it is to a traveller to treasure a blade of grass, an unfamiliar leaf, if he has risked his life to pluck it! It is the same with the trifles of love.

The old lady was not in the drawing-room. When the young girl found herself there, alone with the painter, she brought a chair to stand on, to take down the picture; but perceiving that she could not unhook it without setting her foot on the chest of drawers, she turned to Hippolyte, and said with a blush:

"I am not tall enough. Will you get it down!"

A feeling of modesty, betrayed in the expression of her face and the tones of her voice, was the real motive of her request; and the young man, understanding this, gave her one of those glances of intelligence which are the sweetest language of love. Seeing that the painter had read her soul, Adélaïde cast down her eyes with the instinct of reserve which is the secret of a maiden's heart. Hippolyte, finding nothing to say, and feeling almost timid, took down the picture, examined it gravely, carrying it to the light of the window, and then went away, without saying a word to Mademoiselle Leseigneur but, "I will return it soon."

During this brief moment they both went through one of those storms of agitation of which the effects in the soul may be compared to those of a stone flung into a deep lake. The most delightful waves of thought rise and follow each other, indescribable, repeated, and aimless, tossing the heart like the circular ripples, which for a long time fret the waters, starting from the point where the stone fell.

Hippolyte returned to the studio bearing the portrait. His easel was ready with a fresh canvas, and his palette set, his brushes cleaned, the spot and the light carefully chosen. And till the dinner hour he worked at the painting with the ardour artists throw into their whims. He went again that evening to the Baronne de Rouville's, and remained from nine till eleven. Excepting the different topics of conversation, this evening was exactly like the last. The two old men arrived at the same hour, the same game of piquet was played, the same speeches made by the players, the sum lost by Adélaïde's friend was not less considerable than on the previous evening; only Hippolyte, a little bolder, ventured to chat with the young girl.

A week passed thus, and in the course of it the painter's feelings and Adélaïde's underwent the slow and delightful transformations which bring two souls to a perfect understanding. Every day the look with which the girl welcomed her friend grew more intimate, more confiding, gayer, and more open; her voice and manner became more eager and more familiar. They laughed and talked together, telling each other their thoughts, speaking of themselves with the simplicity of two children who have made friends in a day, as much as if they had met constantly for three years. Schinner wished to be taught piquet. Being ignorant and a novice, he, of course, made blunder after blunder, and, like the old man, he lost almost every game. Without having spoken a word of love the lovers knew that they were all in all to one an other. Hippolyte enjoyed exerting his power over his gentle little friend, and many concessions were made to him by Adélaïde, who, timid and devoted to him, was quite deceived by the assumed fits of temper, such as the least skilled lover and the most guileless girl can affect; and which they constantly play off, as spoilt children abuse the power they owe to their mother's affection. Thus all familiarity between the girl and the old Count was soon put a stop to. She understood the painter's melancholy, and the thoughts hidden in the furrows on his brow, from the abrupt tone of the few words he spoke when the old man unceremoniously kissed Adélaïde's hands or throat.

Mademoiselle Leseigneur, on her part, soon expected her lover to give a short account of all his actions; she was so unhappy, so restless when Hippolyte did not come, she scolded him so effectually for his absence, that the painter had to give up seeing his other friends, and now went nowhere. Adélaïde allowed the natural jealousy of women to be perceived. when she heard that sometimes at eleven o'clock, on quitting the house, the painter still had visits to pay, and was to be seen in the most brilliant drawing-rooms of Paris. This mode of life, she assured him, was bad for his health; then, with the intense conviction to which the accent, the emphasis, and the look of one we love lend so much weight, she asserted that a man who was obliged to expend his time and the charms of his wit on several women at once could not be the object of any very warm affection. Thus the painter was led, as much by the tyranny of his passion as by the exactions of a girl in love, to live exclusively in the little apartment where everything attracted him.

And never was there a purer or more ardent love. On both sides the same trustfulness, the same delicacy, gave their passion increase without the aid of those sacrifices by which many persons try to prove their affection. Between these two there was such a constant interchange of sweet emotion that they knew not which gave or received the most.

As affinity made the union of their souls a close one. The progress of this true feeling was so rapid that two months after the accident to which the painter owed the happiness of knowing Adélaïde , their lives were one life. From early morning the young girl, hearing footsteps over head, could say to herself, "He is there." When Hippolyte went home to his mother at the dinner hour he never failed to look in on his neighbours, and in the evening he flew there at the accustomed hour with a lover's punctuality. Thus the most tyrannical woman or the most ambitious in the matter of love could not have found the smallest fault with the young painter. And Adélaïde tasted of unmixed and unbounded happiness as she saw the fullest realization of the ideal of which, at her age, it is so natural to dream.

The old gentleman now came more rarely; Hippolyte, who had been jealous, had taken his place at the green table, and shared his constant ill-luck at cards. And sometimes, in the midst of his happiness, as he considered Madame de Rouville's disastrous position—for he had had more than one proof of her extreme poverty—an importunate thought would haunt him. Several times he had said to himself as he went home, "Strange! twenty francs every evening?" and he dared not confess to himself his odious suspicions.

He spent two months over the portrait, and when it was finished, varnished, and framed, he looked upon it as one of his best works. Madame la Baronne de Rouville had never spoken of it again. Was this from indifference or pride? The painter would not allow himself to account for this silence. He joyfully plotted with Adélaïde to hang the picture in its place when Madame de Rouville should be out. So one day, during the walk her mother usually took in the Tuileries, Adélaïde for the first time went up to Hippolyte's studio, on the pretext of seeing the portrait in the good light in which it had been painted. She stood speechless and motionless, but in ecstatic contemplation, in which all a woman's feelings were merged. For are they not all comprehended in boundless admiration for the man she loves? When the painter, uneasy at her silence, leaned forward to look at her, she held out her hand, unable to speak a word, but two tears fell from her eyes. Hippolyte took her hand, and covered it with kisses; for a minute they looked at each other in silence, both longing to confess their love, and not daring. The painter kept her hand in his, and the same glow, the same throb, told them that their hearts were both beating wildly.

The young girl, too greatly agitated, gently drew away from Hippolyte, and said, with a look of the utmost simplicity:

"You will make my mother very happy."

"What, only your mother?" he asked.

"Oh, I am too happy."

The painter bent his head and remained silent, frightened at the vehemence of the feelings which her tones stirred in his heart. Then, both understanding the perils of the situation, they went downstairs and hung up the picture in its place. Hippolyte dined for the first time with the Baroness, who, greatly overcome, and drowned in tears, must needs embrace him.

In the evening the old émigré, the Baron de Rouville's old comrade, paid the ladies a visit to announce that he had just been promoted to the rank of vice-admiral. His voyages by land over Germany and Russia had been counted as naval campaigns. On seeing the portrait he cordially shook the painter's hand, and exclaimed, "By Gad! though my old hulk does not deserve to be perpetuated, I would gladly give five hundred pistoles to see myself as like as that is to my dear old Rouville."

At this hint the Baroness looked at her young friend and smiled, while her face lighted up with an expression of sudden gratitude. Hippolyte suspected that the old admiral wished to offer him the price of both portraits while paying for his own. His pride as an artist, no less than his jealousy perhaps, took offence at the thought, and he replied:

"Monsieur, if I were a portrait-painter I should not have done this one."

The admiral bit his lip, and sat down to cards.

The painter remained near Adélaïde, who proposed a dozen hands of piquet, to which he agreed. As he played he observed in Madame de Rouville an excitement over her game which surprised him. Never before had the old Baroness manifested so ardent a desire to win, or so keen a joy in fingering the old gentleman's gold pieces. During the evening evil suspicions troubled Hippolyte's happiness, and filled him with distrust. Could it be that Madame de Rouville lived by gambling? Was she playing at this moment to pay off some debt, or under the pressure of necessity? Perhaps she had not paid her rent. The old man seemed shrewd enough not to allow his money to be taken with impunity. What interest attracted him to this poverty-stricken house, he who was rich? Why, when he had formerly been so familiar with Adélaïde had he given up the rights he had acquired, and which were perhaps his due?

These involuntary reflections prompted him to watch the old man and the Baroness, whose meaning looks and certain sidelong glances cast at Adélaïde displeased him. "Am I being duped?" was Hippolyte's last idea—horrible, scathing, for he believed it just enough to be tortured by it. He determined to stay after the departure of the two old men, to confirm or dissipate his suspicions. He drew out his purse to pay Adélaïde; but carried away by his poignant thoughts, he laid it on the table, falling into a reverie of brief duration; then, ashamed of his silence, he rose, answered some commonplace question from Madame de Rouville, and went close up to her to examine the withered features while he was talking to her.

He went away, racked by a thousand doubts. He had gone down but a few steps when he turned back to fetch the forgotten purse.

"I left my purse here!" he said to the young girl.

"No," she said, reddening.

"I thought it was there," and he pointed to the card-table. Not finding it, in his shame for Adélaïde and the Baroness, he looked at them with a blank amazement that made them laugh, turned pale, felt his waistcoat, and said, "I must have made a mistake. I have it somewhere no doubt."

In one end of the purse there were fifteen louis d'or, and in the other some small change. The theft was so flagrant, and denied with such effrontery, that Hippolyte no longer felt a doubt as to his neighbours' morals. He stood still on the stairs, and got down with some difficulty; his knees shook, he felt dizzy, he was in a cold sweat, he shivered, and found himself unable to walk, struggling, as he was, with the agonizing shock caused by the destruction of all his hopes. And at this moment he found lurking in his memory a number of observations, trifling in themselves, but which corroborated his frightful suspicions, and which, by proving the certainty of this last incident, opened his eyes as to the character and life of these two women.

Had they really waited till the portrait was given them before robbing him of his purse? In such a combination the theft was even more odious. The painter recollected that for the last two or three evenings Adélaïde, while seeming to examine with a girl's curiosity the particular stitch of the worn silk netting, was probably counting the coins in the purse, while making some light jests, quite innocent in appearance, but no doubt with the object of watching for a moment when the sum was worth stealing.

"The old admiral has perhaps good reasons for not marrying Adélaïde, and so the Baroness has tried—"

But at this hypothesis he checked himself, not finishing his thought, which was contradicted by a very just reflection, "If the Baroness hopes to get me to marry her daughter," thought he, "they would not have robbed me."

Then, clinging to his illusions, to the love that already had taken such deep root, he tried to find a justification in some accident. "The purse must have fallen on the floor," said he to himself, "or I left it lying on my chair. Or perhaps I have it about me—I am so absent-minded!" He searched himself with hurried movements, but did not find the ill-starred purse. His memory cruelly retraced the fatal truth, minute by minute. He distinctly saw the purse lying on the green cloth; but then, doubtful no longer, he excused Adélaïde, telling himself that persons in misfortune should not be so hastily condemned. There was, of course, some secret behind this apparently degrading action. He would not admit that that proud and noble face was a lie.

At the same time the wretched rooms rose before him, denuded of the poetry of love which beautifies everything; he saw them dirty and faded, regarding them as emblematic of an inner life devoid of honour, idle and vicious. Are not our feelings written, as it were, on the things about us?

Next morning he rose, not having slept. The heartache, that terrible malady of the soul, had made rapid inroads. To lose the bliss we dreamed of, to renounce our whole future, is a keener pang than that caused by the loss of known happiness, however complete it may have been; for is not Hope better than Memory? The thoughts into which our spirit is suddenly plunged are like a shoreless sea, in which we may swim for a moment, but where our love is doomed to drown and die. And it is a frightful death. Are not our feelings the most glorious part of our life? It is this partial death which, in certain delicate or powerful natures, leads to the terrible ruin produced by disenchantment, by hopes and passions betrayed. Thus it was with the young painter. He went out at a very early hour to walk under the fresh shade of the Tuileries, absorbed in his thoughts, forgetting every thing in the world.

There by chance he met one of his most intimate friends, a school-fellow and studio-mate, with whom he had lived on better terms than with a brother.

"Why, Hippolyte, what ails you?" asked François Souchet, the young sculptor who had just won the first prize, and was soon to set out for Italy.

"I am most unhappy," replied Hippolyte gravely.

"Nothing but a love affair can cause you grief. Money, glory, respect—you lack nothing."

Insensibly the painter was led into confidences, and confessed his love. The moment he mentioned the Rue de Suresne, and a young girl living on the fourth floor, "Stop, stop," cried Souchet lightly. "A little girl I see every morning at the Church of the Assumption, and with whom I have a flirtation. But, my dear fellow, we all know her. The mother is a Baroness. Do you really believe in a Baroness living up four flights of stairs? Brrr! Why, you are a relic of the golden age! We see the old mother here, in this avenue, every day; why, her face, her appearance, tell every thing. What, have you not known her for what she is by the way she holds her bag?"

The two friends walked up and down for some time, and several young men who knew Souchet or Schinner joined them. The painter's adventure, which the sculptor regarded as unimportant, was repeated by him.

"So he, too, has seen that young lady!" said Souchet.

And then there were comments, laughter, innocent mockery, full of the liveliness familiar to artists, but which pained Hippolyte frightfully. A certain native reticence made him uncomfortable as he saw his heart's secret so carelessly handled, his passion rent, torn to tatters, a young and unknown girl, whose life seemed to be so modest, the victim of condemnation, right or wrong, but pronounced with such reckless indifference. He pretended to be moved by a spirit of contradiction, asking each for proofs of his assertions, and their jests began again.

"But, my dear boy, have you seen the Baroness' shawl?" asked Souchet.

"Have you ever followed the girl when she patters off to church in the morning?" said Joseph Bridau, a young dauber in Gros' studio.

"Oh, the mother has among other virtues a certain grey gown, which I regard as typical," said Bixiou, the caricaturist.

"Listen, Hippolyte," the sculptor went on. "Come here at about four o'clock, and just study the walk of both mother and daughter. If after that you still have doubts! well, no one can ever make anything of you; you would be capable of marrying your porter's daughter."

Torn by the most conflicting feelings, the painter parted from his friends. It seemed to him that Adélaïde and her mother must be superior to these accusations, and at the bottom of his heart he was filled with remorse for having suspected the purity of this beautiful and simple girl. He went to his studio, passing the door of the rooms where Adélaïde was, and conscious of a pain at his heart which no man can misapprehend. He loved Mademoiselle de Rouville so passionately that, in spite of the theft of the purse, he still worshiped her. His love was that of the Chevalier des Grieux admiring his mistress, and holding her as pure, even on the cart which carries such lost creatures to prison. "Why should not my love keep her the purest of women? Why abandon her to evil and to vice without holding out a rescuing hand to her?"

The idea of this mission pleased him. Love makes a gain of everything. Nothing tempts a young man more than to play the part of a good genius to a woman. There is something inexplicably romantic in such an enterprise which appeals to a highly-strung soul. Is it not the utmost stretch of devotion under the loftiest and most engaging aspect? Is there not something grand in the thought that we love enough still to love on when the love of others dwindles and dies?

Hippolyte sat down in his studio, gazed at his picture without doing anything to it, seeing the figures through tears that swelled in his eyes, holding his brush in his hand, going up to the canvas as if to soften down an effect, but not touching it. Night fell, and he was still in this attitude. Roused from his moodiness by the darkness, he went downstairs, met the old admiral on the way, looked darkly at him as he bowed, and fled.

He had intended going in to see the ladies, but the sight of Adélaïde's protector froze his heart and dispelled his purpose. For the hundredth time he wondered what interest could bring this old prodigal, with his eighty thousand francs a year, to this fourth story, where he lost about forty francs every evening; and he thought he could guess what it was.

The next and following days Hippolyte threw himself into his work, and to try to conquer his passion by the swift rush of ideas and the ardor of composition. He half succeeded. Study consoled him, though it could not smother the memories of so many tender hours spent with Adélaïde.

One evening, as he left his studio, he saw the door of the ladies' rooms half open. Somebody was standing in the recess of the window, and the position of the door and the staircase made it impossible that the painter should pass without seeing Adélaïde. He bowed coldly, with a glance of supreme indifference; but judging of the girl's suffering by his own, he felt an inward shudder as he reflected on the bitterness which that look and that coldness must produce in a loving heart. To crown the most delightful feast which ever brought joy to two pure souls, by eight days of disdain, of the deepest and most utter contempt!—A frightful conclusion. And perhaps the purse had been found, perhaps Adélaïde had looked for her friend every evening.

This simple and natural idea filled the lover with fresh remorse; he asked himself whether the proofs of attachment given him by the young girl, the delightful talks, full of the love that had so charmed him, did not deserve at least an inquiry; were not worthy of some justification. Ashamed of having resisted the promptings of his heart for a whole week, and feeling himself almost a criminal in this mental struggle, he called the same evening on Madame de Rouville.

All his suspicions, all his evil thoughts vanished at the sight of the young girl, who had grown pale and thin.

"Good heavens! what is the matter?" he asked her, after greeting the Baroness.

Adélaïde made no reply, but she gave him a look of deep melancholy, a sad, dejected look, which pained him.

"You have, no doubt, been working hard," said the old lady. "You are altered. We are the cause of your seclusion. That portrait had delayed some pictures essential to your reputation."

Hippolyte was glad to find so good an excuse for his rudeness.

"Yes," he said, "I have been very busy, but I have been suffering—"

At these words Adélaïde raised her head, looked at her lover, and her anxious eyes had now no hint of reproach.

"You must have thought us quite indifferent to any good or ill that may befall you?" said the old lady.

"I was wrong," he replied. "Still, there are forms of pain which we know not how to confide to any one, even to a friendship of older date than that with which you honour me."

"The sincerity and strength of friendship are not to be measured by time. I have seen old friends who had not a tear to bestow on misfortune," said the Baroness, nodding sadly.

"But you—what ails you?" the young man asked Adélaïde.

"Oh, nothing," replied the Baroness. "Adélaïde has sat up late for some nights to finish some little piece of woman's work, and would not listen to me when I told her that a day more or less did not matter—"

Hippolyte was not listening. As he looked at these two noble, calm faces, he blushed for his suspicions, and ascribed the loss of his purse to some unknown accident.

This was a delicious evening to him, and perhaps to her too. There are some secrets which young souls understand so well. Adélaïde could read Hippolyte's thoughts. Though he could not confess his misdeeds, the painter knew them, and he had come back to his mistress more in love, and more affectionate, trying thus to purchase her tacit forgiveness.

Adélaïde was enjoying such perfect, such sweet happiness, that she did not think she had paid too dear for it with all the grief that had so cruelly crushed her soul. And, yet, this true concord of hearts, this understanding so full of magic charm, was disturbed by a little speech of Madame de Rouville's.

"Let us have our little game," she said, "for my old friend Kergarouët will not let me off."

These words revived all the young painter's fears; he coloured as he looked at Adélaïde's mother, but he saw nothing in her countenance but the expression of the frankest good-nature; no double meaning marred its charm; its keenness was not perfidious, its humour seemed kindly, and no trace of remorse disturbed its equanimity.

He sat down to the card-table. Adélaïde took side with the painter, saying that he did not know piquet, and needed a partner.

All through the game Madame de Rouville and her daughter exchanged looks of intelligence, which alarmed Hippolyte all the more because he was winning; but at last a final hand left the lovers in the old lady's debt.

To feel for some money in his pocket the painter took his hands off the table, and he then saw before him a purse which Adélaïde had slipped in front of him without his noticing it; the poor child had the old one in her hand, and, to keep her countenance, was looking into it for the money to pay her mother. The blood rushed to Hippolyte's heart with such force that he was near fainting.

The new purse, substituted for his own, and which contained his fifteen gold louis, was worked with gilt beads. The rings and tassels bore witness to Adélaïde's good taste, and she had no doubt spent all her little hoard in ornamenting this pretty piece of work. It was impossible to say with greater delicacy that the painter's gift could only be repaid by some proof of affection.

Hippolyte, overcome with happiness, turned to look at Adélaïde and her mother, and saw that they were tremulous with pleasure and delight at their little trick. He felt himself mean, sordid, a fool; he longed to punish himself, to rend his heart. A few tears rose to his eyes; by an irresistible impulse he sprang up, clasped Adélaïde in his arms, pressed her to his heart, and stole a kiss; then with the simple heartiness of an artist, "I ask her for my wife!" he exclaimed, looking at the Baroness.

Adélaïde looked at him with half-wrathful eyes, and Madame de Rouville, somewhat astonished, was considering her reply, when the scene was interrupted by a ring at the bell. The old vice-admiral came in, followed by his shadow, and Madame Schinner. Having guessed the cause of the grief her son vainly endeavored to conceal, Hippolyte's mother had made inquiries among her friends concerning Adélaïde. Very justly alarmed by the calumnies which weighed on the young girl, unknown to the Comte de Kergarouët, whose name she learned from the porter's wife, she went to report them to the vice-admiral; and he, in his rage, declared "he would crop all the scoundrels' ears for them."

Then, prompted by his wrath, he went on to explain to Madame Schinner the secret of his losing intentionally at cards, because the Baronne's pride left him none but these ingenious means of assisting her.

When Madame Schinner had paid her respects to Madame de Rouville, the Baroness looked at the Comte de Kergarouët, at the Chevalier du Halga—the friend of the departed Comtesse de Kergarouët—at Hippolyte, and Adélaïde, and said, with the grace that comes from the heart, "So we are a family party this evening."

PARIS, *May* 1832.

MADAME FIRMIANI

To my dear Alexandre de Berny, from his old friend De Balzac

MANY tales, rich in situations, or made dramatic by the endless sport of chance, carry their plot in themselves, and can be related artistically or simply by any lips without the smallest loss of the beauty of the subject; but there are some incidents of human life to which only the accents of the heart can give life; there are certain anatomical details, so to speak, of which the delicacy appears only under the most skilful infusions of mind. Again, there are portraits which demand a soul, and are nothing without the more ethereal features of the responsive countenance. Finally, there are certain things which we know not how to say, or to depict, without I know not what unconceived harmonies that are under the influence of a day or an hour, of a happy conjunction of celestial signs, or of some occult moral predisposition.

Such revelations as these are absolutely required for the telling of this simple story, in which I would fain interest some of these naturally melancholy and pensive souls which are fed on bland emotions. If the writer, like a surgeon by the side of a dying friend, has become imbued with a sort of respect for the subject he is handling, why should not the reader share this inexplicable feeling? Is it so difficult to throw oneself into that vague, nervous melancholy which sheds grey hues on all our surroundings, which is half an illness, though its languid suffering is sometimes a pleasure?

If you are thinking by chance of the dear friends you have lost; if you are alone, and it is night, or the day is dying, read this narrative; otherwise, throw the book aside, here. If you have never buried some kind aunt, an invalid or poor, you will not understand these pages. To some, they will be odorous as of musk; to others, they will be as colourless, as strictly virtuous as those of Florian. In short, the reader must have known the luxury of tears; must have felt the wordless grief of a memory that drifts lightly by, bearing a shade that is dear but remote; he must possess some of those remembrances that make us at the same time regret those whom the earth has swallowed, and smile over vanished joys.

And now the author would have you believe that for all the wealth of England he would not extort from poetry even one of her fictions to add grace to this narrative. This is a true story, on which you may pour out the treasure of your sensibilities, if you have any.

In these days, our language has as many dialects as there are men in the great human family. And it is a really curious and interesting thing to listen to the different views or versions of one and the same thing, or event, as given by the various species which make up the monograph of the Parisian—the Parisian being taken as a generic term. Thus you might ask a man of the matter-of-fact type, "Do you know Madame Firmiani?" and this man would interpret Madame Firmiani by such an inventory as this: "A large house in the Rue du Bac, rooms handsomely furnished, fine pictures, a hundred thousand francs a year in good securities, and a husband who was formerly receiver-general in the department of Montenotte." Having thus spoken, your matter-of-fact man—stout and roundabout, almost always dressed in black—draws up his lower lip, so as to cover the upper lip, and nods his head, as much as to say, "Very respectable people, there is nothing to be said against them." Ask him no more. Your matter-of-fact people state everything in figures, dividends, or real estate—a great word in their dictionary.

Turn to your right, go and question that young man, who belongs to the lounger species, and repeat your inquiry.

"Madame Firmiani?" says he. "Yes, yes, I know her very well. I go to her evenings. She receives on Wednesdays; a very good house to know." Madame Firmiani is always metamorphosed into a house. The house is not a mere mass of stones architecturally put together; no, this word, in the language of the lounger, has no equivalent. And here your lounger, a dry-looking man, with a pleasant smile, saying clever nothings, but always with more acquired wit than natural wit, bends to your ear, and says with a knowing air:

"I never saw Monsieur Firmiani. His social position consists in managing estates in Italy. But Madame Firmiani is French, and spends her income as a Parisian should. She gives excellent tea! It is one of the few houses where you really can amuse yourself, and where everything they give you is exquisite. It is very difficult to get introduced, and the best society is to be seen in her drawing-rooms." Then the lounger emphasizes his last words by gravely taking a pinch of snuff; he applies it to his nose in little dabs, and seems to be saying: "I go to the house, but do not count on my introducing you."

To folks of this type Madame Firmiani keeps a sort of inn without a sign.

"Why on earth can you want to go to Madame Firmiani's? It is as dull there as it is at Court. Of what use are brains if they do not keep you out of such drawing-rooms, where, with poetry such as is now current, you hear the most trivial little ballad just hatched out."

You have asked one of your friends who comes under the class of petty autocrats—men who would like to have the universe under lock and key, and have nothing done without their leave. They are miserable at other people's enjoyment, can forgive nothing but vice, wrong-doing, and infirmities, and want nothing but protégés. Aristocrats by taste, they are republicans out of spite, simply to discover many inferiors among their equals.

"Oh, Madame Firmiani, my dear fellow, is one of those adorable women whom Nature feels to be a sufficient excuse for all the ugly ones she has created by mistake; she is bewitching, she is kind! I should like to be in power, to be king, to have millions of money, solely (and three words are whispered in your ear). Shall I introduce you to her?"

This young man is a Schoolboy, known for his audacious bearing among men and his extreme shyness in private.

"Madame Firmiani!" cries another, twirling his cane in the air. "I will tell you what I think of her. She is a woman of between thirty and thirty-five, face a little *passée*, fine eyes, a flat figure, a worn contralto voice, dresses a great deal, rouges a little, manners charming; in short, my dear fellow, the remains of a pretty woman which are still worthy of a passion."

This verdict is pronounced by a specimen of the genus Coxcomb, who, having just breakfasted, does not weigh his words, and is going out riding. At such moments a coxcomb is pitiless.

"She has a collection of magnificent pictures in her house. Go and see her," says another; "nothing can be finer."

You have come upon the species Amateur. This individual quits you to go to Pérignon's, or to Tripet's. To him Madame Firmiani is a number of painted canvases.

A Wife.—"Madame Firmiani? I will not have you go there." This phrase is the most suggestive view of all. Madame Firmiani! A dangerous woman! A siren! She dresses well, has good taste; she spoils the night's rest of every wife.—The speaker is of the species Shrew.

AN ATTACHÉ TO AN EMBASSY.—"Madame Firmiani? From Antwerp, is not she? I saw that woman, very handsome, about ten years ago. She was then at Rome."

Men of the order of Attachés have a mania for utterances à la Talleyrand, their wit is often so subtle that their perception is imperceptible. They are like those billiard players who miss the balls with infinite skill. These men are not generally great talkers; but when they talk it is of nothing less than Spain, Vienna, Italy, or Saint-Petersburg. The names of countries act on them like springs; you press them, and the machinery plays all its tunes.

"Does not that Madame Firmiani see a great deal of the Faubourg Saint-Germain?" This is asked by a person who desires claims to distinction. She adds a *de* to everybody's name—to Monsieur Dupin, senior, to Monsieur Lafayette; she flings it right and left and spatters people with it. She spends her life in anxieties as to what is *correct*; but, for her sins, she lives in the unfashionable Marais, and her husband was an attorney—but an attorney in the King's Court.

"Madame Firmiani, monsieur? I do not know her." This man is of the class of Dukes. He recognizes no woman who has not been presented. Excuse him; he was created Duke by Napoleon.

"Madame Firmiani? Was she not a singer at the Italian opera house?"—A man of the genus Simpleton. The individuals of this genus must have an answer to everything. They would rather speak calumnies than be silent.

TWO OLD LADIES (*the wives of retired lawyers*).—THE FIRST (she has a cap with bows of ribbon, her face is wrinkled, her nose sharp, she holds a prayer-book, and her voice is harsh).—"What was her maiden name?—this Madame Firmiani?"

THE SECOND (she has a little red face like a lady-apple, and a gentle voice).—"She was a Cadignan, my dear, niece of the old Prince de Cadignan, and cousin, consequently, to the Duc de Maufrigneuse."

Madame Firmiani then is a Cadignan. Bereft of virtues, fortune, and youth, she would still be a Cadignan; that, like a prejudice, is always rich and living.

AN ECCENTRIC.— "My dear fellow, I never saw any clogs in her ante-room; you may go to her house without compromising yourself, and play there without hesitation; for if there should be any rogues, they will be people of quality, consequently there is no quarreling."

AN OLD MAN OF THE SPECIES OBSERVER.—"You go to Madame Firmiani's, my dear fellow, and you find a handsome woman lounging indolently by the fire. She will scarcely move from her chair; she rises only to greet women, or ambassadors, or dukes—people of importance. She is very gracious, she charms you, she talks well, and likes to talk of everything. She bears every indication of a passionate soul, but she is credited with too many adorers to have a lover. If suspicion rested on only two or three intimate visitors, we might know which was her *cavaliere servente*. But she is all mystery; she is married, and we have never seen her husband; Monsieur Firmiani is purely a creature of fancy, like the third horse we are made to pay for when traveling post, and which we never see; Madame, if you believe the professionals, has the finest contralto voice in Europe, and has not sung three times since she came to Paris; she receives numbers of people, and goes nowhere."

The Observer speaks as an oracle. His words, his anecdotes, his quotations must all be accepted as truth, or you risk being taken for a man without knowledge of the world, without capabilities. He will slander you lightly in twenty drawing-rooms, where he is as essential as the first piece in the bill—pieces so often played to the benches, but which once upon a time were successful. The Observer is a man of forty, never dines at home, and professes not to be dangerous to women; he wears powder and a maroon-coloured coat; he can always have a seat in various boxes at the Théâtre des Bouffons. He is sometimes mistaken for a parasite, but he has held too high positions to be suspected of sponging, and, indeed, possesses an estate, in a department of which the name has never leaked out.

"Madame Firmiani? Why, my dear boy, she was a mistress of Murat's." This gentleman is a Contradictory. They supply the errata to every memory, rectify every fact, bet you a hundred to one, are cock-sure of everything. You catch them out in a single evening in flagrant delicts of ubiquity. They assert that they were in Paris at the time of Mallet's conspiracy, forgetting that half an hour before they had crossed the Beresina. The Contradictories are almost all members of the Legion of Honour; they talk very loud, have receding foreheads, and play high.

"Madame Firmiani, a hundred thousand francs a year? Are you mad? Really some people scatter thousands a year with the liberality of authors, to whom it costs nothing to give their heroines handsome fortunes. But Madame Firmiani is a flirt who ruined a young fellow the other day, and hindered him from making a very good marriage. If she were not handsome, she would be penniless."

This speaker you recognize: he is one of the Envious, and we will not sketch his least feature. The species is as well-known as that of the domestic *felis*. How is the perpetuity of envy to be explained? A vice which is wholly unprofitable!

People of fashion, literary people, very good people, and people of every kind were, in the month of January 1824, giving out so many different opinions on Madame Firmiani that it would be tiresome to report them all. We have only aimed at showing that a man wishing to know her, without choosing, or being able, to go to her house, would have been equally justified in the belief that she was a widow or a wife—silly or witty, virtuous or immoral, rich or poor, gentle or devoid of soul, handsome or ugly; in fact, there were as many Mesdames Firmiani as there are varieties in social life, or sects in the Catholic Church. Frightful thought! We are all like lithographed plates, of which an endless number of copies are taken off by slander these copies resemble or differ from the original by touches so imperceptibly slight that, but for the calumnies of our friends and the witticisms of newspapers, reputation would depend on the balance struck by each hearer between the limping truth and the lies to which Parisian wit lends wings.

Madame Firmiani, like many other women of dignity and noble pride, who close their hearts as a sanctuary end scorn the world, might have been very hardly judged by Monsieur de Bourbonne, an old gentleman of fortune, who had thought a good deal about her during the past winter. As it happened, this gentleman belonged to the Provincial Landowner class, folks who are accustomed to inquire into everything, and to make bargains with peasants. In this business a man grows keen-witted in spite of himself, as a soldier, in the long run, acquires the courage of routine. This inquirer, a native of Touraine and not easily satisfied by the Paris dialects, was a very honourable gentleman who rejoiced in a nephew, his sole heir, for whom he planted his poplars. Their more than natural affection gave rise to much evil-speaking, which individuals of the various species of Tourangeau formulated with much mother wit; but it would be useless to record it; it would pale before that of Parisian tongues. When a man can think of his heir without displeasure, as he sees fine rows of poplars improving every day, his affection increases with each spadeful of earth he turns at the foot of his trees. Though such phenomena of sensibility may be uncommon, they still are to be met with in Touraine.

This much-loved nephew, whose name was Octave de Camps, was descended from the famous Abbé de Camps, so well known to the learned, or to the bibliomaniacs, which is not the same thing.

Provincial folks have a disagreeable habit of regarding young men who sell their reversions with a sort of respectable horror. This Gothic prejudice is had for speculation, which the Government has hitherto found it necessary to encourage. Now, without consulting his uncle, Octave had on a sudden disposed of an estate in favour of the speculative builders. The château of Villaines would have been demolished but for the offers made by his old uncle to the representatives of the demolishing fraternity. To add to the testator's wrath, a friend of Octave's, a distant relation, one of those cousins with small wealth and great cunning, who lead their prudent neighbors to say, "I should not like to go to law with him!" had called, by chance, on Monsieur de Bourbonne and informed him that his nephew was ruined. Monsieur Octave de Camps, after dissipating his fortune for a certain Madame Firmiani, and not daring to confess his sins, had been reduced to giving lessons in mathematics, pending his coming into his uncle's leavings. This distant cousin— a sort of Charles Moor—had not been ashamed of giving this disastrous news to the old country gentleman at the hour when, sitting before his spacious hearth, he was digesting a copious provincial dinner. But would-be legatees do not get rid of an uncle so easily as they could wish. This uncle, thanks to his obstinacy, refusing to believe the distant cousin, came out victorious over the indigestion brought on by the biography of his nephew. Some blows fall on the heart, others on the brain; the blow struck by the distant cousin fell on the stomach, and produced little effect, as the good man had a strong one.

Monsieur de Bourbonne, as a worthy disciple of Saint Thomas, came to Paris without telling Octave, and tried to get information as to his heir's insolvency. The old gentleman, who had friends in the Faubourg Saint-Germain—the Listomères, the Lenoncourts, and the Vandenesses—heard so much slander, so much that was true, and so much that was false concerning Madame Firmiani, that he determined to call on her, under the name of Monsieur de Rouxellay, the name of his place. The prudent old man took care, in going to study Octave's mistress—as she was said to be—to choose an evening when he knew that the young man was engaged on work to be well paid for; for Madame Firmiani was always at home to her young friend, a circumstance that no one could account for. As to Octave's ruin, that, unfortunately, was no fiction.

Monsieur de Rouxellay was not at all like a stage uncle. As an old musketeer, a man of the best society, who had his successes in his day, he knew how to introduce himself with a courtly air, remembered the polished manners of the past, had a pretty wit, and understood almost all the roll of nobility. Though he loved the Bourbons with noble frankness, believed in God as gentlemen believe, and read only the *Quotidienne,* he was by no means so ridiculous as the Liberals of his department would have wished. He could hold his own with men about the Court, so long as he was not expected to talk of *Mosè,* or the play, or romanticism, or local colour, or railways. He had not got beyond Monsieur de Voltaire, Monsieur le Comte de Buffon, Peyronnet, and the Chevalier Gluck, the Queen's private musician.

"Madame," said he to the Marquise de Listomère, to whom he had given his arm to go into Madame Firmiani's room, "if this woman is my nephew's mistress, I pity her. How can she bear to live in the midst of luxury and know that he is in a garret? Has she no soul? Octave is a fool to have invested the price of the estate of Villaines in the heart of a—"

Monsieur de Bourbonne was of a Fossil species, and spoke only the language of a past day.

"But suppose he had lost it at play?"

"Well, madame, he would have had the pleasure of playing."

"You think he has had no pleasure for his money?—Look, here is Madame Firmiani."

The old uncle's brightest memories paled at the sight of his nephew's supposed mistress. His anger died in a polite speech wrung from him by the presence of Madame Firmiani. By one of these chances which come only to pretty women, it was a moment when all her beauties shone with particular brilliancy, the result, perhaps, of the glitter of waxlights, of an exquisitely simple dress, of an indefinable reflection from the elegance in which she lived and moved. Only long study of the petty revolutions of an evening party in a Paris salon can enable one to appreciate the imperceptible shades that can tinge and change a woman's face. There are moments when, pleased with her dress, feeling herself brilliant, happy at being admired and seeing herself the queen of a room full of remarkable men all smiling at her, a Parisian is conscious of her beauty and grace; she grows the lovelier by all the looks she meets; they give her animation, but their mute homage is transmitted by subtle glances to the man she loves. In such a moment a woman is invested, as it were, with supernatural power, and becomes a witch, an unconscious coquette; she involuntarily inspires the passion which is a secret intoxication to herself, she has smiles and looks that are fascinating. If this excitement which comes from the soul lends attractiveness even to ugly women, with what splendor does it not clothe a naturally elegant creature, finely made, fair, fresh, bright-eyed, and, above all, dressed with such taste as artists and even her most spiteful rivals must admit.

Have you ever met, for your happiness, some woman whose harmonious tones give to her speech the charm that is no less conspicuous in her manners, who knows how to talk and to be silent, who cares for you with delicate feeling, whose words are happily chosen and her language pure? Her banter flatters you, her criticism does not sting; she neither preaches nor disputes, but is interested in leading a discussion, and stops it at the right moment. Her manner is friendly and gay, her politeness is unforced, her eagerness to please is not servile; she reduces respect to a mere gentle shade; she never tires you, and leaves you satisfied with her and yourself. You will see her gracious presence stamped on the things she collects about her. In her home everything charms the eye, and you breathe, as it seems, your native air. This woman is quite natural. You never feel an effort, she flaunts nothing, her feelings are expressed with simplicity because they are genuine. Though candid, she never wounds the most sensitive pride; she accepts men as God made them, pitying the vicious, forgiving defects and absurdities, sympathizing with every age, and vexed with nothing because she has the tact to forefend everything. At once tender and lively, she first constrains and then consoles you. You love her so truly, that if this angel does wrong, you are ready to justify her.—Then you know Madame Firmiani.

By the time old Bourbonne had talked with this woman for a quarter of an hour, sitting by her side, his nephew was absolved, he understood that, true or false, Octave's connection with Madame Firmiani no doubt covered some mystery. Returning to the illusions of his youth, and judging of Madame Firmiani's heart by her beauty, the old gentleman thought that a woman so sure of her dignity as she seemed, was incapable of a base action. Her black eyes spoke of so much peace of mind, the lines of her face were so noble, the forms so pure, and the passion of which she was accused seemed to weigh so little on her heart, that, as he admired all the pledges given to love and to virtue by that adorable countenance, the old man said to himself, "My nephew has committed some folly."

Madame Firmiani owned to twenty-five. But the Matter-of-facts could prove that, having been married in 1813 at the age of sixteen, she must be at least eight-and-twenty in 1825. Nevertheless the same persons declared that she had never at any period of her life been so desirable, so perfectly a woman. She had no children, and had never had any; the hypothetical Firmiani, a respectable man of forty in 1813, had, it was said, only his name and fortune to offer her. So Madame Firmiani had come to the age when a Parisian best understands what passion is, and perhaps longs for it innocently in her unemployed hours; she had everything that the world can sell, or lend, or give. The Attachés declared she knew everything, the Contradictories said she had yet many things to learn;

the Observers noticed that her hands were very white, her foot very small, her movements a little too undulating; but men of every species envied or disputed Octave's good fortune, agreeing that she was the most aristocratic beauty in Paris.

Still young, rich, a perfect musician, witty, exquisite; welcomed, for the sake of the Cadignans, to whom she was related through her mother, by the Princesse de Blamont-Chauvry, the oracle of the aristocratic quarter; beloved by her rivals the Duchesse de Maufrigneuse her cousin, the Marquise d'Espard, and Madame de Macumer, she flattered every vanity which feeds or excites love. And, indeed, she was the object of too many desires not to be the victim of fashionable attraction and those delightful calumnies which are wittily hinted behind a fan or in a whispered *aside*. Hence the remarks with which this story opened were necessary to mark the contrast between the real Firmiani and the Firmiani known to the world. Though some women forgave her for being happy, others could not overlook her respectability; now there is nothing so terrible, especially in Paris, as suspicion without foundation; it is impossible to kill it.

This sketch of a personality so admirable by nature can only give a feeble idea of it; it would need the brush of an Ingres to represent the dignity of the brow, the mass of fine hair, the majesty of the eyes, all the thoughts betrayed by the varying hues of the complexion. There was some thing of everything in this woman; poets could see in her both Joan of Arc and Agnes Sorel; but there was also the unknown woman—the soul hidden behind this deceptive mask—the soul of Eve, the wealth of evil, and the treasures of goodness, wrong and resignation, crime and self- sacrifice—the Doña Julia and Haidee of Byron's *Don Juan*.

The old soldier very boldly remained till the last in Madame Firmiani's drawing-room; she found him quietly seated in an armchair, and staying with the pertinacity of a fly that must be killed to be got rid of. The clock marked two in the morning.

"Madame," said the old gentleman, just as Madame Firmiani rose in the hope of making her guest understand that it was her pleasure that he should go. "Madame, I am Monsieur Octave de Camps' uncle."

Madame Firmiani at once sat down again, and her agitation was evident. In spite of his perspicacity, the planter of poplars could not make up his mind whether shame or pleasure made her turn pale. There are pleasures which do not exist without a little coy bashfulness—delightful emotions which the chastest soul would fain keep behind a veil. The more sensitive a woman is, the more she lives to conceal her soul's greatest joys. Many women, incomprehensible in their exquisite caprices, at times long to hear a name spoken by all the world, while they sometimes would sooner bury it in their hearts. Old Bourbonne did not read Madame Firmiani's agitation quite in this light; but forgive him; the country gentleman was suspicious.

"Indeed, monsieur?" said Madame Firmiani, with one of those clear and piercing looks in which we men can never see anything, because they question us too keenly.

"Indeed, madame; and do you know what I have been told—I, in the depths of the country? That my nephew has ruined himself for you; and the unhappy boy is in a garret, while you live here in gold and silks. You will, I hope, forgive my rustic frankness, for it may be useful to you to be informed of the slander."

"Stop, monsieur," said Madame Firmiani, interrupting the gentleman with an imperious gesture, "I know all that. You are too polite to keep the conversation to this subject when I beg you to change it. You are too gallant, in the old-fashioned sense of the word," she added, with a slightly ironical emphasis, "not to acknowledge that you have no right to cross-question me. However, it is ridiculous in me to justify myself. I hope you have a good enough opinion of my character to believe in the utter contempt I feel for money, though I was married without any fortune whatever to a man who had an immense fortune. I do not know whether your nephew is rich or poor; if I have received him, if I still receive him, it is because I regard him as worthy to move in the midst of my friends. All my friends, monsieur, respect each other; they know that I am not so philosophical as to entertain people whom I do not esteem. That, perhaps, shows a lack of charity; but my guardian angel has preserved in me, to this day, an intense aversion for gossip and dishonor."

Though her voice was not quite firm at the beginning of this reply, the last words were spoken by Madame Firmiani with the cool decision of *Célimène* rallying the *Misanthrope*.

"Madame," the Count resumed in a broken voice, "I am an old man—I am almost a father to Octave—I therefore must humbly crave your pardon beforehand for the only question I shall be so bold as to ask you; and I give you my word of honour as a gentleman that your reply will die here," and he laid his hand on his heart with a really religious gesture. "Does gossip speak the truth; do you love Octave?"

"Monsieur," said she, "I should answer any one else with a look. But you, since you are almost a father to Monsieur de Camps, you I will ask what you would think of a woman who, in reply to your question, should say, Yes. To confess one's love to the man we love—when he loves us—well, well; when we are sure of being loved for ever, believe me, monsieur, it is an effort to us and a reward to him; but to any one else!—"

Madame Firmiani did not finish her sentence; she rose, bowed to the good gentleman, and vanished into her private rooms; where the sound of doors opened and shut in succession had language to the ears of the poplar planter.

"Damn it!" said he to himself, "what a woman! She is either a very cunning hussy or an angel;" and he went down to his hired fly in the courtyard, where the horses were pawing the pavement in silence. The coachman was asleep, after having cursed his customer a hundred times.

Next morning, by about eight o'clock, the old gentleman was mounting the stairs of a house in the Rue de l'Observance, where dwelt Octave de Camps. If there was in this world a man amazed, it was the young professor on seeing his uncle. The key was in the door, Octave's lamp was still burning; he had sat up all night.

"Now, you rascal," said Monsieur de Bourbonne, seating himself in an armchair. "How long has it been the fashion to make fools (speaking mildly) of uncles who have twenty-six thousand francs a year in good land in Touraine? and that, when you are sole heir? Do you know that formerly such relations were treated with respect? Pray, have you any fault to find with me? Have I bungled my business as an uncle? Have I demanded your respect? Have I ever refused you money? Have I shut my door in your face, saying you had only come to see how I was? Have you not the most accommodating, the least exacting uncle in France?—I will not say in Europe, it would be claiming too much. You write to me, or you don't write. I live on your professions of affection. I am laying out the prettiest estate in the neighborhood, a place that is the object of envy in all the department; but I do not mean to leave it you till the latest date possible—a weakness that is very pardonable! And my gentleman sells his property, is lodged like a groom, has no servants, keeps no style—"

"My dear uncle—"

"It is not a case of uncle, but of nephew. I have a right to your confidence; so have it all out at once; it is the easiest way, I know by experience. Have you been gambling? Have you been speculating on the Bourse? Come, say, 'Uncle, I am a wretch,' and we kiss and are friends. But if you tell me any lie bigger than those I told, at your age, I will sell my property, buy an annuity, and go back to the bad ways of my youth, if it is not too late."

"Uncle—"

"I went last night to see your Madame Firmiani," said the uncle, kissing the tips of all his fingers together. "She is charming," he went on. "You have the king's warrant and approval, and your uncle's consent, if that is any satisfaction to you. As to the sanction of the Church, that I suppose is unnecessary—the sacraments, no doubt, are too costly. Come, speak out. Is it for her that you have ruined yourself?"

"Yes, uncle."

"Ah! the hussy! I would have bet upon it. In my day a woman of fashion could ruin a man more cleverly than any of your courtesans of to-day. I saw in her a resuscitation of the last century."

"Uncle," said Octave, in a voice that was at once sad and gentle, "you are under a mistake. Madame Firmiani deserves your esteem, and all the adoration of her admirers."

"So hapless youth is always the same!" said Monsieur de Bourbonne, "Well, well! go on in your own way; tell me all the old stories once more. At the same time, you know, I dare say, that I am no chicken in such matters."

"My dear uncle, here is a letter which will explain everything," replied Octave, taking out an elegant letter-case—*her* gift, no doubt. "When you have read it I will tell you the rest, and you will know Madame Firmiani as the world knows her not."

"I have not got my spectacles," said his uncle. "Read it to me."

Octave began: "My dear love—"

"Then you are very intimate with this woman?"

"Why, yes, uncle?"

"And you have not quarrelled?"

"Quarrelled!" echoed Octave in surprise. "We are married—at Gretna Green."

"Well, then, why do you dine for forty sous?"

"Let me proceed."

"Very true. I am listening."

Octave took up the letter again, and could not read certain passages without strong emotion.

"'My beloved husband, you ask me the reason of my melancholy. Has it passed from my soul into my face, or have you only guessed it? And why should you not? Our hearts are so closely united. Besides, I cannot lie, though that perhaps is a misfortune. One of the conditions of being loved is, in a woman, to be always caressing and gay. Perhaps I ought to deceive you; but I would not do so, not even if it were to increase or to preserve the happiness you give me—you lavish on me—under which you overwhelm me. Oh, my dear, my love carries with it so much gratitude! And I must love for ever, without measure. Yes, I must always be proud of you. Our glory—a woman's glory—is all in the man she loves. Esteem, consideration, honour, are they not all his who has conquered everything? Well, and my angel has fallen. Yes, my dear, your last confession has dimmed my past happiness. From that moment I have felt myself humbled through you—you, whom I believed to be the purest of men, as you are the tenderest and most loving. I must have supreme confidence in your still childlike heart to make an avowal which costs me so dear. What, poor darling, your father stole his fortune, and you know it, and you keep it! And you could tell me of this attorney's triumph in a room full of the dumb witnesses of our love, and you are a gentleman, and you think yourself noble, and I am yours, and you are two-and-twenty! How monstrous all through!

"'I have sought excuses for you; I have ascribed your indifference to your giddy youth; I know there is still much of the child in you. Perhaps you have never yet thought seriously of what is meant by wealth, and by honesty. Oh, your laughter hurt me so much! Only think, there is a family, ruined, always in grief, girls perhaps, who curse you day by day, an old man who says to himself every night, "I should not lack bread if Monsieur de Camps' father had only been an honest man."'"

"What!" exclaimed Monsieur de Bourbonne, interrupting him, "were you such an idiot as to tell that woman the story of your father's affair with the Bourgneufs? Women better understand spending a fortune than making one—"

"They understand honesty. Let me go on, uncle!"

"'Octave, no power on earth is authorised to garble the language of honour. Look into your conscience, and ask it by what name to call the action to which you owe your riches.'"

And the nephew looked at his uncle, who beat his head.

"'I will not tell you all the thoughts that beset me; they can all be reduced to one, which is this: I cannot esteem a man who knowingly soils himself for a sum of money whether large or small. Five francs stolen at play, or six times a hundred thousand francs obtained by legal trickery, disgrace a man equally.

I must tell you all: I feel myself sullied by a love which till now was all my joy. From the bottom of my soul there comes a voice I cannot stifle. I have wept to find that my conscience is stronger than my love. You might commit a crime, and I would hide you in my bosom from human justice if I could; but my devotion would go no further. Love, my dearest, is, in a woman, the most unlimited confidence, joined to I know not what craving to reverence and adore the being to whom she belongs. I have never conceived of love but as a fire in which the noblest feelings were yet further purified—a fire which develops them to the utmost.

"'I have but one thing more to say: Come to me poor, and I shall love you twice as much if possible; if not, give me up. If I see you no more, I know what is left to me to do.

"'But, now, understand me clearly, I will not have you make restitution because I desire it. Consult your conscience. This is an act of justice, and must not be done as a sacrifice to love. I am your wife, and not your mistress; the point is not to please me, but to inspire me with the highest esteem. If I have misunderstood, if you have not clearly explained your father's action, in short, if you can regard your fortune as legitimately acquired—and how gladly would I persuade myself that you deserve no blame—decide as the voice of conscience dictates; act wholly for yourself. A man who truly loves, as you love me, has too high a respect for all the holy inspiration he may get from his wife to be dishonourable.

"'I blame myself now for all I have written. A word would perhaps have been enough, and my preaching instinct has carried me away. So I should like to be scolded—not much, but a little. My dear, between you and me are not you the Power! You only should detect your own faults. Well, master mine, can you say I understand nothing about political discussion?'"

"Well, uncle?" said Octave, whose eyes were full of tears.

"I see more writing, finish it."

"Oh, there is nothing further but such things as only a lover may read."

"Very good," said the old man. "Very good, my dear boy. I was popular with the women in my day; but I would have you to believe that I too have loved; *et ego in Arcadiâ*. Still, I cannot imagine why you give lessons in mathematics."

"My dear uncle, I am your nephew. Is not that as much as to say that I have made some inroads on the fortune left to me by my father? After reading that letter a complete revolution took place in me, in one instant I paid up the arrears of remorse. I could never describe to you the state in which I was. As I drove my cab to the Bois a voice cried to me, 'Is that horse yours?' As I ate my dinner, I said to myself, 'Have you not stolen the food?' I was ashamed of myself. My honesty was ardent in proportion to its youth. First I flew off to Madame Firmiani. Ah, my dear uncle, that day I had such joys of heart, such raptures of soul as were worth millions. With her I calculated how much I owed the Bourgneuf family; and I sentenced myself, against Madame Firmiani's advice, to pay them interest at the rate of three per cent. But my whole fortune was not enough to refund the sum. We were both of us lovers enough—husband and wife enough—for her to offer and for me to accept her savings—"

"What, besides all her virtues, that adorable woman can save money!" cried the uncle.

"Do not laugh at her. Her position compels her to some thrift. Her husband went to Greece in 1820, and died about three years ago; but to this day it has been impossible to get legal proof of his death, or to lay hands on the will he no doubt made in favour of his wife; this important document was stolen, lost, or mislaid in a country where a man's papers are not kept as they are in France, nor is there a Consul. So, not knowing whether she may not some day have to reckon with other and malignant heirs, she is obliged to be extremely careful, for she does not wish to have to give up her wealth as Chateaubriand has just given up the Ministry. Now I mean to earn a fortune that shall be mine, so as to restore my wife to opulence if she should be ruined."

"And you never told me—you never came to me. My dear nephew, believe me I love you well enough to pay your honest debts, your debts as a gentleman. I am the Uncle of the fifth act—I will be revenged."

"I know your revenges, uncle; but let me grow rich by my own toil. If you wish to befriend me, allow me a thousand crowns a year until I need capital for some business. I declare at this moment I am so happy that all I care about is to live. I give lessons that I may be no burden on any one.

"Ah, if you could but know with what delight I made restitution. After making some inquiries I found the Bourgneufs in misery and destitution. They were living at Saint Germain in a wretched house. The old father was manager in a lottery office; the two girls did the work of the house and kept the accounts. The mother was almost always ill. The two girls are charming, but they have learnt by bitter experience how little the world cares for beauty without fortune. What a picture did I find there! If I went to the house as the accomplice in a crime, I came out of it an honest man, and I have purged my father's memory. I do not judge him, uncle; there is in a lawsuit an eagerness, a passion which may sometimes blind the most honest man alive. Lawyers know how to legitimatise the most preposterous claims; there are syllogisms in law to humour the errors of conscience, and judges have a right to make mistakes. My adventure was a perfect drama. To have played the part of Providence, to have fulfilled one of these hopeless wishes: 'If only twenty thousand francs a year could drop from heaven!'—a wish we all have uttered in jest; to see a sublime look of gratitude, amazement, and admiration take the place of a glance fraught with curses; to bring opulence into the midst of a family sitting round a turf fire in the evening, by the light of a wretched lamp—No, words cannot paint such a scene. My excessive justice to them seemed unjust. Well, if there be a Paradise, my father must now be happy.—As for myself, I am loved as man was never loved before. Madame Firmiani has given me more than happiness; she has taught me a delicacy of feeling which perhaps I lacked. Indeed, I call her Dear Conscience, one of those loving names that are the out come of certain secret harmonies of spirit. Honesty is said to pay; I hope ere long to be rich myself; at this moment I am bent on solving a great industrial problem, and if I succeed I shall make millions."

"My boy, you have your mother's soul," said the old man, hardly able to restrain the tears that rose at the remembrance of his sister.

At this instant, in spite of the height above the ground of Octave's room, the young man and his uncle heard the noise of a carriage driving up.

"It is she! I know her horses by the way they pull up."

And it was not long before Madame Firmiani made her appearance.

"Oh!" she cried, with an impulse of annoyance on seeing Monsieur de Bourbonne. "But our uncle is not in the way," she went on with a sudden smile. "I have come to kneel at my husband's feet and humbly beseech him to accept my fortune. I have just received from the Austrian Embassy a document proving Firmiani's death. The paper, drawn up by the kind offices of the Austrian envoy at Constantinople, is quite formal, and the will which Firmiani's valet had in keeping for me is subjoined.—There, you are richer than I am, for you have there," and she tapped her husband's breast, "treasures which only God can add to." Then, unable to disguise her happiness, she hid her face in Octave's bosom.

"My sweet niece, we made love when I was young," said the uncle, "but now you love. You women are all that is good and lovely in humanity, for you are never guilty of your faults; they always originate with us."

PARIS, *February* 1831.

PIERRETTE

(Part I of "The Cellibates")

To Mademoiselle Anna de Hanska

DEAR CHILD—you, the joy of a whole house, you, whose white or rose-coloured cape flutters in the summer like a will-o'-the-wisp through the arbours of Wierzchownia, followed by the wistful eyes of your father and mother—how can I dedicate to you a tale full of sadness? but is it not well to tell you of sorrows such as a girl so fondly loved as you are will never know? For some day your fair hands may take them comfort. It is so difficult, Anna, to find in the picture of our manners any incident worthy to meet your eye, that an author has no choice; but perhaps you may discern how happy you are from reading this tale, sent by

Your old friend,
DE BALZAC.

IN October 1827, at break of day, a youth of about sixteen, whose dress proclaimed him to be what modem phraseology insolently calls a proletarian, was standing on a little square in the lower part of the town of Provins. At this early hour he could, without being observed, study the various houses set round the Place in an oblong square. The mills on the streams of Provins were already at work. Their noise, repeated by the echoes from the upper town, and harmonising with the sharp air and the clear freshness of the morning, betrayed the perfect silence—so complete that the clatter of a diligence was audible, still a league away on the highroad.

The two longer rows of houses, divided by an arched avenue of lime-trees, are artless in style, confessing the peaceful and circumscribed life of the townsfolk. In this part of the town there are no signs of trade. At that time there was hardly a carriage-gate suggesting the luxury of the rich—or if there were, it rarely turned on its hinges—excepting that of Monsieur Martener, a doctor who was obliged to keep and use a cab. Some of the fronts were graced by a long vine stem, others with climbing roses growing up to the first floor, and scenting the windows with their large scattered bunches of flowers. One end of this Square almost joins the High Street of the lower town; the other end is shut in by a street parallel with the High Street, and the gardens beyond run down to one of the two rivers that water the valley of Provins.

At this end, the quietest part of the Place, the young work man recognised the house that had been described to him—a front of white stone, scored with seams to represent joins in the masonry, and windows with light iron balconies, decorated with rosettes painted yellow, and closed with grey Venetian shutters. Above this front—a ground floor and a first floor only—three attic windows pierce a slate-roof, and on one of the gables twirls a brand-new weather-cock. This modem weather-cock represents a sportsman aiming at a hare. The front door is reached up three stone steps. On one side of the door an end of leaden pipe spouts dirty water into a little gutter, revealing the kitchen; on the other, two windows, carefully guarded by grey wooden shutters in which heart-shaped holes are cut to admit a little light, seemed to our youth to be those of the dining-room. In the basement secured by the three steps, under each window is an air-opening into the cellars, closed by painted iron shutters pierced with holes in a pattern. Everything was then quite new. An observer, looking at this house freshly repaired, its still raw splendour contrasting with the antique aspect of all the rest, would at once have seen in it the mean ideas and perfect contentment of a retired tradesman.

The young fellow gazed at every detail with an expression of pleasure mingled with sadness; his eyes wandered from the kitchen to the garret with a look that denoted meditation. The pink gleams of sunshine showed in one of the attic windows a cotton curtain which was wanting to the others. Then the lad's face brightened completely; he withdrew a few steps, leaned his back against a lime-tree, and sang, in the drawling tones peculiar to the natives of the West, this ballad of Brittany, published by Bruguière, a composer to whom we owe some charming airs. In Brittany the young swains of the villages sing this song to newly-married couples on their wedding day:—

"We come to wish you every happiness,
To th' maister at your side,
As well as to the bride.

"You, mistress bride, are bound for life and death,
With a bright golden chain,
That none may break in twain.

"Now you to fairs and junkets go no more;
Nay, you must stay at home,
While we may dance and roam.

"And do you know how trusty you must be,
And faithful to your mate,
To love him rathe and late?

"Then take this posy I have made for you.
Alack! for happy hours
Must perish like these flowers."

This national air, as sweet as that arranged by Chateaubriand to the words *Ma sœur, te souvient-il encore?* sung in a little town of la Brie in Champagne, could not fail to arouse irresistible memories in a native of Brittany, so faithfully does it paint the manners, the simplicity, the scenery of that noble old province. There is in it an intangible melancholy, caused by the realities of life, which is deeply touching. And is not this power to awaken a whole world of grave, sweet, sad things by a familiar and often cheerful strain, characteristic of those popular airs which are the superstitions of music, if we accept the word superstition as meaning what remains from the ruin of nations, the flotsam left by revolutions?

As he ended the first verse, the workman, who never took his eyes off the curtain in the attic, saw no one astir. While he was singing the second, it moved a little. As he sang the words, "Take this posy," a young girl's face was seen. A fair hand cautiously opened the window, and the girl nodded to the wanderer as he ended with the melancholy reflection contained in the last two lines:

"Alack! for happy hours
Must perish like these flowers."

The lad suddenly took from under his jacket, and held up to her, a golden-yellow spray of a flower very common in Brittany, which he had picked no doubt in a field in la Brie, where it is somewhat rare—the flower of the furze.

"Why, is it you, Brigaut?" said the girl in a low voice.

"Yes, Pierrette, yes. I am living in Paris; I am walking about France; but I might settle down here, since you are here."

At this moment the window-fastening of the room on the first floor, below Pierrette's, was heard to creak. The girl showed the greatest alarm, and said to Brigaut, "Fly!"

The young fellow jumped like a frog to a bend in the street, round a mill, before entering the wider street that is the artery of the lower town; but in spite of his agility, his hob-nailed shoes, ringing on the paving-cobbles of Provins, made a noise easily distinguished from the music of the mill, and heard by the individual who opened the window.

This person was a woman. No man ever tears himself from the delights of his morning slumbers to listen to a minstrel in a round jacket. None but a maid is roused by a love song. And this was a maid—and an old maid. When she had thrown open her shutters with the action of a bat, she looked about her on all sides, and faintly heard Brigaut's steps as he made his escape. Is there on earth anything more hideous than the matutinal apparition of an ugly old maid at her window? Of all the grotesque spectacles that are the amusement of travellers as they go through little towns, is it not the most unpleasing? It is too depressing, too repulsive to be laughed at.

This particular old maid, whose ear was so keen, appeared bereft of the artifices of all kinds that she used to improve herself; she had no front of false hair, and no collar. Her headgear was the frightful little caul of black sarsnet which old women draw over their skull, showing beyond her night cap, which had been pushed aside in her sleep. This untidiness gave her head the sinister appearance ascribed by painters to witches. The temples, ears, and nape, scarcely concealed, betrayed their withered leanness, the coarse wrinkles were conspicuous for a redness that did not charm the eye, and that was thrown into relief by the comparative whiteness of a bedgown tied at the throat with twisted tapes. The gaps where this bedgown fell open revealed a chest like that of some old peasant woman careless of her ugliness. The fleshless arm might have been a stick covered with stuff. Seen at the window, the lady appeared tall by reason of the strength and breadth of her face, which reminded the spectator of the extravagant size of some Swiss countenances. The chief characteristic of the features, which presented a singular lack of harmony, was a hardness of line, a harshness of colouring, and a lack of feeling in the expression which would have filled a physiognomist with disgust. These peculiarities, visible now, were habitually modified by a sort of business smile, and a vulgar stupidity which aped good-nature so successfully that the people among whom she lived might easily have supposed her to be a kind woman.

She and her brother shared the ownership of this house. The brother was sleeping so soundly in his room that the Opera-house orchestra would not have roused him; and the power of that orchestra is famous! The old maid put her head out of the window, and raised her eyes to that of the attic—eyes of a cold pale blue, with short lashes set in lids that were almost always swollen. She tried to see Pierrette; but recognising the futility of the attempt, she withdrew into her room with a movement not unlike that of a tortoise hiding its head after putting it out of its shell. The shutters were closed again, and the silence of the Square was no more disturbed but by peasants coming into the town, or early risers. When there is an old maid in the house a watch-dog is not needed; not the smallest event occurs without her seeing it, commenting on it, and deducing every possible consequence. Thus this incident was destined to give rise to serious inferences, and to be the opening of one of those obscure dramas which are played out in the family, but which are none the less terrible for being unseen—if indeed the name of drama may be applied to this tragedy of home-life.

Pierrette did not get into bed again. To her Brigaut's arrival was an event of immense importance. During the night—the Eden of the wretched—she escaped from the annoyances and fault-finding she had to endure all day. Like the hero of some German or Russian ballad, to her sleep seemed a happy life, and the day a bad dream. This morning, for the first time in three years, she had had a happy waking. The memories of infancy had sweetly sung their poetry to her soul. She had heard the first verse in her dreams; the second had roused her with a start; at the third she had doubted—the unfortunate are of the school of Saint Thomas; at the fourth verse, standing at her window, bare-foot, and in her shift, she had recognized Brigaut, the friend of her childhood.

Yes, that was indeed the short square jacket with quaint little tails and pockets swinging just over the hips, the classical blue-cloth jacket of the Breton; the waistcoat of coarse knit, the linen shirt buttoned with a golden heart, the wide-rolled collar, the earrings, heavy shoes, trousers of blue drill, mottled in streaks of lighter shades; in short, all the humble and durable items of a poor Breton's costume. The large white horn buttons of the jacket and waistcoat had set Pierrette's heart beating. At the sight of the branch of furze the tears had started to her eyes; then a spasm of terror clutched her heart, crushing the flowers of remembrance that had blossomed for a moment. It struck her that her cousin might have heard her rise and go to the window. She knew the old woman, and made the signal of alarm to Brigaut, which the poor boy had hastened to obey without understanding it. Does not this instinctive obedience betray one of those innocent and mastering affections such as are to be seen once in an age, on this earth where they bloom, like the aloe-trees on Isola Bella, but two or three times in a century? Any one seeing Brigaut fly would have admired the artless heroism of a most artless love.

Jacques Brigaut was worthy of Pierrette Lorrain, who was now nearly fourteen—two children! Pierrette could not help weeping as she saw him take to his heels with the terror inspired by her warning gesture.

She then sat down in a rickety armchair, in front of a looking-glass above a little table. On this she set her elbows, and remained pensive for an hour, trying to recall the Marais, the hamlet of Pen-Hoël, the adventurous voyages on a pond in a boat untied from an old willow-tree by little Jacques; then the old faces—her grandmother and grandfather, her mother's look of suffering, and General Brigaut's handsome head; a whole childhood of careless joy! And this again was a dream—the lights of happiness against a grey background.

She had fine light-brown hair, all in disorder, under a little nightcap tumbled in her sleep, a little cambric cap with frills that she herself had made. On each side curls fell over her temples, escaping from their grey papers. At the back of her head a thick plait hung down to her shoulders. The excessive pallor of her face showed that she was a victim to a girlish ailment to which medical science gives the pretty name of chlorosis, which robs the blood of its natural hue, disturbing the appetite, and betraying much disorderment of the whole system. This waxen hue was apparent in all the flesh tints. The whiteness of her neck and shoulders, the colourlessness of an etiolated plant, accounted for the thinness of her arms crossed in front of her. Pierrette's feet even looked weak and shrunken by disease; her shift, falling only on her calf, showed the relaxed sinews, blue veins, and bloodless muscles. As the cold air chilled her, her lips turned purple. The mournful smile that parted her fairly delicate mouth showed teeth of ivory whiteness, even and small, pretty transparent teeth, in harmony with well-shaped ears and a nose that was elegant, if a little sharp; her face, though perfectly round, was very sweet. All the life of this charming countenance lay in the eyes; the iris, of a bright snuff-brown mottled with black, shone with golden lights round a deep bright retina. Pierrette ought to have been gay; she was sad. Her vanished gaiety lingered in the vivid modeling of her eyes, in the ingenuous form of her brow, and the moulding of her short chin. The long eyelashes lay like brushes on the cheeks worn by debility; the whiteness, too lavishly diffused, gave great purity to the lines and features of her countenance. The ear was a little masterpiece of modelling; it might have been of marble.

Pierrette suffered in many ways. Perhaps you would like to have her story? Here it is.

Pierrette's mother was a Demoiselle Auffray of Provins, half-sister to Madame Rogron, the mother of the present owners of this house. Monsieur Auffray, after marrying for the first time at the age of eighteen, took a second wife at the age of sixty-nine. The child of his first marriage was an only daughter, ugly enough, who, when she was sixteen, married an innkeeper of Provins named Rogron. By his second marriage old Auffray had another daughter, but she was very pretty. Thus the quaint result was an enormous difference in age between Monsieur Auffray's two daughters. The child of his first wife was fifty when the second was born. By the time her father gave her a sister Madame Rogron had two children of her own, both of full age.

The uxorious old man's younger child was married for love, at eighteen, to a Breton officer named Lorrain, a captain in the Imperial Guard. Love often begets ambition. The captain, eager to get his colonelcy, exchanged into the line. While the Major and his wife, comfortable enough with the allowance given them by Monsieur and Madame Auffray, were living handsomely in Paris, or running about Germany as the Emperor's wars or truces might guide them, old Auffray, a retired grocer at Provins, died suddenly, before he had time to make his will. The good man's estate was so cleverly manipulated by the innkeeper and his wife that they absorbed the larger part of it, leaving to old Auffray's widow no more than the house in the little Square and a few acres of land. This widow, little Madame Lorrain's mother, was but eight-and-thirty when her husband died. Like many other widows, she had an unwholesome wish to marry again. She sold to her stepdaughter, old Madame Rogron, the land and house she had inherited under her marriage settlement, to marry a young doctor named Néraud, who ran through her fortune, and she died of grief in great poverty two years afterwards.

Thus Madame Lorrain's share of the Auffray property had in great part disappeared, being reduced to about eight thousand francs.

Major Lorrain died on the field of honour at Montereau, leaving his widow, then one-and-twenty, burdened with a little girl fourteen months old, and with no fortune but the pension she could claim from Government, and whatever money might come to her from Monsieur and Madame Lorrain, tradespeople at Pen-Hoël, a town of la Vendée, in the district known as le Marais. These Lorrains, the parents of the deceased officer, and Pierrette's paternal grandfather and grandmother, sold building-timber, slates, tiles, cornices, pipes, and the like. Their business was a poor one, either from their incapacity or from ill-luck, and brought them in a bare living. The failure of the great house of Colinet at Nantes, brought about by the events of 1814, which caused a sudden fall in the price of colonial produce, resulted in a loss to them of eighty thousand francs they had placed on deposit. Their daughter-in-law was therefore warmly received; the Major's widow brought with her a pension of eight hundred francs, an enormous sum at Pen-Hoël. When her half-sister and brother-in-law Rogron sent her the eight thousand francs due to her, after endless formalities, prolonged by distance, she placed the money in the Lorrains' hands, taking a mortgage, however, on a little house they owned at Nantes, let for a hundred crowns a year, and worth, perhaps, ten thousand francs.

Young Madame Lorrain died there after her mother's second and luckless marriage, in 1819, and almost at the same time as her mother. This daughter of the old man and his young wife was small, fragile, and delicate; the damp air of the Marais did not agree with her. Her husband's family, eager to keep her there, persuaded her that nowhere else in the world would she find a place healthier or pleasanter than the Marais, the scene of Charette's exploits. She was so well taken care of, nursed, and coaxed, that her death brought honour to the Lorrains.

Some persons asserted that Brigaut, an old Vendéen, one of those men of iron who served under Charette, Mercier, the Marquis de Montauran, and the Baron du Guénic in the wars against the Republic, counted for much in young Madame Lorrain's submission. If this were so, it was certainly for the sake of a most loving and devoted soul. And, indeed, all Pen-Hoël could see that Brigaut, respectfully designated as the Major—having held that rank in the Royalist army—spent his days and his evenings in the Lorrains' sitting-room by the side of the Emperor's Major's widow. Towards the end the curé of Pen-Hoël allowed himself to speak of this matter to old Madame Lorrain; he begged her to persuade her daughter-in-law to marry Brigaut, promising to get him an appointment as justice of the peace to the district of Pen-Hoël, by the intervention of the Vicomte de Kergarouët. But the poor woman's death made the scheme useless.

Pierrette remained with her grandparents, who owed her four hundred francs a year, naturally spent on her maintenance. The old people, now less and less fit for business, had an active and pushing rival in trade, whom they could only abuse, without doing anything to protect themselves. The Major, their friend and adviser, died six months after young Madame Lorrain, perhaps of grief, or perhaps of his wounds; he had had seven-and-twenty. Their bad neighbour, as a good man of business, now aimed at ruining his rivals, so as to extinguish all competition. He got the Lorrains to borrow on their note of hand, foreseeing that they could never pay, and so forced them, in their old age, to become bankrupt. Pierrette's mortgage was second to a mortgage held by her grandmother, who clung to her rights to secure a morsel of bread for her husband. The house at Nantes was sold for nine thousand five hundred francs, and the costs came to fifteen hundred francs. The remaining eight thousand francs came to Madame Lorrain, who invested them in a mortgage in order to live at Nantes in a sort of almshouse, like that of Sainte-Périne in Paris, called Saint-Jacques, where the two old people found food and lodging at a very moderate rate.

As it was impossible that they should take with them their little destitute grandchild, the old Lorrains bethought them of her uncle and aunt Rogron, to whom they wrote. The Rogrons of Provins were dead. Thus the letter from the Lorrains to the Rogrons would seem to be lost. But if there is anything here below which can take the place of Providence, is it not the General Post-Office? The genius of the Post, immeasurably superior to that of the Public, outdoes in inventiveness the imagination of the most brilliant novelist. As soon as the Post has charge of a letter, worth, on delivery, from three to ten sous, if it fails at once to find him or her to whom it should be delivered, it displays a mercenary solicitude which has no parallel but in the boldest duns. The Post comes, goes, hunts through the eighty-six departments. Difficulties incite the genius of its officials, who, not unfrequently, are men of letters, and who then throw themselves into the pursuit with the ardour of the mathematicians at the National Observatory; they rummage the kingdom. At the faintest, gleam of hope the Paris offices are on the alert again. You often sit amazed as you inspect the scrawls that meander over the letter, back and front—the glorious evidence of the administrative perseverance that animates the Post-Office. If a man were to undertake what the Post has accomplished, he would have spent ten thousand francs in travelling, in time and in money, to recover twelve sous. The Post certainly has more intelligence than it conveys.

The letter written by the Lorrains to Monsieur Rogron, who had been dead a year, was transmitted by the Post to Monsieur Rogron, his son, a haberdasher in the Rue Saint Denis, Paris. This is where the genius of the Post-Office shines. An heir is always more or less puzzled to know whether he has really scraped up the whole of his inheritance, whether he has not forgotten some debt or some fragments. The Revenue guesses everything; it even reads character. A letter addressed to old Rogron of Provins was bound to pique the curiosity of Rogron *junior* of Paris, or of Mademoiselle Rogron, his heirs. So the Revenue earned its sixty centimes.

The Rogrons, towards whom the Lorrains held out beseeching hands though they were in despair at having to part from their granddaughter, thus became the arbiters of Pierrette Lorrain's fate. It is indispensable, therefore, to give some account of their antecedents and their character.

Old Rogron, the innkeeper at Provins, on whom old Auffray had bestowed the child of his first marriage, was hot-faced, with a purple-veined nose, and cheeks which Bacchus had over-laid with his crimson and bulbous blossoms. Though stout, short, and pot-bellied, with stumpy legs and heavy hands, he had all the shrewdness of the Swiss innkeeper, resembling that race. His face remotely suggested a vast hail-stricken vineyard. Certainly he was not handsome; but his wife was like him. Never were a better matched couple. Rogron liked good living and to have pretty girls to wait on him. He was one of the sect of Egoists whose ways are brutal, and who give themselves up to their vices and do their will in the face of Israel. Greedy, mercenary, and by no means refined, obliged to be the purveyor to his own fancies, he ate up all he earned till his teeth failed him. Then avarice remained. In his old age he sold his inn, collected, as we have seen, all his father-in-law's leavings, and retired to the little house in the Square, which he bought for a piece of bread of old Auffray's widow, Pierrette's grandmother.

Rogron and his wife owned about two thousand francs a year, derived from the letting of twenty-seven plots of land in the neighbourhood of Provins, and the interest on the price of their inn, which they had sold for twenty thousand francs. Old Auffray's house, though in a very bad state, was used as it was for a dwelling by the innkeepers, who avoided repairing it as they would have shunned the plague; old rats love cracks and ruins. The retired publican, taking a fancy for gardening, spent his savings in adding to his garden; he extended it to the bank of the river, making a long square shut in by two walls, and ending with a stone embankment, below which the water-plants, left to run wild, displayed their abundant flowers.

Early in their married life the Rogron couple had a son and a daughter, with two years between them; everything degenerates; their children were hideous. Put out to nurse in the country as cheaply as possible, these unhappy little ones came home with the wretched training of village life, having cried long and often for their foster-mother; who went to work in the fields, and who left them meanwhile shut up in one of the dark, damp, low rooms which form the dwelling of the French peasant. By this process the children's features grew thick, and their voices harsh; they were far from flattering their mother's vanity, and she tried to correct them of their bad habits by a severity which, by comparison with their father's, seemed tenderness itself. They were left to play in the yards, stables, and outhouses of the inn, or to run about the town; they were sometimes whipped; sometimes they were sent to their grandfather Auffray, who loved them little. This injustice was one of the reasons that encouraged the Rogrons to secure a large share of the "old rascal's" leavings. Meanwhile, however, Rogron sent his boy to school; and he paid a man, one of his carters, to save the lad from the conscription. As soon as his daughter Sylvie was twelve years old, he sent her to Paris as an apprentice in a house of business. Two years later, his son Jérôme-Denis was packed off by the same road. When his friends the carriers, who were his allies, or the inn customers asked him what he meant to do with his children, old Rogron explained his plans with a brevity which had this advantage over the statements of most fathers, that it was frank:

"When they are of an age to understand me, I shall just give them a kick you know where, saying, 'Be off and make your fortune,'" he would reply, as he drank, or wiped his mouth with the back of his hand. Then looking at the inquirer with a knowing wink, "Ha, ha!" he would add, "they are not greater fools than I am. My father gave me three kicks, I shall give them but one. He put a louis into my hand, I will give them ten; so they will be better off than I was.—That's the right way. And after I am gone, what is left will be left; the notaries will find them fast enough. A pretty joke, indeed, if I am to keep myself short for the children's sake! They owe their being to me; I have brought them up; I ask nothing of them; they have not paid me back, heh, neighbour? I began life as a carter, and that did not hinder me from marrying that old rascal Auffray's daughter."

Sylvie was placed as an apprentice, with a premium of a hundred crowns for her board, with some tradespeople in the Rue Saint-Denis, natives of Provins. Two years later she was paying her way; though she earned no money, her parents had nothing to pay for her food and lodging. This, in the Rue Saint-Denis, is called being "at par:" Two years later Sylvie was earning a hundred crowns a year. In the course of that time her mother had sent her a hundred francs for pocket-money. Thus, at the age of nineteen, Mademoiselle Sylvie Rogron was independent. When she was twenty, she was second "young lady" in the house of Julliard, raw silk merchants, at the sign of the *Ver chinois* (or Silkworm), in the Rue Saint-Denis.

The history of the brother was like the sister's. Little Jérôme-Denis Rogron was placed with one of the largest wholesale mercers in the Rue Saint-Denis, the *maison Guépin* at the *Trois Quenouilles*. While Sylvie, at twenty-one, was forewoman with a thousand francs a year, Jérôme-Denis, better served by luck, was, at eighteen, head shop-clerk, earning twelve hundred, with the Guépins, also natives of Provins. The brother and sister met every Sunday and holiday, and spent the day in cheap amusements. They dined outside Paris; they went to Saint-Cloud, Meudon, Belleville, or Vincennes.

At the end of 1815 they united the money they had earned by the sweat of their brow, and bought of Madame Guenée the business and good-will of a famous house, the *Sur de famille*, one of the best known retail haberdashers. The sister kept the cash, the shop, and the accounts; the brother was both buyer and head-clerk, as Sylvie was for some time her own forewoman. In 1821, after five years' hard work, competition had become so lively in the haberdashery business that the brother and sister had scarcely been able to pay off the purchase money and keep up the reputation of the house.

Though Sylvie Rogron was at this time but forty, her ugliness, her constant toil, and a peculiarly crabbed expression, arising as much from the shape of her features as from her anxieties, made her look like a woman of fifty. Jérôme-Denis Rogron, a the age of thirty-eight, had the most idiotic face that ever bent over a counter to a customer. His low forehead, crushed by fatigue, was seamed by three arid furrows. His scanty grey hair, cut very short, suggested the unutterable stupidity of a cold-blooded animal; in the gaze of his blue-grey eyes there was neither fire nor mind. His round, flat face aroused no sympathy, and did not even bring a smile to the lips of those who study the varieties of Parisian physiognomy; it was depressing. And while, like his father, he was short and thick, his shape, not having the coarse obesity of the innkeepcr, showed in every detail an absurd flabbiness. His father's excessive redness gave place in him to the flaccid lividness acquired by people who live in airless backshops, in the barred coops that serve as counting-houses, always folding and unfolding skeins of thread, paying or receiving money, harrying clerks, or repeating the same phrases to customers. The small intelligence of this brother and sister had been completely sunk in mastering their business, in debit and credit, and in the study of the rules and customs of the Paris market. Thread, needles, ribbon, pins, buttons, tailors' trimmings, in short, the vast list of articles constituting Paris haberdashery, had filled up their memory. Letters to write and answer, bills and stock-taking, had absorbed all their capabilities.

Outside their line of business they knew absolutely nothing; they did not even know Paris. To them Paris was something spread out round the Rue Saint-Denis. Their narrow nature found its field in their shop. They knew very well how to nag their assistants and shop-girls and find them at fault. Their joy consisted in seeing all their hands as busy on the counters as mice's paws, handling the goods or folding up the pieces. When they heard seven or eight young voices of lads and girls simpering out the time-honoured phrases with which shop-assistants reply to a customer's remarks, it was a fine day, nice weather. When ethereal blue brought life to Paris, and Parisians out walking thought of no haberdashery but what they wore, "Bad weather for business," the silly master would observe. The great secret, which made Rogron the object of his apprentices' admiration, was his art in tying, untying, re-tying, and making up a parcel. Rogron could pack a parcel and look out at what was going on in the street, or keep an eye on his shop to its furthest depths; he had seen everything by the time he handed it to the buyer, saying, "Madame—nothing more this morning?"

But for his sister, this simpleton would have been ruined. Sylvie had good sense and the spirit of trade. She advised her brother as to his purchases from the manufacturers, and relentlessly sent him off to the other end of France to make a sou of profit on some article. The shrewdness, of which every woman possesses more or less, having no duty to do for her heart, she had utilized it in speculation. Stock to be paid for! this thought was the piston that worked this ma chine and gave it appalling energy. Rogron was never more than head-assistant; he did not understand his business as a whole; personal interest, the chief motor of the mind, had not carried him forward one step. He often stood dismayed when his sister desired him to sell some article at a loss, foreseeing that it would go out of fashion; and afterwards he guilelessly admired her. He did not reason well or ill; he was incapable of reasoning; but he had sense enough to submit to his sister, and he did so for a reason that had nothing to do with business. "She is the eldest," he would say. Physiologists and moralists may possibly find in such a persistently solitary life, reduced to satisfying mere needs, and deprived of money and pleasure in youth, an explanation of the animal expression of face, the weak brain, and idiotic manner of this haberdasher. His sister had always hindered his marrying, fearing perhaps that she might lose her influence in the house, and seeing a source of expense and ruin in a wife certainly younger, and probably less hideous, than herself.

Stupidity may betray itself in two ways—it is talkative or it is mute. Mute stupidity may be endured; but Rogron's was talkative. The tradesman had fallen into the habit of scolding his assistants, of expatiating to them on the minutiæ of the haberdashery business and selling to "the trade," ornamenting his lectures with the flat jokes that constitute the *bagout,* the gab of the shops. (This word *bagout*, used formerly to designate the stereotyped repartee, has given way before the soldier's slang word *blague* or humbug.) Rogron, to whom his little domestic audience were bound to listen, Rogron, very much pleased with himself, had finally adopted a set of phrases of his own. The chatterbox believed himself eloquent. The need for explaining to customers the thing they want, for finding out their wishes, for making them want the thing they do not want, loosens the tongue of the counter-jumper. The retail dealer at last acquires the faculty of pouring out sentences in which words have no meaning, but which answer their purpose. Then he can explain to his customers methods of manufacture unknown to them, and this gives him a sort of short-lived superiority over the purchaser; but apart from the thousand and one explanations necessitated by the thousand and one articles he sells, he is, so far as thought is concerned, like a fish on straw in the sunshine.

Rogron and Sylvie—a pair of machines illicitly baptized—had neither potentially nor actively the feelings which give life to the heart. These two beings were utterly dry and tough, hardened by toil, by privations, by the remembrance of their sufferings during a long and weariful apprenticeship. Neither he nor she had pity for any misfortune. They were not implacable, but impenetrable with regard to anybody in difficulties. To them virtue, honour, loyalty, every human feeling was epitomized in the regular payment of their accounts. Close-fisted, heartless, and sordidly thrifty, the brother and sister had a terrible reputation among the traders of the Rue Saint-Denis.

But for their visits to Provins, whither they went thrice a year, at times when they could shut the shop for two or three days, they would never have got shop-lads and girls. But old Rogron packed off to his children every unhappy creature intended by its parents to go into trade; he carried on for them a business in apprentices in Provins, where he vaunted with much vanity his children's fortune. The parents, tempted by the remote hope of having their son or daughter well taught and well looked after, and the chance of seeing a child some day step into Rogron junior's business, sent the youth who was in the way to the house kept by the old bachelor and old maid. But as soon as the apprentices, man or maid, for whom the fee of a hundred crowns was always paid, saw any way of escaping from these galleys, they fled with a glee which added to the terrible notoriety of the Rogrons. The indefatigable innkeeper always supplied them with fresh victims.

From the age of fifteen Sylvie Rogron, accustomed to grimace over the counter, had two faces—the amiable mask of the saleswoman and the natural expression of a shrivelled old maid. Her assumed countenance was a marvelous piece of mimicry; she smiled all over; her voice turned soft and insinuating, and held the customers under a commercial spell. Her real face was what she had shown between the two half-opened shutters. It would have scared the bravest of the Cossacks of 1815, though they dearly loved every variety of Frenchwoman.

When the letter came from the Lorrains, the Rogrons, in mourning for their father, had come into possession of the house they had almost stolen from Pierrette's grandmother, of the innkeeper's acquired land, and finally of certain sums derived from usurious loans in mortgages on land in the hands of peasant owners whom the old drunkard hoped to dispossess. The charge on the business was paid off. The Rogrons had stock to the value of about sixty thousand francs in the shop, about forty thousand francs in their cash-box or in assets, and the value of their good will. Seated on the bench, covered with striped green worsted velvet, and fitted into a square recess behind the cash-desk, with just such another desk opposite for the forewoman, the brother and sister held council as to their plans. Every tradesman hopes to retire. If they realized their whole stock and business, they ought to have about a hundred and fifty thousand francs, without counting their inheritance from old Rogron. Thus by investing in the funds the capital at their disposal, each of them would have three to four thousand francs a year, even if they devoted the price of the business—which would no doubt be paid in instalments—to restoring their paternal home. So they might go to Provins and live there in a house of their own.

Their forewoman was the daughter of a rich farmer at Donnemarie, who was burdened with nine children; thus he was obliged to place them all in business, for his wealth, divided among nine, would be little enough for each. But in five years the farmer lost seven of his children, consequently the forewoman had become an interesting person; so much so, that Rogron had attempted, but vainly, to make her his wife. The young lady manifested an aversion for the master which nullified all his manœuvres. On the other hand, Mademoiselle Sylvie did not encourage the plan; she even opposed her brother's marriage, and wanted rather to have so clever a woman as their successor. Rogron's marriage she postponed till they should be settled at Provins.

No passer-by can understand the motive-power that underlies the cryptogamic lives of certain shopkeepers; as we look at them we wonder, "On what, and why do they live? What becomes of them? Where did they come from?" We lose ourselves in vacancy as we try to account for them. To discover the little poetry that germinates in these brains and vivifies these existences, we must dig into them; but we soon reach the tufa on which everything rests. The Paris shopkeeper feeds on hopes more or less likely to be realised, and without which he would evidently perish: one dreams of building or managing a theatre, another struggles for the honors of the Maine; this one has a castle in the air three leagues from Paris, a so-called park, where he plants coloured plaster statues and arranges fountains that look like an end of thread, and spends immense sums; that one longs for promotion to the higher grades of the National Guard. Provins, an earthly paradise, excited in the two haberdashers the fanaticism which the inhabitants of every pretty town in France feel for their home. And to the glory of Champagne, it may be said that this affection is amply justified. Provins, one of the most charming spots in France, rivals Frangistan and the valley of Cashmere; not only has it all the poetry of Saadi, the Homer of Persia, but it also has pharmaceutical treasures for medical science. The crusaders brought roses from Jericho to this delightful valley, where, by some chance, the flowers developed new qualities without losing anything of their colour. And Provins is not only the Persia of France; it might be Baden, Aix, Bath; it has mineral waters.

This is the picture seen year after year, which now and again appeared in a vision to the haberdashers on the muddy pavement of the Rue Saint-Denis

After crossing the grey flats that lie between la Ferté-Gaucher and Provins—a desert, but a fertile one, a desert of wheat—you mount a hill. Suddenly, at your feet, you see a town watered by two rivers; at the bottom of the slope spreads a green valley broken by graceful lines and retreating distances. If you come from Paris you take Provins lengthways; you see the everlasting French highroad running along the foot of the hill and close under it, owning its blind man and its beggars, who throw in an accompaniment of lamentable voices when you pause to gaze at this unexpectedly picturesque tract of land. If you arrive from Troyes, you come in from the plain. The castle and the old town, with its rampart, climb the shelves of the hill. The new town lies below.

There are upper and lower Provins; above, a town in the air, with steep streets and fine points of view, surrounded by hollow roads like ravines between rows of walnut-trees, furrowing the narrow hilltop with deep cuttings: a silent town this, clean and solemn, overshadowed by the imposing ruins of the stronghold;

then, behind a town of mills, watered by the Voulzie and the Durtain, two rivers of Brie, narrow, sluggish, and deep; a town of inns and trade, of retired tradespeople, traversed by diligences, chaises and heavy carts. These two towns—or this town—with its historical associations, with the melancholy of its ruins, the gaiety of its valley, its delightful ravines full of unkempt hedgerows and wildflowers, its river terraced with gardens, has so sure a hold on the love of its children that they behave like the sons of Auvergne, of Savoy, of France. Though they leave Provins to seek their fortune, they always come back to it. The phrase, "To die in one's burrow," made for rabbits and faithful souls, might be taken by the natives of Provins as their motto.

And so the two Rogrons thought only of their beloved Provins. As they sold thread, the brother saw the old town. While packing cards covered with buttons, he was gazing at the valley. He rolled and unrolled tape, but he was following the gleaming course of the rivers. As he looked at his pigeon-holes, he was climbing the sunk roads whither of old he fled to evade his father's rage, to eat walnuts, and to cram on blackberries. The little Square at Provins above all filled his thoughts; he would beautify the house; he dreamed of the front he would rebuild, the bedrooms, the sitting-room, the billiard-room, the dining-room; then of the kitchen garden, which he would turn into an English garden with a lawn, grottoes, fountains, statues, and what not?

The rooms in which the brother and sister slept on the second floor of the house, three windows wide and six stories high—there are many such in the Rue Saint-Denis—had no furniture beyond what was strictly necessary; but not a soul in Paris had finer furniture than this haberdasher. As he walked in the streets he would stand in the attitude of an ecstatic, looking at the handsome pieces on show and examining hangings with which he filled his house. On coming home he would say to his sister, "I saw a thing in such or such a shop that would just do for us!" The next day he would buy another, and invariably he gave up one month the choice of the month before. The revenue would not have paid for his architectural projects; he wanted everything, and always gave the preference to the newest thing. When he studied the balconies of a newly-built house, and the doubtful at tempts at exterior decoration, he thought the mouldings, sculpture, and ornament quite out of place. "Ah!" he would say to himself, "those fine things would look much better at Provins than they do there." As he digested his breakfast on his doorstep, leaning his back against the shop side, with a hazy eye the haberdasher saw a fantastic dwelling, golden in the sunshine of his dream; he walked in a garden, listening to his fountain as it splashed in a shower of diamonds on a round flag of limestone. He played billiards on his own table; he planted flowers.

When his sister sat, pen in hand, lost in thought, and for getting to scold the shopmen, she was seeing herself receiving the townsfolk of Provins, gazing at herself in the tall mirrors of her drawing-room, and wearing astounding caps. Both brother and sister were beginning to think that the atmosphere of the Rue Saint-Denis was unwholesome, and the smell of the mud in the market made them long for the scent of the roses of Provins. They suffered alike from home sickness and monomania, both thwarted by the necessity for selling their last remnants of thread, reels of silk, and buttons. The promised land of the valley of Provins attracted these Israelites all the more strongly because they had for a long time really suffered, and had crossed with gasping breath the sandy deserts of haberdashery.

The letter from the Lorrains arrived in the middle of a meditation on that beautiful future. The haberdashers scarcely knew their cousin Pierrette Lorrain. The settlement of Auffray's estate, long since, by the old innkeeper, had taken place when they were going into business, and Rogron never said much about his money matters. Having been sent to Paris so young, the brother and sister could hardly remember their aunt Lorrain. It took them an hour of genealogical discussion to recall their aunt, the daughter of their grandfather Auffray's second wife, and their mother's half-sister. They then remembered that Madame Lorrain's mother was the Madame Néraud who had died of grief. They concluded that their grandfather's second marriage had been a disastrous thing for them, the result being the division of Auffray's estate between two families. They had, indeed, heard sundry recriminations from their father, who was always somewhat of the grudging publican. The pair studied the Lorrains' letter through the medium of these reminiscences, which were not in Pierrette's favour. To take charge of an orphan, a girl, a cousin, who in any case would be their heiress in the event of their neither of them marrying,—this was matter for discussion. The question was regarded from every point of view. In the first place, they had never seen Pierrette. Then it would be very troublesome to have a young girl to look after. Would they not be binding themselves to provide for her? It would be impossible to send her away if they did not like her. Would they not have to find her a husband? And if, after all, Rogron could find "a shoe to fit him" among the heiresses of Provins, would it not be better to keep all they had for his children? The shoe that would fit her brother, according to Sylvie, was a rich girl, stupid and ugly, who would allow her sister-in-law to rule her. The couple decided that they would refuse.

Sylvie undertook to reply. Business was sufficiently pressing to retard this letter, which she did not deem urgent, and indeed the old maid thought no more about it when the forewoman consented to buy the business and stock-in-trade of the *Sur de famille.*

Sylvie Rogron and her brother had gone to settle in Provins four years before the time when Brigaut's appearance brought so much interest into Pierrette's life. But the doings of these two persons in the country require a description no less than their life in Paris; for Provins was fated to be as evil an influence for Pierrette as her cousins' commercial antecedents.

When a small tradesman who had come to Paris from the provinces returns to the country from Paris, he inevitably brings with him some notions; presently he loses them in the habits of the place where he settles down, and where his fancies for innovations gradually sink. Hence come those slow, small, successive changes which are gradually scratched by Paris on the surface of country-town life, and which are the essential stamp of the change of a retired shopkeeper into a confirmed provincial. This change is a real distemper. No small tradesman can pass without a shock from perpetual talk to utter silence, from the activity of his Paris life to the stagnation of the country. When the good folks have earned a little money, they spend a pertain amount on the passion they have so long been hatching, and work off the last spasms of an energy which cannot be stopped short at will. Those who have never cherished any definite plan, travel, or throw themselves into the political interests of the municipality. Some go out shooting or fishing, and worry their farmers and tenants. Some turn usurers, like old father Rogron, or speculate, like many obscure persons.

The dream of this brother and sister is known to you; they wanted to indulge their magnificent fancy for handling the trowel, for building a delightful house. This fixed idea had graced the Square of lower Provins with the frontage which Brigaut had just been examining, the interior arrangements of the house, and its luxurious furniture. The builder drove never a nail in without consulting the Rogrons, without making them sign the plans and estimates, without explaining in lengthy detail the structure of the object under discussion, where it was made, and the various prices. As to anything unusual, it had always been introduced by Monsieur Tiphaine or Madame Julliard the younger, or Monsieur Garceland, the Maire. Such a resemblance with some wealthy citizen of Provins always carried the day in the builder's favour.

"Oh, if Monsieur Garceland has got one we will have it!" said Mademoiselle Sylvie. "It must be right; he had good taste."

"Sylvie, he suggests we should have ovolos in the cornice of the passage."

"You call that an ovolo?'

"Yes, mademoiselle."

"But why? What a queer name! I never heard it before."

"But you have seen them?'

"Yes."

"Do you know Latin?"

"No."

"Well, it means egg-shaped; the ovolo is egg-shaped."

"You are a queer crew, you architects!" cried Rogron. "That, no doubt, is the reason you charge so much; you don't throw away your egg-shells!"

"Shall we paint the passage?" asked the builder.

"Certainly not!" cried Sylvie. "Another five hundred francs!"

"But the drawing-room and the stairs are so nice, it is a pity not to decorate the passage," said the builder. "Little Madame Lesourd had hers painted last year."

"And yet her husband, being crown prosecutor, cannot stay at Provins—"

"Oh! he will be President of the Courts here some day," said the builder.

"And what do you think is to become of Monsieur Tiphaine then?"

"Monsieur Tiphaine! He has a pretty wife; I am not uneasy about him. Monsieur Tiphaine will go to Paris."

"Shall we paint the corridor?"

"Yes; the Lesourds will, at any rate, see that we are as good as they are," said Rogron.

The first year of their residence in Provins was wholly given up to these discussions, to the pleasure of seeing the workmen busy, to the surprises and information of all kinds that they got by it, and to the attempts made by the brother and sister to scrape acquaintance with the most important families in the town.

The Rogrons had never had any kind of society; they had never gone out of their shop; they knew literally no one in Paris, and they thirsted for the pleasure of visiting. On their return they found first Monsieur and Madame Julliard, of the *Ver chinois*, with their children and grandchildren; then the Guépin family, or, to be exact, the Guépin clan; the grandson still kept the shop of the *Trois Quenouilles*; and finally, Madame Guénée, who had sold them the business of the *Sur de famille*; her three daughters were married in Provins. These three great tribes—the Julliards, the Guépins, and the Guenées—spread over the town like couch-grass on a lawn. Monsieur Garceland, the Maire, was Monsieur Guépin's son-in-law. The Curé, Monsieur l'Abbé Péroux, was own brother to Madame Julliard, who was a Péroux. The President of the Court, Monsieur Tiphaine, was brother to Madame Guénée, who signed herself "*née* Tiphaine."

The queen of the town was Madame Tiphaine *junior*, the handsome only daughter of Madame Roguin, who was the wealthy wife of a notary of Paris; but he was never mentioned. Delicate, pretty, and clever, married to a provincial husband by the express management of her mother, who would not have her with her, and had taken her from school only a few days before her marriage, Melanie felt herself an exile at Provins, where she behaved admirably well. She was already rich, and had great expectations. As to Monsieur Tiphaine, his old father had advanced his eldest daughter, Madame Guénée, so much money on account of her share of the property, that an estate worth eight thousand francs a year, at about five leagues from Provins, would fall to the President. Thus the Tiphaines, who had married on twenty thousand francs a year, exclusive of the President's salary and residence, expected some day to have twenty thousand francs a year more. They were not out of luck, people said.

Madame Tiphaine's great and only object in life was to secure her husband's election as deputy. Once in Paris, the deputy would be made judge, and from the Lower Court she promised herself he should soon be promoted to the High Court of Justice. Hence she humoured everybody's vanity, and strove to please; more difficult still, she succeeded. The young woman of two-and-twenty received twice a week, in her handsome house in the old town, all the citizen class of Provins. She had not yet taken a single awkward step on the slippery ground where she stood. She gratified every conceit, patted every hobby; grave with serious folks, and a girl with girls, of all things a mother with the mothers, cheerful with the young wives, eager to oblige, polite to all; in short, a pearl, a gem, the pride of Provins. She had not yet said the word, but all the electors of the town awaited the day when their dear President should be old enough, to nominate him at once. Every voter, sure of his talents, made him his man and his patron. Oh yes, Monsieur Tiphaine would get on; he would be Keeper of the Seals, and he would promote the interests of Provins.

These were the means by which Madame Tiphaine had been so fortunate as to obtain her ascendency over the little town of Provins. Madame Guénée, Monsieur Tiphaine's sister, after seeing her three daughters married—the eldest to Monsieur Lesourd the public prosecutor, the second to Monsieur Martener the doctor, and the third to Monsieur Auffray the notary—had herself married again Monsieur Galardon, the collector of taxes. Mesdames Lesourd, Martener, and Auffray, and their mother Madame Galardon, regarded the President as the wealthiest and cleverest man in the family. The public prosecutor, Monsieur Tiphaine's nephew by marriage, had the greatest interest in getting his uncle to Paris, so as to be made President himself. Hence these four ladies—for Madame Galardon adored her brother—formed a little court about Madame Tiphaine, taking her opinion and advice on every subject.

Then Monsieur Julliard's eldest son, married to the only daughter of a rich farmer, was taken with a sudden passion, a *grande passion*, secret and disinterested, for the President's wife—that angel dropped from the sky of Paris. Melanie, very wily, incapable of burdening herself with a Julliard, but perfectly capable of keeping him as an Amadis and making use of his folly, advised him to start a newspaper to which she was the Egeria. So for two years now Julliard, animated by his romantic passion, had managed a paper and run a diligence for Provins. The newspaper, entitled *La Ruche, The Beehive,* included literary, archæological, and medical papers concocted in the family. The advertisements of the districts paid the expenses; the subscriptions—about two hundred—were all profit. Melancholy verses sometimes appeared in it, unintelligible to the country people, and addressed "To Her!!!" with the three points of admiration. Thus the young Julliard couple, singing the merits of Madame Tiphaine, had allied the clan Julliard to that of the Guénées. Thenceforward the President's drawing-room, of course, led the society of the town. The very few aristocrats who lived at Provins met in a single house in the old town, that of the old Comtesse de Bréautey.

During the first six months after their transplanting, the Rogrons, by favour of their old-time connection with the Julliards, the Guépins, and the Guénées, and by emphasizing their relationship to Monsieur Auffray the notary—a great-grandnephew of their grandfather's—were received at first by Madame Julliard the elder and Madame Galardon; then, not without difficulty, they found admission to the beautiful Madame Tiphaine's drawing-room. Everybody wished to know something about the Rogrons before inviting them to call. It was a little difficult to avoid receiving tradespeople of the Rue Saint-Denis, natives of Provins, who had come back to spend their money there. Nevertheless, the instinct of society is always to bring together persons of similar fortune, education, manners, acquaintance, and character. Now the Guépins, the Guénées, and the Julliards were of a higher grade, and of older family, than the Rogrons—the children of a money-lending innkeeper who could not be held blameless in his private life, nor with regard to the Auffray inheritance. Auffray the notary, Madame Galardon's son-in-law, knew all about it; the estate had been wound up in his predecessor's office. Those older merchants, who had retired twelve years since, had found themselves on the level of education, breeding, and manners of the circle to which Madame Tiphaine imparted a certain stamp of elegance, of Paris varnish. Everything was homogeneous; they all understood each other, and knew how to conduct themselves, and talk so as to be agreeable to the rest. They knew each other's characters, and were accustomed to agree. Having been once received by Monsieur Garceland the Maire, the Rogrons flattered themselves that they should soon be on intimate terms with the best society of the town. Sylvie learned to play boston. Rogron, far too stupid to play any game, twirled his thumbs and swallowed his words when once he had talked about his house. But the words acted like medicine; they seemed to torture him cruelly; he rose, he looked as if he were about to speak; he took fright and sat down again, his lips comically convulsed. Sylvie unconsciously displayed her nature at games. Fractious and complaining whenever she lost, insolently triumphant when she won, contentious and fretful, she irritated her adversaries and her partners, and was a nuisance to everybody.

Eaten up with silly and undisguised envy, Rogron and his sister tried to play a part in a town where a dozen families had formed a net of close meshes; all their interests, all their vanities made, as it were, a slippery floor on which newcomers had to tread very cautiously to avoid running up against some thing or getting a fall. Allowing that the rebuilding of their house might cost thirty thousand francs, the brother and sister between them would still have ten thousand francs a year. They fancied themselves very rich, bored their acquaintances to death with their talk of future splendour, and so gave the measure of their meanness, their crass ignorance, and their idiotic jealousy. The evening they were introduced to Madame Tiphaine the beauty—who had already watched them at Madame Garceland's, at her sister-in-law's, Madame Galardon's, and at the elder Madame Julliard's—the queen of Provins said in a confidential tone to Julliard *junior,* who remained alone with her and the President a few minutes after everyone was gone:

"You all seem to be much smitten with these Rogons?"

"I!" said the Amadis of Provins; "they bore my mother; they overpower my wife; and when Mademoiselle Sylvie was sent, thirty years ago, as an apprentice to my father, even then he could not endure her."

"But I have a very great mind," said the pretty lady, putting a little foot on the bar of the fender, "to give them to understand that my drawing-room is not an inn-parlour."

Julliard cast up his eyes to the ceiling as much as to say:

"Dear Heaven, what wit, what subtlety!"

"I wish my company to be select, and if I admit the Rogrons it will certainly not be that."

"They have no heart, no brain, no manners," said the President. "When after having sold thread for twenty years, as my sister did, for instance—"

"My dear, your sister would not be out of place in any drawing-room," said Madame Tiphaine, in a parenthesis.

"If people are so stupid as to remain haberdashers to the end," the President went on; "if they do not cast their skin; if they think that 'Comtes de Champagne' means 'accounts for wine,' as the Rogrons did this evening, they should stay at home."

"They are noisome!" said Julliard. "You might think there was only one house in Provins. They want to crush us, and, after all, they have hardly enough to live on."

"If it were only the brother," said Madame Tiphaine, "we might put up with him. He is not offensive. Give him a Chinese puzzle, and he would sit quietly in a corner. It would take him the whole winter to put up one pattern. But Mademoiselle Sylvie! What a voice—like a hyena with a cold! What lobster's claws! Do not repeat anything of this, Julliard."

When Julliard was gone, the little lady said to her husband:

"My dear, there are enough of the natives that I am obliged to receive; these two more would be the death of me; and with your permission, we will deprive ourselves of the pleasure."

"You are the mistress in your own house," said the President, "but we shall make many enemies. The Rogrons will join the Opposition, which hitherto has had no solidity in Provins. That Rogron is already hanging on to Baron Gouraud and Vinet the lawyer."

"Heh!" said Mélanie, with a smile, "they will do you service then. Where there are no enemies, there is no triumph. A Liberal conspiracy, an illegal society, a fight of some kind, would bring you into the foreground."

The President looked at his young wife with a sort of alarmed admiration.

Next day every one at Madame Garceland's said in every one else's ear that the Rogrons had not had a success at Madame Tiphaine's, and her remark about the inn-parlour was much applauded. Madame Tiphaine took a month before returning Mademoiselle Sylvie's visit. This rudeness is much remarked on in the country. Then, at Madame Tiphaine's, when playing boston with the elder

Madame Julliard, Sylvie made a most unpleasant scene about a splendid *misère* hand, on which her erewhile mistress caused her to lose—maliciously and on purpose, she declared. Sylvie, who loved to play nasty tricks on others, could never accept a return in kind. Madame Tiphaine, therefore, set the example of making up the card-parties before the Rogrons arrived, so that Sylvie was reduced to wandering from table to table, watching others play, while they looked at her askance with meaning glances. At old Madame Julliard's, whist was now the game, and Sylvie could not play it. The old maid at last understood that she was an outlaw, but without understanding the reason. She believed herself to be an object of jealousy to everybody.

Ere long the Rogrons were asked nowhere; but they persistently spent their evenings at various houses. Clever people made game of them, without venom, quite mildly, leading them to talk utter nonsense about the *ovolos* in their house, and about a certain cellaret for liqueurs, matchless in Provins. Meanwhile they gave themselves the final blow. Of course, they gave a few sumptuous dinners, as much in return for the civilities they had received as to show off their splendour. The guests came solely out of curiosity. The first dinner was given to Monsieur and Madame Tiphaine, with whom the Rogrons had not once dined; to Messieurs and Mesdames Julliard, father and son, mother and daughter-in-law; to Monsieur Lesourd, Monsieur the Curé, Monsieur and Madame Galardon. It was one of those provincial spreads, where the guests sit at table from five o'clock till nine. Madame Tiphaine had introduced the grand Paris style to Provins, the well-bred guests going away as soon as coffee had been served. She had some friends that evening at home, and tried to steal away, but the Rogrons escorted the couple to the very street; and when they returned, bewildered at having failed to keep the President and his wife, the other guests explained Madame Tiphaine's good taste, and imitated it with a promptitude that was cruel in a country town.

"They will not see our drawing-room lighted up!" cried Sylvie, "and candle-light is like rouge to it."

The Rogrons had hoped to give their guests a surprise. No one hitherto had been admitted to see this much-talked-of house. And all the frequenters of Madame Tiphaine's drawing-room impatiently awaited her verdict as to the marvels of the "*Palais* Rogron."

'Well," said little Madame Martener, "you have seen the Louvre? Tell us all about it."

"But all—like the dinner—will not amount to much."

"What is it like?"

"Well, the front door, of which we were, of course, required to admire the gilt-iron window frames that you all know, opens into a long passage through the house, dividing it unequally, since there is but one window to the street on the right, and two on the left. At the garden end this passage has a glass door to steps leading down to the lawn, a lawn with a decorative pedestal supporting a plaster cast of the Spartacus, painted to imitate bronze. Behind the kitchen the architect has contrived a little pantry, under the staircase, which we were not spared seeing. The stair, painted throughout like yellow-veined marble, is a hollow spiral, just like the stairs that in a café lead from the ground floor to the entresol. This trumpery structure of walnut wood, really dangerously light, and with banisters picked out with brass, was displayed to us as one of the seven new wonders of the world. The way to the cellars is beneath.

"On the other side of the passage, looking on the street, is the dining-room, opening by folding doors into the drawing-room, of the same size, but looking on to the garden."

"So there is no hall?" said Madame Auffray.

"The hall, no doubt, is the long passage where you stand in a draught," replied Madame Tiphaine. "We have had the eminently national, liberal, constitutional, and patriotic notion," she went on, "of making use only of wood grown in France! In the dining-room, the floor, laid in a neat pattern, is of walnut wood. The sideboards, table, and chairs are also in walnut. The window curtains are of white cotton with red borders, looped back with vulgar ropes over enormous pegs with elaborate dull-gilt rosettes, the mushroom-like object standing out against a reddish paper. These magnificent curtains run on rods ending in huge scrolls, and are held up by lions' claws in stamped brass, one at the top of each pleat.

"Over one of the sideboards is a regular café clock, draped, as it were, with a sort of napkin in bronze gilt, an idea that quite enchants the Rogrons. They tried to make me admire this device; and I could find nothing better to say than that if it could ever be proper to hang a napkin round a clock face, it was, no doubt, in a dining-room. On this sideboard are two large lamps, like those which grace the counters of grand restaurants. Over the other is a highly decorative barometer, which seems to play an important part in their existence; Rogron gazes at it as he might gaze at his bride-elect. Between the windows the builder has placed a white earthenware stove in a hideously ornate niche. The walls blaze with a splendid paper in red and gold, such as you will see in these same restaurants, and Rogron chose it there no doubt on the spot.

"Dinner was served in a set of white-and-gold china; the dessert service is bright blue with green sprigs; but they opened the china closet to show us that they had another service of stoneware for everyday use. The linen is in large cupboards facing the sideboards. Everything is varnished, shining, new, and harsh in colour. Still, I could accept the dining-room; it has a character of its own which, though not pleasing, is fairly representative of that of the owners; but there is no enduring the five engravings—those black-and-white things against which the Minister of the Interior ought really to get a decree; they represent Poniatowski leaping into the Elster, the Defence of the Barrière de Clichy, Napoleon himself pointing a gun, and two prints of Mazeppa, all in gilt frames of a vulgar pattern suitable to the prints, which are enough to make one loathe popularity. Oh! how much I prefer Madame Julliard's pastels representing fruits, those capital pastels which were done in the time of Louis XV, and which harmonise with the nice old dining-room and its dark, rather worm-eaten panels, which are at least characteristic of the country, and suit the heavy family silver, the antique china, and all our habits. The country is provincial; it becomes ridiculous when it tries to ape Paris. You may perhaps retort, '*Vous êtes orfévre, Monsieur Josse!*'—'You are to the manner born.' But I prefer this old room of my father-in-law Tiphaine's, with its heavy curtains of green-and-white damask, its Louis XV chimney-piece, its scroll pattern pier glass, its old beaded mirrors and time-honoured card-tables; my jars of old Sèvres, old blue, mounted in old gilding; my clock with its impossible flowers, my out-of-date chandelier, and my tapestried furniture to all the splendour of their drawing- room."

"What is it like?" said Monsieur Martener, delighted with the praise of the country so ingeniously brought in by the pretty Parisenne.

"The drawing-room is a fine red—as red as Mademoiselle Sylvie when she is angry at losing a *misère*.

"Sylvie-red," said the President, and the word took its place in the vocabulary of the district.

"The window-curtains—red! the furniture the chimney-piece—red marble veined with yellow! the candelabra and clock—red marble veined with yellow, and mounted in a heavy vulgar style; Roman lamp-brackets supported on Greek foliage! From the top of the clock a lion stares down on you, stupidly, as the Rogrons stare; a great good-natured lion, the ornamental lion so called, which will long continue to dethrone real lions; he spends his life clutching a black ball exactly like a deputy of the left. Perhaps it is a Constitutional allegory. The dial of this clock is an extraordinary piece of work.

"The chimney glass is framed with appliqué ornaments, which look poor and cheap, though they are a novelty. But the upholsterer's genius shines most in a panel of red stuff of which the radiating folds all centre in a rosette in the middle of the chimney-board—a romantic poem composed expressly for the Rogrons, who display it with ecstasy. From the ceiling hangs a chandelier, carefully wrapped in a green cotton shroud, and with reason; it is in the very worst taste, raw-toned bronze, with even more detestable tendrils of brown gold. Under it a round tea-table of marble, with more yellow than ever in the red, displays a shining metal tray, on which glitter cups of painted china—such painting!—arranged round a cut-glass sugar-basin, so bold in style that our grandchildren will open their eyes in amazement at the gilt rings round the edge and the diamond pattern on the sides, like a mediæval quilted doublet, and at the tongs for taking the sugar, which probably no one will ever use.

"This room is papered with red flock-paper imitating velvet, divided into panels by a beading of gilt brass, finished at the corners with enormous palms. A chromo-lithograph hangs on each panel, framed most elaborately in plaster casting of garlands to imitate fine wood-carving. The furniture of elm-root, upholstered with satin-cloth, classically consists of two sofas, two large easy-chairs, six armchairs, and six light chairs. The console is graced by an alabaster vase, called *à la Medicis,* under a glass shade, and by the much-talked-of liqueur-case. We were told often enough that 'there is not such another in Provins.' In each window bay, hung with splendid red silk curtains and lace curtains besides, stands a card-table. The carpet is Aubusson; the Rogrons have not failed to get hold of the crimson ground with medallions of flowers, the vulgarest of all the common patterns.

"The room looks uninhabited; there are no books or prints—none of the little things that furnish a table," and she looked at her own table covered with fashionable trifles, albums, and the pretty toys that were given her. "There are no flowers, none of the little nothings that fade and are renewed. it is all as cold and dry as Mademoiselle Sylvie. Buffon is right in saying that the style is the man, and certainly drawing-rooms have a style!"

Pretty Madame Tiphaine went on with her description by epigrams; and from this specimen, it is easy to imagine the rooms in which the brother and sister really lived on the first floor, which they also displayed to their guests. Still, no one could conceive of the foolish expenses into which the cunning builder had dragged the Rogrons; the mouldings of the doors, the elaborate inside shutters, the plaster ornaments on the cornices, the fancy painting, the brass-gilt knobs and bells, the ingenious smoke-consuming fireplaces, the contrivances for the prevention of damp, the sham inlaid wood on the staircase, the elaborate glass and smith's work—in short, all the fancy-work which adds to the cost of building, and delights the common mind, had been lavished without stint.

No one would go to the Rogrons' evenings; their pretensions were still-born. There were abundant reasons for refusing; every day was taken up by Madame Garceland, Madame Galardon, the two Julliard ladies, Madame Tiphaine, the Sous-préfet, etc. The Rogrons thought that giving dinners was all that was needed to get into society; they secured some young people who laughed at them, and some diners-out, such as are to be found in every part of the world; but serious people quite gave them up. Sylvie, alarmed at the clear loss of forty thousand francs swallowed up without any return in the house she called her dear house, wanted to recover the sum by economy. So she soon ceased to give dinners that cost from thirty to forty francs, without the wine, as they failed to realise her hope of forming a circle—a thing as difficult to create in the country as it is in Paris. Sylvie dismissed her cook, and hired a country girl for the coarser work. She herself cooked "to amuse herself."

Thus, fourteen months after their return home, the brother and sister had drifted into a life of isolation and idleness. Her banishment from "the world" had roused in Sylvie's soul an intense hatred of the Tiphaines, Julliards, Auffrays, and Garcelands—in short, of everybody in Provins society, which she stigmatised as a *clique*, with which she was on the most distant terms. She would gladly have set up a rival circle; but the second-rate citizen class was composed entirely of small tradespeople, never free but on Sundays and holidays; or of persons in ill-odour, like Vinet the lawyer and Doctor Néraud; or of rank Bonapartists, like General Gouraud; and Rogron very rashly made friends with these, though the upper set had vainly warned him against them. The brother and sister were obliged to sit together by the fire of their dining-room stove, talking over their business, the faces of their customers, and other equally amusing matters.

The second winter did not come to an end without their being almost crushed by its weight of dullness. They had the greatest difficulty in spending the hours of their day. As they went to bed at night, they thought, "One more over!"

They spun out the morning by getting up late and dressing slowly. Rogron shaved himself every morning; he examined his face and described to his sister the changes he fancied he noted in it; he squabbled with the maid over the temperature of the hot water; he wandered into the garden to see if the flowers were sprouting; he ventured down to the river-bank, where he had built a summer-house; he examined the wood work of the house. Had it warped? Had the settling split any of the panels? Was the paint wearing well? Then he came in to discuss his anxieties as to a sick hen, or some spot where the damp had left stains, talking to his sister, who affected hurry in laying the table while she scolded the maid. The barometer was the most useful article in the house to Rogron; he consulted it for no reason, tapped it familiarly like a friend, and then said, "Vile weather!" to which his sister would reply, "Pooh, the weather is quite seasonable." If anybody called, he would boast of the excellence of this instrument.

Their breakfast took up some little time. How slowly did these two beings masticate each mouthful. And their digestion was perfect; they had no cause to fear cancer of the stomach. By reading the *Ruche* and the *Constitutionnel* they got on to noon. They paid a third of the subscription to the Paris paper with Vinet and Colonel Gouraud. Rogron himself carried the paper to the Colonel, who lived in the Square, lodging with Monsieur Martener; the soldier's long stories were an immense delight to him. Rogron could only wonder why the Colonel was considered dangerous. He was such an idiot as to speak to him of the ostracism under which he lived, and retail the sayings of the "clique." God only knows what the Colonel—who feared no one, and was as redoubtable with the pistol as with the sword—had to say of "la Tiphaine" and "her Julliard," of the ministerial officials of the upper town—"men brought over by foreigners, capable of anything to stick in their places, cooking the lists of votes at the elections to suit themselves," and the like.

At about two o'clock Rogron sallied forth for a little walk. He was quite happy when a shopkeeper, standing at his door, stopped him with a "How d'ye do, Père Rogron?" He gossiped, and asked, "What news in the town?" heard and repeated scandal, or the tittle-tattle of Provins. He walked to the upper town, or in the sunk roads, according to the weather. Sometimes he met other old men airing themselves in like manner. Such meetings were happy events.

There were at Provins certain men who were out of conceit with the life of Paris, learned and modest men, living with their books. Imagine Rogron's frame of mind when he listened to a supernumerary judge named Desfondrilles, more of an archæologist than a lawyer, saying to a man of education, old Monsieur Martener, the doctor's father, as he pointed to the valley:

"Will you tell me why the idlers of all Europe flock to Spa rather than to Provins, when the waters of Provins are acknowledged to be superior by the whole French faculty of medicine, and to have effects and an energy worthy of the medical properties of our roses?"

'What do you expect?" replied the man of the world, "it is one of the caprices of Caprice, and just as inexplicable. The wines of Bordeaux were unknown a hundred years ago. Maréchal Richelieu, one of the grandest figures of the last century, the Alcibiades of France, was made governor of Guyenne. His chest was delicate—the world knew why—the wine of the country strengthened and restored him to health. Bordeaux at once made a hundred millions of francs a year, and the Marshal extended the Bordeaux district as far as Angoulême and as far as Cahors, in short, to forty leagues in every direction! Who knows where the vineyards of Bordeaux end?—And there is no equestrian statue of the Marshal at Bordeaux!"

"Ah! if such an event should take place at Provins in this century or the next," Monsieur Desfondrilles went on, "I hope that either on the little Square in the lower town, or on the castle, or somewhere in the upper town, some bas-relief will be seen representing the head of Monsieur Opoix, the rediscoverer of the mineral waters of Provins!"

"But, my dear sir, it would perhaps be impossible to rehabilitate Provins," said old Monsieur Martener. "The town is bankrupt."

At this Rogron opened his eyes wide, and exclaimed:

"What!"

"Provins was formerly a capital which, in the twelfth century, held its own as a rival to Paris, when the Counts of Champagne held their court here as King René held his in Provence," replied the man of learning. "In those days civilisation, pleasure, poetry, elegance, women—in short, all the splendour of social life was not exclusively restricted to Paris. Towns find it as hard as houses of business to rise again from ruin. Nothing is left to Provins but the fragrance of its historic past and that of its roses—and a sous-préfecture."

"Oh! to think what France might be if she still had all her feudal capitals!" said Desfondrilles. "Can our sous-préfets fill the place of the poetic, gallant, and warlike race of Thibault, who made Provins what Ferrara was in Italy, what Weimar was in Germany, and what Munich would like to be in our day?"

"Provins was a capital?" asked Rogron.

"Why, where have you dropped from?" said Desfondrilles the archæologist.

The lawyer struck the pavement of the upper town where they were standing with his stick: "Do not you know," he cried, "that all this part of Provins is built on crypts?"

"Crypts?"

"Yes, to be sure, crypts of unaccountable loftiness and extent. They are like cathedral aisles, full of pillars."

"Monsieur Desfondrilles is writing a great antiquarian work in, which he intends to describe these singular structures," said old Martener, seeing the lawyer mount his hobby.

Rogron came home enchanted to think that his house stood in this valley. The crypts of Provins kept him occupied for five or six days in exploring them, and for several evenings afforded a subject of conversation to the old couple. Thus Rogron generally picked up something about old Provins, about the intermarriages of the families, or some stale political news which he retailed to his sister. And a hundred times over in the course of his walk—several times even of the same person—he would ask, 'Well, what is the news? What has happened lately?" When he came in he threw himself on a sofa in the drawing-room as if he were tired out, but really he was only weary of his own weight.

He got on to dinner-time by going twenty times to and fro between the drawing-room and the kitchen, looking at the clock, opening and shutting doors. So long as the brother and sister spent the evenings in other houses they got through the hours till bedtime, but after they were reduced to staying at home the evening was a desert to traverse. Sometimes people on their way home, after spending the evening out, as they crossed the little Place, heard sounds in the Rogrons' house as if the brother were murdering the sister; they recognised them as the terrific yawns of a haberdasher driven to bay. The two machines had nothing to grind with their rusty wheels, so they creaked.

The brother talked of marrying, but with a sense of despair. He felt himself old and worn; a wife terrified him. Sylvie, who understood the need for a third person in the house, then remembered their poor cousin, for whom no one in Provins had ever inquired, for everybody supposed that little Madame Lorrain and her daughter were both dead. Sylvie Rogron never lost anything; she was too thoroughly an old maid to mislay anything, whatever it might be. She affected to have found the letter from the Lorrains so as to make it natural that she should mention Pierrette to her brother, and he was almost happy at the possibility of having a little girl about the house. Sylvie wrote to the old Lorrains in a half-business-like, half-affectionate tone, attributing the delay in her answer to the winding up of their affairs, to their move back to Provins, and settling there. She affected to be anxious to have her little cousin with her, allowing it to be understood that if Monsieur Rogron should not marry,

Pierrette would some day inherit twelve thousand francs a year. It would be needful to have been, like Nebuchadnezzar, to some extent a wild beast, shut up in a cage in a beast-garden with nothing to prey on but butcher's meat brought in by the keeper, or else a retired tradesman with no shop-clerks to nag, to imagine the impatience with which the brother and sister awaited their cousin Lorrain. Three days after the despatch of the letter they were already wondering when the child would arrive, Sylvie discerned in her so-called generosity to her penniless cousin a means of changing the views of Provins society with regard to herself. She called on Madame Tiphaine, who had stricken them with her disapproval, and who aimed at creating an upper class at Provins, like that at Geneva, and blew the trumpet to announce the advent of her cousin Pierrette, the child of Colonel Lorrain, pitying her woes, and congratulating herself as a lucky woman on having a pretty young heiress to introduce in society.

"You have been a long time discovering her," remarked Madame Tiphaine, who sat enthroned on a sofa by her fire side.

Madame Garceland, in a few words spoken in an undertone during a deal, revived the story of the Auffray property. The notary related the innkeeper's iniquities.

"Where is the poor little thing?" asked the President politely.

"In Brittany," said Rogron.

"But Brittany is a wide word!" remarked Monsieur Lesourd, the public prosecutor.

"Her grandfather and grandmother wrote to us.—When was it, my dear?" asked Rogron.

Sylvie, absorbed in asking Madame Garceland where she had bought the stuff for her dress, did not foresee the effect of her answer, and said, "Before we sold our business."

"And you answered three days ago, Mademoiselle Sylvie!" exclaimed the notary.

Sylvie turned as red as the hottest coals in the fire.

"We wrote to the Institution of Saint-Jacques," replied Rogron.

"There is a sort of asylum there for old people," said a lawyer, who had been supernumerary judge at Nantes. "But she cannot be there, for they only take in persons who are past sixty."

"She is there with her grandmother Lorrain," said Rogron.

"She had a little money, the eight thousand francs left her by your father—no I mean your grandfather," said the notary, blundering intentionally.

"Indeed!" said Rogron, looking stupid, and not understanding this sarcasm.

"Then you knew nothing of your first cousin's fortune or position?" asked the President.

"If Monsieur Rogron had known it, he would not have left her in a place which is no more than a respectable workhouse," said the judge severely. "I remember now that a house belonging to Monsieur and Madame Lorrain was sold at Nantes under an execution; and Mademoiselle Lorrain lost her claims, for I was the commissioner in charge."

The notary spoke of Colonel Lorrain, who, if he were alive, would indeed be astonished to think of his child being in an institution like that of Saint-Jacques. The Rogrons presently withdrew, thinking the world very spiteful. Sylvie perceived that her news had had no success; she had ruined herself in everybody's opinion; henceforth she had no hope of making her way in the higher society of Provins.

From that day the Rogrons no longer dissembled their hatred of the great citizen families of Provins, and of all their adherents. The brother now repeated all the Liberal fables which Lawyer Vinet and Colonel Gouraud had crammed him with about the Tiphaines, the Guénées, the Garcelands, the Guépins, and the Julliards.

"I tell you what, Sylvie, I don't see why Madame Tiphaine should turn a cold shoulder on the Rue Saint-Denis: the best of her beauty was made there. Madame Roguin, her mother, is a cousin of the Guillaumes of the *Cat and Racket*, who gave over their business to their son-in-law Joseph Lebas. Her father is that notary, that Roguin, who failed in 1819, and ruined the Birotteaus. So Madame Tiphaine's money is stolen wealth; for what is a notary's wife who takes her own settlement out of the fire and allows her husband to become a fraudulent bankrupt A pretty thing indeed! Ah! I understand! She got her daughter married to live here at Provins through her connections with the banker du Tillet. And these people are proud!—Well! However, that is what the world is!"

On the day when Denis Rogron and his sister Sylvie thus broke out in abuse of the clique, they had, without knowing it, become persons of importance, and were on the highroad to having some society; their drawing-room was on the point of becoming a centre of interests which only needed a stage. The retired haberdasher assumed historical and political dignity, for, still without knowing it, he gave strength and unity to the hitherto unstable elements of the Liberal party at Provins. And this was the way of it: The early career of the Rogrons had been anxiously observed by Colonel Gouraud and the advocate Vinet, who had been thrown together by their isolation and their agreement of ideas. These two men professed equal patriotism, and for the same reasons—they wanted to acquire importance. But though they were anxious to be leaders, they lacked followers. The Liberals of Provins comprised an old soldier who sold lemonade; an innkeeper; Monsieur Cournant, a notary, Monsieur Auffray's rival; Monsieur Néraud, a physician, Doctor Martener's rival; and some independent persons, farmers scattered about the neighbourhood, and holders of national stock. The Colonel and the lawyer, glad to attract an idiot whose money might help them in their manuvres, who would support their subscriptions, who, in some cases, would take the bull by the horns, and whose house would be useful as a town-hall for the party, took advantage of the Rogrons' hostility towards the aristocrats of the place. The Colonel, the lawyer, and Rogron had a slight bond in their joint subscription to the *Constitutionnel*; it would not be difficult for the Colonel to make a Liberal of the ex-haberdasher, though Rogron knew so little of political history that he had not heard of the exploits of Sergeant Mercier; he thought he was a friend and brother.

The impending arrival of Pierrette hastened the hatching of certain covetous dreams to which the ignorance and folly of the old bachelor and old maid had given rise. The Colonel, seeing that Sylvie had lost all chance of getting her foot into the circle of the Tiphaines, had an idea. Old soldiers have seen so many horrors in so many lands, so many naked corpses grimacing hideously on so many battle-fields, that an ugly face has no terrors for them, so the Colonel took steady aim at the old maid's fortune. This officer, a short, fat man, wore rings in his ears, which were already graced by bushy tufts of hair. His floating grey whiskers were such as in 1799 had been called "fins." His large, good-natured, red face was somewhat frost-bitten, as were those of all who escaped at the Beresina. His huge, prominent stomach had the flattened angle below characteristic of an old cavalry officer; Gouraud had commanded the second regiment of Hussars. His grey moustache covered a huge mouth—a perfect trap—the only word to describe that abyss; he did not eat, he devoured! A sword-cut had shortened his nose. His speech was in consequence thick and deeply nasal, like that ascribed to Capuchin friars. His hands, which were small, short, and broad, were such as make a woman say, "You have the hands of a thorough scamp." His legs, below such a huge body, looked frail. Within this active but clumsy body lay a cunning spirit, entire experience of life and things, hidden under the apparent carelessness of a soldier, and utter contempt for the conventionalities of society. Colonel Gouraud had the pension of the Cross of the Legion of Honour, and two thousand four hundred francs a year as half-pay—a thousand crowns a year in all for his whole income.

The lawyer, tall and lean, had no talent but his political opinions, and no income but the meagre profits of his business. At Provins solicitors plead their own cases. In view of his opinions, the Court listened with small favour to Maître Vinet; and the most Liberal farmers, when entangled in lawsuits, would rely on an attorney in favour with the Bench rather than employ Vinet. This man was said to have led astray a rich girl living near Coulommiers, and to have compelled her parents to let her marry him. His wife was one of the Chargebœufs, an old family of nobles in la Brie, who took their name from the exploit of a squire in Saint Louis' expedition to Egypt. She had incurred her parents' displeasure, and they, to Vinet's knowledge, had arranged to leave their whole fortune to their eldest son, charged, no doubt, with a reversion in favour of his sister's children. Thus this man's first ambitious scheme came to nothing. The lawyer soon haunted by poverty, and ashamed of not having enough to enable his wife to keep up appearances, had made vain efforts to get his foot into a ministerial career; but the rich branch of the Chargebœufs refused to assist him. These Royalists were strictly moral, and disapproved of a compulsory marriage; besides, their would-be relation's name was Vinet; how could they favour any one so common? So the lawyer was handed on from one branch to another when he tried to utilise his wife's interest with her relations. Madame Vinet found no assistance but from one of the family, a widowed Madame Chargebœuf, with a daughter, quite poor, who lived at Troyes. And a day came when Vinet remembered the kind reception his wife met with from this lady.

Rejected by the whole world, full of hatred of his wife's family, of the Government which refused him an appointment, and of the society of Provins, which would have nothing to say to him, Vinet accepted his poverty. His venom fermented and gave him energy to endure. He became a Liberal on perceiving that his fortune was bound up with the triumph of the Opposition, and vegetated in a wretched little house in the upper town, which his wife seldom quitted. This girl, born to a better fate, lived absolutely alone in her home with her one child. There are cases of poverty nobly met and cheerfully endured; but Vinet, eaten up by ambition, and feeling that he had wronged a young creature, cherished a dark indignation; his conscience expanded to admit every means to success. His face, still young, changed for the worse. People were sometimes terrified in Court at the sight of his flat viperine head, with its wide mouth, and eyes that glittered through his spectacles; at hearing his sharp, shrill, rasping voice, that wrung their nerves. His muddy complexion, patchy with sickly hues of yellow and green, revealed his suppressed ambitions, his perpetual mortifications and hidden penury. He could argue and harangue; he had no lack of point and imagery; he was leaned and crafty. Accustomed to indulge his imagination for the sake of rising by hook or by crook, he might have made a politician. A man who hesitates at nothing so long as it is legal is a strong man, and in this lay Vinet's strength.

This coming athlete of parliamentary debate—one of the men who were to proclaim the supremacy of the House of Orleans—had a disastrous influence over Pierrette's fate. At present he wanted to provide himself with a weapon by founding a newspaper at Provins. After having studied the Rogrons from afar, with the assistance of the Colonel, he ended by reckoning on the brother. And this time he reckoned with his host; his poverty was to come to an end after seven dolorous years, during which more than one day had come round without bread. On the day when Gouraud announced to Vinet, on the little Square, that the Rogrons had broken with the citizen aristocracy and official circles of the old town, the lawyer nudged him significantly in the ribs.

"This wife or that, ugly or handsome, it must be all the same to you," said he. "You should marry Mademoiselle Rogron, and then we could get something done here—"

"I was thinking of it. But they have sent for the daughter of poor Colonel Lorrain—their heiress," said Gouraud.

"You could make them leave you their money by will. You would have a very nicely fitted house."

"And the child, after all! Well, we shall see," said the Colonel, with a jocose and deeply villainous leer, which showed a man of Vinet's temper how small a thing a little girl was in the eyes of this old soldier.

Since her grandparents had gone into the asylum where they were forlornly ending their days, Pierrette, young and full of pride, was so dreadfully miserable at living there on charity, that she was happy to learn that she had some rich connections. On hearing that she was leaving, Brigaut, the Major's son, the companion of her childhood, who was now a joiner's apprentice at Nantes, came to give her the money needful for her journey by coach—sixty francs, all the savings of his odd earnings painfully hoarded; Pierrette accepted it with the sublime indifference of true friendship, showing that she, in similar circumstances, would have been hurt by thanks. Brigaut had gone every Sunday to Saint-Jacques to play with Pierrette, and to comfort her. The sturdy young workman had already gone through his delightful apprenticeship to the perfect and devoted care that we give to the object of our involuntary choice and affection. More than once ere now, Pierrette and he, on a Sunday, sitting in a corner of the garden, had sketched their childish dreams on the veil of the future; the young craftsman, mounted on his plane, traveled round the world, making a fortune for Pierrette, who waited for him.

So, in the month of October 1824, when Pierrette had almost completed her eleventh year, she was placed in the care of the guard of the diligence from Nantes to Paris by the two old people and the young apprentice, all three dreadfully sad. The guard was requested to put her into the coach for Provins, and to take great care of her. Poor Brigaut! he ran after the diligence like a dog, looking at his dear Pierrette as long as he could. In spite of the child's signals, he ran on for a league beyond the town, and when he was exhausted, his eyes sent a last tearful glance at Pierrette, who cried when she could see him no more. Pierrette put her head out of the window, and discerned her friend standing squarely, and watching the heavy vehicle that left him behind.

The Lorrains and Brigaut had so little knowledge of life that the little Bretonne had not a sou left when she arrived in Paris. The guard, to whom the child prattled of rich relations, paid her expenses at an inn in Paris, made the guard of the Troyes coach repay him, and desired him to deliver Pierrette to her family and collect the debt, exactly as if she were a parcel by carrier.

Four days after leaving Nantes, at about nine o'clock one Monday evening, a kind, burly old guard of the Messageries Royales took Pierrette by the hand, and, while the coach was unloading in the High Street such passengers and parcels as were to be deposited at Provins, he led her, with no luggage but two frocks, two pairs of stockings, and two shifts, to the house pointed out to him by the office clerk as that of Mademoiselle Rogron.

"Good-morning, mademoiselle, and gents all," said the guard. "I have brought you a cousin of yours, and here she be, and a pretty dear too. You have forty-seven francs to pay. Though your little girl has no weight of baggage, please to sign my way-book."

Mademoiselle Sylvie and her brother gave way to their delight and astonishment.

"Begging your pardon," said the guard, "my coach is waiting—sign my sheet and give me forty-seven francs and sixty centimes, and what you please for me and the guard from Nantes, for we have taken as much care of her as if she were our own. We have paid out for her bed and food, her place in the coach here, and other little things."

"Forty-seven francs and twelve sous?" exclaimed Sylvie.

"You're never going to beat me down?" cried the guard.

"But where is the invoice?" said Rogron.

"The invoice!—Here is my way-bill."

"You can talk afterwards, pay now!" said Sylvie to her brother; "you see, you cannot help paying."

Rogron went to fetch forty-seven francs twelve sous.

"And nothing for us—for my pal and me?" said the guard.

Sylvie produced a two-franc piece from the depths of hers old velvet bag, where her keys lurked in bunches.

"Thank you—keep it," said the man. "We would rather have looked after the little girl for her own sake." He took up his sheet and went out, saying to the servant girl: "A nice place this is! There are crocodiles of that sort without going to Egypt for 'em."

"Those people are horribly coarse!" said Sylvie, who had heard his speech.

"Dame! they took care of the child," replied Adèle, with her hands on her hips.

"We are not obliged to live with him," said Rogron.

"Where is she to sleep?" asked the maid.

Such was the reception that met Pierrette Lorrain on her arrival at her cousins' house, while they looked at her with a bewildered air. She was flung on their hands like a parcel, with no transition between the wretched room in which she had lived with her grandparents and her cousins' dining-room, which struck her as palatial. She stood there mute and shy. To any one but these retired haberdashers, the little Bretonne would have been adorable in her frock of coarse blue serge, a pink cotton apron, her blue stockings, thick shoes, and white kerchief; her little red hands were covered by knitted mittens of red wool edged with white that the guard had bought for her. Her little Brittany cap. which had been washed in Paris—it had got tumbled in the course of the journey from Nantes—really looked like a glory round her bright face. This native cap, made of fine cambric, with a stiff lace border ironed into flat pleats, deserves a description, it is so smart and so simple. The light, filtered through the muslin and lace, casts a half shadow, a twilight softness, on the face; it gives it the virginal grace which painters try to find on their palettes, and which Leopold

I HAVE BROUGHT YOU A COUSIN OF YOURS, AND HERE SHE BE

Robert has succeeded in lending to the Raphael-like face of the woman holding a child in his picture of the *Reapers.* Within this setting of broken lights shone an artless rose and white face, beaming with vigorous health. The heat of the room brought the blood to her head, and it suffused the edge of her tiny ears with fire, tingeing her lips and the tip of a finely cut nose, while by contrast it made her bright complexion look brighter than before.

'Well, have you nothing to say to us?" said Sylvie. "I am your cousin Sylvie, and that is your cousin Denis."

"Are you hungry?" asked Rogron.

"When did you leave Nantes?" asked Sylvie.

"She is dumb," said Rogron.

"Poor child, she has very few clothes to her back!" observed sturdy Adèle, as she untied the bundle wrapped in a handkerchief belonging to old Lorrain.

"Kiss your cousin," said Sylvie. Pierrette kissed Rogron. "Yes, kiss your cousin," said Rogron. Pierrette kissed Sylvie.

"She is scared by the journey, poor little thing; perhaps she is sleepy," said Adèle.

Pierrette felt a sudden and invincible aversion for her two relations, a feeling she had never before known. Sylvie and the maid went to put the little girl to bed in the room on the second floor where Brigaut was to see the cotton curtain. There were in this attic a small bed with a pole painted blue, from which hung a cotton curtain, a chest of drawers of walnut wood, with no marble top, a smaller table of the same wood, a looking-glass, a common bed-table, and three wretched chairs. The walls and sloping roof to the front were covered with a cheap blue paper flowered with black. The floor was painted and waxed, and struck cold to the feet. There was no carpet but a thin bedside rug made of selvages. The chimney-shelf, of cheap marble, was graced with a mirror, two candlesticks of copper gilt and a vulgar alabaster vase with two pigeons drinking to serve as handles; this Sylvie had had in her room in Paris.

"Shall you be comfortable here, child?" asked Sylvie.

"Oh! it is beautiful!" replied the little girl in her silvery treble.

"She is not hard to please," muttered the sturdy peasant woman to herself. "I had better warm the bed, I suppose?" she asked.

"Yes," said Sylvie, "the sheets may be damp."

Adèle brought a head kerchief of her own when she came up with the warming-pan; and Pierrette, who had hitherto slept in sheets of coarse Brittany linen, was amazed at the soft cotton sheets. When the little girl was settled and in bed, Adèle, as she went downstairs, could not help exclaiming, "All her things put together are not worth three francs, mademoiselle!"

Since adopting her system of strict economy, Sylvie always made the servant sit in the dining-room, so as to have but one lamp and one fire. When Colonel Gouraud and Vinet came, Adèle withdrew to her kitchen. Pierrette's arrival kept them talking for the rest of the evening.

"We must get her some clothes to-morrow," said Sylvie. "She has hardly a stitch."

"She has no shoes but those thick ones she had on, and they weigh a pound," said Adèle.

"They wear them so in those parts," said Rogron.

"How she looked at the room, which is none so fine neither, for a cousin of yours, mademoiselle!"

"So much the better; hold your tongue. You see she is delighted with it."

"Lord above us! what shifts! They must rub her skin raw. But none of these things are of any use," said Adèle, turning out the contents of Pierrette's bundle.

Till ten o'clock master, mistress, and maid were busy deciding of what stuff and at what price the shifts should be made, how many pairs of stockings and of what quality, and how many under-petticoats would be needed, and calculating the cost of Pierrette's wardrobe.

"You will not get off for less than three hundred francs," said Rogron to his sister, as he carried the price of each article in his head from long practice, and added up the total from memory.

"Three hundred francs!" exclaimed Sylvie.

"Yes, three hundred; work it out yourself."

The brother and sister began again, and made it three hundred francs without the sewing.

"Three hundred francs at one cast of the net!" cried Sylvie, who went to bed on the idea so ingeniously expressed by this proverbial figure of speech.

Pierrette was one of those children of love whom love has blessed with tenderness, cheerfulness, brightness, generosity, and devotedness; nothing had as yet chilled or crushed her heart; it was almost wildly sensitive, and the way she was received by her relations weighed on it painfully. Though Brittany had to her been a home of poverty, it had also been a home of affection. Though the old Lorrains were the most unskilful traders, they were the simplest, most loving, most caressing souls in the world, as all disinterested people are. At Pen-Hoël their little grand-daughter had had no teaching but that of nature. Pierrette went as she would in a boat on the pools, she ran about the village or the fields with her companion Jacques Brigaut, exactly like Paul and Virginia. Both the children, spoiled and petted by every one, and as free as the air, ran after the thousand joys of childhood; in summer they went to watch the fishermen, they caught insects, plucked flowers, and gardened; in winter they made slides, built smart snow-palaces and snow-men, or made snow balls to pelt each other. They were everywhere welcome; everybody smiled on them.

When it was time that they should learn something, misfortunes came. Jacques, left destitute by his father's death, was apprenticed by his relations to a cabinet-maker, and maintained by charity, as Pierrette was soon after in the asylum of Saint-Jacques. But even in this almshouse, pretty little Pierrette had been made much of, loved, and kindly treated by all. The child, thus accustomed to so much affection, no longer found, in the home of these longed-for and wealthy relations, the look, the tone, the words, the manner which she had hitherto met with in every one, even in the guards of the diligences. Thus her amazement, already great, was complicated by the changed moral atmosphere into which she had been plunged. The heart can turn suddenly cold and hot as the body can. The poor child longed to cry without knowing what for. She was tired, and she fell asleep.

Accustomed to rise very early, like all country-bred children, Pierrette awoke next morning two hours before the cook. She dressed, trotted about her room over her cousin's head, looked out on the little Square, and was going downstairs; she was astonished at the splendour of the staircase; she examined every detail—the rosettes, the brass-work, the mouldings, the painting, etc. Then she went down; she could not open the garden door, so she came up again; went down once more when Adèle was about, and sprang into the garden. She took possession of it, ran to the river, was amazed by the summer-house, went into the summer-house; she had enough to see and wonder at in all she saw till her cousin Sylvie was up. During breakfast Sylvie said to her:

"So it was you, little bird, who were trotting up and down stairs at daybreak, and making such a noise? You woke me so completely that I could not get to sleep again. You must be very quiet, very good, and learn to play without making a sound. Your cousin does not like noise."

"And you must take care about your feet," said Rogron. "You went into the summer-house with muddy shoes, and left your footsteps printed on the floor. Your cousin likes everything to be clean. A great girl like you ought to be cleanly. Were you not taught to be clean in Brittany? To be sure, when I went there to buy flax it was dreadful to see what savages they were!—She has a fine appetite at any rate," said Rogron, turning to his sister; "you might think she had not seen food these three days."

And so, from the very first, Pierrette felt hurt by her cousins' remarks, hurt without knowing why. Her frank and upright nature, hitherto left to itself, had never been used to reflect; incapable, therefore, of understanding wherein her cousins were wrong, she was doomed to tardy enlightenment through suffering.

After breakfast, the couple, delighted by Pierrette's astonishment, and eager to enjoy it, showed her their fine drawing room, to teach her to respect its splendour. Unmarried people as a result of their isolation, and prompted by the craving for something to interest them, are led to supply the place of natural affections by artificial affections—the love of dogs, cats, or canary birds, of their servant or their spiritual director. Thus Rogron and Sylvie had an immoderate affection for the house and furniture that had cost them so much. Sylvie had taken to helping Adèle every morning, being of opinion that the woman did not know how to wipe furniture, to brush it, and make it look like new. This cleaning was soon her constant occupation. Thus, far from diminishing in value, the furniture was improved. Then the problem was to use it without wearing it out, without staining it, without scratching the wood or chilling the polish. This idea ere long became an old maid's monomania. Sylvie kept in a closet woollen rags, wax, varnish, and brushes; she learned to use them as skillfully as a polisher; she had feather brooms and dusters, and she could rub without fear of hurting herself, she was so strong! Her clear, blue eye, as cold and hard as steel, constantly peered under the furniture, and you were more likely to find a tender chord in her heart than a speck of flue under a chair.

After what had passed at Madame Tiphaine's, Sylvie could not possibly shirk the outlay of three hundred francs. During the first week Sylvie was wholly occupied, and Pierrette constantly amused, by the frocks to be ordered and tried on, the shifts and petticoats to be cut out and made by needle-women working by the day. Pierrette did not know how to sew.

"She has been nicely brought up!" cried Rogron. "Do you know nothing, child?"

Pierrette, who only knew how to love, answered but by a pretty childish shrug.

"What did you do all day in Brittany?" asked Rogron.

"I played," she replied guilelessly. "Everybody played with me. Grandmamma and grandpapa—and everybody told me stories. Oh! they were very fond of me."

"Indeed!" replied Rogron, "and so you lived like a lady."

Pierrette did not understand this tradesman's wit. She opened her eyes wide.

"She is as stupid as a wooden stool," said Sylvie to Mademoiselle Borain, the best workwoman in Provins.

"So young!" said the needlewoman, looking at Pierrette, whose delicate little face looked up at her with a knowing expression.

Pierrette liked the workwoman better than her cousins; she put on pretty airs for them, watched them sewing, said quaint things—the flowers of childhood, such as Rogron and Sylvie had already silenced by fear, for they liked to impress all dependants with a wholesome alarm. The sewing-women were charmed with Pierrette. The outfit, however, was not achieved without some terrible interjections.

"That child will cost us the eyes in our heads!" said Sylvie to Rogron.

"Hold yourself up child, do. The deuce is in it! the clothes are for you, not for me," said she to Pierrette, when she was being measured or fitted.

"Come, let Mademoiselle Borain do her work; you won't pay her day's wages!" she exclaimed, seeing the child ask the head needlewoman to do something for her.

"Mademoiselle," asked Mademoiselle Borain, "must this seam be back-stitched?"

"Yes; make everything strongly; I do not want to have such a piece of work again in a hurry."

But it was the same with the little cousin as with the house. Pierrette was to be as well dressed as Madame Garceland's little girl. She had fashionable little boots of bronze kid, like the little Tiphaine girl. She had very fine cotton stockings, stays by the best maker, a frock of blue reps, a pretty cape lined with white silk, all in rivalry with young Madame Julliard's little girl. And the underclothes were as good as the outside show, Sylvie was so much afraid of the keen and scrutinising eye of the mothers of children. Pierrette had pretty shifts of fine calico. Mademoiselle Borain said that Madame the Sous-préfète's little girls wore cambric drawers with embroidery and frilling—the latest thing, in short; Pierrette had frilled drawers. A charming drawn bonnet was ordered for her of blue velvet lined with white satin, like the little Martener girl's. Thus Pierrette was the smartest little person in Provins. On Sunday, on coming out from church, all the ladies kissed her. Mesdames Tiphaine, Garceland, Galardon, Auffray, Lesourd, Martener, Guépin, and Julliard doted on the sweet little Bretonne. This excitement flattered old Sylvie's vanity, and in her lavishness she thought less of Pierrette than of gratified pride.

However, Sylvie was fated to find offence in her little cousin's success, and this was how it came about. Pierrette was asked out, and, still to triumph over her neighbours, Sylvie allowed her to go. Pierrette was called for to play games and have dolls' dinner-parties with these ladies' children. Pierrette was a much greater success than the Rogrons; Mademoiselle Sylvie was aggrieved that Pierrette was in demand at other houses, but that no one came to see Pierrette at home. The artless child made no secret of her enjoyment at the houses of the Tiphaines, the Marteners, the Galardons, the Julliards, the Lesourds, the Auffrays, and the Garcelands, whose kindness contrasted strangely with the vexatiousness of her cousins. A mother would have been glad of her child's happiness; but the Rogrons had taken Pierrette to please themselves, not to please her; their feelings, far from being paternal, were tainted with egoism and a sort of commercial interest.

The beautiful outfit, the fine Sunday clothes, and the everyday frocks began Pierrette's misfortunes. Like all children free to amuse themselves and accustomed to follow the dictates of fancy, she wore out her shoes, boots, and frocks with frightful rapidity, and, above all, her frilled drawers. A mother when she scolds her child thinks of the child only; she is only hard when driven to extremities, and when the child is in the wrong; but in this great clothes question, the cousins' money was the first consideration; that was the real point, and not Pierrette. Children have a dog-like instinct for discerning injustice in those who rule them; they feel without fail whether they are tolerated or loved. Innocent hearts are more alive to shades than to contrasts; a child that does not yet understand evil knows when you offend the sense of beauty bestowed on it by nature. The lessons that Pierrette brought upon herself as to the behaviour of a well-bred young lady, as to modesty and economy, were the corollary of this main idea—"Pierrette is ruining us."

These scoldings, which had a fatal issue for Pierrette, led the old couple back into the familiar commercial ruts from which their home-life at Provins had led them to wander, and in which their nature could expand and blossom. After being used to domineer, to make remarks, to give orders, to scold their clerks sharply, Rogron and his sister were perishing for lack of victims. Small natures require despotism to exercise their sinews, as great souls thirst for equality to give play to their heart. Now narrow minds can develop as well through persecution as through benevolence; they can assure themselves of their power by tyrannising cruelly or beneficently over others; they go the way their nature guides them. Add to this the guidance of interest, and you will have the key to most social riddles. Pierrette now became very necessary to her cousins' existence. Since her arrival the Rogrons had been absorbed in her outfit, and then attracted by the novelty of companionship. Every new thing, a feeling, or even a tyranny, must form its set, its creases. Sylvie began by calling Pierrette "my child;" she gave up "my child" for "Pierrette" unqualified. Her reproofs, at first sourly gentle, became hard and sharp. As soon as they had started on this road, the brother and sister made rapid progress. They were no longer dull. It was not a deliberate scheme of malice and cruelty; it was the instinct of unreasoning tyranny. They believed that they were doing good to Pierrette, as of old to their apprentices.

Pierrette, whose sensitiveness was genuine, noble, and overstrung, the very antipodes of the Rogrons' aridity, had a horror of being blamed; it struck her so cruelly that tears rose at once to her large, clear eyes. She had a hard struggle to suppress her engaging liveliness, which charmed every one out of the house. She might indulge it before the mothers of her little friends; but at home, by the end of the first month she began to sit silent, and Rogron asked her if she were ill. At this strange question she flew off to the bottom of the garden to cry by the river, into which her tears fell, as she was one day to fall in the torrent of society.

One day, in spite of her care, the little girl tore her best reps frock at Madame Tiphaine's, where she had gone to play one fine day. She at once burst into tears, foreseeing the scolding that awaited her at home. On being questioned, she let fall a few words about her terrible cousin Sylvie in the midst of her tears. Pretty Madame Tiphaine had some stuff to match, and she herself put in a new front breadth. Mademoiselle Rogron heard of the trick, as she called it, played on her by that limb of a little girl. From that day she would never let Pierrette visit any of the ladies.

The new life which Pierrette was to lead at Provins was fated to fall into three very distinct phases. The first lasted three months, during which she enjoyed a kind of happiness, divided between the old people's cold caresses, and the scoldings, which she found scorching. The prohibition that kept her from seeing her little friends, emphasizing the necessity for beginning to learn everything that a well-brought-up girl should know, put an end to the first phase of Pierrette's life at Provins, the only period when she found existence endurable.

The domestic changes produced at the Rogrons' house by Pierrette's residence there were studied by Vinet and the Colonel with the cunning of a fox bent on getting into a fowl-house, and uneasy at discovering a new creature on the scene. They both paid calls at long intervals, so as not to scare Mademoiselle Sylvie; they found various excuses for chatting with Rogron, and made themselves masters of the situation with an air of reserve and dignity that the great Tartufe might have admired. The Colonel and the lawyer spent at the Rogrons' the evening of the very day when Sylvie had refused, in very harsh terms, to let Pierrette go to Madame Tiphaine's. On hearing of her refusal, the Colonel and the lawyer looked at each other as folks who know their Provins.

"She positively tried to make a fool of you?" said the lawyer "We warned Rogron long ago of what has now happened. There is no good to be got out of those people."

"What can you expect of the Anti-national Party?" cried the Colonel, curling up his moustache and interrupting Vinet. "If we had tried to get you away from them, you might have thought that we had some malicious motive for speaking to you so. But why, mademoiselle, if you are fond of a little game, should you not play boston in the evenings at home in your own house? Is it impossible to find any one in the place of such idiots as the Julliards? Vinet and I play boston; we will find a fourth. Vinet might introduce his wife to you; she is very nice, and she is one of the Chargebœufs. You will not be like those apes in the upper town; you will not expect a good little housewife, who is compelled by her family's disgraceful conduct to do all her own house work, to dress like a Duchess,—and she has the courage of a lion and the gentleness of a lamb."

Sylvie Rogron displayed her long yellow teeth in a smile at the Colonel, who endured the horrible phenomenon very well, and even assumed a flattering air.

"If there are but four of us, we cannot play boston every evening," replied she.

'Why, where else have I to go—an old soldier like me, who has nothing to do, and lives on his pensions? The lawyer is free every evening. Besides, you will have company, I promise you," he added, with a mysterious air.

"You have only to declare yourselves frankly opposed to the Ministerial party in Provins, and hold your own against them," said Vinet. "You would see how popular you would be in Provins; you would have a great many people on your side. You would make the Tiphaines furious by having an Opposition salon. Well, then, let us laugh at others, if others laugh at us. The 'clique' do not spare you, I can tell you."

"What do they say?" asked Sylvie.

In country towns there is always more than one safety-valve by which gossip finds a vent from one set into another. Vinet had heard all that had been said about the Rogrons in the drawing-rooms from which the haberdashers had been definitively banished. The supernumerary judge Desfondrilles, the archæologist was of neither party. This man, like some other independent members of society, repeated everything he heard, out of provincial habit, and Vinet had had the benefit of his chit-chat. The malicious lawyer repeated Madame Tiphaine's pleasantries, with added venom. As he revealed the practical jokes of which Sylvie and Rogron had been the unconscious victims, he stirred the rage and aroused the revengeful spirit of these two arid souls, craving some aliment for their mean passions.

A few days later Vinet brought his wife, a well-bred woman, shy, neither plain nor pretty, very meek, and very conscious of her misfortune. Madame Vinet was fair, rather worn by the cares of her penurious housekeeping, and very simply dressed. No woman could have better pleased Sylvie. Madame Vinet put up with Sylvie's airs, and gave way to her like a woman accustomed to give way. On her round forehead, her rose-pink cheeks, in her slow, gentle eyes, there were traces of those deep reflections, that clear-sighted thoughtfulness, which women who are used to suffering bury under perfect silence. The influence of the Colonel, displaying for Sylvie's behoof *courtieresque* graces that seemed wrung from his soldierly roughness, with that of the wily Vinet, soon made itself felt by Pierrette. The child, the pretty squirrel, shut up in the house, or going out only with old Sylvie, was every instant checked by a "Don't touch that, Pierrette!" and by incessant sermons on holding herself up. Pierrette stooped and held her shoulders high; her cousin wanted her to be as straight as herself, and she was like a soldier presenting arms to his Colonel; she would sometimes give her little slaps on her back to make her hold herself up. The free and light-hearted child of the Marais learned to measure her movements and imitate an automaton.

One evening, which marked the beginning of the second period, Pierrette, whom the three visitors had not seen in the drawing-room during the evening, came to kiss her cousins and courtesy to the company before going to bed. Sylvia coldly offered her cheek to the pretty little thing, as if to be kissed and have done with it. The action was so cruelly significant that tears started from Pierrette's eyes.

"Have you pricked yourself, my little Pierrette?" said the abominable Vinet.

"What is the matter with you?" asked Sylvie severely.

"Nothing," said the poor child, going to kiss Rogron.

"Nothing?" repeated Sylvie. "You cannot be crying for nothing!"

"What is it, my little pet?" said Madame Vinet.

"My rich cousin Sylvie does not treat me so well as my poor grandmother!"

"Your grandmother stole your money," said Sylvie, "and your cousin will leave you hers."

The Colonel and Vinet exchanged covert glances.

"I would rather be robbed and loved," said Pierrette.

"Very well, you shall be sent back to the place you came from."

"But what has the dear child done?" asked Madame Vinet.

Vinet fixed his eye on his wife, with that terrible cold, fixed stare that belongs to those who rule despotically. The poor lonely woman, unceasingly punished for not having the one thing required of her—namely, a fortune—took up her cards again.

"What has she done?" cried Sylvie, raising her head with a jerk so sudden, that the yellow wall-flowers in her cap were shaken. "She does not know what to do next to annoy us. She opened my watch to examine the works, and touched the wheel, and broke the mainspring. Madam listens to nothing. All day long I am telling her to take care: what she is about, and I might as well talk to the lamp."

Pierrette, ashamed of being reprimanded in the presence of strangers, went out of the room very gently.

"I cannot think how to quell that child's turbulence," said Rogron.

"Why, she is old enough to go to school," said Madame Vinet.

Another look from Vinet silenced his wife, to whom he had been careful not to confide his plans and the Colonel's with regard to the bachelor couple.

"That is what comes of taking charge of other people's children," cried Gouraud. "You might have some of your own yet, you or your brother; why do you not both marry?"

Sylvie looked very sweetly at the Colonel; for the first time in her life she beheld a man to whom the idea that she might marry did not seem absurd.

"Madame Vinet is right!" cried Rogron, "that would keep Pierrette quiet. A master would not cost much."

The Colonel's speech so entirely occupied Sylvie that she did not answer her brother.

"If only you would stand the money for the Opposition paper we were talking about, you might find a tutor for your little cousin in the responsible editor. We could get that poor schoolmaster who was victimized by the encroachments of the priests. My wife is right; Pierrette is a rough diamond that needs polishing," said Vinet to Rogron.

"I fancied that you were a Baron," said Sylvie to the Colonel, after a long pause, while each player seemed meditative.

"Yes. But having won the title in 1814, after the battle of Nangis, where my regiment did wonders, how could I find the money or the assistance needed to get it duly registered? The barony, like the rank of general, which I won in 1815, must wait for a revolution to secure them to me."

"If you could give a mortgage as your guarantee for the money," said Rogron presently, "I could do it."

"That could be arranged with Cournant," replied Vinet. "The newspaper would lead to the Colonel's triumph, and make your drawing-room more powerful than those of Tiphaine and Co."

"How is that?" asked Sylvie.

At this moment, while Madame Vinet was dealing, and the lawyer explaining all the importance that the publication of an independent paper for the district of Provins must confer on Rogron, the Colonel, and himself, Pierrette was bathed in tears. Her heart and brain were agreed; she thought Sylvie far more to blame than herself. The little Bretonne instinctively perceived how unfailing charity and benevolence should be. She hated her fine frocks and all that was done for her. She paid too dear for these benefits. She cried with rage at having given her cousins a hold over her, and determined to behave in such a way as to reduce them to silence, poor child! Then she saw how noble Brigaut had been to give her his savings. She thought her woes had reached a climax, not knowing that at that moment new misfortunes were being plotted in the drawing-room.

A few days later Pierrette had a writing-master. She was to learn to read, write, and do sums. Pierrette's education involved the house of Rogron in fearful disaster. There was ink on the tables, on the furniture, and on her clothes; writing-books and pens strewn everywhere, powder on the upholstery, books torn and dog-eared while she was learning her lessons. They already spoke to her—and in what a way!—of the necessity for earning her living and being a burden on no one. As she heard these dreadful warnings, Pierrette felt a burning in her throat; she was choking, her heart beat painfully fast. She was obliged to swallow down her tears; for each one was reckoned with as an offence against her magnanimous relations. Rogron had found the occupation that suited him. He scolded Pierrette as he had formerly scolded his shopmen; he would fetch her in from the midst of her play to compel her to study; he heard her repeat her lessons; he was the poor child's fierce tutor. Sylvie, on her part, thought it her duty to teach Pierrette the little she knew of womanly accomplishments.

Neither Rogron nor his sister had any gentleness of nature. These narrow souls, finding a real pleasure in bullying the poor little thing, changed unconsciously from mildness to the greatest severity. This severity was, they said, the consequence of the child's obstinacy; she had begun too late to learn, and was dull of apprehension. Her teachers did not understand the art of giving lessons in a form suited to the pupil's intelligence, which is what should distinguish private from public education. The fault lay far less with Pierrette than with her cousins. It took her an immensely long time to learn the beginnings. For the merest trifle she was called stupid and silly, foolish and awkward. Incessantly ill-used by hard words, Pierrette never met any but cold looks from the two old people. She fell into the stolid dullness of a sheep; she dared do nothing when she found her actions misjudged, misunderstood, misinterpreted. In everything she awaited Sylvie's orders, and the expression of her cousin's will, keeping her thoughts to herself and shutting herself up in passive obedience. Her bright colour began to fade. Sometimes she complained of aches and pains. When Sylvie asked her, Where? the poor child, who felt generally ailing, replied, "All over."

"Was ever such a thing heard of as aching all over? If you were ill all over, you would be dead!" retorted Sylvie.

"You may have a pain in your chest," said Rogron the expositor, "or in your teeth, or your head, or your feet, or your stomach, but no one ever had pains everywhere. What do you mean by 'all over?' Pain all over is pain nowhere. Do you know what you are doing? You are talking for talking's sake."

Pierrette at last never spoke, finding that her artless girlish remarks, the flowers of her opening mind, were met with commonplace retorts which her good sense told her were ridiculous.

"You are always complaining, and you eat like a fasting friar!" said Rogron.

The only person who never distressed this sweet fragile flower was the sturdy servant Adèle. Adèle always warmed the little girl's bed, but in secret, since one evening when, being discovered in the act of thus "spoiling" her master's heiress, she was scolded by Sylvie.

"Children must be hardened; that is the way to give them strong constitutions. Have we been any the worse for it, my brother and I?" said Sylvie. "You will make Pierrette a peeky coddle!"—*une picheline*, a word of the Rogron vocabulary to designate weakly and complaining persons.

The little angel's caressing expressions were regarded as mere acting. The roses of affection that budded so fresh and lovely in this young soul, and longed to open to the day, were mercilessly crushed. Pierrette felt the hardest blows on the tenderest spots of her heart. If she tried to soften these two savage natures by her pretty ways, she was accused of expressing her tenderness out of self-interest. "Tell me plainly what you want," Rogron would exclaim roughly; "you are certainly not coaxing me for nothing."

Neither the sister nor the brother recognised affection, and Pierrette was all affection.

Colonel Gouraud, anxious to please Mademoiselle Rogron, declared her right in all that concerned Pierrette. Vinet no less supported the old cousins in their abuse of Pierrette; he ascribed all the reported misdeeds of this angel to the obstinacy of the Breton character, and said that no power, no strength of will, could ever conquer it. Rogron and his sister were flattered with the utmost skill by these two courtiers, who had at last succeeded in extracting from Rogron the surety money for the newspaper, the *Provins Courrier,* and from Sylvie five thousand francs, as a shareholder. The Colonel and Vinet now took the field. They disposed of a hundred shares at five hundred francs each to the electors who held State securities, and whom the Liberal journals filled with alarms, to farmers, and to persons who were called independent. They even extended their ramifications over the whole department, and beyond it, to some adjacent townships. Each shareholder subscribed for the paper, of course. Then the legal and other advertisements were divided between the *Ruche* and the *Courrier.* The first number contained a grandiloquent column in praise of Rogron, who was represented as the Laffitte of Provins.

As soon as the public mind found a leader, it became easy to perceive that the coming elections would be hotly contested. Madame Tiphaine was in despair.

"Unfortunately," said she, as she read an article attacking her and Monsieur Julliard, "unfortunately, I forgot that there is always a rogue not far away from a dupe, and that folly always attracts a clever man of the fox species."

As soon as the newspaper was to be seen for twenty leagues round, Vinet had a new coat and boots, and a decent waistcoat and trousers. He displayed the famous white hat affected by Liberals, and showed his collar and cuffs. His wife engaged a servant, and appeared dressed as became the wife of an influential man; she wore pretty caps.

Vinet, out of self-interest, was grateful. He and his friend Cournant, notary to the Liberal side, and Auffray's opponent, became the Rogrons' advisers, and did them two great services. The leases granted by old Rogron their father, in 1815, under unfortunate circumstances, were about to fall in. Horticulture and market-gardening had lately developed enormously in the Provins district. The pleader and the notary made it their business to effect an increase of fourteen hundred francs a year on granting the new leases. Vinet also won for them two lawsuits against two villages, relating to plantations of trees, in which the loss of five hundred poplars was involved. The money for the poplars, with the Rogrons' savings, which for the last three years had amounted to six thousand francs deposited at compound interest, was skilfully laid out in the purchase of several plots of land. Finally, Vinet proposed and carried out the eviction of certain peasant proprietors, to whom Rogron the elder had lent money, and who had killed themselves with cultivating and manuring their land to enable them to repay it, but in vain.

Thus the damage done to the Rogrons' capital by the reconstruction of their house was to a great extent remedied. Their estates in the immediate neighbourhood of the town, chosen by their father as innkeepers know how to choose, cut up into small holdings of which the largest was less than five acres, and let to perfectly solvent tenants, themselves owners of some plots of land mortgaged to secure the farm rents, brought in at Martinmas, in November 1826, five thousand francs. The taxes were paid by the tenants, and there were no buildings to repair or insure against fire.

The brother and sister each possessed four thousand six hundred francs in the five per cents; and as their selling value was above par, Vinet exhorted them to invest the money in land, promising them—seconded by the notary—that they should not lose a farthing of interest by the transfer.

By the end of this second period life was so intolerable to Pierrette—the indifference of all about her, the senseless fault finding and lack of affection in her cousins became so virulent, she felt so plainly the cold chill of the tomb blowing upon her, that she entertained the daring project of going away, on foot, with no money, to Brittany to rejoin her grandfather and grandmother. Two events prevented this: Old Lorrain died, and Rogron was appointed Pierrette's guardian by a family council held at Provins. If her old grandmother had died first, it is probable that Rogron, advised by Vinet, would have called upon the grandfather to repay the child's eight thousand francs, and have reduced him to beggary.

"Why, you may inherit Pierrette's money," said Vinet with a hideous smile. "You can never tell who will live or who will die."

Enlightened by this speech, Rogron left the widow Lorrain no peace as Pierrette's debtor till he had made her secure to the little girl the capital of the eight thousand francs by a deed of gift, of which he paid the cost.

Pierrette was strangely affected by this loss. Just as the blow fell on her she was to be prepared for her first Communion, the other event which by its obligations tied her to Provins. This necessary and simple ceremony was to bring about great changes for the Rogrons. Sylvie learned that the curé, Monsieur Péroux, was instructing the little Julliards, the Lesourds, Garcelands, and others. She made it therefore a point of honour to put Pierrette under the guidance of the Abbé Péroux's superior, Monsieur Habert, a man who was said to belong to the Jesuit Congregation—very zealous for the interests of the Church, much dreaded in Provins, and hiding immense ambition under the strictest severity of principle. The priest's sister, an unmarried woman of about thirty, had a school for girls in the town. The brother and sister were much alike; both lean, sallow, atrabilious, with black hair.

Pierrette, a Bretonne nurtured in the practice and poetry of the Catholic faith, opened her heart and ears to the teaching of this imposing priest. Suffering predisposes the mind to devoutness; and most young girls, prompted by instinctive tenderness, lean towards mysticism, the obscurer side of religion. So the priest sowed the seed of the Gospel and the dogmas of the Church in good ground. He completely changed Pierrette's frame of mind. Pierrette loved Jesus Christ as presented to girls in the Sacrament, as a celestial bridegroom; her moral and physical sufferings now had their meaning; she was taught to see the hand of God in everything. Her soul, so cruelly stricken in this house, while she could not accuse her cousins, took refuge in the sphere whither fly all who are wretched, borne on the wings of the three Christian virtues. She gave up the idea of flight. Sylvie, amazed at the alteration produced in Pierrette by Monsieur Habert, became curious. And so, while preparing the child for her first Communion, Monsieur Habert won to God the hitherto wandering soul of Mademoiselle Sylvie. Sylvie became a bigot.

Denis Rogron, over whom the supposed Jesuit could get no hold—for at that time the spirit of his late lamented Majesty Constitution the First was in some simpletons supreme above that of the Church—Denis remained faithful to Colonel Gouraud, Vinet, and Liberalism.

Mademoiselle Rogron, of course, made acquaintance with Mademoiselle Habert, with whom she was in perfect sympathy. The two old maids loved each other like two loving sisters. Mademoiselle Habert proposed to take Pierrette under her care, and spare Sylvie the trouble and vexations of educating a child; but the brother and sister replied that Pierrette's absence would make the house feel too empty. The Rogrons' attachment to their little cousin seemed excessive.

On seeing Mademoiselle Habert in possession, Colonel Gouraud and Vinet ascribed to the ambitious priest, on his sister's behalf, the matrimonial scheme imagined by the Colonel.

"Your sister wants to see you married," said the lawyer to the ex-haberdasher.

"And to whom?" said Rogron.

"To that old sibyl of a schoolmistress," cried the Colonel, curling his moustache.

"She has said nothing to me about it," said Rogron blankly. A woman so determined as Sylvie was sure to make great progress in the ways of salvation. The priest's influence soon grew in the house, supported as it was by Sylvie, who managed her brother. The two Liberals, very legitimately alarmed, understood that if the priest had determined to get Rogron for his sister's husband—a far more suitable match than that of Sylvie and the Colonel—he would urge Sylvie to the excessive practice of religion, and make Pierrette go into a convent. They would thus lose the reward of eighteen months of efforts, meanness, and flattery. They took a terrible dumb hatred of the priest and his sister, and yet, if they were to keep up with them step for step they felt the necessity of remaining on good terms with them.

Monsieur and Mademoiselle Habert, who played both whist and boston, came every evening. Their assiduity excited that of the others. The lawyer and the soldier felt that they were pitted against adversaries stronger than themselves, a preconception which Monsieur Habert and his sister fully shared. This situation was in itself a battle. Just as the Colonel gave to Sylvie a foretaste of the unhoped-for joys of an offer of marriage—for she had brought herself to regard Gouraud as a man worthy of her—so Mademoiselle Habert wrapped the retired haberdasher in the cotton wool of her attentions, her speeches, and her looks. Neither party could say to itself the great word of great politicians, "Divide the spoil!" each insisted on the whole prize.

Besides, the two wily foxes of the opposition at Provins—an Opposition that was growing in strength—were rash enough to believe themselves stronger than the Priesthood; they were the first to fire. Vinet, whose gratitude was stirred up by the claw-fingers of self-interest, went to fetch Mademoiselle de Chargebœuf and her mother. The two women, who had about two thousand francs a year, lived very narrowly at Troyes. Mademoiselle Bathilde de Chargebœuf was one of those splendid women who believe in marrying for love, and change their minds towards their five-and-twentieth year on finding themselves still unwedded. Vinet succeeded in persuading Madame de Chargebœuf to combine her two thousand francs with the thousand crowns he was making now that the newspaper was started, and to come and live with him at Provins, where Bathilde, he said, might marry a simpleton named Rogron, and, so clever as she was, rival handsome Madame Tiphaine.

The reinforcement of Vinet's household and ideas by the arrival of Madame and Mademoiselle de Chargebœuf gave the utmost cohesion to the Liberal party. This coalition brought consternation to the aristocracy of Provins and the Tiphaine party. Madame de Bréautey, in dismay at seeing two women of family so misled, begged them to come to see her. She bewailed the blunders committed by the Royalists, and was furious with those of Troyes on learning the poverty of this mother and daughter.

"What! was there no old country gentleman who would marry that dear girl, born to rule a château?" cried she. "They had let her run to seed, and now she will throw herself at the head of a Rogron!"

She hunted the department through and failed to find one gentleman who would marry a girl whose mother had but two thousand francs a year. Then the "clique" of the Tiphaines and the Sous-préfet also set to work, but too late, to discover such a man. Madame de Bréautey inveighed loudly against the selfishness that was eating up France, the result of materialism and of the power conferred on money by the laws; the nobility was nothing in these days! Beauty was nothing! Rogrons and Vinets were defying the King of France!

Bathilde had the indisputable advantage over her rival not merely of beauty, but of dress. She was dazzlingly fair. At five-and-twenty her fully-developed shoulders and splendid modelling were exquisitely full. The roundness of her throat, the slenderness of her articulations, the splendour of her fine fair hair, the charm of her smile, the elegant shape of her head, the dignity and outline of her face, her fine eyes under a well-moulded brow, her calm and well-bred movements, and her still girlish figure, all were in harmony. She had a fine hand and a narrow foot.

Her robust health gave her, perhaps, the look of a handsome inn-servant; "but that should be no fault in Rogron's eyes," said pretty Madame Tiphaine.

The first time Mademoiselle de Chargebœuf was seen she was dressed simply enough. Her dress of brown merino, edged with green embroidery, was cut low; but a kerchief of tulle, neatly drawn down by invisible strings, covered her shoulders, back, and bust, a little open at the throat, though fastened by a brooch and chain. Under this fine network Bathilde's beauty was even more attractive, more suggestive. She took off her velvet bonnet and her shawl on entering, and showed pretty ears with gold eardrops. She had a little cross and heart on black velvet round her neck, which contrasted with its whiteness like the black that fantastic nature sets round the tail of a white Angora cat. She was expert in all the arts of girls on their promotion: twisting her fingers to arrange curls that are not out of place, displaying her wrists by begging Rogron to button her cuff, which the hapless man, quite dazzled, bluntly refused to do, hiding his agitation under assumed indifference. The bashfulness of the only passion our haberdasher was ever to know in his life always gave it the demeanor of hatred. Sylvie, as well as Céleste Habert, misunderstood it; not so the lawyer, the superior man of this company of simpletons, whose only enemy was the priest, for the Colonel had long been his ally.

Gouraud, on his part, thenceforth behaved to Sylvie as Bathilde did to Rogron. He appeared in clean linen every evening; he wore velvet collars, which gave effect to his martial countenance, set off by the corners of his white shirt collar; he adopted white drill waistcoats, and had a new frock-coat made of blue cloth, on which his red rosette was conspicuous, and all under pretence of doing honour to the fair Bathilde. He never smoked after two o'clock. His grizzled hair was brushed down in a wave over his ochre-colored skull. In short, he assumed the appearance and attitude of a party chief, of a man who was prepared to rout the enemies of France—in one word, the Bourbons—with tuck of drum.

The satanical pleader and the cunning Colonel played a still more cruel trick on Monsieur and Mademoiselle Habert than that of introducing the beautiful Mademoiselle de Chargebœuf, who was pronounced by the Liberal party and by the Bréauteys to be ten times handsomer than the beautiful Madame Tiphaine. These two great country-town politicians had it rumoured from one to another that Monsieur Habert agreed with them on all points. Provins before long spoke of him as a "Liberal priest." Called up before the Bishop, Monsieur Habert was obliged to give up his evenings with the Rogrons, but his sister still went there. Thence forth the Rogron drawing-room was a fact and a power.

And so, by the middle of that year, political intrigues were not less eager than matrimonial intrigues in the Rogrons' rooms. While covert interests, buried out of sight, were fighting wildly for the upper hand, the public struggle won disastrous notoriety. Everybody knows that the Villèle ministry was overthrown by the elections of 1826. In the Provins constituency, Vinet, the Liberal candidate—for whom Monsieur Cournant had obtained his qualification by the purchase of some land of which the price remained unpaid—came very near beating Monsieur Tiphaine. The President had a majority of only two.

Mesdames Vinet and de Chargebœuf, Vinet and the Colonel, were sometimes joined by Monsieur Cournant and his wife; then by Néraud the doctor, a man whose youth had been very "stormy," but who now took serious views of life; he had devoted himself to science, it was said, and if the Liberals were to be believed, was a far cleverer man than Monsieur Martener. To the Rogrons their triumph was as inexplicable as their ostracism had been.

The handsome Bathilde de Chargebœuf, to whom Vinet spoke of Pierrette as an enemy, was horribly disdainful to the child. The humiliation of this poor victim was necessary to the interest of all. Madame Vinet could do nothing for the little girl who was being brayed in the mortar of the pitiless egotisms which the lady at last understood. But for her husband's imperative desire she would never have come to the Rogrons; it grieved her too much to see their ill-usage of the pretty little thing who clung to her, understanding her secret good-will, and begged her to teach her such or such a stitch or embroidery pattern. Pierrette had shown that when she was thus treated she understood and succeeded to admiration. But Madame Vinet was no longer of any use, so she came no more.

Sylvie, who still cherished the notion of marriage, now regarded Pierrette as an obstacle. Pierrette was nearly fourteen; her sickly fairness, a symptom that was quite overlooked by the ignorant old maid, made her lovely. Then Sylvie had the bright idea of indemnifying herself for the expenses caused by Pierrette by making a servant of her. Vinet, as representing the interests of the Chargebœufs, Mademoiselle Habert, Gouraud, all the influential visitors, advised Sylvie by all means to dismiss Adèle. Could not Pierrette cook and keep the house in order? When there was too much to be done, she need only engage the Colonel's housekeeper, a very accomplished person, and one of the best cooks in Provins. Pierrette ought to learn to cook and to polish the floors, said the baleful lawyer, to sweep, keep the house neat, go to market, and know the price of things. The poor little girl, whose unselfishness was as great as her generosity, offered it herself, glad to pay thus for the hard bread she ate under that roof.

Adèle went. Thus Pierrette lost the only person who might perhaps have protected her. Strong as she was, from that hour she was crushed body and soul. The old people had less mercy on her than on a servant: she was their property! She was scolded for mere nothings, for a little dust left on the corner of a chimney-shelf or a glass shade. These objects of luxury that she had so much admired became odious to her. In spite of her anxiety to do right, her relentless cousin Sylvie always found some fault with everything she did. In two years Pierrette never heard a word of praise or of affection. Her whole happiness consisted in not being scolded. She submitted with angelic patience to the dark moods of these two unmarried beings, to whom the gentler feelings were all unknown, and who made her suffer every day from her dependency. This life in which the young girl was gripped, as it were, between the two haberdashers as in the jaws of a vice, increased her malady. She had such violent fits of inexplicable distress, such sudden bursts of secret grief, that her physical development was irremediably checked. And thus, by slow degrees, through terrible though concealed sufferings, Pierrette had come to the state in which the friend of her childhood had seen her as he stood on the little Square and greeted her with his Breton ballad.

Before entering on the story of the domestic drama in the Rogrons' house, to which Brigaut's arrival gave rise, it will be necessary, to avoid digressions, to account for the lad's settling at Provins, since he is in some sort a silent personage on the stage.

Brigaut, as he fled, was alarmed not merely by Pierrette's signal, but also by the change in his little friend; hardly could he recognise her, but for the voice, eyes, and movements which recalled his lively little playfellow, at once so gay and so loving. When he had got far away from the house, his legs quaked under him, his spine felt on fire! He had seen the shadow of Pierrette, and not Pierrette herself. He made his way up to the old town, thoughtful and uneasy, till he found a spot whence he could see the Place and the house where Pierrette lived; he gazed at it sadly, lost in thought as in finite as the troubles into which we plunge without knowing where they may end. Pierrette was ill; she was unhappy; she regretted Brittany! What ailed her? All these questions passed again and again through Brigaut's mind, and racked his breast, revealing to him the extent of his affection for his little adopted sister.

It is very rarely that a passion between two children of different sexes remains permanent. The charming romance of Paul and Virginia no more solves the problem of this strange moral fact than does that of Brigaut and Pierrette. Modern history offers the single illustrious exception of the sublime Marchesa di Pescara and her husband, who, destined for each other by their parents at the age of fourteen, adored each other, and were married. Their union gave to the sixteenth century the spectacle of boundless conjugal affection, never clouded. The Marchesa, a widow at four-and-thirty, beautiful, witty, universally beloved, refused monarchs, and buried herself in a convent, where she never saw, never heard, any one but nuns.

Such perfect love as this blossomed suddenly in the heart of the poor Breton artisan. Pierrette and he had so often been each other's protectors, he had been so happy in giving her the money for her journey, he had almost died of running after the diligence, and Pierrette had not known it! The memory of it had often warmed him during the chill hours of his toilsome life these three years past. He had improved himself for Pierrette; he had learned his craft for Pierrette; he had come to Paris for Pierrette, intending to make a fortune for her. After being there a fortnight, he could no longer control his longing to see her; he had walked from Saturday evening till Monday morning. He had intended to return to Paris, but the pathetic appearance of his little friend held him fast to Provins. A wonderful magnetism disputed, it is true, in spite of so many instances—acted on him without his knowing it; and tears filled his eyes, while they also dimmed Pierrette's sight. If to her he was Brittany and all her happy childhood, to him Pierrette was life! At sixteen Brigaut had not yet learned to draw or give the section of a moulding; there were many things he did not know; but at piecework he had earned from four to five francs a day. So he could live at Provins; he would be within reach of Pierrette; he would finish learning his business by working under the best cabinetmaker in the town, and watch over the little girl.

Brigaut made up his mind at once. He flew back to Paris, settled his accounts, collected his pass, his luggage, and his tools. Three days later he was working for Monsieur Frappier, the best carpenter in Provins. Energetic workmen, steady, and averse to turbulency and taverns, are rare enough to make a master glad to get a young fellow like Brigaut. To conclude his story on that score, by the end of a fortnight he was foreman, lodging and boarding with Frappier, who taught him arithmetic and linear drawing. The carpenter lived in the High Street, about a hundred yards from the little oblong Place, at the end of which stood the Rogrons' house.

Brigaut buried his love in his heart, and was not guilty of the smallest indiscretion. He got Madame Frappier to tell him the history of the Rogrons;

from her he learned how the old innkeeper had set to work to get the money left by old Auffray. Brigaut was fully informed as to the character of the haberdasher and his sister. One morning he met Pierrette at market with Mademoiselle Sylvie, and shuddered to see her with a basket on her arm full of provisions. He went to see Pierrette again at church on Sunday, where the girl appeared in all her best; there, for the first time, Brigaut understood that Pierrette was Mademoiselle Lorrain.

Pierrette saw her friend, but she made him a mysterious signal to keep himself out of sight. There was a world of meaning in this gesture, as in that by which, a fortnight since, she had bidden him vanish. What a fortune he would have to make in ten years to enable him to marry the companion of his childhood, to whom the Rogrons would leave a house, a hundred acres of land, and twelve thousand francs a year, not to mention their savings! The persevering Breton would not tempt fortune till he had acquired the knowledge he still lacked. So long as it was theory alone, it was all the same whether he learned in Paris or at Provins, and he preferred to remain near Pierrette, to whom he also purposed to explain his plans and the sort of help she might count on. Finally, he would certainly not leave her till he understood the secret of the pallor which had already dimmed the life of the feature which generally retains it longest the eyes; till he knew what caused the sufferings that gave her the look of a girl bowing before the scythe of Death, and about to be cut down.

Her two pathetic signals, which were not false to their friendship, but which enjoined the greatest caution, struck terror into the lad's heart. Evidently Pierrette desired him to wait, and not to try to see her, or there would be danger and peril for her. As she came out of church she gave him a look, and Brigaut saw that her eyes were full of tears. The Breton would more easily have squared the circle than have guessed what had happened in the Rogrons' house since his arrival.

It was not without lively apprehensions that Pierrette came down from her room that day when Brigaut had plunged into her morning dream like another dream. Having risen and opened her window, Mademoiselle Rogron must have heard the song and its words—compromising, no doubt, in the ears of an old maid; but Pierrette knew nothing of the causes that made her cousin so alert. Sylvie had good reasons for getting up and running to the window. For about a week past strange secret events and cruel pangs of feeling had agitated the principal figures in the Rogron salon. These unknown events, carefully concealed by all concerned, were to fall on Pierrette like an icy avalanche.

The realm of mysteries, which ought perhaps to be called the foul places of the human heart, lies at the bottom of the greatest revolutions, political, social, or domestic; but in speaking of them it may be extremely useful to explain that their algebraical expression, though accurate, is not faithful so far as form is concerned. These deep calculations do not express themselves so brutally as history reports them. Any attempt to relate the circumlocutions, the rhetorical involutions, the long colloquies, in which the mind designedly darkens the light it casts, the honeyed words diluting the venom of certain insinuations, would mean writing a book as long as the noble poem called *Clarissa Harlowe.*

Mademoiselle Habert and Mademoiselle Rogron were equally desirous of marrying; but one was ten years younger than the other, and probability allowed Céleste Habert to think that her children would inherit the Rogrons' whole fortune. Sylvie was almost forty-two, an age at which marriage has its risks. In confiding their ideas to each other to secure mutual approbation, Céleste Habert, on a hint from the vindictive Abbé, had enlightened Sylvie as to the possibilities of the position. The Colonel, a violent man, with the health of a soldier, a burly bachelor of forty-five, would no doubt act on the moral of all fairy tales: they lived happy, and had many children. This form of happiness alarmed Sylvie; she was afraid of dying—a fear which tortures unmarried women to the utmost.

But the Martignac ministry was now established—the second victory which upset the Villèle administration. Vinet's party held their head high in Provins. Vinet, now the leading advocate of la Brie, carried all before him, to use a colloquialism. Vinet was a personage; the Liberals prophesied his advancement; he would certainly be a deputy or public prosecutor. As to the Colonel, he would be Mayor of Provins. Oh! to reign as Madame Garceland reigned, to be the Mayoress! Sylvie could not resist this hope; she determined to consult a doctor, though it might cover her with ridicule. The two women, one triumphant, and the other sure of having her in leading-strings, invented one of those stratagems which women advised by a priest, are so clever in planning. To consult Monsieur Néraud, the Liberal physician, Monsieur Martener's rival, would be a blunder. Céleste Habert proposed to Sylvie to hide her in a dressing-closet while she, Mademoiselle Habert, consulted Monsieur Martener, who attended the school, on her own account. Whether he were Céleste's accomplice or no, Martener told his client that there was some, though very little, danger for a woman of thirty. "But with your constitution," he added, "you have nothing to fear."

"And if a woman is past forty?" asked Mademoiselle Céleste Habert.

"A woman of forty who has been married and had children need fear nothing."

"But an unmarried woman, perfectly well conducted—for example, Mademoiselle Rogron?"

"Well conducted! There can be no doubt," said Monsieur Martener. "In such a case the safe birth of a child is a miracle which God certainly works sometimes, but rarely."

"And why?" asked Céleste Habert.

Whereupon the doctor replied in a terrific pathological description, explaining that the elasticity bestowed by Nature on the muscles and joints in youth ceased to exist at a certain age, particularly in women whose occupations had made them sedentary for some years, like Mademoiselle Rogron.

"And so, after forty no respectable woman ought to marry?"

"Or she should wait," replied the doctor. "But then it is hardly a marriage; it is a partnership. What else could it be?"

In short, it was proved by this consultation, clearly, scientifically, seriously, and rationally, that after the age of forty a virtuous maiden should not rush into matrimony.

When Monsieur Martener had left, Mademoiselle Céleste Habert found Mademoiselle Rogron green and yellow, her eyes dilated,—in fact, in a frightful state.

"Then you truly love the Colonel?" said she.

"I still hoped," said the old maid.

"Well, then, wait," said Mademoiselle Habert, who knew that time would be avenged on the Colonel.

The morality of this marriage was also doubtful. Sylvie went to sound her conscience in the confessional. The stern director expounded the views of the Church, which regards marriage only as a means of propagating the race, reprobates second marriages, and scorns passions that have no social aim. Sylvie Rogron's perplexity was great. These mental struggles gave strange force to her passion, and lent it the unaccountable charm which forbidden joys have always had for women since the time of Eve.

Mademoiselle Rogron's disturbed state could not escape the lawyer's keen eye. One evening, after cards, Vinet went up to his dear friend Sylvie, took her hand, and led her to sit down with him on one of the sofas.

"Something ails you," he said in her ear.

She gloomily bent her head. The pleader let Rogron leave the room, sat alone with the old maid, and got her to make a clean breast of it.

"Well played, Abbé! But you have played my game for me," he said to himself after hearing of all the private consultations Sylvie had held, of which the last was the most alarming.

This sly legal fox was even more terrible in his explanations than the doctor had been; he advised the marriage, but only ten years hence for greater safety. The lawyer vowed that all the Rogron fortune should be Bathilde's. He rubbed his hands, and his very face grew sharper as he ran after Madame and Mademoiselle de Chargebœuf, whom he had left to start homewards with their servant armed with a lantern.

The influence exerted by Monsieur Habert, the physician of the soul, was entirely counteracted by Vinet, the physician of the purse. Rogron was by no means devout, so the man of the Church and the man of the Law, the two black gowns, pulled him opposite ways. When he heard of the victory carried off by Mademoiselle Habert, who hoped to marry Rogron, over Sylvie, hanging between the fear of death and the joy of becoming a baroness, Vinet perceived the possibility of removing the Colonel from the scene of battle. He knew Rogron well enough to find some means of making him marry the fair Bathilde. Rogron had not been able to resist the blandishments of Mademoiselle de Chargebœuf; Vinet knew that the first time Rogron should be alone with Bathilde and himself their engagement would be settled. Rogron had come to the point of staring at Mademoiselle Habert, so shy was he of looking at Bathilde.

Vinet had just seen how much Sylvie was in love with the Colonel. He understood the depth of such a passion in an old maid, no less eaten up by bigotry, and he soon hit on a plan for ruining at one blow both Pierrette and the Colonel, getting rid of one by means of the other.

Next morning, on coming out of Court, he met the Colonel and Rogron walking together, their daily habit.

When these three men were seen together, their conjunction always made the town talk. This triumvirate, held in horror by the Sous-préfet, the Bench, and the Tiphaine partisans, made a triad of which the Liberals of Provins were proud. Vinet edited the *Courrier* single-handed; he was the head of the party; the Colonel, the responsible manager of the paper, was its arm; Rogron, with his money, formed the sinews; he was considered as the link between the managing committee at Provins and the managing committee in Paris. To hear the Tiphaines, these three men were always plotting something against the Government, while the Liberals admired them as defenders of the people. When the lawyer saw Rogron returning to the Square, brought homewards by the dinner-hour, he took the Colonel's arm and hindered him from accompanying the ex-haberdasher.

"Look here, Colonel," said he, "I am going to take a great weight off your shoulders. You can do better than marry Sylvie; if you go to work the right way, in two years' time you may marry little Pierrette Lorrain."

And he told him the results of the Jesuit's manuvring.

"What a clever stroke—and reaching so far?" said the Colonel.

"Colonel," said Vinet gravely, "Pierrette is a charming creature; you may be happy for the rest of your days. You have such splendid health, that such a match would not, for you, have the usual drawbacks of an ill-assorted marriage; still, do not imagine that this exchange of a terrible life for a pleasant one will be easy to effect. To convert your lady-love into your confidante is a manœuvre as dangerous as, in your profession, it is to cross a river under the enemy's fire. Keen as you are as a cavalry officer, you must study the position, and carry out your tactics with the superior skill which has won us our present position. If I should one day be public prosecutor, you may command the department. Ah! if only you had a vote, we should be further on our way. I might have bought the votes of those two officials by indemnifying them for the loss of their places, and we should have had a majority. I should be sitting by Dupin, Casimir Périer, and—"

The Colonel had for some time past been thinking of Pierrette, but he hid the thought with deep dissimulation; his roughness to Pierrette was only on the surface. The child could not imagine why the man who called himself her father's old comrade treated her so ill, when, if he met her alone, he put his hand under her chin and gave her a fatherly caress. Ever since Vinet had confided to him Mademoiselle Sylvie's terror of marriage, Gouraud had sought opportunities of seeing Pierrette alone, and then the rough officer was as mild as a cat; he would tell her how brave her father was, and say what a misfortune for her his death had been.

A few days before Brigaut's arrival, Sylvie had found Gouraud and Pierrette together. Jealousy had then entered into her soul with monastic vehemence. Jealousy, which is above all passions credulous and suspicious, is also that in which fancy has most power; but it does not lend wit, it takes it away; and in Sylvie jealousy gave birth to very strange ideas. She conceived that the man who had sung the words "Mistress Bride" to Pierrette must be the Colonel; and

Sylvie thought she had reason to ascribe this serenade to the Colonel, because during the last week Gouraud's manner seemed to have undergone a change. This soldier was the only man who, in the solitude in which she had lived, had ever troubled himself about her; hence she watched him with all her eyes, all her understanding; and by dint of indulging in hopes alternately flourishing and blighted, she had given them so much scope that they produced the effect on her of a moral mirage. To use a fine but vulgar expression, by dint of looking she often saw nothing. By turns she rejected and struggled victoriously against the notion of this chimerical rivalry. She instituted comparisons between herself and Pierrette; she was forty, and her hair was grey; Pierrette was a deliciously white little girl, with eyes tender enough to bring warmth to a dead heart. She had heard it said that men of fifty were fond of little girls like Pierrette.

Before the Colonel had sown his wild oats and frequented the Rogrons' drawing-room, Sylvie had heard at the Tiphaines' parties strange reports of Gouraud and his doings. Old maids in love have the exaggerated Platonic notions which girls of twenty are apt to profess; they have never lost the hard-and-fast ideas which cling to all who have no experience of life, nor learnt how social forces modify, erode, and coerce such fine and lofty notions. To Sylvie the idea of being deceived by her Colonel was a thought that hammered at her brain.

So from the hour, that morning, which every celibate spends in bed between waking and rising, the old maid had thought of nothing but herself and Pierrette and the song which had aroused her by the words, "Mistress Bride." Like a simpleton, instead of peeping at the lover through the Venetian shutters, she had opened her window, without reflecting that Pierrette would hear her. If she had but had the common wit of a spy, she would have seen Brigaut, and the fateful drama then begun would not have taken place.

Pierrette, weak as she was, removed the wooden bars which fastened the kitchen shutters, opened the shutters, and hooked them back, then she opened the passage door leading into the garden. She took the various brooms needed for sweeping the carpet, the dining-room floor, the passage, the stairs, in short, for cleaning everything with such care and exactitude as no servant, not even a Dutch one, would give to her work; she hated the least reproof. To her, happiness consisted in seeing Sylvie's little blue eyes, colourless and cold, with a look—not indeed of satisfaction, that they never wore—only calm when she had examined everything with the owner's eye, the inscrutable glance which sees what escapes the keenest observer.

By the time Pierrette returned to the kitchen her skin was moist; then she put everything in order, lighted the stove so as to have live charcoal, made the fire in her cousins' rooms, and put hot water for their toilet, though she had none for hers. She laid the table for breakfast and lighted the dining-room stove. For all these various tasks she had to go to the cellar to fetch brushwood, leaving a cool place to go to a hot one, or a hot place to go into the cold and damp. These sudden changes, made with the reckless haste of youth, merely to avoid a hard word, or to obey some order, aggravated the state of her health beyond remedy. Pierrette did not know that she was ill. Still she felt the beginnings of sufferings; she had strange longings, and hid them; a passion for raw salad, which she devoured in secret. The innocent child had no idea that this state meant serious disease, and needed the greatest care. Before Brigaut's arrival, if Néraud, who might accuse, himself of her grandmother's death, had revealed this mortal peril to the little girl, she would have smiled; she found life too bitter not to smile at death. But within these last few minutes, she, who added to her physical ailments the Breton home-sickness—a moral sickness so well known, that colonels of regiments reckon on it in the Bretons who serve in their regiments—she loved Provins. The sight of that gold-coloured flower, that song, the presence of the friend of her childhood, had revived her as a plant long deprived of water recovers after hours of rain. She wanted to live; she did not believe that she had suffered!

She timidly stole into Sylvie's room, lighted the fire, left the hot-water pot, spoke a few words, went to awake her guardian, and then ran downstairs to take in the milk, the bread, and the other provisions supplied by the tradesmen. She stood for some time on the doorstep, hoping that Brigaut would have the wit to return; but Brigaut was already on the road to Paris. She had dusted the drawing-room and was busy in the kitchen, when she heard heir cousin Sylvie coming downstairs. Mademoiselle Rogron made her appearance in a Carmelite grey silk dressing-gown, on her head a tulle cap decorated with bows, her false curls put on askew, her night dress showing above the wrapper, her feet slipshod in her slippers. She inspected everything, and came to her little cousin, who was waiting to know what they would have for breakfast.

"So there you are, Miss Ladylove!" said Sylvie to Pierrette, in a half-merry, half-mocking tone.

"I beg your pardon, cousin?"

"You crept into my room like a sneak and out again in the same way; but you must have known that I should have something to say to you."

"To me?"

"You have had a serenade this morning like a princess, neither more nor less."

"A serenade?" exclaimed Pierrette.

"A serenade?" echoed Sylvie, mimicking her. "And you have a lover."

"Cousin, what do you mean by a lover?" Sylvie evaded the question, and said:

"Do you dare to say, mademoiselle, that a man did not come under our windows and talk to you of marriage!"

Persecution had taught Pierrette the cunning indispensable to slaves; she boldly replied, "I do not know what you mean—"

"Dog—" added the old maid in vinegar tones.

"Cousin," said Pierrette humbly.

"And you did not get up, I suppose, and did not go bare foot to your window? Enough to give you some bad illness. Well, catch it, and serve you right!—And I suppose you did not talk to your lover?"

"No, cousin."

"I knew you had a great many faults, but I did not know you told lies. Think of what you are about, mademoiselle. You will have to tell your cousin Denis and me all about the scene of this morning, and explain it too; otherwise your guardian will have to take strong measures."

The old maid, devoured by jealousy and curiosity, was trying intimidation. Pierrette did as all people must who are enduring beyond their strength—she kept silence. Silence is to all creatures thus attacked the only means of salvation; it fatigues the Cossack charges of the envious, the enemy's savage rushes; it results in a crushing and complete victory. What is more complete than silence? It is final. Is it not one of the modes of the Infinite?

Sylvie looked stealthily at Pierrette. The child coloured; but instead of flushing all over, the red lay in patches on her cheeks, in burning spots of symptomatic hue. On seeing these signals of ill-health, a mother would at once have changed her note; she would have taken the child on her knee, have questioned her, have acquired long since a thousand proofs of Pierrette's perfect and beautiful innocence, have suspected her weakness, and understood that the blood and humours diverted from their course were thrown back on the lungs after disturbing the digestive functions. Those eloquent scarlet patches would have warned her of imminent and mortal danger. But an old maid to whom the feelings that guard the family, the needs of childhood, the care required in early womanhood were all unknown, could have none of the indulgence and the pity that are inspired by the thousand incidents of married and maternal life. The sufferings of misery, instead of softening her heart, had made it callous.

"She blushes—she has done wrong!" thought Sylvie. So Pierrette's silence received the worst construction.

"Pierrette," said she, "before your cousin Denis comes down we will have a little talk.—Come," she went on in a milder tone. "Shut the door to the street. If any one comes, they will ring; we shall hear."

In spite of the damp fog rising from the river, Sylvie led Pierrette along the gravelled path that zigzagged between the grass-plots, to the edge of the terrace built in a so-called picturesque style of broken rockwork planted with flags and other water-plants. The old cousin now changed her tactics; she would try to catch Pierrette by gentleness. The hyena would play the cat.

"Pierrette," said she, "you are no longer a child; you will soon set foot in your fifteenth year, and it would not be at all astonishing if you had a lover."

"But, cousin," said Pierrette, raising her eyes of angelic sweetness to her cousin's cold, sour face, for Sylvie had put on her saleswoman expression, "what is a lover?"

It was impossible to Sylvie to define to her brother's ward with accuracy and decency what she meant by a lover; instead of regarding the question as the result of adorable innocence, she treated it as mendacious.

"A lover, Pierrette, is a man who loves you and wishes to marry you."

"Ah!" said Pierrette. "In Brittany when two persons are agreed, we call the young man a suitor!"

"Well, understand that there is not the smallest harm in confessing your feeling for a man, my child. The harm is in secrecy. Have you, do you think, taken the fancy of any man who comes here?"

"I do not think so."

"You do not love one of them?"

"Quite sure?"

"Quite sure."

"Look me in the face, Pierrette." Pierrette looked at her cousin.

"And yet a man spoke to you from the Square this morning?"

Pierrette looked down.

"You went to your window, you opened it, and spoke to him."

"No, cousin; I wanted to see what the weather was like, and I saw a countryman in the Square."

"Pierrette, since your first Communion you have improved greatly, you are obedient and pious, you love your relations and God; I am pleased with you, but I never have told you so for fear of inflaming your pride."

The horrible woman mistook the dejection, the submission, the silence of wretchedness for virtues! One of the sweetest things that brings comfort to the sufferer, to martyrs, to artists, in the midst of the Divine wrath roused in them by envy and hatred, is to meet with praise from some quarter whence they have always had blame and bad faith. So Pierrette looked up at her cousin with attentive eyes, and felt ready to forgive her all the pain she had caused her.

"But if it is all mere hypocrisy, if I am to find in you a serpent I have cherished in my bosom, you would be an infamous, a horrible creature!"

"I do not think I have anything to blame myself for," said Pierrette, feeling a dreadful pang at her heart on this sudden transition from unexpected praise to the terrible accent of the hyena.

"You know that lying is a mortal sin?"

"Yes, cousin."

'Well, then, you stand before God!" said the old maid, pointing with a solemn gesture to the gardens and the sky. "Swear to me that you do not know that countryman."

"I will not swear," said Pierrette.

"Ah! he was not a countryman! Little viper!"

Pierrette fled across the garden like a startled fawn, appalled by this moral dilemma. Her cousin called to her in an awful voice.

"The bell," she replied.

"What a sly little wretch!" said Sylvie to herself. "She has a perverse nature, and I am sure now that the little serpent has twisted herself round the Colonel. She has heard us say that he is a Baron. A Baroness, indeed! Little fool! Oh! I will be rid of her by placing her as an apprentice, and pretty soon too!"

Sylvie was so lost in thought that she did not see her brother coming down the walk and contemplating the mischief done by the frost to his dahlias.

"Well, Sylvie, what are you thinking about there? I thought you were looking at the fishes; sometimes they jump out of the water."

"No," said she.

"Well, how did you sleep?" and he proceeded to tell her his dreams of the past night. "Do not you think that my face looks patchy?" a favourite word with the Rogrons. Since Rogron had loved—nay, we will not profane the word—had desired Mademoiselle de Chargebœuf, he had been very anxious about his appearance and himself.

At this moment Pierrette came down the steps and called to them that breakfast was ready. On seeing her little cousin; Sylvie's complexion tuned green and yellow; all her bile rose. She examined the passage, and said that Pierrette ought to have polished it with foot-brushes.

"I will polish it if you wish," replied the angel, not knowing how injurious this form of labour is to a young girl.

The dining-room was above blame. Sylvie sat down, and all through breakfast affected to want things that she never would have thought of in a calmer frame of mind, seeking for them simply to make Pierrette rise to fetch them, and always just as the poor child was beginning to eat. But mere nagging was not enough; she sought some subject for fault finding, and fumed with internal rage at finding none. If they had been eating eggs, she would certainly have complained of the boiling of hers. She hardly replied to her brother's silly talk, and yet she looked only at him; her eyes avoided Pierrette, who was keenly aware of this behavior.

Pierrette brought in the coffee for her cousins in a large silver cup, which served to heat the milk in, mixed with cream, in a saucepan of hot water. The brother and sister then added, to their taste, the black coffee which was made by Sylvie. When she had carefully prepared this dainty, Sylvie detected in it a faint cloud of coffee dust; she care fully skimmed it off the tawny mixture and looked at it, leaning over it to examine it more minutely. Then the storm burst.

"What is the matter?" asked Rogron.

"The matter! Miss, here, has put ashes in my coffee. Ashes in coffee are so nice! … Well, well! It is not astonishing; no one can do two things at once. Much she was thinking of the coffee! A blackbird might have flown through the kitchen, and she would not have heeded it this morning! How should she see the ashes flying? And then—only her cousin's!—Much she cares about it!"

She went on in this way, while she elaborately laid on the edge of her plate some fine coffee that had passed through the filter, mixed with some grains of sugar that had not melted.

"But, cousin, that is coffee," said Pierrette.

"So I am a liar now?" exclaimed Sylvie, looking at Pierrette, and scorching her by a fearful flash that her eyes could dart when she was angry.

These temperaments, which passion has never exhausted, have at command a great supply of the vital fluid. This phenomenon of extreme brightness in her eye under the influence of rage was all the more confirmed in Mademoiselle Rogron because formerly, in her shop, she had had occasion to try the power of her gaze by opening her eyes enormously wide, always to fill her dependants with salutary terror.

"I will teach you to give me the lie," she went on; "you, who deserve to be sent away from table to feed by yourself in the kitchen."

"What is the matter with you both?" cried Rogron. "You are as cross as two sticks this morning."

"Oh, my lady knows what I mean! I am giving her time to make up her mind before speaking to you about it, for I am much kinder to her than she deserves."

Pierrette looked through the window out on to the Square, so as not to meet her cousin's eyes, which frightened her.

"She pays no more heed than if I were talking to this sugar-basin! And she has sharp ears too; she can speak from the top of the house to answer some one below. … She is that perverse! Your ward is aggravating beyond words, and you need look for nothing good from her; do you hear me, Rogron?"

"What has she done that is so wicked?" asked her brother. "At her age too! It is beginning young!" cried the old maid in a fury.

Pierrette rose to clear away, just to keep herself in countenance; she did not know which way to look. Though such language was nothing new to her, she never could get used to it. Her cousin's rage made her feel as though she had committed some crime. She wondered what her rage would be if she knew of Brigaut's escapade. Perhaps they would keep Brigaut away. All the thousand ideas of a slave crowded on her at once, thoughts swift and deep, and she resolved to resist by absolute silence as to an incident in which her conscience could see no evil.

She had to endure words so cruel, so harsh, insinuations so insulting, that on her return to the kitchen she was seized with cramp in the stomach and a violent attack of sickness. She dared not complain; she was not sure of getting any care. She turned pale and faint, said that she felt ill, and went up to bed, clinging to the banisters at every step, and believing that her last hour had come. "Poor Brigaut!" thought she.

"She is ill," said Rogron.

"She ill! It is all megrims," said Sylvie, loud enough to be overheard. "She was not ill this morning, I can tell you!"

This last shot was too much for Pierrette, who crept to bed in tears, praying to God to remove her from this world.

For a month past Rogron had no longer carried the *Constitutionnel* to Gouraud; the Colonel obsequiously came to fetch the newspaper, to make talk, and take Rogron out when the weather was fine. Sylvie, sure of seeing the Colonel, and being able to question him, dressed herself coquettishly. The old maid thought she achieved this by putting on a green gown, a little yellow cashmere shawl bordered with red, and a white bonnet with meagre grey feathers. At the hour when the Colonel was due, she settled herself in the drawing-room with her brother, making him keep on his dressing-gown and slippers.

"It is a fine morning, Colonel," said Rogron, hearing Gouraud's heavy step; "but I am not dressed, my sister perhaps wanted to go out, she left me to mind the house; wait for me."

Rogron went off, leaving Sylvie with the Colonel.

"Where are you going? you are dressed like a goddess," observed Gouraud, seeing a certain solemnity of expression on the old maid's battered face.

"Yes, I was going out; but as the child is not well, I must stay at home."

"What is the matter with her?"

"I do not know; she asked to go to bed."

Gouraud's cautiousness, not to say his distrust, was constantly on the alert as a result of his collusion with Vinet. The lawyer evidently had the best of it. He edited the paper, he ruled it as a master, and applied the profits to the editing; whereas the Colonel, the responsible stalking-horse, got little enough. Who was to be the député? Vinet. Who the great electioneer? Vinet. Who was always consulted? Vinet.

Then he knew, at least as well as Vinet, the extent and depth of the passion consuming Rogron for the fair Bathilde de Chargebœuf. This passion was becoming a mania, as all the lowest passions of men do. Bathilde's voice made the old bachelor thrill. Rogron, thinking only of his desire, concealed it; be dared not hope for such a match. The Colonel, to sound him, had told Rogron that he was about to propose for Bathilde's hand; Rogron had turned pale at the mere thought of such a formidable rival; he had become cold to Gouraud, almost hostile. Thus Vinet in every way ruled the roast, while he, the Colonel, was tied to the house only by the doubtful bond of a love which, on his part, was but feigned, and on Sylvie's as yet unconfessed. When the lawyer had divulged the priest's manœuvre and advised him to throw over Sylvie and pay his addresses to Pierrette, Vinet had humoured his inclinations; still, as the Colonel analysed the true purport of this suggestion, and examined the ground on which he stood, he fancied he could discern in his ally some hope of making mischief between him and Sylvie, and taking advantage of the old maid's fears to make the whole of Rogron's fortune fall into Mademoiselle de Chargebœuf's hands.

Hence, when Rogron left him alone with Sylvie, the Colonel's acumen seized on the slight indications which betrayed some uneasiness in Sylvie. He saw that she had planned to be under arms and alone with him for a minute. Gouraud, who already vehemently suspected Vinet of playing him some malignant trick, ascribed this conference to a secret suggestion of this legal ape; he put himself on his guard, as when he had been making a reconnaissance in the enemy's country, keeping an eye on the whole prospect, listening for the least sound, his mind alert, his hand on his weapon. It was the Colonel's weakness never to believe a word said by a woman; and when the old maid spoke of Pierrette, and said she was in bed at midday, he concluded that Sylvie had simply put her in disgrace in her room out of jealousy.

"The child is growing very pretty," said he, in an indifferent tone.

"Yes, she will be pretty," replied Mademoiselle Rogron.

"You ought now to send her to a shop in Paris," added the Colonel. "She would make a fortune. They look out for very pretty girls now in the milliners' shops."

"Is that really your advice?" asked Sylvie, in an anxious voice.

"Good! I have hit it!" thought the Colonel. "Vinet's advice that Pierrette and I should marry by-and-by was only intended to place me in this old witch's black-books.—Why," he said aloud, "what do you expect to do with her? Do you not see a perfectly lovely girl, Bathilde de Chargebœuf, of noble birth, well connected, and left to become an old maid. No one will have anything to say to her. Pierrette has nothing; she will never marry. Do you suppose that youth and beauty have any attraction for me, for instance?—for me, who, as Captain of Artillery in the Imperial Guard from the first day when the Emperor had a guard, have had my feet in every capital in Europe, and known the prettiest women in them all?—Youth and beauty—they are deuced common and silly. Don't talk of them to me!"

"At eight-and-forty," he went on, adding to his age, "when a man has gone through the retreat from Moscow and the dreadful campaign in France, his loins are a bit weary; I am an old fellow. Now, a wife like you would cosset me and take care of me; her fortune, added to my few thousand francs of pension, would secure me suitable comfort for my old age, and I should like her a thousand times better than a minx who would give me no end of trouble, who would be thirty and have her passions when I should be sixty and have the rheumatism.

At my time of life we think of these things. And, between you and me, I may add that if I marry, I should hope to have no children."

Sylvie's face was transparent to the Colonel all through this speech, and her reply was enough to assure him of Vinet's perfidy.

"So you are not in love with Pierrette?" she exclaimed.

"Bless me! Are you crazy, my dear Sylvie?" cried he. "When we have lost all our teeth, is it the time to crack nuts? Thank God, I still have my wits, and know myself."

Sylvie would not then say more about herself; she thought herself very wily in using her brother's name.

"My brother," said she, "had thought of your marrying her."

"Your brother can never have had such a preposterous notion. A few days ago, to find out his secret, I told him that I was in love with Bathilde; he turned as white as your collar."

"Is he in love with Bathilde?" said Sylvie.

"Madly! And Bathilde certainly loves only his money."— ("One for you, Vinet," thought Gouraud).—"What should have made him speak of Pierrette?—No, Sylvie," he went on, taking her hand and pressing it with meaning, "since you have led to the subject"—he went close to her—"well"—he kissed her hand; he was a cavalry colonel, and had given proofs of courage—"know this: I want no wife but you. Though the marriage will look like a marriage for money, I feel true affection for you."

"But it was I who wished that you should marry Pierrette; and if I were to give her my money—what then, Colonel?"

"But I do not want to have a wretched home, or to see, ten years hence, some young whippersnapper, such as Julliard, hovering round my wife, and writing verses to her in the newspaper. I am too much a man on that score; I will never marry a woman out of all proportion too young."

"Well, Colonel, we will talk that over seriously," said Sylvie, with a glance she thought amorous, and which was very like that of an ogress. Her cold, raw purple lips parted over her yellow teeth, and she fancied she was smiling.

"Here I am," said Rogron, and he led away the Colonel, who bowed courteously to the old maid.

Gouraud was determined to hasten his marriage with Sylvie, and so become master of the house; promising himself that, through the influence he would acquire over Sylvie during the honeymoon, he would get rid both of Bathilde and of Céleste Habert. So, as they walked, he told Rogron that he had been making fun of him the other day; that he had no intentions of winning Bathilde's heart, not being rich enough to take a wife who had no money. Then he confided his projects; he had long since chosen Sylvie for her admirable qualities; in short, he aspired to the honour of becoming his brother-in-law.

"Oh, Colonel! Oh, Baron! If only my consent were needed, it would be done as soon as legal delays should allow!" cried Rogron, delighted to find himself relieved of this terrible rival.

Sylvie spent the whole morning examining her own rooms to see if there were accommodation for a couple. She determined on building a second story for her brother, and having the first floor for herself and her husband; but she also promised herself, in accordance with the notions of every old maid, to put the Colonel to some tests, so as to judge of his heart and habits before making up her mind. She still had doubts, and wanted to make sure that Pierrette had no intimacy with the Colonel.

At dinner-time the girl came down to lay the cloth. Sylvie had been obliged to do the cooking, and had spotted her gown, exclaiming, "Curse Pierrette!" For it was evident, indeed, that if Pierrette had cooked the dinner, Sylvie would not have had a grease-stain on her silk dress.

"So here you are, you little coddle. You are like the blacksmith's dog that sleeps under the forge and wakes at the sound of a saucepan. So you want me to believe that you are ill, you little story-teller!"

The one idea, "You did not confess the truth as to what took place this morning, therefore everything you say is a lie," was like a hammer with which Sylvie was prepared to hit incessantly on Pierrette's head and heart.

To Pierrette's great astonishment, Sylvie sent her, after dinner, to dress for the evening. The liveliest imagination is no match for the energy which suspicion gives to the mind of an old maid. In such a case, the old maid beats politicians, attorneys and notaries, bill-brokers and misers. Sylvie promised herself that she would consult Vinet after looking well about her. She meant to keep Pierrette in the room, so as to judge for herself by the child's face whether the Colonel had told the truth.

The first to come were Madame de Chargebœuf and her daughter. By her cousin Vinet's advice, Bathilde had dressed with twice her usual elegance. She wore a most becoming blue cotton-velvet gown, the clear kerchief as before, bunches of grapes in garnets and gold for earrings, her hair in ringlets, the artful necklet, little black satin shoes, grey silk stockings, and Suède gloves, and then queenly airs and girlish coquettishness enough to catch every Rogron in the river. Her mother, calm and dignified, had preserved, as had Bathilde, a certain aristocratic impertinence by which these two women redeemed everything, betraying the spirit of their caste. Bathilde was gifted with superior intelligence, though Vinet alone had been able to discern it after the two months that these ladies had spent in his house. When he had sounded the depths of this girl, depressed by the uselessness of her youth and beauty, but enlightened by the contempt she felt for the men of a period when money was their sole idol, Vinet exclaimed in surprise:

"If I had but married you, Bathilde, by this time I should have been Keeper of the Seals; I would have called myself Vinet de Chargebœuf, and have sat on the right."

Bathilde had no vulgar aims in her wish to be married; she would not marry for motherhood, nor for the sake of having a husband; she would marry to be free, to have a "responsible publisher," as it were—to be called Madame, and to act as men act. Rogron to her was a name; she thought she could make something of this imbecile creature—a député, who might vote while she pulled the wires; she wanted to be revenged on her family, who had paid little heed to a penniless girl. Vinet, admiring and encouraging her ideas, had greatly extended and strengthened them.

"My dear cousin," said he, explaining to her the influence exerted by women, and pointing out the sphere of action proper to them, "do you suppose that Tiphaine, a profoundly mediocre man, can by his own merits rise to sit on the lower bench in Paris? It is Madame Tiphaine who got him returned as deputy; it is she who will carry him to Paris. Her mother, Madame Roguin, is a cunning body, who does what she pleases with du Tillet the banker, one of Nucingen's chief allies, both of them close friends of Keller's; and these three houses do great services to the Government or its most devoted adherents; the offices are on the best possible terms with these lynxes of the financial world, and men like those know all Paris. There is nothing to hinder Tiphaine from rising to be the Presiding Judge of one of the higher Courts.—Marry Rogron; we will make him deputy for Provins as soon as I have secured for myself some other constituency in Seine-et-Marne. Then you will have a receivership—one of those places where Rogron will have nothing to do but to sign his name. We will stick to the Opposition if it triumphs; but if the Bourbons remain in power, O how gently we will incline towards the centre! Besides, Rogron will not live for ever, and you can marry a title by-and-by. And then, if you are in a good position, the Chargebœufs will help us. Your poverty—like mine—has, no doubt, enabled you to estimate what men are worth; they are to be made use of only as post-horses. A man or a woman can take us from one stage to the next!"

Vinet had made a little Catherine de Medici of Bathilde. He left his wife at home, happy with her two children, and always attended Madame de Chargebœuf and Bathilde to the Rogrons'. He appeared in all his glory as the tribune of Champagne. He wore neat gold spectacles, a silk waistcoat, a white cravat, black trousers, thin boots, a black coat made in Paris, a gold watch and chain. Instead of the Vinet of old—pale, lean, haggard, and gloomy—he exhibited the Vinet of the day, in all the bravery of a political personage; sure of his luck, he trod with the decision peculiar to a busy advocate familiar with the caverns of justice. His small, cunning head was so smartly brushed, and his clean-shaven chin gave him such a finished though cold appearance, that he looked quite pleasing, in the style of Robespierre. He might certainly become a delightful public prosecutor, with an elastic, dangerous, and deadly flow of eloquence, or an orator, with all the subtlety of Benjamin Constant. The acrimony and hatred which had formerly animated him had turned to perfidious softness. The poison had become medicine.

"Good-evening, my dear, how are you?" said Madame de Chargebœuf to Sylvie.

Bathilde went straight to the fireplace, took off her hat, looked at herself in the glass, and put her pretty foot on the bar of the fender to display it to Rogron.

"What ails you, monsieur?" said she, looking at him. "You give me no greeting? Well, indeed! I may put on a velvet frock for your benefit …"

She stopped Pierrette, bidding her put her hat on a chair, and the girl took it from her, Bathilde resigning it to her as though Pierrette had been the housemaid.

Men are thought very fierce, and so are tigers; but neither tigers, nor vipers, nor diplomates, nor men of law, nor executioners, nor kings, can in their utmost atrocities come near the gentle cruelty, the poisoned sweetness, the savage scorn of young ladies to each other when certain of them think themselves superior to others in birth, fortune, or grace, and when marriage is in question, or precedence, or, in short, any feminine rivalry. The "Thank you, mademoiselle," spoken by Bathilde to Pierrette, was a poem in twelve cantos.

Her name was Bathilde, the other's was Pierrette; she was a Chargebœuf, the other a Lorrain! Pierrette was undersized and fragile, Bathilde was tall and full of vitality! Pierrette was fed by charity, Bathilde and her mother lived on their own money! Pierrette wore a stuff frock with a deep tucker, Bathilde dragged the serpentine folds of her blue velvet; Bathilde had the finest shoulders in the department, and an arm like a queen's, Pierrette's shoulder-blades and arms were skinny; Pierrette was Cinderella, Bathilde the fairy; Bathilde would get married, Pierrette would die a maid! Bathilde was worshiped, Pierrette had no one to love her! Bathilde had her hair dressed—she had taste, Pierrette hid her hair under a little cap, and knew nothing of the fashions! *Epilogue*—Bathilde was everything, Pierrette was nothing. The proud little Bretonne perfectly understood this cruel poem.

"Good-evening, child," said Madame de Chargeuf from the summit of her grandeur, and with an accent given by her narrow pinched nose.

Vinet put the crowning touch to these insulting civilities by looking at Pierrette and saying, on three notes, "Oh, oh, oh! How fine we are this evening, Pierrette!"

"I!" said the poor child. "You should say that to your cousin, not to me. She is beautiful!"

"Oh, my cousin is always beautiful," replied the lawyer. "Do not you say so, Père Rogron?" he added, turning to the master of the house, and shaking hands with him.

"Yes," said Rogron.

"Why force him to say what he does not think? I never was to his taste," replied Bathilde, placing herself in front of Rogron. "Is not that the truth?—Look at me."

Rogron looked at her from head to foot, and gently closed his eyes, like a cat when its poll is scratched.

"You are too beautiful," said he, "too dangerous to look at."

"Why?"

Rogron gazed at the fire-logs and said nothing.

At this moment Mademoiselle Habert came, followed by the Colonel. Céleste Habert, everybody's enemy now, had none but Sylvie on her side; but each one showed her all the greater consideration, politeness, and amiable attention because all were undermining her, so that she doubted between this display of civil interest and the distrust which her brother had implanted in her. The priest, though standing apart from the theatre of war, guessed everything; and so, when he perceived that his sister's hopes were at an end, he became one of the Rogrons' most formidable antagonists,

The reader can at once imagine what Mademoiselle Habert was like on being told that even if she had not been mistress—arch-mistress—of a school, she would still always have looked like a governess. Governesses have a particular way of putting on their caps. Just as elderly Englishwomen have monopolised the fashion of turbans, so governesses have the monopoly of these caps; the crown of the cap towers above the flowers, the flowers are more than artificial; stored carefully in a wardrobe, this cap is always new and always old, even on the first day. These old maids make it a point of honour to be like a painter's lay-figure; they sit on their haunches, not on their chairs. When they are spoken to they turn their whole body; and when their gowns creak, we are tempted to believe that the springs of the machinery are out of order. Mademoiselle Habert, a type of her kind, had a hard eye, a set mouth, and under her chin, furrowed with wrinkles, the limp and crumpled capstrings wagged and frisked as she moved. She had an added charm in two moles, rather large and rather brown, with hairs that she left to grow like untied clematis. Finally, she took snuff, and without grace.

They sat down to the toil of boston. Sylvie had opposite to her Mademoiselle Habert, and the Colonel sat on one side, opposite Madame de Chargebœuf. Bathilde placed herself near her mother and Rogron. Sylvie put Pierrette between herself and the Colonel. Rogron opened another card-table in case Monsieur Néraud should come, and Monsieur Cournant and his wife. Vinet and Bathilde could both play whist, which was Monsieur and Madame Cournant's game. Ever since the Chargebœuf ladies—as they say in Provins—had been in the habit of coming to the Rogrons', the two lamps blazed on the chimney-piece between the candelabra and the clock, and the tables were lighted by wax lights at two francs a pound, which, however, was paid by winnings at cards.

"Now, Pierrette, my child, take your sewing," said Sylvie with treacherous gentleness, seeing her watch the Colonel's play.

In public she always pretended to treat Pierrette very kindly. This mean deceit irritated the honest Bretonne, and made her despise her cousin. Pierrette fetched her embroidery; but as she set the stitches, she looked now and then at the Colonel's game. Gouraud seemed not to know that there was a little girl at his side. Sylvie began to think this indifference extremely suspicious. At a certain moment in the game the old maid declared misers in hearts; the pool was full of counters, and there were twenty-seven sous in it besides. The Cournants and Néraud had come. The old supernumerary judge, Desfondrilles—a man in whom the Minister of Justice had discerned the qualifications for a judge when appointing him examining magistrate, but who was never thought clever enough for a superior position—had for the last two months forsaken the

Tiphaines, and shown a leaning towards Vinet's party. He was now standing in front of the fire, holding up his coat-tails, and gazing at the gorgeous drawing-room in which Mademoiselle de Chargebœuf shone; for the setting of crimson looked as if it had been contrived on purpose to show off the beauty of this magnificent young woman. Silence reigned; Pierrette watched the play, and Sylvie's attention was diverted by the excitement of the game.

"Play that," said Pierrette to the Colonel, pointing to a heart.

The Colonel led from a sequence in hearts; the hearts lay between him and Sylvie; the Colonel forced the ace, though it was guarded in Sylvie's hand by five small cards.

"It is not fair play! Pierrette saw my hand, and the Colonel allowed her to advise him!"

"But, mademoiselle," said Céleste, "it was the Colonel's game to lead hearts since he found that you had one!"

The speech made Desfondrilles smile; he was a keen observer, who amused himself with watching all the interests at stake in Provins, where he played the part of *Rigaudin* in Picard's play of *la Maison en loterie.*

"It was the Colonel's game," Cournant put in, without knowing anything about it.

Sylvie shot at Mâdemoiselle Habert a look of old maid against old maid, villainous but honeyed.

"Pierrette, you saw my hand," said Sylvie, fixing her eyes on the girl.

"No, cousin."

"I was watching you all," said the archælogical judge; "I can bear witness that the little girl saw no one's hand but the Colonel's."

"Pooh! these little girls know very well how to steal a glance with their sweet eyes," said Gouraud in alarm.

"Indeed!" said Sylvie.

"Yes," replied Gouraud; "she may have looked over your hand to play you a trick. Was it not so, my beauty?"

"No," said the honest Bretonne. "I am incapable of such a thing! In that case I should have followed my cousin's game."

"You know very well that you are a story-teller and a little fool into the bargain," said Sylvie. "Since what took place this morning, who can believe a word you say? You are a ..."

Pierrette did not wait to hear her cousin end the sentence in her presence. Anticipating a torrent of abuse, she rose, went out of the room without a light, and up to her room. Sylvie turned pale with rage, and muttered between her teeth, "I will pay her out!"

'Will you pay your losses?" said Madame de Chargebœuf. At this moment poor Pierrette hit her head against the passage door which the judge had left open.

"Good! That serves her right!" cried Sylvie.

'What has happened?" asked Desfondrilles.

"Nothing that she does not deserve," replied Sylvie.

"She has given herself some severe blow," said Mademoiselle Habert.

Sylvie tried to evade paying her stakes by rising to see what Pierrette had done; but Madame de Chargebœuf stopped her.

"Pay us first," said she, laughing; "by the time you return you will have forgotten all about it."

This suggestion, based on the bad faith the ex-haberdasher showed in the matter of her gambling debts, met with general approval. Sylvie sat down and thought no more of Pierrette; and no one was surprised at her indifference. All the evening Sylvie was absent-minded. When cards were over, at about half-past nine, she sank into an easy-chair by the fire, and only rose to take leave of her guests. The Colonel tortured her; she did not know what to think about him.

"Men are so false!" said she to herself as she fell asleep.

Pierrette had given herself a frightful blow against the edge of the door, just over her ear, where girls part their hair to put the forepart into curl-papers. Next morning there was a bad purple-veined bruise.

"God has punished you," said Sylvie at breakfast; "you disobeyed me, you showed a great want of respect in not listening to me, and in going away in the middle of my sentence. You have no more than you deserve."

"Still," said Rogron, "you should put on a rag dipped in salt and water."

"Pooh! It is nothing!" said Sylvie.

The poor child had come to the point when she thought her guardian's remark a proof of interest.

The week ended as it had begun, in constant torment. Sylvie became ingenious, and carried her refinement of tyranny to an extreme pitch. The Illinois, Cherokees, and Mohicans might have leant of her. Pierrette dared not complain of her indefinite misery and the pain she suffered in her head. At the bottom of Sylvie's displeasure lay the girl's refusal to tell anything about Brigaut; and Pierrette, with Breton obstinacy, was determined to keep a very natural silence. Every one can imagine what a glance she gave Brigaut, who, as she believed, would be lost to her if he were discovered, and whom she instinctively longed to keep near her, happy in knowing that he was at Provins. What a delight to her to see Brigaut again! The sight of the companion of her childhood was to her like the view an exile gets from afar of his native land; she looked on him as a martyr gazes at the sky when, during his torments, his eyes, blessed with double sight, see through to heaven.

Pierrette's parting glance had been so perfectly intelligible to the Major's son, that while he planed his boards, opened his compasses, took his measurements, and fitted his pieces, he racked his brains for some means of corresponding with Pierrette. Brigaut at last hit on this extremely simple plan. At a certain hour at night Pierrette must let down a string, and he would tie a letter to the end of it. In the midst of her terrible sufferings from two maladies, an abscess which was forming in her head, and her general disorderment, Pierrette was sustained by the idea of corresponding with Brigaut. The same desire agitated both hearts; though apart, they understood each other! At every pang that made her heart flutter, at every pain that shot through her brain, Pierrette said to herself, "Brigaut is at hand!" and then she could suffer without complaining.

On the next market-day after their first meeting in the church, Brigaut looked out for his little friend. Though he saw that she was pale, and trembling like a November leaf about to drop from the bough, without losing his head he went to bargain for some fruit at the stall where the terrible Sylvie was beating down the price of her purchases. Brigaut contrived to slip a note into Pierrette's hand, and he did it naturally, while jesting with the market woman, and with all the dexterity of a rake, as if he had never done anything else, so coolly did he manage it, in spite of the hot blood that sang in his ears and surged boiling from his heart, almost bursting the veins and arteries. On the surface he had the determination of an old housebreaker, and within the quaking heart of innocence, like mothers sometimes in their mortal anguish, when they are gripped between two dangers, between two precipices. Pierrette felt Brigaut's dizziness; she crushed the paper into her apron pocket; the pallor of her cheeks changed to the cherry redness of a fierce fire. These two children each unconsciously went through sensations enough for ten commonplace love-affairs. That instant left in their souls a wellspring of emotions. Sylvie, who did not recognise the Breton accent, could not suspect a lover in Brigaut, and Pierrette came home with her treasure.

The letters of these two poor children were destined to serve as documents in a horrible legal squabble; for, but for that fatal circumstance, they never would have been seen. This is what Pierrette read that evening in her room:

"My Dear Pierrette,—At midnight, when everybody is asleep, but when I shall be awake for your sake, I will come every night under the kitchen window. You can let down out of your window a string long enough to reach me, which will make no noise, and tie to the end of it whatever you want to write to me. I will answer you in the same way. I knew that you had been taught to read and write by those wretched relations who were to do you so much good, and who are doing you so much harm! You, Pierrette, the daughter of a Colonel who died for France, are compelled by these monsters to cook for them! That is how your pretty colour and your fine health have vanished. What has become of my Pierrette? What have they done to her? I can see plainly that you are not happy.

"Oh! Pierrette, let us go back to Brittany. I can earn enough to give you everything you need; you may have three francs a day, for I earn from four to five, and thirty sous are plenty for me. Oh! Pierrette, how I have prayed to God for you since seeing you again. I have asked Him to give me all your pain, and to grant you all the pleasures.

"What have you to do with them that they keep you? Your grandmother is more to you than they are. These Rogrons are venomous; they have spoilt all your gaiety. You do not even walk at Provins as you used to move in Brittany. Let us go home to Brittany. In short, here I am to serve you, to do your bidding; and you must tell me what you wish. If you want money, I have sixty crowns of ours, and I shall have the grief of sending them to you by the string instead of kissing your dear hands respectfully when I give you the money. Ah! my dear Pierrette, the blue sky has now for a long time been dark to me. I have not had two hours of joy since I put you into that ill-starred diligence; and when I saw you again, like a shade, that witch of a cousin disturbed our happiness. However, we shall have the comfort of praying to God together every Sunday; He will perhaps hear us the better. Not good-bye, dear Pierrette, only till to-night."

This letter agitated her so greatly that she sat for above an hour reading and re-reading it; but she reflected, not without pain, that she had nothing to write with. So she made up her mind to the difficult expedition from her attic to the dining-room, where she could find ink, pen, and paper; and she accomplished it without waking Sylvie. A few minutes before midnight she had finished this letter, which was also produced in Court:—

"My Friend,—Oh yes, my friend! For there is no one but you, Jacques, and, my grandmother, who loves me. God forgive me, but you are the only two persons I love, one as much as the other, neither more nor less. I was too little to remember my mother; but you, Jacques, and my grandmother, and my grandfather too, God rest his soul, for he suffered much from his ruin, which was mine too—in short, you are the only two remaining, and I love you as much as I am wretched! So to know how much I love you, you would have to know how much I suffer; but I do not wish that—it would make you too unhappy. I am spoken to as you would not speak to a dog; I am treated as if I were dirt; and in vain I examine myself as if I were before God, I cannot see that I am in fault towards them. Before you sang the bride's song to me I saw that God was good in my misery; for I prayed to Him to take me out of this world, and as I felt very ill, I said to myself, 'God has heard me!'

"But since you have come, Brigaut, I want to go away with you to Brittany to see my grandmamma, who loves me, though they tell me she has robbed me of eight thousand francs. Brigaut, if they are really mine, can you get them? But it is all a lie; if we had eight thousand francs, grandmamma would not be at Saint-Jacques. I would not trouble that good saintly woman's last days by telling her of my miseries; it would be enough to kill her. Ah! if she could know that they make her grandchild wash the pots and pans—she who would say to me, 'Leave that alone, my darling,' when I tried to help her in her troubles; 'leave it, leave it, my pet; you will spoil your pretty little hands.' Well, my nails are clean at any rate! Many times I cannot carry the market basket, and the handle saws my arm as I come home from market.

"At the same time, I do not think that my cousins are cruel; but it is their way always to be scolding, and it would seem that I can never get away from them. My cousin Rogron is my guardian. One day when I meant to run away, as I was too miserable, and I told them so, my cousin Sylvie answered that the police would go after me, that the law was on my guardian's side; and I saw very clearly that cousins can no more take the place of our father and mother than the Saints can take the place of God.—My poor Jacques, what use could I make of your money? Keep it for our journey. Oh! how I have thought of you and Pen-Hoël and the large pool. We ate our cake first, out there, for I think I am getting worse. I am very ill, Jacques. I have such pains in my head that I could scream, and in my back and my bones; sometimes round my loins that half kills me; and I have no appetite but for nasty things, leaves and roots, and I like the smell of printed paper. There are times when I should cry if I were alone, for I may not do anything as I wish; I am not even allowed to cry. I have to hide myself to offer up my tears to Him from whom we receive those mercies which we call our afflictions. Was it not He who inspired you with the good idea of coming to sing the bride's song under my window?—Oh! Jacques, cousin Sylvie, who heard you, told me I had a lover. If you will be my lover, love me very much; I promise always to love you, as in the past, and to be your faithful servant,

"PIERRETTE LORRAIN.

"You will always love me, won't you?"

The girl had taken a crust of bread from the kitchen, in which she made a hole to stick her letter in, so as to weight the thread. At midnight, after opening her window with excessive caution, she let down her note with the bread, which could make no noise by tapping against the wall or the shutters. She felt the thread pulled by Brigaut, who broke it, and then went stealthily away. When he was in the middle of the Square she could see him, though indistinctly, in the starlight; but he could gaze at her in the luminous band projected by the candle. The two young things remained there for an hour; Pierrette signaling to him to go away, he going and she remaining, and he returned to his post, while Pierrette again waved to him to be gone. This was several times repeated, till the girl shut her window, got into bed, and blew out her light.

Once in bed, she went to sleep, happy though suffering; she had Brigaut's letter under her pillow. She slept the sleep of the persecuted, a sleep blessed by the angels, the sleep of golden and far-away glories full of the arabesques of heaven, which Raphael dreamed of and drew.

Her delicate physical nature was so responsive to her moral nature that Pierrette rose next morning as glad and light as a lark, beaming and gay. Such a change could not escape Sylvie's eye; this time, instead of scolding her, she proceeded to watch her with the cunning of a raven.

"What makes her so happy?" was suggested by jealousy, and not by tyranny. If Sylvie had not been possessed by the idea of the Colonel, she would certainly have said as usual, "Pierrette, you are very turbulent, or very heedless of what is said to you." The old maid determined to spy on Pierrette, as only old maids can spy. The day passed in gloom and silence, like the hour before a storm.

"So you are no longer so ailing, miss?" said Sylvie at dinner. "Did not I tell you that she shams it all to worry us?" she exclaimed, turning to her brother, without waiting for Pierrette's reply.

"On the contrary, cousin, I have a sort of fever—"

"What sort of fever? You are as gay as a linnet. You have seen some one again perhaps?"

Pierrette shuddered, and kept her eyes on her plate.

"*Tartuffe!*" cried Sylvie. "At fourteen! Already! What a nature! Why, you will be a wretch indeed!"

"I do not know what you mean," replied Pierrette, raising her fine luminous hazel eyes to her cousin's face.

"This evening," said Sylvie, "you will remain in the dining-room to sew by a candle. You are in the way in the drawing-room, and I will not have you looking over my hand to advise your favourites."

Pierrette did not flinch.

"Hypocrite!" exclaimed Sylvie as she left the room.

Rogron, who could not understand what his sister was talking about, said to Pierrette, "What is the matter between you two? Try, Pierrette, to please your cousin; she is most indulgent, most kind; and if she is put out with you, certainly you must be wrong. Why do you squabble? For my part, I like a quiet life. Look at Mademoiselle Bathilde; you should try to copy her."

Pierrette could bear it all; Brigaut would come, beyond doubt, at midnight to bring his answer, and this hope was her viaticum for the day. But she was exhausting her last strength. She did not go to sleep; she sat up listening to the clocks strike the hours, and fearing to make a sound. At last twelve struck; she softly opened her window, and this time she used a string she had made long enough by tying several bits together. She heard Brigaut's step, and when she drew up the string she read the following letter, which filled her with joy:—

"My Dear Pierrette,—If you are in such pain, you must not tire yourself by sitting up for me. You will be sure to hear me call like a *Chouan*. My father luckily taught me to imitate their cry. So I shall repeat it three times, and you will know that I have come, and that you must let down the string, but I shall not come again for some few days. I hope then to have good news for you. Oh! Pierrette, not death! What are you thinking of? All my heart quaked; I thought I was dead myself at the mere idea. No, my Pierrette, you shall not die; you shall live happy, and soon be rescued from your persecutors. If I should not succeed in what I am at tempting, to save you, I would go to the lawyers and declare in the face of heaven and earth how you are treated by your cruel relations.

"I am certain that you have only to endure a few days more: take patience. Pierrette, Brigaut is watching over you, as he did in the days when we went to slide on the pond, and I pulled you out of the deep hole where we were so nearly lost together. Good-bye, my dear Pierrette; in a few days we shall be happy, please God. Alas! I dare not tell you of the only thing that may hinder our meeting. But God loves us! So in a few days I shall be able to see my dear Pierrette in liberty, without a care, without any one hindering my looking at you, for I am very hungry to see you, O Pierrette! Pierrette, who condescend to love me and to tell me so. Yes, Pierrette, I will be your lover, but only when I have earned the grand fortune you deserve, and till then I will be no more to you than a devoted servant whom you may command. Adieu.

"JACQUES BRIGAUT."

This was what the young fellow did not tell Pierrette. He had written the following letter to Madame Lorrain at Nantes:—

"MADAME LORRAIN,—Your granddaughter will die, killed by ill-usage, if you do not come to claim her back. I hardly knew her again; and to enable you to judge for yourself of the state of things, I enclose in this letter one from Pierrette to me. You are reported here to have your grandchild's fortune, and you ought to justify yourself on this point. In short, if you can, come quickly; we may yet be happy, and later you will find Pierrette dead.—I remain, with respect, your humble servant,

"JACQUES BRIGAUT.

"At Monsieur Frappier's, Master joiner, Grand' Rue, Provins."

Brigaut only feared lest Pierrette's grandmother might be dead.

Though this letter from him, whom in her innocence she called her lover, was almost inexplicable to Pierrette, she accepted it with virgin faith. Her heart experienced the feeling which travellers in the desert know when they see from afar the palm grove round a well. In a few days her miseries would be ended, Brigaut said it; she slept on the promise of her childhood's friend; and yet, as she laid this letter with the former one, a dreadful thought found dreadful expression:

"Poor Brigaut," said she to herself, "he does not know the hole I have my feet in!"

Sylvie had heard Pierrette; she had also heard Brigaut below the window; she sprang up, rushed to look out on the Square through the shutter slats, and saw a man going away towards the house where the Colonel lived. In front of that Brigaut stopped. The old maid gently opened her door, went upstairs, was amazed at seeing a light in Pierrette's room, peeped through the keyhole, and could see nothing.

"Pierrette," said she, "are you ill?"

"No, cousin," said Pierrette, startled.

"Then why have you a light in your room at midnight? Open your door. I must know what you are about."

Pierrette, barefoot, opened the door, and Sylvie saw the skein of twine which Pierrette, never dreaming of being caught, had neglected to put away. Sylvie pounced upon it.

"What do you use that for?"

"Nothing, cousin."

"Nothing?" said she. "Very good. Lies again! You will not find that the way to heaven. Go to bed; you are cold."

She asked no more, but disappeared, leaving Pierrette terror-stricken by such leniency. Instead of an outbreak, Sylvie had suddenly made up her mind to steal a march on the Colonel and Pierrette, to possess herself of the letters, and confound the couple who were deceiving her. Pierrette, inspired by danger, put the two letters inside her stays and covered them with calico.

This was the end of the loves of Pierrette and Brigaut.

Pierrette was glad of her friend's decision, for Sylvie's suspicions would be disconcerted by having nothing to feed on. And, in fact, Sylvie spent three nights out of her bed and three evenings in watching the innocent Colonel, without discovering anything in Pierrette's room, or in the house or out of it, that hinted at their having any understanding. She sent Pierrette to confession, and took advantage of her absence to hunt through everything in the child's room as dexterously and as keenly as the spies and searchers at the gates of Paris. She found nothing. Her rage rose to the climax of human passion. If Pierrette had been present, she would certainly have beaten her without ruth. To a woman of this temper, jealousy was not so much a feeling as a possession; she breathed, she felt her heart beat, she had emotions in a way hitherto completely unknown to her; at the least movement she was on the alert, she listened to the faintest sounds, she watched Pierrette with gloomy concentration.

"That little wretch will be the death of me!" she would say. Sylvie's severity to the child became at last the most refined cruelty, and aggravated the miserable state in which Pierrette lived. The poor little thing was constantly in a fever, and the pain in her head became intolerable. By the end of a week she displayed to the frequenters of the Rogrons' house a face of suffering which must certainly have softened any less cruel egotism; but Doctor Néraud, advised perhaps by Vinet, did not call for more than a week. The Colonel, suspected by Sylvie, was afraid she might break off their marriage if he showed the smallest anxiety about Pierrette; Bathilde accounted for her indisposition by simple causes, in no way dangerous.

At last, one Sunday evening, when the drawing-room was full of company, Pierrette could not endure the pain; she fainted completely away; and the Colonel, who was the first to observe that she had lost consciousness, lifted her up and carried her on to a sofa.

"She did it on purpose," said Sylvie, looking at Mademoiselle Habert and the other players.

"Your cousin is very ill, I assure you," said the Colonel.

"She was very well in your arms," retorted Sylvie, with a hideous smile.

"The Colonel is right," said Madame de Chargebœuf; "you ought to send for a doctor. This morning in church every one was talking of Mademoiselle Lorrain's state as they came out—it is obvious."

"I am dying," said Pierrette.

Desfondrilles called to Sylvie to unfasten the girl's frock. Sylvie complied, saying, "It is all a sham!"

She undid the dress, and was going to loosen the stays. Then Pierrette found superhuman strength; she sat up, and exclaimed, "No, no; I will go to bed."

Sylvie had touched her stays, and had felt the papers. She allowed Pierrette to escape, saying to everybody, "Well, do you think she is so very ill? It is all put on; you could never imagine the naughtiness of that child."

She detained Vinet at the end of the evening; she was furious, she was bent on revenge; she was rough with the Colonel as he bid her good-night. Gouraud shot a glance at Vinet that seemed to pierce him to the very bowels, and mark the spot for a bullet. Sylvie begged Vinet to remain. When they were alone, the old maid began:

"Never in my life, nor in all my days, will I marry the Colonel!"

"Now that you have made up your mind, I may speak. The Colonel is my friend; still, I am yours rather than his. Rogron has done me services I can never forget. I am as firm a friend as I am an implacable enemy. Certainly, when once I am in the Chamber you will see how I shall rise, and I will make Rogron a Receiver-General.—Well, swear to me never to repeat a word of our conversation!" Sylvie nodded assent. "In the first place, our gallant Colonel is an inveterate gambler."

"Indeed!" said Sylvie.

"But for the difficulties this passion has got him into, he might perhaps have been a Marshal of France," the lawyer went on. "So he might squander all your fortune. But he is a deep customer. Do not believe that married people have or have not children, and you know what will happen to you. No. If you wish to marry, wait till I am in the Chamber, and then you can marry old Desfondrilles, who will be president of the Court here. To revenge yourself, make your brother marry Mademoiselle de Chargebœuf; I will undertake to get her consent; she will have two thousand francs a year, and you will be as nearly connected with the Chargebœufs as I am. Take my word for it, the Chargebœufs will call us cousins some day."

"Gouraud is in love with Pierrette," replied Sylvie.

"He is quite capable of it," said Vinet; "and quite capable of marrying her after your death."

"A pretty little scheme!" said she.

"I tell you he is as cunning as the devil. Make your brother marry, and announce that you intend to remain unmarried and leave your money to your nephews or nieces; you will thus hit Pierrette and Gouraud by the same blow, and you will see how foolish he will look."

"To be sure," cried the old maid; "I can catch them. She shall go into a shop, and will have nothing. She has not a penny. Let her do as we did, and work."

Vinet having got his idea into Sylvie's head, and knowing her obstinacy, left the house. The old maid ended by thinking that the plan was her own.

Vinet found the Colonel outside, smoking a cigar while he waited for him.

"Hold hard!" said the Colonel. "You have pulled me to pieces, but there are stones enough in the ruins to bury you."

"Colonel!"

"There is no 'Colonel' in the case. I am going to lead you a dance. In the first place, you will never be deputy—"

"Colonel!"

"I can command ten votes, and the election depends on—"

"Colonel, just listen to me. Is there no one in the world but old Sylvie? I have just been trying to clear you. You are accused and proved guilty of writing to Pierrette; she has seen you coming out of your house at midnight to stand below the girl's window—"

"Well imagined!"

"She means her brother to marry Bathilde, and will keep her fortune for their children."

"Will Rogron have any?"

"Yes," said Vinet. "But I promise to find you a young and agreeable woman with a hundred and fifty thousand francs.—Are you mad? Can you and I afford to quarrel? Things have turned against you in spite of me; but you do not know me."

'Well, we must learn to know each other," replied the Colonel. "Get me a wife with fifty thousand crowns before the elections—otherwise, your servant. I do not like awkward bedfellows, and you have pulled all the blankets to your side. Good-night."

"You will see," said Vinet, shaking hands affectionately with the Colonel.

At about one in the morning three clear, low hoots, like those of an owl, admirably mimicked, sounded in the Place; Pierrette heard them in her fevered sleep. She got up, quite damp, opened her window, saw Brigaut, and threw out a ball of silk, to which he tied a letter.

Sylvie, excited by the events of the evening and her own deliberations, was not asleep; she was taken in by the owl's cry.

"Ah! what a bird of ill-omen!—But, hark! Pierrette is out of bed. What does she want?"

On hearing the attic window open, Sylvie rushed to her own window and heard Brigaut's paper rustle against the shutters. She tied her jacket strings, and nimbly mounted the stairs to Pierrette's room; she found her untying the silk from round the letter.

"So I have caught you!" cried the old maid, going to the window, whence she saw Brigaut take to his heels. "Give me that letter."

"No, cousin," said the girl, who, by one of the stupendous inspirations of youth, and sustained by her spirit, rose to the dignity of resistance which we admire in the history of some nations reduced to desperation.

"What, you will not?" cried Sylvie, advancing on her cousin, and showing her a hideous face full of hatred, and distorted by rage.

Pierrette drew back a step or two to have time to clutch her letter in her hand, which she kept shut with invincible strength. On seeing this, Sylvie seized Pierrette's delicate white hand in her lobster's claws and tried to wrench it open. It was a fearful struggle, an infamous struggle, as everything is that dares to attack thought, the only treasure that God has set beyond the reach of power, and keeps as a secret bond between the wretched and himself.

The two women, one dying, the other full of vigour, looked steadfastly at each other. Pierrette's eyes flashed at her torturer such a look as the Templar's who received on his breast the blows from a mace in the presence of Philippe le Bel. The King could not endure that fearful gleam, and retired appalled by it; Sylvie, a woman, and a jealous woman, answered that magnetic glance by an ominous glare. Awful silence reigned. The Bretonne's clenched fingers resisted her cousin's efforts with the tenacity of a steel vice. Sylvie wrung Pierrette's arm, and tried to open her hand; as this had no effect, she vainly set her nails in the flesh. Finally, madness reinforced her anger; she raised Pierrette's fist to her teeth to bite her fingers and subdue her by pain. Pierrette still defied her with the terrifying gaze of innocence. The old maid's fury was roused to such a pitch that she was blind to all else; gripping Pierrette's arm, she beat the girl's fist on the window-sill, and on the marble chimney-piece, as we beat a nut to crack it and get at the kernel."

"Help, help!" cried Pierrette; "I am being killed."

"So you scream, do you, when I find you with a lover in the middle of the night?"

And she hit again and again without mercy.

"Help, help!" cried Pierrette, whose fist was bleeding.

At this moment there were violent blows on the street door. Both equally exhausted, the two women ceased.

Rogron, aroused and anxious, not knowing what was happening, had got out of bed, gone to his sister's room, and not found her; then he was alarmed, went down and opened the door, and was almost upset by Brigaut, followed by what seemed a phantom.

At the same instant Sylvie's eyes fell on Pierrette's stays; she remembered having felt the papers in them; she threw herself on them like a tiger on his prey, twisted the stays round her hand, and held them up with a smile, as an Iroquois smiles at his foe before scalping him.

"I am dying—" said Pierrette, dropping on her knees. "Who will save me?"

"I will," cried a woman with white hair, turning on Pierrette an aged, parchment face in which a pair of grey eyes sparkled.

"Ah, grandmother, you have come too late!" cried the poor child, melting into tears.

Pierrette went to fall on her bed, bereft of all her strength, and half killed by the reaction, which in a sick girl was inevitable after such a violent struggle. The tall withered apparition took her in her arms as a nurse takes a child, and went out, followed by Brigaut, without saying a word to Sylvie, at whom, by a tragic glance, she hurled majestic accusation. The sight of this dignified old woman in her Breton costume, shrouded in her *coiffe*, which is a sort of long cloak made of black cloth, and accompanied by the terrible Brigaut, appalled Sylvie: she felt as if she had seen death.

She went downstairs, heard the door shut, and found herself face to face with her brother, who said to her, "They have not killed you then?"

"Go to bed," said Sylvie. "To-morrow morning we will see what is to be done."

She got into bed again, unpicked the stays, and read Brigaut's two letters, which utterly confounded her. She went to sleep in the strangest perplexity, never dreaming of the terrible legal action to which her conduct was to give rise.

Brigaut's letter to the widow Lorrain had found her in the greatest joy, which was chequered when she read it. The poor old woman, now past seventy, had been dying of grief at having to live without Pierrette at her side; she only comforted herself for her loss by the belief that she had sacrificed herself to her grandchild's interests. She had one of those ever young hearts to which self-sacrifice gives strength and vitality. Her old husband, whose only joy Pierrette had been, had grieved for the child; day after day he had looked for her and missed her. It was an old man's sorrow; the sorrow old men live on, and die of at last.

Everybody can therefore imagine the joy felt by this poor woman, shut up in an almshouse, on hearing of one of those actions which, though rare, still are heard of in France.

After his failure François Joseph Collinet, the head of the house of Collinet, sailed for America with his children. He was a man of too much good feeling to sit down at Nantes, ruined and bereft of credit, in the midst of the disasters caused by his bankruptcy. From 1814 till 1824 this brave merchant, helped by his children and by his cashier, who remained faithful to him, and lent him the money to start again, valiantly worked to make a second fortune. After incredible efforts, that were crowned by success, by the eleventh year he was able to return to Nantes and rehabilitate himself, leaving his eldest son at the head of the American house. He found Madame Lorrain of Pen-Hoël at Saint-Jacques, and beheld the resignation with which the most hapless of his fellow-victims endured her penury.

"God forgive you!" said the old woman, "since you give me on the brink of the grave the means of securing my grandchild's happiness. I, alas! can never see my poor old man's credit re-established."

Monsieur Collinet had brought to his creditor her capital and interest at trade rates, altogether about forty-two thousand francs. His other creditors, active, wealthy, and capable men, had kept themselves above water, while the Lorrains' overthrow had seemed to old Collinet irremediable; he had now promised the widow that he would rehabilitate her husband's good name, finding that it would involve an expenditure of only about forty thousand francs more. When this act of generous restitution became known on 'Change at Nantes, the authorities were eager to re-open its doors to Collinet before he had surrendered to the Court at Rennes; but the merchant declined the honour, and submitted to all the rigour of the Commercial Code.

Madame Lorrain, then, had received forty-two thousand francs the day before the post brought her Brigaut's letters. As she signed her receipt, her first words were:

"Now I can live with my Pierrette, and let her marry poor Brigaut, who will make a fortune out of my money!"

She could not sit still; she fussed and fidgeted, and wanted to set out for Provins. And when she had read the fatal letters, she rushed out into the town like a mad thing, asking how she could get to Provins with the swiftness of lightning. She set out by mail when she heard of the Governmental rapidity of that conveyance. From Paris she took the Troyes coach; she had arrived at eleven that evening at Frappier's, where Brigaut, seeing the old Bretonne's deep despair, at once promised to fetch her granddaughter, after describing Pierrette's state in a few words. Those few words so alarmed the old woman that she could not control her she ran out to the Square. When Pierrette screamed, her grandmother's heart was pierced by the cry as keenly as was Brigaut's. The two together would no doubt have roused all the inhabitants, if Rogron, in sheer terror, had not opened the door. This cry of a girl in extremity filled the old woman with strength as great as her horror; she carried her dear Pierrette all the way to Frappier's, where his wife had hastily arranged Brigaut's room for Pierrette's grandmother. So in this miserable lodging, on a bed scarcely made, they laid the poor child; she fainted away, still keeping her hand closed, bruised and bleeding as it was, her nails set in the flesh. Brigaut, Frappier, his wife, and the woman contemplated Pierrette in silence, all lost in unutterable astonishment.

"Why is her hand covered with blood?" was the grandmother's first question.

Pierrette, overcome by the sleep which follows such an extreme exertion of strength, and knowing that she was safe from any violence, relaxed her fingers. Brigaut's letter fell out as an answer.

"They wanted to get my letter," said Brigaut, falling on his knees and picking up the note he had written, desiring his little friend to steal softly out of the Rogrons' house. He piously kissed the little martyr's hand.

Then there was a thing which made the joiners shudder: it was the sight of old Madame Lorrain, a sublime spectre standing by her child's bedside. Horror and vengeance fired with fierce expression the myriad wrinkles that furrowed her skin of ivory yellow; on her brow, shaded by thin grey locks, sat divine wrath. With the powerful intuition granted to the aged as they approach the tomb, she read all Pierrette's life, of which indeed she had been thinking all the way she had come.

She understood the malady that threatened the life of her darling. Two large tears gathered painfully in her grey-and-white eyes, which sorrow had robbed of lashes and eye brows; two beads of grief that gave a fearful moisture to those eyes, and swelled and rolled over those withered cheeks without wetting them.

"They have killed her!" she said at last, clasping her hands.

She dropped on her knees, which hit two sharp blows on the floor; she was making a vow, no doubt, to Sainte-Anne d'Auray, the most powerful Madonna of Brittany.

"A doctor from Paris," she next said to Brigaut. "Fly there, Brigaut. Go!"

She took the artisan by the shoulders and turned him round with a despotic gesture.

"I was coming at any rate, my good Brigaut," she said, calling him back. "I am rich.—Here!" She untied the ribbon that fastened her bodice across her bosom, took out a paper, in which were wrapped forty-two banknotes, and said, "Take as much as you need; bring back the greatest doctor in Paris."

"Keep that," said Frappier; "he could not change a bank-note at this hour. I have money; the diligence will pass presently, he will be sure to find a place in it. But would it not be better first to consult Monsieur Martener, who will give us the name of a Paris physician? The diligence is not due for an hour; we have plenty of time."

Brigaut went off to rouse Monsieur Martener. He brought the doctor back with him, not a little surprised to find Mademoiselle Lorrain at Frappier's.

Brigaut described to him the scene that had just taken place at the Rogrons'. The loquacity of a despairing lover threw light on this domestic drama, though the doctor could not suspect its horrors or its extent. Martener gave Brigaut the address of the famous Horace Bianchon, and Jacques and his master left the room on hearing the approach of the diligence.

Monsieur Martener sat down, and began by examining the bruises and wounds on the girl's hand, which hung out of bed.

"She did not hurt herself in such a way," said he.

"No, the dreadful creature I was so unhappy as to trust her with was torturing her," said the grandmother. "My poor Pierrette was crying out, 'Help! Murder!' It was enough to touch the heart of an executioner."

"But why?" said the doctor, feeling Pierrette's pulse. "She is very ill," he went on, bringing the light close to the bed. "We shall hardly save her," said he, after looking at her face. "She must have suffered terribly, and I cannot understand their having left her without care."

"It is my intention," said the old woman, "to appeal to justice. Had these people, who wrote to ask me for my granddaughter, saying that they had twelve thousand francs a year, any right to make her their cook and give her work far beyond her strength?"

"They did not choose to see that she was obviously suffering from one of the ailments to which young girls are some times subject, and needed the greatest care!" cried Monsieur Martener.

Pierrette was roused, partly by the light held by Madame Frappier so as to show her face more clearly, and partly by the dreadful pain in her head, caused by reactionary collapse after her struggle.

"Oh, Monsieur Martener, I am very ill," said she, in her pretty voice.

"Where is the pain, my child?" said the doctor.

"There," she replied, pointing to a spot on her head above the left ear.

"There is an abscess!" cried the doctor, after feeling Pierrette's head for some time, and questioning her as to the pain.

"You must tell us everything, my dear, to enable us to cure you. Why is your hand in this state? You did not injure it like this yourself?"

Pierrette artlessly told the tale of her struggle with her cousin Sylvie.

"Make her talk to you," said the doctor to her grandmother, "and learn all about it. I will wait till the surgeon arrives from Paris, and we will call in the head surgeon of the hospital for a consultation. It seems to me very serious. I will send a soothing draught to give Mademoiselle some sleep. She needs rest."

The old Bretonne, left alone with her grandchild, made her tell everything, by exerting her influence over her, and explaining to her that she was rich enough for all three, so that Brigaut need never leave them. The poor child confessed all her sufferings, never dreaming of the lawsuit she was leading up to. The monstrous conduct of these two loveless beings, who knew nothing of family affection, revealed to the old woman worlds of torment, as far from her conception as the manners of the savage tribes must have been to the first travellers who penetrated the savannas of America.

Her grandmother's presence, and the certainty of living with her for the future in perfect ease, lulled Pierrette's mind as the draught lulled her body. The old woman watched by her, kissing her brow, hair, and hands, as the holy women may have kissed Jesus while laying Him in the sepulchre.

By nine in the morning Monsieur Martener went to the President of the Courts, and related to him the scene of the past night between Sylvie and Pierrette, the moral and physical torture, the cruelty of every kind inflicted by the Rogrons on their ward, and the two fatal maladies which had been developed by this ill-usage. The President sent for the notary, Monsieur Auffray, a connection of Pierrette's on her mother's side.

At this moment the war between the Vinet party and the Tiphaine party was at its height. The gossip circulated in Provins by the Rogrons and their adherents as to the well-known liaison between Madame Roguin and du Tillet the banker, and the circumstances of Monsieur Roguin's bankruptcy—Madame Tiphaine's father was said to have committed forgery—hit all the more surely because, though it was scandal, it was not calumny. Such wounds pierce to the bottom of things; they attacked self-interest in its most vital part. These statements, repeated to the partisans of Tiphaine by the same speakers who also reported to the Rogrons all the sarcasms uttered by the "beautiful Madame Tiphaine" and her friends, added fuel to their hatred, complicated as it was with political feeling.

The irritation caused in France at that time by party spirit, which had waxed excessively violent, was everywhere bound up, as it was at Provins, with imperiled interests and offended with antagonistic private feelings. Each coterie eagerly pounced on anything that might damage its rival. Party animosity was not less implicated than personal conceit in even trivial questions, which were often carried to great lengths. A whole town threw itself in some dispute, raising it to the dignity of a political contest. And so the President discerned, in the action between Pierrette and the Rogrons, a means of confuting, discrediting, and humiliating the owners of that drawing-room where plots were hatched against the monarchy, and where the Opposition newspaper had had its birth.

He sent for the public prosecutor. Then Monsieur Lesourd, Monsieur Auffray the notary—appointed the legal guardian of Pierrette—and the President of the Court discussed in the greatest privacy, with Monsieur Martener, what steps could be taken. The legal guardian was to call a family council (a formality of French law), and, armed with the evidence of the three medical men, would demand the dismissal of Rogron from his guardianship. The case thus formulated would be brought before the tribunal, and then Monsieur Lesourd would get it carried into the Criminal Court by demanding an inquiry.

By mid-day all Provins was in a stir over the strange reports of what had taken place at the Rogrons' in the course of the past night. Pierrette's screams had been remotely heard in the Square, but they had not lasted long; no one had got up; but everybody had asked in the morning, "Did you hear the noise and screaming at about one o'clock? What was it?" Gossip and comment had given such magnitude to the horrible drama that a crowd collected in front of Frappier's shop, everybody cross-questioning the honest joiner, who described the girl's arrival at his house with her hand bleeding and her fingers mangled.

At about one in the afternoon a post-chaise, containing Doctor Bianchon, by whom sat Brigaut, stopped at Frappier's door, and Madame Frappier went off to the hospital to fetch Monsieur Martener and the head surgeon. Thus the reports heard in the town received confirmation.

The Rogrons were accused of having intentionally maltreated their young cousin, and endangered her life. The news reached Vinet at the Law Courts; he left his business and hurried to the Rogrons'. Rogron and his sister had just finished breakfast. Sylvie had avoided telling her brother of her defeat during the night; she allowed him to question her, making no reply but: "It does not concern you." And she bustled to and fro between the kitchen and dining-room to avoid all discussion.

She was alone when Vinet walked in.

"Do you know nothing of what is going on?" asked the lawyer.

"No," said Sylvie.

"You are going to have a criminal action brought against you for the way in which matters stand with Pierrette."

"A criminal action!" said Rogron, coming in. "Why? What for?"

"In the first place," said Vinet, looking at Sylvie, "tell me exactly, without subterfuge, all that took place last night, as though you were before God, for there is some talk of cutting off Pierrette's hand."

Sylvie turned ashy pale and shivered.

"Then there was something!" said the lawyer.

Mademoiselle Rogron told the story, trying to justify herself; but on being cross-questioned, related all the details of the horrible conflict.

"If you have only broken her fingers, you will only appear in the Police Court; but if her hand has to be amputated, you will find yourself brought up at the Assizes. The Tiphaines will do anything to get you there."

Sylvie, more dead than alive, confessed her jealousy, and, which was even harder to bring out, how her suspicions had blundered.

"What a case for trial!" exclaimed Vinet. "You and your brother may be ruined by it; you will be thrown over by many of your friends even if you gain it. If you do not come out clear, you will have to leave Provins."

"Oh! my dear Monsieur Vinet—you who are such an able lawyer," cried Rogron, horrified, "advise us, save us!"

Vinet dexterously fomented the fears of these two fools to the utmost, and declared positively that Madame and Mademoiselle de Chargebœuf would hesitate to go to their house again. To be forsaken by these two ladies would be a fatal condemnation. In short, after an hour of magnificent manuvring, it was agreed that in order to induce Vinet to save the Rogrons, he must have an interest at stake in defending him in the eyes of all Provins. In the course of the evening Rogron's engagement to marry Mademoiselle de Chargebœuf was to be announced. The banns were to be published on Sunday. The marriage-contract would at once be drawn up by Cournant, and Mademoiselle Rogron would figure in it as abandoning, in consideration of this alliance, the capital of her share of the estate by a deed of gift to her brother, reserving only a life-interest. Vinet impressed on Rogron and his sister the necessity of having a draft of this deed drawn up two or three days before that event, so as to put Madame and Mademoiselle de Chargebœuf under the necessity, in public opinion, of continuing their visits to the Rogrons.

"Sign that contract, and I will undertake to get you out of the scrape," said the lawyer. "It will no doubt be a hard fight, but I will go into it body and soul, and you will owe me a very handsome taper."

"Yes, indeed," said Rogron.

By half-past eleven the lawyer was empowered to act for them, alike as to the contract and as to the management of the case. At noon the President was informed that a summons was applied for by Vinet against Brigaut and the widow Lorrain for abducting Pierrette Lorrain, a minor, from the domicile of her guardian. Thus the audacious Vinet took up the offensive, putting Rogron in the position of a man having the law on his side. This, indeed, was the tone in which the matter was commented on in the Law Courts. The President postponed hearing the parties till four o'clock. The excitement of the town over all these events need not be described. The President knew that the medical consultation would be ended by three o'clock; he wished that the legal guardian should appear armed with the physicians' verdict.

The announcement of Rogron's engagement to the fair Bathilde de Chargebœuf, and of the deed of gift added by Sylvie to the contract, promptly made the Rogrons two enemies—Mademoiselle Habert and the Colonel, who thus saw all their hopes dashed. Céleste Habert and the Colonel remained ostensibly friends to the Rogrons, but only to damage them more effectually. So, as soon as Monsieur Martener spoke of the existence of an abscess on the brain in the haberdashers' hapless victim, Céleste and the Colonel mentioned the blow Pierrette had given herself that evening when Sylvie had driven her out of the room, and remembered Mademoiselle Rogron's cruel and barbarous remarks. They related various instances of the old maid's utter indifference to her ward's sufferings. Thus these friends of the couple admitted serious wrong, while affecting to defend Sylvia and her brother.

Vinet had foreseen this storm; but Mademoiselle de Chargebœuf was about to acquire the whole of the Rogrons' fortune, and he promised himself that in a few weeks he should see her living in the nice house on the Place, and reign conjointly with her over Provins; for he was already scheming for a coalition with the Bréauteys to serve his own ambitions.

From twelve o'clock till four all the ladies of the Tiphaine faction—the Garcelands, the Guépins, the Julliards, Mesdames Galardon, Guénée, and the sous-préfet's wife—all sent to inquire after Mademoiselle Lorrain. Pierrette knew nothing whatever of this commotion in the town on her behalf. In the midst of acute suffering she felt ineffably happy at finding herself between her grandmother and Brigaut, the objects of her affection. Brigaut's eyes were constantly full of tears, and the old woman petted her beloved grandchild.

God knows the grandmother spared the three men of science none of the details she had heard from Pierrette about her life with the Rogrons! Horace Bianchon expressed his indignation in unmeasured terms. Horrified by such barbarity, he insisted that the other doctors of the town should be called in;

so Monsieur Néraud was present, and was requested, as being Rogron's friend, to contradict if he could the terrible inferences derived from the consultation, which, unfortunately for Rogron, were unanimously subscribed to. Néraud, who was already credited with having made Pierrette's maternal grandmother die of grief, was in a false position, of which Martener adroitly took advantage, delighted to overwhelm the Rogrons, and also to compromise Monsieur Néraud, his antagonist. It is needless to give the text of this document, which also was produced at the trial. If the medical terms of Molière's age were barbarous, those of modern medicine have the advantage of such extreme plain speaking, that an account of Pierrette's maladies, though natural, and unfortunately common, would shock the ear. The verdict was indisputably final, attested by so famous a name as that of Horace Bianchon.

After the Court sitting was over, the President remained in his place, while Pierrette's grandmother came in with Monsieur Auffray, Brigaut, and a considerable crowd. Vinet appeared alone. This contrast struck the spectators, including a vast number of merely inquisitive persons. Vinet, who had kept his gown on, raised his hard face to the President, settling his spectacles as he began in his harsh, sawing tones to set forth that certain strangers had made their way into the house of Monsieur and Mademoiselle Rogron by night, and had carried away the girl Lorrain, a minor. Her guardian claimed the protection of the Court to recover his ward.

Monsieur Auffray, as the guardian appointed by the Court, rose to speak.

"If Monsieur le Président," said he, "will take into his consideration this consultation, signed by one of the most eminent Paris physicians, and by all the doctors and surgeons of Provins, he will perceive how unreasonable is Monsieur Rogron's claim, and what sufficient reasons induced the minor's grandmother to release her at once from her tormentors. The facts are these: A deliberate consultation, signed unanimously by a celebrated Paris doctor, sent for in great haste, and by all the medical authorities of the town, ascribe the almost dying state of the ward to the ill-treatment she had received at the hands of the said Rogron and his sister. As a legal formality a family council will be held, with the least possible delay, and consulted on the question whether the guardian ought not to be held disqualified for his office. We petition that the minor shall not be sent back to her guardian's house, but shall be placed in the hands of any other member of the family whom Monsieur le Président may see fit to designate."

Vinet wanted to reply, saying that the document of the consultation ought to be communicated to him that he might contravene it.

"Certainly not to Vinet's side," said the President severely, "but perhaps to the public prosecutor. The case is closed."

At the foot of the petition the President wrote the following injunction:

"Inasmuch as that by a consultation unanimously signed by the medical faculty of this town and by Doctor Bianchon of the medical faculty of Paris, it is proved that the girl Lorrain, a minor, claimed by her guardian Rogron, is in a very serious state of sickness brought on by the ill-usage and cruelty inflicted on her in the house of her guardian and his sister,

"We, President of the Lower Court of Justice at Provins,

"Decree on the petition, and enjoin that until the family council shall have been held which, as the provisional guardian appointed by the law declares, is at once to be convened, the said minor shall not re-enter her guardian's residence, but shall be transferred to that of the guardian appointed by the law.

"And in the second place, in consideration of the minor's present state of health, and the traces of violence which, in the opinion of the medical men, are to be seen on her person, we commission the chief physician and chief surgeon of the Hospital of Provins to attend her; and in the event of the cruelty being proved to have been constant, we reserve all the rights and powers of the law, without prejudice to the civil action taken by Auffray, the legalised temporary guardian."

This terrible injunction was pronounced by Monsieur le Président Tiphaine with a loud voice and distinct utterance.

"Why not the hulks at once?" said Vinet. "And all this fuss about a little girl who carried on an intrigue with a carpenter's apprentice! If this is the way the case is conducted," he added insolently, "we shall apply for other judgment on the plea of legitimate suspicions."

Vinet left the Court, and went to the chief leaders of his party to explain the position of Rogron, who had never given his little cousin a finger-flip, and whom the tribunal had treated, as he declared, less as Pierrette's guardian than as the chief voter in Provins.

To hear him, the Tiphaines were making much ado about nothing. The mountain would bring forth a mouse. Sylvie, an eminently religious and well-conducted person, had detected an intrigue between her brother's ward and a carpenter's boy, a Breton named Brigaut. The young rascal knew very well that the girl would have a fortune from her grandmother, and wanted to tamper with her.

Vinet to talk of tampering! ... Mademoiselle Rogron, who had kept the letters in which this little slut's wickedness was made clear, was not so much to blame as the Tiphaines tried to make her seem. Even if she had been betrayed into violence to obtain a letter, which could easily be accounted for by the irritation produced in her by Breton obstinacy, in what was Rogron to blame?

The lawyer thus made the action a party matter, and contrived to give it political colour. And so, from that evening, there were differences of opinion on the question.

"If you hear but one bell, you hear but one note," said the wise-heads. "Have you heard what Vinet has to say? He explains the case very well."

Frappier's house was regarded as unsuitable for Pierrette on account of the noise, which would cause her much pain in the head. Her removal from thence to her appointed guardian's house was as desirable from a medical as from a legal point of view. This business was effected with the utmost care, and calculated to make a great sensation. Pierrette was placed on a stretcher with many mattresses, carried by two men, escorted by a Grey Sister holding in her hand a bottle of ether, followed by her grandmother, Brigaut, Madame Auffray, and her maid. The people stood at the windows and in the doors to see the little procession pass. No doubt the state in which Pierrette was seen and her death-like pallor gave immense support to the party adverse to the Rogrons. The Auffrays were bent on showing to all the town how right the President had been in pronouncing his injunction. Pierrette and her grandmother were established on the second floor of Monsieur Auffray's house. The notary and his wife lavished on them the generosity of the amplest hospitality; they made a display of it. Pierrette was nursed by her grandmother, and Monsieur Martener came to see her again the same evening, with the surgeon.

From that evening dated much exaggeration on both sides. The Rogrons' room was crowded. Vinet had worked up the Liberal faction in the matter. The two Chargebœuf ladies dined with the Rogrons, for the marriage contract was to be signed forthwith. Vinet had had the banns put up at the Mairie that morning. He treated the business of Pierrette as a mere trifle. If the Court of Provins could not judge it dispassionately, the superior Court would judge of the facts, said he, and the Auffrays would think twice before rushing into such an action. Then the connection between the Rogrons and the Chargebœufs was of immense weight with certain people. To them the Rogrons were as white as snow, and Pierrette an excessively wicked little girl whom they had cherished in their bosom.

In Madame Tiphaine's drawing-room vengeance was taken on the horrible scandals the Vinet party had promulgated for the last two years. The Rogrons were monsters, and the guardian would find himself in the Criminal Court. In the Square, Pierrette was perfectly well; in the upper town, she must infallibly die; at the Rogrons', she had a few scratches on her hand; at Madame Tiphaine's, she had her fingers smashed; one would have to be cut off.

Next day the *Courrier de Provins* had an extremely clever article, well written, a masterpiece of innuendo mixed up with legal demurs, which placed the Rogrons above suspicion. The *Ruche,* which came out two days later, could not reply without risk of libel; but it said that in a case like the present, the best thing was to leave justice to take its course.

The family council was constituted by the Justice of the Peace of the Provins district, as the legal President, in the first place, of Rogron and the two Auffrays, Pierrette's next-of-kin; then of Monsieur Ciprey, a nephew of Pierrette's maternal grandmother. He added to these Monsieur Habert, the young girl's director, and Colonel Gouraud, who had always given himself out to be a comrade of her father's, Colonel Lorrain. The Justice's impartiality was highly applauded in including in this family council Monsieur Habert and the Colonel, whom all the town regarded as great friends of the Rogrons. In the difficult position in which he found himself, Rogron begged to be allowed the support of Maître Vinet on the occasion. By this manœuvre, evidently suggested by Vinet, he succeeded in postponing the meeting of the family council till the end of December.

At that date the President and his wife were in Paris, living with Madame Roguin, in consequence of the sitting of the Chambers. Thus the Ministerial party at Provins was bereft of its head. Vinet had already quietly made friends with the worthy examining judge, Monsieur Desfondrilles, in case the business should assume the penal or criminal aspect that Tiphaine had endeavored to give it.

For three hours Vinet addressed the family council; he proved an intrigue between Brigaut and Pierrette, to justify Mademoiselle Rogron's severity; he pointed out how natural it was that the guardian should have left his ward under the control of a woman; he dwelt on his client's non-interference in the mode of Pierrette's education as conducted by Sylvie. But in spite of Vinet's efforts, the meeting unanimously decided on abolishing Rogron's guardianship. Monsieur Auffray was appointed Pierrette's guardian, and Monsieur Ciprey her legal guardian.

They heard the evidence given by Adèle the maid, who incriminated her former master and mistress; by Mademoiselle Habert, who repeated Sylvie's cruel remarks the evening when Pierrette had given herself the dreadful blow that everybody had heard, and the comments on Pierrette's health made by Madame de Chargebœuf. Brigaut produced the letter he had received from Pierrette, which established their innocence. It was proved that the deplorable state in which the minor now was resulted from the neglect of her guardian, who was responsible in all that related to his ward. Pierrette's illness had struck everybody, even persons in the town who did not know the family. Thus the charge of cruelty against Rogron was fully sustained. The matter would be made public.

By Vinet's advice Rogron put in a protest against the confirmation by the Court of the decision of the family council. The Minister of Justice now intervened, in consequence of the increasingly critical condition of Pierrette Lorrain. This singular case, though put on the lists forthwith, did not come up for trial till near the month of March 1828.

By that time the marriage of Rogron to Mademoiselle de Chargebœuf was an accomplished fact. Sylvie was living on the second floor of the house, which had been arranged to accommodate her and Madame de Chargebœuf; for the first floor was entirely given up to Madame Rogron. The beautiful Madame Rogron now succeeded to the beautiful Madame Tiphaine. The effect of this marriage was enormous. The town no longer came to Mademoiselle Sylvie's salon, but to the beautiful Madame Rogron's.

Monsieur Tiphaine, the President of the Provins Court, pushed by his mother-in-law, and supported by du Tillet and by Nucingen, the Royalist bankers, found an opportunity of being useful to the Ministry. He was one of the most highly respected speakers of the Centre, was made a judge of the Lower Court in the Seine district, and. got his nephew Lesourd nominated President in his place at Provins. This appointment greatly annoyed Monsieur Desfondrilles, still an archæologist, and more supernumerary than ever. The Keeper of the Seals sent a protégé of his own to fill Lesourd's place. Thus Monsieur Tiphaine's promotion did not lead to any advancement in the legal forces at Provins.

Vinet took advantage of these circumstances very cleverly. He had always told the good folks of Provins that they were only serving as a step-ladder to Madame Tiphaine cunning and ambition. The President laughed in his sleeve at his friends. Madame Tiphaine secretly disdained the town of Provins; she would never come back to it.

Monsieur Tiphaine *père* presently died; his son inherited the estate of le Fay, and sold his handsome house in the upper town to Monsieur Julliard. This sale showed how little he intended to come back to Provins. Vinet was right! Vinet had been a true prophet! These facts had no little influence on the action relating to Rogron's guardianship.

The horrible martyrdom so brutally inflicted on Pierrette by two imbecile tyrants—which led, medically speaking, to her being subjected by Monsieur Martener, with Bianchon's approval, to the terrible operation of trepanning; the whole dreadful drama, reduced to judicial statements, was left among the foul medley known to lawyers as outstanding cases. The action dragged on through the delays and inextricable intricacies of "proceedings," constantly checked by the quibbles of a contemptible lawyer, while the calumniated Pierrette languished in suffering from the most terrible pains known to medical science. We could not avoid these details as to the strange variations in public opinion and the slow march of justice, before returning to the room where she was living—where she was dying.

Monsieur Martener and the whole of the Auffray family were in a very few days completely won by Pierrette's adorable temper, and by the old Bretonne, whose feelings, ideas, and manners bore the stamp of an antique Roman type. This matron of the Marais was like one of Plutarch's women.

The doctor desired to contend with Death, at least, for his prey; for from the first the Paris and provincial physicians had agreed in regarding Pierrette as past saving. Then began between the disease and the doctor, aided by Pierrette's youth, one of those struggles which medical men alone know; the reward, in the event of success, is not in the pecuniary profit, or even in the rescued sufferer; it lies in sweet satisfaction of conscience, and in a sort of ideal and invisible palm of victory gathered by every true artist from the joyful certainty of having achieved a fine work. The physician makes for healing as the artist makes for the beautiful, urged on by a noble sentiment which we call virtue. This daily recurring battle had extinguished in this man, though a provincial, the squalid irritation of the warfare going on between the Vinet party and that of the Tiphaines, as happens with men who have to fight it out with great suffering.

Monsieur Martener had at first wished to practise his profession in Paris; but the activity of the great city, the callousness produced at last in a doctor's mind by the terrific number of sick people and the multitude of serious cases, had appalled his gentle soul, which was made for a country life. He was in bondage, too, to his pretty birthplace. So he had come back to Provins to marry and settle there, and take almost tender care of a population he could think of as a large family. All the time Pierrette was ill he could not bear to speak of her illness. His aversion to reply when every one asked for news of the poor child was so evident, that at last nobody questioned him about her. Pierrette was to him what she could not help being—one of those deep, mysterious poems, immense in its misery, such as occur in the terrible life of a physician. He had for this frail girl an admiration of which he would betray the secret to no one.

This feeling for his patient was infectious, as all true sentiments are; Monsieur and Madame Auffray's house, so long as Pierrette lived in it, was peaceful and still. Even the children, who of old had had such famous games with Pierrette, understood, with childlike grace, that they were not to be noisy or troublesome. They made it a point of honour to be good because Pierrette was ill.

Monsieur Auffray's house is in the upper town, below the ruined castle; built, indeed, on one of the cliff-like knolls formed by the overthrow of the old ramparts. From thence the residents have a view over the valley as they walk in a little orchard supported by the thick walls rising straight up from the lower town. The roofs of the houses rise to the level of the wall that upholds this garden. Along this terrace is a walk ending at the glass-door of Monsieur Auffray's study. At the other end are a vine-covered arbour and a fig-tree, sheltering a round table, a bench, and some chairs, all painted green.

Pierrette had a room over that of her new guardian. Madame Lorrain slept there on a camp-bed by her grandchild's side. From her window Pierrette could see the beautiful valley of Provins, which she hardly knew—she had so rarely been out of the Rogrons' sinister dwelling. Whenever it was fine, she liked to drag herself, on her grandmother's arm, as far as this arbour. Brigaut, who now did no work, came three times a day to see his little friend; he was absorbed in grief, which made him indifferent to life; he watched for Monsieur Martener with the eagerness of a spaniel, always went in with him and came out with him.

It would be difficult to imagine all the follies every one was ready to commit for the dear little invalid. Her grandmother, drunk with grief, hid her despair; she showed the child the same smiling face as at Pen-Hoël. In her wish to delude herself, she made her a Breton cap such as Pierrette had worn when she came to Provins, and put it on her; the girl then looked to her more like herself; she was sweet to behold, with her face framed in the aureole of cambric edged with starched lace. Her face, as white as fine white porcelain, her forehead on which suffering set a semblance of deep thoughtfulness, the purity of outline refined by sickness, the slowness and occasional fixity of her gaze, all made Pierrette a master-work of melancholy.

The child was waited on with fanatical devotion; she was so tender, so loving. Madame Martener had sent her piano to Madame Auffray, her sister, thinking it might amuse Pierrette, to whom music was rapture. It was a poem to watch her listening to a piece by Weber, Beethoven, or Hérold, her eyes raised to heaven in silence, regretting, no doubt, the life she felt slipping from her. Monsieur Péroux the curé and Monsieur Habert, her two priestly comforters, admired her pious resignation.

Is it not a strange fact, worthy of the attention alike of philosophers and of mere observers, that a sort of seraphic perfection is characteristic of youths and maidens marked amid the crowd with the red cross of death, like saplings in a forest? He who has witnessed such a death can never remain or become an infidel. These beings exhale, as it were, a heavenly fragrance, their looks speak of God, their voice is eloquent in the most trivial speech, and often sounds like a divine instrument, expressing the secrets of futurity. When Monsieur Martener congratulated Pierrette on having carried out some disagreeable prescription, this angel would say in the presence of all, and with what a look!— "I wish to live, dear Monsieur Martener, less for my own sake than for my grandmother's, for my poor Brigaut's, and for you all, who will be sorry when I die."

The first time she took a walk, in the month of November, under a bright Martinmas sun, escorted by all the family, Madame Auffray asked her if she were tired.

"Now that I have nothing to bear but the pain God sends me, I can endure it. I find strength to bear suffering in the joy of being loved."

This was the only time she ever alluded, even so remotely, to her horrible martyrdom at the Rogrons'; she never spoke of them; and as the remembrance could not fail to be painful, no one mentioned their name.

"Dear Madame Auffray," said she one day at noon on the terrace, while gazing at the valley lighted up by brilliant sunshine and dressed in the russet tints of autumn, "my dying days in your house will have brought me more happiness than all the three years before."

Madame Auffray looked at her sister, Madame Martener, and said to her in a whisper:

"How she would have loved!"

And, indeed, Pierrette's tone and look gave her words unutterable meaning.

Monsieur Martener kept up a correspondence with Doctor Bianchon, and tried no serious treatment without his approbation. He hoped first to restore the girl to normal health, and then to enable the abscess to discharge itself through the ear. The more acute her pain was, the more hopeful he felt. With regard to the first point he had some success, and that was a great triumph. For some days Pierrette recovered her appetite, and could satisfy it with substantial food, for which her unhealthy state had hitherto given her great aversion; her colour improved, but the pain in her head was terrible. The doctor now begged the great physician, his consultee, to come to Provins. Bianchon came, stayed two days, and advised an operation; he threw himself into all poor Martener's anxiety, and went himself to fetch the famous Desplein. So the operation was performed by the greatest surgeon of ancient or modern times; but this terrible augur said to Martener as he went away with Bianchon, his best-beloved pupil:

"You can save her only by a miracle. As Horace has told you, necrosis has set in. At that age the bones are still so tender."

The operation was performed early in March 1828. All that month Monsieur Martener, alarmed by the fearful torments Pierrette endured, made several journeys to Paris; he consulted Desplein and Bianchon, to whom he even suggested a treatment resembling that known as lithotrity—the insertion of a tubular instrument into the skull, by which a heroic remedy might be introduced to arrest the progress of decay. The daring Desplein dared not attempt this surgical feat, which only despair had suggested to Martener.

When the doctor returned from his last journey to Paris, his friends thought him crestfallen and gloomy. One fatal evening he was compelled to announce to the Auffray family, to Madame Lorrain, to the confessor, and to Brigaut, who were all present, that science could do no more for Pierrette, that her life was in the hands of God alone. Her grandmother took a vow and begged the curé to say, every morning at daybreak, before Pierrette rose, a mass which she and Brigaut would attend.

The case came up for trial. While the Rogrons' victim lay dying, Vinet was calumniating her to the Court. The Court ratified the decision of the family council, and the lawyer immediately appealled. The newly-appointed public prosecutor delivered an address which led to an inquiry. Rogron and his sister were obliged to find sureties to avoid being sent to prison. The inquiry necessitated the examination of Pierrette herself. When Monsieur Desfondrilles went to the Auffrays' house, Pierrette was actually dying; the priest was at her bedside, and she was about to take the last sacrament. At that moment she was entreating all the assembled family to forgive her cousins as she herself forgave them, saying, with excellent good sense, that judgment in such cases belonged to God alone.

"Grandmother," said she, "leave all you possess to Brigaut"—Brigaut melted into tears—"and," Pierrette went on, "give a thousand francs to good Adèle, who used to warm my bed on the sly. If she had stayed with my cousins, I should be alive ..."

It was at three o'clock on Easter Tuesday, on a beautiful day, that this little angel ceased to suffer. Her heroic grandmother insisted on sitting by her all night with the priests, and sewing her winding-sheet on her with her old hands. Towards evening Brigaut left the house and went back to Frappier's.

"I need not ask you the news, my poor boy," said the carpenter.

"Père Frappier—yes; it is all over with her, and not with me!"

The apprentice looked round the workshop at all the wood store with gloomy but keen eyes.

"I understand, Brigaut," said the worthy Frappier. "There—that is what you want," and he pointed to some two-inch oak planks.

"Do not help me, Monsieur Frappier," said the Breton. "I will do it all myself."

Brigaut spent the night in planing and joining Pierrette's coffin, and more than once he ripped off with one stroke a long shaving wet with his tears. His friend Frappier smoked and watched him. He said nothing to him but these few words when his man put the four sides together:

"Make the lid to slide in a groove, then her poor friends will not hear you nail it down."

At daybreak Brigaut went for lead to line the coffin. By a singular coincidence the sheets of lead cost exactly the sum he had given to Pierrette for her journey from Nantes to Provins. The brave Breton, who had borne up under the dreadful pain of making a coffin for the beloved companion of his childhood, overlaying each funereal board with all his memories, could not endure this coincidence; he turned faint, and could not carry the lead; the plumber accompanied him and offered to go with him and solder down the top sheet as soon as the body should be laid in the coffin.

The Breton burned his plane and all the tools he had used for the work, he wound up his accounts with Frappier, and bade him good-bye.

The heroism which enabled the poor fellow, like the grandmother, to busy himself with doing the last services to the dead, led to his intervening in the crowning scene which put a climax to the Rogrons' tyranny.

Brigaut and the plumber arrived at Monsieur Auffray's just in time to decide by brute force a horrible and shameful legal question. The chamber of the dead was full of people, and presented a strange scene to the two workmen. The Rogrons stood hideous by the victim's corpse to torture it even in death. The body of the poor girl, sublime in its beauty, lay on her grandmother's camp-bed. Pierrette's eyes were closed, her hair smoothly braided, her body sewn into a winding-sheet of coarse cotton.

By this bed, her hair in disorder, on her knees with out stretched hands and a flaming face, old Madame Lorrain was crying out:

"No, no; it shall never be!"

At the foot of the bed were the guardian Monsieur Auffray, the Curé Monsieur Péroux, and Monsieur Habert. Tapers were still burning. Opposite the grandmother stood the hospital surgeon and Monsieur Néraud, supported by the smooth-tongued and formidable Vinet. A registrar was present. The surgeon had on his dissecting apron; one of his assistants had opened his roll of instruments and was handing him a scalpel.

This scene was disturbed by the noise made by the fall of the coffin, which Brigaut and the plumber dropped; and by Brigaut himself, who, entering first, was seized with horror on seeing old Madame Lorrain in tears.

"What is the matter?" asked Brigaut, placing himself by her side, and convulsively clutching a chisel he had brought with him.

"The matter!" said the old woman. "They want to open my child's body, to split her skull—to rend her heart after her death as they did in her lifetime!"

"Who?" said Brigaut, in a voice to crack the drum of the lawyer's ears.

"The Rogrons."

"By the God above us!—"

"One moment, Brigaut," said Monsieur Auffray, seeing the Breton brandish his chisel.

"Monsieur Auffray," said Brigaut, as pale as the dead girl, "I listen to you because you are Monsieur Auffray. But at this moment I would not listen to—"

"Justice!" Auffray put in.

"Is there such a thing as Justice?" cried Brigaut.

"That—that is Justice!" he went on, threatening the lawyer, the surgeon, and the clerk with his chisel that flashed in the sunlight.

"My good fellow," said the curé, "Monsieur Rogron's lawyer has appealled to Justice. His client lies under a serious accusation, and it is impossible to refuse a suspected person the means of clearing himself. According to Monsieur Rogron's advocate, if this poor child died of the abscess on the brain, her former guardian must be regarded as guiltless; for it is proved that Pierrette for a long time concealed the blow she had given herself—"

"That will do!" said Brigaut.

"My client—"Vinet began.

"Your client," cried the Breton, "shall go to hell, and I to the scaffold; for if one of you makes an attempt to touch her whom your client killed—if that sawbones does not put his knife away, I will strike him dead."

"This is overt resistance;" said Vinet; "we shall lay it before the Court."

The five strangers withdrew.

"Oh, my son!" said the old woman, starting up and throwing her arms round Brigaut's neck, "let us bury her at once; they will come back."

"When once the lead is soldered," said the plumber, "perhaps they will not dare."

Monsieur Auffray hurried off to his brother-in-law, Monsieur Lesourd, to try to get this matter settled. Vinet wished for nothing better. Pierrette once dead, the action as to the guardianship, which was not yet decided, must die a natural death, without any possibility of argument either for or against the Rogrons; the question remained an open one. So the shrewd lawyer had perfectly foreseen the effect his demand would produce.

At noon Monsieur Desfondrilles reported to the Bench on the inquiry relating to the Rogrons, and the Court pronounced a verdict of no case, on self-evident grounds.

Rogron dared not show his face at Pierrette's funeral, though all the town was present. Vinet tried to drag him there; but the ex-haberdasher feared the excitement of universal reprobation.

Brigaut, after seeing the grave filled up in which Pierrette was laid, left Provins and went on foot to Paris. He addressed a petition to the Dauphiness to be allowed, in consideration of his father's name, to enlist in the Royal Guard, and was soon afterwards enrolled. When an expedition was fitted out for Algiers, he again wrote to the Dauphiness, begging to be ordered on active service. He was then sergeant; Marshal Bourmont made him sub-lieutenant of the Line. The Major's son behaved like a man seeking death. But death has hitherto respected Jacques Brigaut, who has distinguished himself in all the recent expeditions without being once wounded. He is now at the head of a battalion in the Line. There is not a more taciturn or a better officer. Off duty he is speechless, walks alone, and lives like a machine. Every one understands and respects some secret sorrow. He has forty-six thousand francs, left him by old Madame Lorrain, who died in Paris in 1829.

Vinet was elected député in 1830, and the services he has done to the new Government have earned him the place of Prosecutor-General. His influence is now so great that he will always be returned as député. Rogron is Receiver-General in the town where Vinet exercises his high functions, and by a singular coincidence Monsieur Tiphaine is the chief President of the Supreme Court there; for the Judge unhesitatingly attached himself to the new dynasty of July. The ex-beautiful Madame Tiphaine lives on very good terms with the beautiful Madame Rogron. Vinet and President Tiphaine agree perfectly.

As to Rogron, utterly stupid, he says such things as this:

"Louis Philippe will never be really King until he can create nobles."

This speech is obviously not his own.

His failing health allows Madame Rogron to hope that ere long she may be free to marry General the Marquis de Montriveau, a peer of France, who is Governor of the department, and attentive to her. Vinet is always in a hurry to condemn a man to death; he never believes in the innocence of the accused. This man, born to be a public prosecutor, is considered one of the most amiable men of his district, and is not less successful in Paris and in the Chamber; at Court he is the exquisite courtier.

General Baron Gouraud, that noble relic of our glorious armies, has married—as Vinet promised that he should—a Demoiselle Matifat, five-and-twenty years of age, the daughter of a druggist in the Rue des Lombards, who had a fortune of fifty thousand crowns. He is Governor—as Vinet prophesied—of a department close to Paris. He was made a peer of France as the reward of his conduct in the riots under Casimir Périer's Ministry. Baron Gouraud was one of the generals who took the Church of Saint-Merry, delighted to "rap the knuckles" of the civilians who had bullied them for fifteen years; and his zeal won him the Grand Cordon of the Legion of Honour.

None of those who were implicated in Pierrette's death have any remorse. Monsieur Desfondrilles is still an archæologist; but, to promote his own election, Attorney-General Vinet took care to have him appointed President of the Court. Sylvie holds a little court, and manages her brother's affairs; she lends at high interest, and does not spend more than twelve hundred francs a year.

From time to time, in the little Square, when some son of Provins comes home from Paris to settle there, and is seen coming out of Mademoiselle Rogron's house, some former partisan of the Tiphaines will say, "The Rogrons had a very sad affair once about a ward …"

"A mere party question," President Desfondrilles replies. "Monstrous tales were given out. Out of kindness of heart they took this little Pierrette to live with them, a nice child enough, without a penny; just as she was growing up she had some intrigue with a joiner's apprentice, and would come to her window barefoot to talk to the lad, who used to stand just there, do you see? The lovers sent each other notes by means of a string. As you may suppose, in her state, and in the months of October and November, that was quite enough to upset a little pale-faced girl. The Rogrons behaved admirably; they never claimed their share of the child's inheritance; they gave everything to the grandmother. The moral of it all, my friends, is that the devil always punishes us for a good action."

"Oh! this is quite another story; old Frappier told it in a very different way!"

"Old Frappier consults his cellar more than his memory," remarked a frequenter of Mademoiselle Rogron's drawing room.

"But then old Monsieur Habert—"

"Oh! you know about his share in the matter?"

"Why, he wanted to get his sister married to Monsieur Rogron, the Receiver-General."

Two men daily think of Pierrette. Martener and Major Brigaut, who alone know the terrible truth.

To give that truth immense proportions, it is enough to recall the fact that if we change the scene to the Middle Ages, and to the vast theatre of Rome, a sublime girl, Beatrice Cenci, was dragged to the scaffold for reasons and by intrigues almost the same as those which brought Pierrette to the tomb. Beatrice Cenci found none to defend her but an artist —a painter. And to-day history and living people, on the evidence of Guido Reni's portrait, condemn the Pope, and regard Beatrice as one of the most pathetic victims of infamous passions and factions.

And we may agree that the law would be a fine thing for social roguery, if there were no God.

November 1830.

THE VICAR OF TOURS

(Part II of "The Cellibates")

To DAVID, Sculptor

The duration of the work on which I write your name—doubly illustrious in our age—is most uncertain, while you inscribe mine on bronze, which outlives nations even when stamped only by the vulgar die of the coiner. Will not numismatists be puzzled by the many crowned heads in your studio, when they find among the ashes of Paris these lives, prolonged by you beyond the life of nations, in which they will fancy they discover dynasties? Yours is this divine prerogative—mine be the gratitude.

De Balzac.

In the early autumn of 1826 the Abbé Birotteau, the principal personage of this story, was caught in a shower on his way home from the house where he had spent the evening. He was just crossing, as fast as his burly weight permitted, a little deserted square known as the Close, lying behind the apse of Saint-Gatien at Tours.

The Abbé Birotteau, a short man of apoplectic build, and now sixty years of age, had already had several attacks of gout. Hence, of all the minor miseries of human life, that which the worthy man held in most horror was the sudden wetting of his shoes with their large silver buckles, and the immersion of their soles. In fact, notwithstanding the flannel lining in which he packed his feet in all weathers, with the care a priest always takes of himself, they often got a little damp; then, next day, the gout unfailingly gave him proof of its constancy.

However, as the cobbles in the Close are always dry, and as the Abbé had won three francs and ten sous at whist from Madame de Listomère, he submitted to the rain with resignation from the middle of the Place de l'Archevêché, where it had begun to fall heavily. Moreover, at this moment he was brooding over his chimera, a longing already twelve years old, a priest's day-dream! A dream which, recurring every evening, now seemed likely to find fulfilment; in short, he was too well wrapped in the fur sleeves of a canon's robes to be sensitive to the severities of the weather. In the course of this evening the accustomed guests who met at Madame de Listomère's had as good as promised him a nomination to the canon's stall at present vacant in the Metropolitan Chapter of Saint-Gatien, by proving to him that no one better deserved it than he, whose claims were indisputable, though so long ignored. If he had lost at cards, if he had heard that the canonry was given to the Abbé Poirel, his rival, the good man would have found the rain very cold; he might have abused life. But he was in one of those rare moments when delightful sensations make us forget everything. Though he hastened his pace, it was in obedience to a mechanical impulse, and truth—so indispensable in a tale of domestic life—requires us to say that he was thinking neither of the shower nor of the gout.

There were formerly round this Close, on the side by the Grand' Rue, a number of houses standing within a wall, and belonging to the Cathedral, inhabited by certain dignitaries of the Chapter. Since the sequestration of ecclesiastical property, the town has taken the alley dividing these houses as a public way, by the name of Rue de la Psalette, leading from the Close to the High Street. The name itself shows that here formerly dwelt the precentor with his schools and those who were within his jurisdiction. The left side of the street is formed of one large house, its garden walls being bridged by the flying buttresses of Saint-Gatien, which spring from the ground of its strip of garden, making it doubtful whether the Cathedral were built before or after that ancient dwelling. But, by examining the mouldings and the shape of the windows, the arch of the doorway, and the external architecture of the house, darkened by time, an archæologist detects that it had always been part and parcel of the magnificent church to which it is wedded. An antiquarian—if there were one at Tours, one of the least literary towns of France—might even discern at the entrance to the passage from the Close some traces of the covered archway which of old served as an entry to these priestly dwellings, and which must have harmonised in character with the main edifice.

This house, being to the north of Saint-Gatien, lies always in the shadow of this vast Cathedral, on which time has cast its gloomy mantle, stamped wrinkles, and set its damp chill, its mosses, and straggling weeds. And it is perennially wrapped in the deepest silence, broken only by the tolling of the bells, the chanted service heard through the Cathedral walls, or the cawing of jackdaws nesting at the top of the belfries. The spot is a desert of masonry, a solitude full of individuality, in which none could dwell but beings absolutely mindless, or gifted with immense strength of soul.

The house in question had always been the home of Abbés, and belonged to an old maid named Mademoiselle Gamard. Although during the Terror the property had been bought from the nation by Mademoiselle Gamard's father, as the worthy maiden had for twenty years past let the rooms to priests, no one, at the Restoration, could take it ill that a bigot should not surrender a piece of national property; religious persons may have supposed that she meant to bequeath it to the Chapter, and the worldly saw no change in its uses.

It was to this house, then, that the Abbé Birotteau was making his way; he had lived in it for two years. His rooms there had been till then, as the canonry was now, the object of his desires, and his *hoc erat in votis* for a dozen years before. To board with Mademoiselle Gamard and to be made a canon were the two great aims of his life; and perhaps they completely sum up the ambitions of a priest who, regarding himself as a pilgrim to eternity, can in this world wish for no more than a good room, a good table, clean clothes, shoes with silver buckles—all-sufficient for his animal needs—and a canonry to satisfy his pride, the indefinable feeling which will accompany us, no doubt, into the presence of God, since there are grades of rank among the saints.

But the Abbé Birotteau's desire for the rooms he now occupied, so trivial a feeling in the eyes of the worldly wise, had been to him a perfect passion, a passion full of obstacles, and, like the most criminal passions, full of hopes, joys, and remorse.

The arrangements and space in her house did not allow Mademoiselle Gamard to take more than two resident boarders. Now, about twelve years before the day when Birotteau went to lodge with this maiden lady, she had undertaken to preserve in health and contentment Monsieur l'Abbé Troubert and Monsieur l'Abbé Chapeloud. The Abbé Troubert still lived, the Abbé Chapeloud was dead, and Birotteau had been his immediate successor.

The late Abbé Chapeloud, in his lifetime Canon of Saint-Gatien, had been the Abbé Birotteau's intimate friend. Every time the priest had gone into the canon's rooms he had unfailingly admired them, the furniture, and the books. This admiration one day gave birth to a desire to possess these fine things. The Abbé Birotteau had found it impossible to smother this desire, which often made him dreadfully unhappy when he reflected that only the death of his best friend could satisfy this hidden covetousness, which nevertheless constantly increased.

The Abbé Chapeloud and his friend Birotteau were not rich. Both sons of peasants, they had nothing but the poor emolument doled out to priests, and their small savings had been spent in tiding over the evil days of the Revolution. When Napoleon re-established Catholic worship, the Abbé Chapeloud was made Canon of Saint-Gatien, and the Abbé Birotteau became *vicaire*, or mass-priest, of the Cathedral. It was then that Chapeloud went to board with Mademoiselle Gamard. When Birotteau first called on the Canon in his new residence, he thought the rooms delightfully arranged, but that was all. The beginnings of this concupiscence for furniture were like those of a real passion in a young man, which often at first is no more than cold admiration of the woman he subsequently loves for ever.

These rooms, reached by a stone staircase, were on the side of the house looking south. The Abbé Troubert inhabited the ground floor, and Mademoiselle Gamard the first floor of the main front to the street. When Chapeloud went in, the rooms were bare and the ceilings blackened by smoke. The chimney fronts, clumsily carved in stone, had never been painted. All the furniture the poor canon could at first put in consisted of a bed, a table, some chairs, and his few books. The apartment was like a fine woman in rags.

But two or three years later, an old lady having left the Abbé Chapeloud two thousand francs, he laid out the money in the purchase of an oak bookcase, saved from the destruction of an old château pulled down by the *Bande noire* (a company who bought old buildings to demolish), and remarkable for carvings worthy of the admiration of artists. The Abbé made the purchase, fascinated less by its cheapness than by its exact correspondence in size with the dimensions of his corridor. His savings then allowed him completely to restore this corridor, until now abandoned to neglect. The floor was carefully waxed, the ceiling whitewashed, the wood-work painted and grained to imitate the tone and knots of oak. A marble chimney-shelf replaced the old one. The Canon had taste enough to hunt up and find some old armchairs of carved walnut wood. Then a long ebony table and two little Boulle cabinets gave this library a finish full of character.

Within two years, the liberality of various devout persons, and the bequests of pious penitents, though small, had filled the shelves of the bookcase hitherto vacant. Finally, an uncle of Chapeloud's, an old Oratorian, left him his collection in folio of the *Fathers of the Church*, and several other large works of value to an ecclesiastic.

Birotteau, more and more surprised by the successive transformations in this formerly bare corridor, by degrees became involuntarily covetous. He longed to possess this study, so perfectly adapted to the gravity of priestly habits. This passion grew day by day. Spending whole days, as he often did, in working in this snuggery, he could appreciate the silence and peace of it, after having at first admired its comfortable arrangement. For the next few years the Abbé Chapeloud used this retreat as an oratory which his lady friends delighted to embellish. Later, again, a lady presented to the Canon a piece of furniture in worsted work for his bedroom, at which she had long been stitching under the amiable priest's eyes without his suspecting its purpose. Then Birotteau was as much dazzled by the bedroom as by the library.

Finally, three years before his death, the Abbé Chapeloud had completed the comfort of his rooms by decorating the drawing-room. Though simply furnished with red Utrecht velvet, this had been too much for Birotteau. From the day when the Canon's friend first saw the red silk curtains, the mahogany furniture, the Aubusson carpet that graced this large room, freshly painted, Chapeloud's apartment became to him the object of a secret monomania. To live there, to sleep in the great bed with silk curtains in which the Canon slept, and have all his comforts about him as Chapeloud had, seemed to Birotteau perfect happiness; he looked for nothing beyond. Every feeling which envy and ambition arouse in the souls of other men, was, in that of the Abbé Birotteau, centered in the deep and secret longing with which he wished for a home like that created for himself by the Abbé Chapeloud. When his friend fell ill, it was no doubt sincere affection that brought Birotteau to see him; but on first hearing of the Canon's sickness, and while sitting with him, there rose from the depths of his soul a thousand thoughts, of which the simplest formula was always this, "If Chapeloud dies, I can have his rooms." Still, as Birotteau had a good heart, strict principles, and a narrow intellect, he never went so far as to conceive of means for getting his friend to leave him his library and furniture.

The Abbé Chapeloud, an amiable and indulgent egoist, guessed his friend's mania—which it was not difficult to do, and forgave it—which for a priest would seem less easy. Still, Birotteau, whose friendship remained unaltered, never ceased to walk day after day with the Canon up and down the same path in the Mall at Tours without curtailing by a single minute the time devoted to this exercise for the last twenty years. Birotteau thought of his involuntary wishes as sins, and would have been capable, in sheer contrition, of the utmost devotion for Chapeloud's sake.

The Canon paid his debt to this sincere and artless brotherliness by saying, a few days before his death, to the priest, who was reading to him from the

HE RANG AGAIN, A VERY SIGNIFICANT PEAL

Quotidienne, "You will get the rooms this time. I feel that it is all over with me."

In fact, by his will, the Abbé Chapeloud left his library and furniture to Birotteau. The possession of these much-longed-for things, and the prospect of being taken as a boarder by Mademoiselle Gamard, greatly softened Birotteau's grief at the loss of his friend the Canon. He would not perhaps have called him to life again, but he wept for him. For several days he was like Gargantua, whose wife died in giving birth to Pantagruel, and who knew not whether to rejoice over his son's birth or to lament at having buried his good Badebec, and made the mistake of rejoicing at his wife's death and deploring the birth of Pantagruel.

The Abbé Birotteau spent the first days of his grief in verifying the volumes of *his* library, and enjoying the use of *his* furniture, examining them, and saying in a tone, which, unfortunately, could not be recorded, "Poor Chapeloud!" In short, his joy and his grief were so absorbing that he felt no distress at seeing the canonry bestowed on another, though the lamented Chapeloud had always hoped that Birotteau might be his successor. Mademoiselle Gamard received the Abbé with pleasure as a boarder, and he thus enjoyed thenceforth all the delights of material existence that the deceased Canon had so highly praised.

Incalculable advantages! For, to hear the late departed Canon Chapeloud, not one of the priests who dwelt in the town of Tours, not even the Archbishop himself, could be the object of care so delicate or so precise as that lavished by Mademoiselle Gamard on her two boarders. The first words spoken by the Canon to his friend as they walked in the Mall had almost always referred to the excellent dinner he had just eaten; and it was a rare thing if, in the course of the seven walks they took in the week, he did not happen to say at least fourteen times, "That good woman has certainly a vocation for taking charge of the priesthood."

"Only think," said the Canon to Birotteau, "for twelve successive years clean linen, albs, surplices, bands—nothing has ever been missing. I always find everything in its place and in sufficient numbers, all smelling of orris-root. My furniture is constantly polished, and so well wiped that for a long time past I have not known what dust means. Did you ever see a speck in my rooms? Then the fire-logs are well chosen, the smallest things are all good; in short, it is as if Mademoiselle Gamard always had an eye on my room. I cannot recollect in ten years ever having had to ring twice for anything whatever. That I call living! never to have to look for a thing, not even for one's slippers; always to find a good fire and a good table. Once my bellows put me out, the nozzle had got burned; I had not to complain twice. The very next day Mademoiselle had bought me a nice pair of bellows and the pair of tongs you see me use to put the fire together."

Birotteau's only reply was, "Smelling of orris-root!" That smelling of orris-root always struck him. The Canon's words painted a really ideal state of happiness to the poor priest whose bands and albs nearly turned his brain; for he had no sense of order, and not unfrequently forgot to bespeak his dinner. And so, whenever he caught sight of Mademoiselle Gamard at Saint-Gatien, either while going round for the offertory or while reading mass, he never failed to give her a gentle and kindly glance such as Saint Theresa may have raised to heaven.

Though the comfort which every creature desires, and of which he had so often dreamed, had now fallen to his lot, as it is difficult for any man, even for a priest, to live without a hobby, for the last eighteen months the Abbé Birotteau had substituted for his two gratified passions a craving for a canonry. The title of canon had become to him what that of a peer must be to a plebeian minister. And the probability of a nomination, the hopes he had just been encouraged in at Madame de Listomère's, had so effectually turned his brain that it was only on reaching home that he discovered that he had left his umbrella at her house. Perhaps, indeed, but for the rain that fell in torrents, he would not have remembered it then, so completely was he absorbed in repeating to himself all that had been said on the subject of his preferment by the members of the party at Madame de Listomère's—an old lady with whom he spent every Wednesday evening.

The Abbé rang sharply as a hint to the maid not to keep him waiting. Then he shrank into the corner by the door so as to be splashed as little as possible; but the water from the roof ran off precisely on the toes of his shoes, and the gusts of wind blew on to, him squalls of rain not unlike a repeated shower bath. After calculating the time necessary for coming from the kitchen to pull the latch-string under the door, he rang again, a very significant peal. "They cannot have gone out," thought he, hearing not a sound within. And for the third time he rang, again and again, a peal that sounded so sharply through the house, and was so loudly repeated by every echo in the Cathedral, that it was impossible not to be roused by this assertive jangle. And a few moments after it was not without satisfaction, mingled with annoyance, that he heard the maid's wooden shoes clattering over the pebbly stone floor. Still, the gouty priest's troubles were not over so soon as he thought. Instead of pulling the latch, Marianne was obliged to unlock the door with the huge key, and draw back the bolts.

"How can you leave me to ring three times in such weather?" said he to Marianne.

"Why, sir, as you see, the house was locked up. Everybody has been in bed a long time; it has struck a quarter to ten. Mademoiselle must have thought you had not gone out."

"But you yourself saw me go out. Besides, Mademoiselle knows very well that I go to Madame de Listomère's every Wednesday."

"Well, sir, I only did as Mademoiselle told me," replied Marianne, locking the door again.

These words were a blow to the Abbé, which he felt all the more keenly for the intense bliss of his day-dream. He said nothing, but followed Marianne to the kitchen, to fetch his bedroom candle, which he supposed would have been brought down there. But instead of going to the kitchen, Marianne lighted the Abbé up to his rooms, where he found the candlestick on a table outside the door of the red drawing-room, in a sort of ante-room, formed of the stair landing, which the Canon had shut in for the purpose by a large glass partition. Dumb with surprise, he hurried into his bedroom, found no fire on the hearth, and called Marianne, who had not yet had time to go downstairs.

"You have not lighted my fire?" said he.

"I beg your pardon, sir; it must have gone out again."

Birotteau looked again at the hearth, and saw plainly that the ashes had been piled there since the morning.

"I want to dry my feet," he went on; "make up the fire."

Marianne obeyed with the haste of a woman who wants to go to sleep. While the Abbé himself hunted for his slippers, failing to see them in the middle of his bed-rug, as usual, he made certain observations as to the way Marianne was dressed, which proved to a demonstration that she had not just got out of bed, as she had asserted. And he then remembered that for about a fortnight past he had been weaned from all the little attentions that had made life so endurable for the last eighteen months. Now, as it is in the nature of narrow minds to argue from minute things, he at once gave himself up to deep reflections on these four incidents, imperceptible to anybody else, but to him nothing less than four catastrophes. The oversight as to his slippers, Marianne's falsehood with regard to the fire, the unaccustomed removal of his candlestick to the table in the ante-room, and the long waiting so ingeniously inflicted on him on the threshold in the rain, were ominous of a complete wreck of his happiness.

When the fire was blazing on the dogs, when his night-lamp was lighted, and Marianne had left him without inquiring as usual, "Does Monsieur need anything further?" the Abbé sank gently into his departed friend's roomy and handsome easy-chair; still, his action as he dropped into it was somewhat melancholy. The worthy man was oppressed by the presentiment of terrible disaster. His eyes fell in succession on the handsome timepiece, the chest of drawers, the chairs, curtains, and rugs, the four-post bed, the holy-water shell and the crucifix, on a Virgin by le Valentin, on a Christ by Lebrun—in short, on all the details of the room; the expression of his face betrayed the pangs of the tenderest farewell that a lover ever looked at his first mistress, or an old man at his latest plantation. The Abbé had just detected—a little late, it is true—the symptoms of a covert persecution to which he had for about three months been subjected by Mademoiselle Gamard, whose ill-will would no doubt have been suspected sooner by a man of keener intelligence.

Have not all old maids a certain talent for emphasising the acts and words suggested to them by hatred? They scratch as cats do. And not only do they hurt, but they take pleasure in hurting, and in making their victim see that they can hurt. While a man of the world would not have allowed himself to be clawed a second time, the worthy Birotteau had taken several scratches in the face before he had conceived of malignant purpose.

Immediately, with the inquisitorial shrewdness acquired by priests, accustomed as they are to direct consciences and to investigate trifles from the shades of the confessional, the Abbé Birotteau set to work to formulate the following proposition—as though it were the basis of a religious controversy.—Granting that Mademoiselle Gamard may have forgotten Madame de Listomère's evening—that Marianne had neglected to light my fire—that they thought I was at home; as it is certain that I, *myself*, must have taken my candlestick downstairs this morning!!!—it is impossible that Mademoiselle Gamard, seeing it in her sitting-room, could have supposed I had gone to bed. *Ergo*, Mademoiselle Gamard left me at the door in the rain on purpose; and by having the candlestick carried up to my rooms she meant me to know it.—"What does it mean?" he said aloud, carried away by the gravity of the case, as he rose to take off his wet clothes, and put on his dressing-gown and his nightcap. Then he went from the bed to the fire gesticulating and jerking out such comments as these, in various tones of voice, all ended in a falsetto pitch as though to represent points of interrogation.

'What the deuce have I done? Why does she owe me a grudge?—Marianne cannot have forgotten my fire; Mademoiselle must have told her not to light it! I should be childish not to see from the tone and manner she assumes towards me that I have been so unfortunate as to displease her.— Nothing of the kind ever happened to Chapeloud!—It will be impossible for me to live in the midst of the annoyances that … At my age too!"

He went to bed, hoping to clear up on the morrow the cause of the hatred which was destroying for ever the happiness he had enjoyed for two years after wishing for it so long. Alas! the secret motives of Mademoiselle Gamard's feeling against him were destined to remain for ever unknown to him; not because they were difficult to guess, but because the poor man had not the simple candour which enables great minds and thorough scoundrels to recognise and judge themselves. Only a man of genius or a master of intrigue ever says to himself, "I was to blame." Interest and talent are the only conscientious and lucid counsellors.

Now, the Abbé Birotteau, whose kindliness went to the pitch of silliness, whose knowledge was a sort of veneer laid on by patient work, who had no experience whatever of the world and its ways, and who lived between the altar and the confessional, chiefly engaged in deciding trivial cases of conscience in his capacity of confessor to the schools of the town and to some noble souls who appreciated him—the Abbé Birotteau was, in short, to be regarded as a big baby to whom the greater part of social customs were absolutely unknown. At the same time, the selfishness natural to all human beings, reinforced by the egoism peculiar to a priest, and by that of the narrow life of a provincial town, had insensibly grown strong in him without his suspecting it. If any one had taken enough interest in searching the good man's soul to show him that, in the infinitely small details of his existence and the trivial duties of his private life, he failed essentially in the self-sacrifice he professed, he would have punished and mortified himself in all sincerity.

But those whom we offend, even unwittingly, reck not of our innocence; they desire and achieve revenge. Thus Birotteau, weak as he was, was doomed to suffer under the hand of that great distributive Justice which always trusts the world to carry out its sentences, known to many simpletons as the misfortunes of life.

There was this difference between Canon Chapeloud and the Abbé: one was a witty and ingenious egotist, the other an honest and clumsy one. When Monsieur Chapeloud had come to board with Mademoiselle Gamard, he could perfectly well gauge his landlady's character. The confessional had enlightened him as to the bitterness infused into an old maid's heart by the misfortune of finding herself outside society; his behaviour to Mademoiselle Gamard was shrewdly calculated. The lady being no more than eight-and-thirty, still had those little pretensions which, in such discreet persons, turn in later years into a high opinion of themselves.

The Canon understood that, to live comfortably with Mademoiselle Gamard, he must always show her the same respect and attention, and be more infallible than the Pope. To attain this end he established no points of contact between himself and her beyond what the strictest politeness required, and those necessarily subsisting between two persons living under the same roof. Thus, though he and the Abbé Troubert regularly took their three meals a day, he had never appeared at breakfast, but had accustomed Mademoiselle Gamard to send up to him, in his bed, a cup of coffee with milk. Then, he had avoided the boredom of supper by always taking tea at some house where he spent the evening. Thus he rarely saw his landlady at any time of the day excepting at dinner, but he always came into the room a few minutes before the hour. During this polite little visit, every day of the twelve years he had spent under her roof he had asked her the same questions and received the same answers. How Mademoiselle Gamard had slept during the night, the breakfast, little domestic events, the appearance of her face, the health of her person, the weather, the length of the Church services, the incidents of the morning's Mass, the health of this or that priest, constituted the themes of this daily dialogue.

During dinner he always indulged her with indirect flattery, going on from the quality of the fish, the excellence of some seasoning, or the merits of a sauce, to those of Mademoiselle Gamard and her virtues as a housekeeper. He was sure of soothing all the old maid's conceits when he praised the art with which her preserves were made, her gherkins pickled, and the excellence of her jam, her pies, and other gastronomical inventions. Finally, the wily Canon never quitted her yellow drawing-room without remarking that there was not another house in Tours where the coffee was so good as that he had just been drinking.

Thanks to this perfect comprehension of Mademoiselle Gamard's character, and this science of life as practised by the Canon for those twelve years, no grounds had ever occurred for a discussion on any matter of domestic discipline. The Abbé Chapeloud had from the first discerned every angle, every rasping edge, every asperity in this old maid, and had so regulated the effect of the tangents where they inevitably met, as to secure from her every concession needed for peace and happiness in life. And Mademoiselle Gamard would always say that Canon Chapeloud was a most amiable man, very easy to live with, and full of wit.

As to the Abbé Troubert, the bigot never by any chance spoke of him. Troubert had so completely fallen into the routine of her life, like a satellite in the orbit of its planet, that he had become to her a sort of mongrel creature between those of the human and those of the canine species; he filled a place in her mind exactly below that occupied by her friends and that filled by a fat asthmatic pug-dog to which she was tenderly devoted; she managed him completely, and their interests became so inextricably knit that many persons of Mademoiselle Gamard's circle supposed that the Abbé Troubert had an eye to the old maid's fortune, and was attaching her to him by his constant patience, guiding her all the more effectually because he affected to obey her, never allowing her to see in him the faintest wish to rule her.

When the Canon died, the old maid, anxious to have a boarder of quiet habits, naturally thought of this priest. The Canon's will had not yet been opened when Mademoiselle Gamard was already meditating giving the departed Canon's upper rooms to her worthy Abbé Troubert, whom she thought but poorly lodged on the ground floor. But when the Abbé Birotteau came to discuss with her the written conditions of her terms, she found that he was so much in love with the lodgings for which he had long cherished a passion he might now avow, that she did not venture to propose an exchange, and affection gave way before the pressure of interest. To console her favourite Abbé, Mademoiselle substituted a parquet flooring in a neat pattern for the white Château-Renaud tiles in the ground-floor rooms, and rebuilt a chimney that smoked.

The Abbé Birotteau had seen his friend Chapeloud constantly for twelve years, without its ever having occurred to him to wonder why he was so excessively circumspect in his intercourse with the old maid. When he came to live under this saintly damsel's roof he felt like a lover on the verge of happiness. Even if he had not been blinded by natural stupidity, his eyes were too much dazzled by contentment for him to be capable of gauging Mademoiselle Gamard or of considering the due measure of his daily relations with her. Mademoiselle Gamard, seen from afar, through the prism of the material enjoyment the Abbé dreamed of finding with her, appeared to him an admirable creature, a perfect Christian, an essentially charitable soul, the woman of the Gospel, the wise Virgin graced with the humble and modest virtues which shed celestial fragrance over life. And thus, with all the enthusiasm of a man who has reached a long-wished-for goal, with the simplicity of a child and the silly heedlessness of an old man devoid of worldly experience, he came into Mademoiselle Gamard's life as a fly is caught in a spider's web.

So the first day he was to dine and sleep in the old maid's house he lingered in her drawing-room, as much in the wish to make acquaintance with her as in the inexplicable embarrassment that often troubles shy people and makes them fear lest they should be rude if they break off a conversation to leave the room. So there he remained all the evening. Another old maid, a friend of Birotteau's, Mademoiselle Salomon de Villenoix, came in the evening. Then Mademoiselle Gamard had the joy of arranging a game of boston. The Abbé, as he went to bed, thought he had had a very pleasant evening.

As yet he knew Mademoiselle Gamard and the Abbé Troubert but very little, and saw only the surface. Few persons show their faults unveiled at first. Generally everybody tries to assume an attractive exterior. So Birotteau conceived the delightful purpose of devoting his evenings to Mademoiselle Gamard instead of spending them elsewhere. The lady had some few years since conceived a desire which revived more strongly every day. This desire, common to old men, and even to pretty women, had become in her a passion like that of Birotteau for his friend Chapeloud's rooms, and was rooted in the old maid's heart by the feelings of pride, egoism, envy, and vanity which are innate in the worldly-minded. This story repeats itself in every age. You have but slightly to enlarge the circle at the bottom of which these personages are about to move, to find the co-efficient motive of events which happen in the highest ranks of society.

Mademoiselle Gamard spent her evenings at six or eight different houses by turns. Whether it was that she was annoyed at having to seek company, and thought that at her age she had a right to expect some return; whether her conceit was affronted by her having no circle of her own; or whether it was that her vanity craved the compliments and amusements she saw her friends enjoying,—all her ambition was to make her *salon* a centre of union towards which a certain number of persons would tend every evening with pleasure. When Birotteau and his friend Mademoiselle Salomon had spent a few evenings in her room with the faithful and patient Abbé Troubert, one night, as she came out of Saint-Gatien, Mademoiselle Gamard said to the kind friends of whom she had hitherto considered herself the slave, that those who cared to see her might very well come once a week to her house, where a sufficient party met already to make up a game of boston; that she could not leave her new boarder, the Abbé Birotteau, alone; that Mademoiselle Salomon had not yet missed a single evening of the week; that she belonged to her boarders; and that, etc., etc.

Her speech was all the more humbly haughty and volubly sweet because Mademoiselle Salomon de Villenoix belonged to the most aristocratic circle in Tours! Though Madmoiselle Salomon came solely for the Abbé's sake, Mademoiselle Gamard triumphed in having her in her drawing- room. Thanks to the Abbé Birotteau, she found herself on the eve of succeeding in her great scheme of forming a circle which might become as numerous and as agreeable as were those of Madame de Listomère, of Mademoiselle Merlin de la Blottière, and other devout persons in a position to receive the pious society of Tours. But, alas! the Abbé Birotteau brought Mademoiselle Gamard's hopes to an overthrow.

Now, if any persons, who have attained in life the enjoyment of a long-wished-for happiness, have entered into the gladness the Abbé must have felt in lying down to rest in Chapeloud's bed, they must also form a slight notion of Mademoiselle Gamard's chagrin at the ruin of her cherished scheme. After accepting his good fortune patiently enough for six months, Birotteau deserted his home, carrying with him Mademoiselle Salomon.

In spite of unheard-of efforts, the ambitious Gamard had secured no more than five or six recruits, whose fidelity was very problematical, and at least four unfailing visitors were needed for regular boston. She was consequently obliged to make honourable amends and return to her old friends, for old maids are too poor company to themselves not to crave the doubtful pleasures of society.

The causes of this defection are easily imagined. Though the Abbé was one of those to whom Paradise shall one day be opened in virtue of the words, "Blessed are the poor in spirit," he, like many fools, could not endure the weariness inflicted on him by other fools. Unintelligent persons are like weeds that thrive in good ground; they love to be amused in proportion to the degree in which they weary themselves. Being the incarnation of the dullness they suffer from, the craving they perpetually feel to be divorced from themselves produces the mania for excitement, the need to be where they are not, which characterises them as it does other creatures who lack feeling, or whose lot is a failure, or who suffer by their own fault. Without understanding too clearly the vacuity and nullity of Mademoiselle Gamard, or discerning the smallness of her mind, poor Birotteau discovered, too late for happiness, the faults she had in common with all old maids, as well as those personal to herself.

What is evil, in other people, contrasts so strongly with what is good, that it generally strikes the eye before inflicting a wound. This moral phenomenon might at need justify the tendency that leads us all more or less to evil speaking. Socially speaking, it is so natural to satirise the faults of others, that we ought to forgive the severe gossip to which our own absurdities give rise, and wonder at nothing but calumny.

But the good Abbé's eyes were never at the precise focus which enables the worldly wise to see and at once evade their neighbour's sharp tongues; to discover his landlady's faults, he was obliged to endure the warning given by nature to all its creatures, that of suffering.

Old maids, having never bent their temper or their lives to other lives and other tempers, as woman's destiny requires, have for the most part a mania for making everything about them bend to them. In Mademoiselle Gamard this feeling had degenerated into despotism, but this despotism could only be exerted in small things. For instance—out of a thousand cases—the basket of counters and fish placed on the boston table for the Abbé Birotteau must be left on the spot where she had put it, and the Abbé irritated her extremely by moving it, as he did almost every evening. What was the cause of this touchiness foolishly provoked by mere trifles, and what was its object? No one could say; Mademoiselle Gamard herself did not know.

Though very lamblike by nature, the new boarder did not like to feel the crook too often, any more than a sheep, especially a crook set with nails. Without understanding Canon Troubert's amazing patience, Birotteau was anxious to escape the bliss which Mademoiselle Gamard was bent on seasoning to her own taste, for she thought she could compound happiness as she could preserves; but the luckless priest set to work very clumsily, as a result of his perfectly artless nature. So the separation was not effected without some clawing and pricking, to which the Abbé Birotteau tried to seem insensible.

By the end of the first year of his life under Mademoiselle Gamard's roof the Abbé had fallen into his old habits, spending two evenings a week at Madame de Listomère's, three with Mademoiselle Salomon, and the other two with Mademoiselle Merlin de la Blottière. These ladies moved in the aristocratic sphere of Tours society, to which Mademoiselle Gamard was not admitted. So the landlady was excessively indignant at the Abbé's defection, which made her aware of her small importance: any kind of selection implying some contempt for the rejected object.

"Monsieur Birotteau did not find us good enough company," the Abbé Troubert would say to Mademoiselle Gamard's friends when she was obliged to give up her "evenings." "He is a wit, a *gourmet!* He must have fashion, luxury, brilliant conversation, the tittle-tattle of the town."

And such words always prompted Mademoiselle Gamard to praise the Canon's excellent temper at the expense of Birotteau's.

"He is not so clever when all is said," she remarked. "But for Canon Chapeloud he would never have been received by Madame de Listomère. Oh, I lost a great deal when the Abbé Chapeloud died. What an amiable man! and so easy to live with! Indeed, in twelve years we never had the smallest difficulty or disagreement."

Mademoiselle Gamard painted so unflattering a portrait of Monsieur Birotteau that her innocent boarder was regarded by this citizen circle, secretly hostile to the aristocratic class, as an essentially fractious man, very difficult to get on with. Then for a few weeks the old maid had the satisfaction of hearing herself pitied by her female friends, who, without believing a word of what they said repeated again and again,

"How can you, who are so gentle and so kind, have inspired him with such dislike?—" or, "Be comforted, dear Mademoiselle Gamard, every one knows you too well—" and so forth.

Delighted, nevertheless, to escape spending an evening each week in the Close—the most deserted and gloomy spot in all Tours, and the most remote from the centre of life— they all blessed the Abbé.

Love or hatred must constantly increase between two persons who are always together; every moment fresh reasons are found for loving or hating better. Thus to Mademoiselle Gamard the Abbé Birotteau became unendurable. Eighteen months after taking him as a boarder, just when the good man believed he had found the peace of contentment in the silence of aversion, and prided himself on having come so comfortably to terms with the old woman, to use his expression, he was to her the object of covert persecution and calmly planned animosity.

The four capital facts of the closed door, the forgotten slippers, the lack of fire, the candlestick taken to his rooms, alone could betray the terrible enmity of which the last effects were not to fall on him till the moment when they would be irremediable. As he went to sleep, the good Abbé racked his brain, but vainly—and, indeed, he must soon have come to the bottom of it—to account for Mademoiselle Gamard's singularly uncivil behaviour. In point of fact, as he had originally acted very logically, obeying the natural law of his egoism, he could not possibly form a guess as to how he had offended his landlady. While great things are simple to understand, and easy to express, the mean things of life need much detail. The incidents which constitute the prologue, as it were, to this parochial drama, in which the passions will be seen not less violent than if they had been excited by important interests, necessitated this long introduction, and any exact historian would have found it difficult to abridge the trivial tale.

When he awoke next morning, the Abbé's thoughts were so much set on the canonry, that he forgot the four circumstances which, the evening before, had appeared to him to be sinister prognostics of a future full of disaster. Birotteau was not the man to get up without a fire; he rang to announce to Marianne that he was awake, and wanted her; then, as he was wont, he lay lost in a somnolent, half-dreamy state, during which, as a rule, the woman made the fire, and dragged him gently from his last doze by a hum of inquiry and quiet bustle—a sort of music that he liked.

Half an hour went by, and Marianne had not appeared. The Abbé, already half a Canon, was about to ring again, when he stayed his hand on hearing a man's step on the stairs. In fact, the Abbé Troubert, after discreetly tapping at the door, at Birotteau's bidding came in. This call did not surprise him; the priests were in the habit of paying each other a visit once a month. The Canon was at once amazed that Marianne should not yet have lighted his quasi-colleague's fire. He opened a window, called Marianne in a rough tone, and bid her come up at once; then, turning to his brother priest, he said, "If Mademoiselle should hear that you have no fire, she would give Marianne a good scolding."

After this speech he inquired for Birotteau's health, and asked him, in an insinuating voice, whether he had any recent news that could encourage his hope of being made a Canon. The Abbé explained to him what was being done, and guilelessly told him who the personages were that Madame de Listomère was canvassing, not knowing that Troubert had never forgiven that lady for not inviting him to her house—him—Canon Troubert, twice designate to be made Vicar-General of the diocese.

It would be impossible to meet with two figures offering so many points of contrast as those of these two priests. Troubert, tall and lean, had a bilious yellow hue, while Birotteau was what is familiarly called crummy. His face, round and florid, spoke of good-nature devoid of ideas; while Troubert's, long and furrowed by deep wrinkles wore at times an expression of irony and scorn; still, attentive examination was needed to discover these feelings. The Canon was habitually and absolutely placid, his eyelids almost always lowered over a pair of orange-hazel eyes, whose glance was at will very clear and piercing. Red hair completed this countenance, which was constantly clouded under the shroud cast over his features by serious meditations. Several persons had at first supposed him to be absorbed in high and rooted ambition; but those who thought they knew him best had ended by demolishing this opinion, representing him as stultified by Mademoiselle Gamard's tyranny, or worn by long fasting. He rarely spoke, and never laughed. When he happened to be pleasurably moved, a faint smile appeared and lost itself in the furrows on his cheeks.

Birotteau, on the other hand, was all expansiveness, all openness; he liked tidbits, and could be amused by a trifle with the artlessness of a man free from gall and malice. The Abbé Troubert at first sight inspired an involuntary feeling of dread, while the Vicar made every one who looked at him smile kindly. When the tall Canon stalked solemnly along the cloisters and aisles of Saint-Gatien, his brow bent, his eye stern, he commanded respect; his bowed figure harmonised with the yellow vaulting of the cathedral; there was something monumental in the folds of his gown, and worthy of the sculptor's art. But the good little Abbé moved without dignity, trotted and pattered, looking as if he rolled along.

And yet the two men had one point of resemblance. While Troubert's ambitious looks, by making the world afraid of him, had perhaps contributed to condemn him to the modest dignity of a mere Canon, Birotteau's character and appearance seemed to stamp him for ever as no more than a *vicaire* of the Cathedral. The Abbé Troubert meanwhile, at the age of fifty, by the moderation of his conduct, by the apparently total absence of any ambition in his aims, and by his saintly life, had dispelled the fears his superiors had conceived of his supposed cleverness and his alarming exterior. Indeed, for a year past, his health had been seriously impaired, so that his early promotion to the dignity of Vicar-General to the Archbishop seemed probable. His rivals even hoped for his appointment, to enable them the more effectually to prepare for their own, during the short span of life that might yet be granted him by a malady that had become chronic. Birotteau's triple chin, far from suggesting the same hopes, displayed to the candidates who were struggling for the canonry all the symptoms of vigorous health, and his gout seemed to them the proverbial assurance of a long life.

The Abbé Chapeloud, a man of great good sense, whose amiability had secured him the friendship of persons in good society and of the various heads of the diocese, had always opposed the elevation of the Abbé Troubert, secretly and with much address; he had even hindered his admission to any of the salons where the best set in Tours were wont to meet, though during his lifetime Troubert always treated him with great respect, and on all occasions showed him the utmost deference. This persistent submissiveness had not availed to change the deceased Canon's opinion; during his last walk with Birotteau, he had said to him once more:

"Do not trust that dry pole Troubert! He is Sixtus V reduced to the scale of a bishopric."

This was Mademoiselle Gamard's friend and messmate, who, the very day after that on which she had, so to speak, declared war with poor Birotteau, had come to call on him with every mark of friendliness.

"You must excuse Marianne," said Troubert as she came in. "I fancy she did my room first. My place is very damp, and I coughed a great deal during the night.—You are very healthily situated here," he added, looking up at the mouldings.

"Oh, I am lodged like a Canon!" replied Birotteau with a smile.

"And I like a curate," replied the humble priest.

"Yes, but before long you will be lodged in the Archbishop's Palace," said the good Abbé, who only wanted that everybody should be happy.

"Oh! or in the graveyard. God's will be done!" and Troubert looked up to heaven with a resigned air. "I came," he went on, "to beg you to lend me the *General Clergy List*. No one but you has the book at Tours."

"Take it out of the bookcase," replied Birotteau, reminded by the Canon's last words of all the joys of his life.

The tall priest went into the library, and remained there all the time the Abbé was dressing. Presently the breakfast-bell rang, and Birotteau, reflecting that but for Troubert's visit he would have had no fire to get up by, said to himself, "He is a good man!"

The two priests went down together, each armed with an enormous folio, which they laid on one of the consoles in the dining-room.

"What in the world is that?" asked Mademoiselle Gamard in sharp tones, addressing Birotteau. "You are not going to lumber up my dining-room with old books, I hope!"

"They are some books I wanted," said the Abbé Troubert. "Monsieur is kind enough to lend them to me."

"I might have guessed that," said she with a scornful smile. "Monsieur Birotteau does not often study such big books."

"And how are you, mademoiselle?" asked the Abbé in a piping voice.

"Why, not at all well," she replied curtly. "You were the cause of my being roused from my first sleep, and I felt the effects all night." And as she seated herself, Mademoiselle Gamard added, "Gentlemen, the milk will get cold."

Astounded at being so sourly received by his hostess when he expected her to apologise, but frightened, as timid people are, by the prospect of a discussion, especially when they themselves are the subject of it, the poor Abbé took his place in silence. Then, recognising in Mademoiselle Gamard's face the obvious symptoms of a bad temper, he sat warring with his common-sense, which advised him not to submit to her want of manners, while his nature prompted him to avoid a quarrel. Birotteau, a prey to this internal struggle, began by seriously studying the broad-green stripes painted on the oilcloth cover, which, from immemorial habit, Mademoiselle Gamard always left on the table during breakfast, heedless of the frayed edges and scars innumerable that covered this cloth. The two boarders were seated opposite each other, in cane armchairs at each end of the table, a royal square; the place between them being occupied by the landlady, who towered above the table from a chair mounted on runners, padded with cushions, and backing on the dining-room stove. This room and the common sitting-room were on the ground. floor, under the Abbé Birotteau's bedroom and drawing-room. When the Abbé had received from Mademoiselle Gamard his cup of sweetened coffee, he felt chilled by the utter silence in which he was doomed to perform the usually cheerful function of breakfast. He dared not look either at Troubert's expressionless face, nor at the old maid's threatening countenance; so, to do something, he turned to the pug-dog, over burdened with fat, lying near the stove on a cushion whence it never stirred, finding always on the left a little plate of dainties, and on the right a saucer of clean water.

"Well, my pet," said he, "so you want your coffee?"

This personage, one of the most important members of the household, but not a troublesome one since he never barked now, and left the conversation to his mistress, looked up at Birotteau with his little eyes buried in the folds of fat that wrinkled his face. Then he cunningly shut them again.

To give the measure of the priest's discomfiture, it must be explained that, being gifted with a voice and volubility as resonant and meaningless as the sound of an india-rubber ball, he asserted, without being able to give the faculty any reason for his opinion, that speech favoured digestion. Mademoiselle Gamard, who shared this theory of hygiene, had never hitherto failed to converse during meals, notwithstanding their misunderstanding; but now for some few days the Abbé had racked his wits in vain to ask her insidious questions which might loosen her tongue. If the narrow limits to which this story is restricted would allow of a report in full of one of these conversations which always provoked the Abbé Troubert's bitter and sardonic smiles, it would give a perfect picture of the Bœotian existence of provincials. Some clever men might perhaps be even pleased to know the extraordinary amplitude given by the Abbé Birotteau and Mademoiselle Gamard to their personal opinions on politics, religion, and literature. There would certainly be some very funny things to tell: such as their reasons, in 1820, for doubting the death of Napoleon, or the conjectures which led them to believe in the survival of Louis XVII, smuggled away in a hollow log of wood. Who would not have laughed to hear them asserting, with arguments peculiarly their own, that the King of France alone spent the money collected in taxes; that the Chambers met to destroy the Clergy; that more than thirteen hundred thousand persons had perished on the scaffold during the Revolution? Then they discussed the press, knowing nothing of how many newspapers were issued, having not the smallest idea of what this modern power is. Finally, Monsieur Birotteau listened respectfully to Mademoiselle Gamard when she asserted that a man fed on an egg every morning would infallibly die at the end of a year, and that it had been known; that a soft roll eaten without drinking for a few days would cure sciatica; that all the workmen who had been employed in the destruction of the Abbey of Saint-Martin had died within six months; that a certain préfet had done his utmost in Bonaparte's time to ruin the towers of Saint-Gatien, and a thousand other absurd stories.

But at the present juncture Birotteau felt his tongue dead within him; so he resigned himself to eating without trying to converse. He soon thought that such silence was perilous to his digestion, and boldly said, "This is excellent coffee!" But the courageous act fell flat.

After looking at the narrow strip of sky above the garden, between the two black buttresses of Saint-Gatien, the Abbé again was brave enough to remark, "It will be finer to-day than it was yesterday."

At this Mademoiselle Gamard did no more than cast one of her most ingratiating glances at Monsieur Troubert, and then turn her eyes full of terrible severity on Birotteau, who was happily looking down.

No being of the female sex was better able to assume the elegiac attitude of an old maid than Mademoiselle Sophie Gamard; but to do justice in describing a person whose character will give the greatest interest to the trivial events of this drama, and to the antecedent lives of the figures playing a part in it, it will be well here to epitomise the ideas of which the old maid is the outcome. The habits of life form the soul, and the soul forms the countenance. If in society, as in the universe, everything must have a purpose, there yet are on this earth some existences of which the use and purpose are undiscoverable; morality and political economy alike reject the individual that consumes without producing, that fills a place on earth without diffusing either good or evil—for evil, no doubt, is a form of good of which the results are not immediately manifest. Very rarely does an old maid fail to place herself by her own act in this class of unproductive creatures. Now if the consciousness of work done gives productive beings a sense of satisfaction which helps them to endure life, the knowledge that they are a burden on others, or even merely useless, must produce the contrary effect, and give to the inert a contempt for them selves as great as that they provoke in others. This stern social reprobation is one of the causes which, unknown to themselves, contribute to implant in their soul the grievance which is stamped on their faces.

A prejudice, not perhaps without a basis of truth, every where gives rise—and in France more than elsewhere—to marked disfavour being felt towards a woman with whom no man has chosen to share his fortunes, or to endure the woes of life. And an age comes to unmarried women when the world, rightly or wrongly, condemns them on the strength of the disdain to which they are victims. If ugly, the amiability of their nature ought to have redeemed the imperfections of their persons; if pretty, their loneliness must have its cause in serious reasons. It is hard to decide which of the two classes is most to be contemned. If their single life is deliberately chosen, if it is a determination to be independent, neither men nor mothers can forgive them for having shirked the sacrifice of woman by refusing to know the passions that make their sex pathetic. To reject its sufferings is to forego its poetry, to cease to deserve the sweet consolations to which a mother has always uncontested rights. Then the generous feelings, the exquisite qualities of woman, can only be developed by constant exercise. When she remains unmarried, a creature of the female sex is a self-contradiction: egoistical and cold, she fills us with horror.

This pitiless verdict is unfortunately too just for old maids to misinterpret its motives. These ideas germinate in their heart as naturally as the effects of their desolate life are imprinted on their features. Thus they wither, because the constant expansion, or the happiness that blooms in a woman's face and lends softness to her movements, has never existed in them. Then they grow harsh and discontented, because a creature that fails of its purpose is unhappy, it suffers, and suffering brings forth viciousness. In fact, before an unmarried woman spites herself for her loneliness, she accuses the whole world, and from accusation there is but one step to the desire for revenge.

Again, the ill-grace that disfigures their persons is an inevitable outcome of their life. Never having felt the necessity to please, elegance and good taste are unknown to them. This feeling gradually leads them to choose everything to suit their own convenience at the cost of what might be agreeable to others. Without quite understanding their dissimilarity to other women, at last they observe it and suffer from it. Jealousy is an indelible passion in the female heart. Old maids are jealous for nothing, and know only the woes of the single passion which men can forgive in women because it flatters them. Thus tormented on every side, and compelled to reject the development of their nature, old maids are always conscious of a moral uneasiness to which they never become accustomed. Is it not hard at any age, especially for a woman, to read a feeling of repugnance on every face, when it ought to have been her fate to inspire none but sensations of kindliness in the hearts of those about her? Hence an old maid's glance is always askance, not so much from modesty as from fear and shame.

Now, it is impossible that a person perpetually at war with herself, or at loggerheads with life, should leave others in peace, and never envy their happiness. This world of gloomy ideas lay complete in Mademoiselle Gamard's dull grey eyes; and the broad, dark circle in which they were set spoke of the long struggles of her solitary life. All the wrinkles on her face were straight lines. The form of her brow, head, and cheeks was characterized by rigidity and hardness. Without heeding them, she left the hairs, once brown, of two or three moles on her chin to grow as they would. Her thin lips scarcely covered her long but sufficiently white teeth. She was dark, and her hair had once been black, but terrible headaches had turned it white. This disaster led her to wear a front; but not knowing how to put it on so as to conceal the junction, there often was a small gap between her cap-border and the black ribbon that fastened this half-wig, very carelessly curled. Her gown, of thin silk in summer, of merinos in winter, and always of Carmelite brown, fitted her ungraceful figure and thin arms rather too closely. Her collar, always limp, betrayed a throat whose reddish skin was as finely lined as an oak leaf looked at in the light.

Her parentage accounted for the faults of her figure. She was the daughter of a dealer in fire-logs, a peasant who had risen in the world. At eighteen she might have been fresh and plump, but not a trace was now left either of the white skin or the fine colour she boasted of having then had. The hues of her complexion had acquired the dull pallor common enough in very devout persons. An aquiline nose was of all her features that which most strongly expressed the despotism of her ideas, just as the flatness of her forehead revealed her narrowness of mind. Her movements had an odd abruptness bereft of all grace; and only to see her pull her handkerchief out of her bag and loudly blow her nose would have told you what her character and habits were. Fairly tall, she held herself very upright, justifying the remark of a naturalist, who explains the stiffness of old maids physiologically by declaring that all their joints anchylose. She walked so that the motion did not distribute itself equally over her whole person, or produce the graceful undulations that are so attractive in a woman; she moved all of a piece, so to speak, seeming to lift herself at every step, like the statue of the Commendatore. In her moments of good-humour she would give it out, as all old maids do, that she could have been married, but that, happily, she had found out her lover's faithlessness in time, and she thus, without knowing it, passed judgment on her heart in favour of her sense of self-interest.

This typical figure of an old maid was suitably set against a background of the grotesque pattern, representing Turkish landscapes, of a satin wall-paper with which the dining-room was hung. Mademoiselle Gamard habitually occupied this room, ornamented by two consoles and a barometer. In the place occupied by each priest was a little footstool in worsted work of faded hues.

The public sitting-room, where she received company, was worthy of her. The room will be at once familiar when it is known that it went by the name of the yellow drawing-room; the hangings were yellow, the furniture and wall-paper yellow; on the chimney-shelf, in front of a mirror with a gilt frame, candlesticks and a clock in cut glass reflected a hard glitter to the eye. As to Mademoiselle Gamard's private sanctum, no one had ever been allowed to enter it. It could only be conjectured that it was full of the odds and ends, the shabby furniture, the rags and tatters, so to speak, which old, maids collect and cling to so fondly.

This was the woman who was destined to exert the greatest influence over the Abbé Birotteau's latter days. Having failed to exercise the energies bestowed on woman in the way intended by nature, and urged by the need of expending them, this old maid had thrown them into the sordid intrigue, the petty tittle-tattle of provincial life, and the selfish scheming which at last exclusively absorbs all old maids.

Birotteau, for his woe, had developed in Sophie Gamard the only feelings this unhappy creature could possibly know, those of hatred; these, till now latent, as a result of the calm monotony of a country-town life, whose horizon was to her more especially narrow, were presently to become all the more intense for being wreaked on small things, and in a narrow sphere of activity. Birotteau was one of those men who are predestined to suffer everything, because, as they never foresee anything, they can avoid nothing; everything falls on them.

"Yes, it will be fine," the Canon replied after a pause, seeming to come out of his meditations and to wish to fulfil the laws of good manners.

Birotteau, frightened at the time that had elapsed between the remark and the reply, since he, for the first time in his life, had swallowed his coffee without speaking, left the dining-room, where his heart was held as in a vice. Feeling his cup of coffee lie heavy on his stomach, he went to walk, sadly enough, up and down the narrow box-edged paths which marked out a star in the garden. But as he turned after his first round, he saw the Abbé Troubert and Mademoiselle Gamard standing at the glass door of the drawing-room; he with his arms crossed, as motionless as the statue on a tomb, she leaning against the shutter-door. Both, as they watched him, seemed to be counting the number of his steps.

To a timid person there is nothing so distressing as being the object of inquisitive inspection; when it is made by the eyes of hatred, the sort of suffering it inflicts becomes an intolerable martyrdom. Presently the Abbé fancied that he was hindering Mademoiselle Gamard and the Canon from taking their walk. This notion, inspired alike by fear and by good-nature, acquired such proportions, that he abandoned the place. He went away, already thinking no more of his canonry, so greatly was he worried by the woman's maddening tyranny.

By chance, and happily for him, he was kept very busy at Saint-Gatien, where there were several funerals, a marriage, and two baptisms. This enabled him to forget his troubles. When his appetite warned him of the dinner hour, he took out his watch in some alarm, seeing that it was some minutes past four. He knew Mademoiselle Gamard's punctuality, so he hurried home.

He saw the first course brought down again as he passed the kitchen. Then on going into the dining-room, the old maid said to him in a tone of voice which betrayed alike the harshness of a reproof and the glee of finding her boarder in fault, "It is half-past four, Monsieur Birotteau; you knew we should not wait for you."

The priest looked at the dining-room clock, and the arrangement of the gauze wrapper, intended to protect it from dust, showed him that his landlady had wound it in the course of the morning, and had allowed herself the pleasure of setting it faster than the clock of Saint-Gatien's. There was nothing to be said. The least word of the suspicion he had conceived would have sprung the most terrible and plausible of those explosions of eloquence which Mademoiselle Gamard, like all women of her class, could give vent to in such cases.

The thousand-and-one vexations that a maid-servant can inflict on her master, or a wife on her husband, in the daily course of private life, were imagined by Mademoiselle Gamard, who heaped them on her boarder. The way in which she plotted her conspiracies against the poor Abbé's domestic comfort bore the stamp of deeply malignant genius. She contrived never to be in the wrong.

By the end of a week after the opening of this tale, his life in the house, and his position towards Mademoiselle Gamard, revealed to him a plot, hatching for six months past. So long as the old maid had been covert in her revenge, and the priest could voluntarily keep up his self-deceit, refusing to believe in her malevolent purpose, the moral effects had made no great progress in him. But since the incidents of the displacement of the candlestick and the clock put too fast, Birotteau could no longer doubt that he was living under the rule of an aversion that kept an ever-watchful eye on him. From this he rapidly sank into despair, for ever seeing Mademoiselle Gamard's lean and talon-like fingers ready to claw his heart.

The old maid, happy in living on a sentiment so teeming with excitement as revenge is, delighted in hovering and wheeling above the Abbé as a bird of prey hovers and circles over a field mouse before seizing it. She had long plotted a scheme which the bewildered priest could not possibly guess, and which she soon began to unfold, showing the genius that can be displayed in small things by isolated beings whose soul, incapable of apprehending the grandeur of true piety, has lost itself in the trivialities of devotion. The last and most frightful aggravation of his torments was that the nature of them prohibited Birotteau, an effusive man who loved to be pitied and comforted, from enjoying the little solace of relating them to his friends. The small amount of tact he owed to his shyness made him dread appearing ridiculous by troubling himself about such silly trifles. At the same time, these silly trifles made up his whole life, the life he loved, full of busy vacuity and vacuous business, a dull, grey life, in which too strong a feeling was a misfortune, and the absence of all excitement is happiness. Thus the poor Abbé's paradise had suddenly become a hell. In short, his torments were intolerable.

The terror with which he contemplated an explanation with Mademoiselle Gamard grew daily, and the secret misfortunes which blighted every hour of his old age injured his health. One morning, as he put on his speckled blue stockings, he observed that the circumference of his calf had shrunk by eight lines. Appalled at such a terribly unmistakable symptom, he determined to make an effort to persuade the Abbé Troubert to intervene officially between himself and Mademoiselle Gamard.

When he found himself in the presence of the imposing Canon, who came out of a study crammed with papers, where he was always at work, admitting nobody, to receive him in a bare room, the Abbé was almost ashamed to speak of Mademoiselle Gamard's petty aggravations to a man who seemed so seriously occupied. But after having suffered all the misery of mental deliberation which humble, weak, or irresolute persons go through, even with regard to trifles, he made up his mind to explain the position to the Canon, not without feeling his heart swollen by extraordinary throbs. Troubert listened with a cold, grave air, trying, but in vain, to control some smiles, which, to intelligent eyes, might have betrayed the satisfaction of a secret desire. A flash sparkled in his eye when Birotteau described to him, with the eloquence lent by true emotion, the bitterness that was incessantly poured out for him; but Troubert at once covered his eyes with his hands, a gesture common to great thinkers, and preserved his habitually dignified attitude.

When the Abbé ceased speaking he would have been puzzled indeed if he had tried to read any sign of the feelings he imagined he should incite in this mysterious priest, on his face, mottled now with yellow patches—yellower than even his usual bilious complexion. After a moment's silence, the Canon made one of those replies of which every word must have been carefully studied to give them their full bearing, but which subsequently showed to capable persons the amazing depth of his mind and the power of his intellect.

He finally crushed Birotteau by saying that all these things surprised him the more, because, but for his brother's explanation, he would never have discerned them. He ascribed this dullness of perception to his important occupations, to his work, and to the supremacy of certain lofty thoughts, which did not allow of his heeding the trivialities of life. He pointed out, but without assuming the airs of wishing to censure the conduct of a man whose years and learning commanded his respect, that "the hermits of old rarely thought about their food, or their dwelling in the deserts, where they gave themselves up to holy contemplation," and that "in our days the priest could, in mind, make a desert for himself in every place." Then, returning to Birotteau, he remarked that "such squabbles were a quite new thing to him. During twelve years nothing of the kind had ever arisen between Mademoiselle Gamard and the venerated Abbé Chapeloud. As for himself, he could, no doubt, act as moderator between the priest and their landlady, since his friendship for her did not overstep the limits imposed by the laws of the Church on its faithful ministers; but then justice would require that he should also hear Mademoiselle Gamard. At the same time, he discerned no change in her; he had always seen her thus; he had willingly yielded to some of her vagaries, knowing that the excellent woman was kindness and sweetness itself; these little caprices of temper were to be ascribed to the sufferings caused by a pulmonary trouble, of which she never spoke, resigning herself to it as a true Christian." He ended by saying that "when he should have lived a few years longer with Mademoiselle, he would appreciate her better, and recognize the beauties of her admirable character."

The Abbé Birotteau came away bewildered. Under the absolute necessity of taking counsel with himself alone, he gauged Mademoiselle Gamard by himself. The poor man thought that by absenting himself for a few days this woman's hatred would burn itself out for lack of fuel. So he determined to go, as he had done before now, to spend some time at a country place where Madame de Listomère always went at the end of the autumn, a season when, in Touraine, the sky is usually clear and mild. Poor man! He was thus carrying out secret wishes of his terrible enemy, whose schemes could not be thwarted by anything short of monk-like endurance; while he, guessing nothing, and not knowing his own business even, was doomed to fall like a lamb under the first blow from the butcher.

Lying on the slope between the town of Tours and the heights of Saint-Georges, facing the south, and sheltered by cliffs, Madame de Listomère's estate combined all the charms of the country with the pleasures of the town. It was not more than a ten-minutes' drive from the Bridge of Tours to the gate of this house, known as *l'Alouette* (the Lark)—an immense convenience in a place where no one will disturb himself for any earthly thing, not even in quest of pleasure.

The Abbé Birotteau had been about ten days at l'Alouette, when one morning, at the breakfast hour, the lodge-keeper came to tell him that Monsieur

Caron wished to speak with him. Monsieur Caron was a lawyer employed by Mademoiselle Gamard. Birotteau, not remembering this, and conscious of no litigious difficulty to be settled with anybody in the world, left the table, not without some anxiety, to meet the lawyer; he found him sitting modestly on the parapet of a terrace.

"Your intention of remaining no longer as a resident under Mademoiselle Gamard's roof being now quite evident—" the man of business began.

"Dear me, monsieur," cried Birotteau, interrupting him, "I never thought of leaving her."

"And yet, monsieur," the lawyer went on, "you must certainly have expressed yourself to that effect to Mademoiselle, since she has sent me to inquire whether you intend remaining long in the country. The event of a prolonged absence not having been provided for in your agreement, might give rise to some discussion. Now, as Mademoiselle Gamard understands it, your board—"

"Monsieur," said Birotteau in surprise, and again interrupting the lawyer, "I did not think it could be necessary to take steps, almost legal in their nature, to—"

"Mademoiselle Gamard, wishing to preclude any difficulty," said Monsieur Caron, "has sent me to come to an understanding with you."

"Very well, if you will be so obliging as to call again tomorrow, I, on my part, will have taken advice."

"So be it," said Caron with a bow.

The scrivener withdrew. The hapless priest, appalled by the pertinacity of Mademoiselle Gamard's persecution, went back to Madame de Listomère's dining-room looking quite upset. At his mere appearance every one asked him, 'Why, Monsieur Birotteau, what is the matter?"

The Abbé, greatly distressed, sat down without answering, so overwhelmed was he by the vague vision of his misfortune. But after breakfast, when several of his friends had gathered round a good fire in the drawing-room, Birotteau artlessly told them the tale of his catastrophe. The hearers, who were just beginning to be bored by their stay in the country, were deeply interested in an intrigue so completely in keeping with provincial life. Everybody took the Abbé's part against the old maid.

'Why!" cried Madame de Listomère, "do you not plainly see that the Abbé Troubert wants your rooms?"

In this place the historian would have a right to sketch this lady's portrait; but it occurs to him that even those persons to whom Sterne's cognomology is unknown could surely not utter the three words MADAME DE LISTOMÈRE without seeing her—noble and dignified, tempering the austerity of piety by the antique elegance of monarchical and classic manners and polite distinction; kind, but a little formal; speaking slightly through her nose; allowing herself to read *la Nouvelle Héloïse*, and to go to the play; still wearing her own hair.

"The Abbé Birotteau must certainly not yield to that nagging old woman!" cried Monsieur de Listomère, a lieutenant in the navy, spending a holiday with his aunt. "If the Abbé has any courage, and will follow my advice, he will soon have recovered his peace of mind."

In short, everybody began to analyse Mademoiselle Gamard's proceedings with the acumen peculiar to provincials, who, it certainly cannot be denied, possess the talent of laying bare the most secret human actions.

"You have not hit the mark," said an old landowner who knew the country. "There is something very serious under this which I have not yet mastered. The Abbé Troubert is far too deep to be so easily seen through. Our good friend Birotteau is only at the beginning of his troubles. In the first place, would he be happy and left in peace even if he gave up his rooms to Troubert? I doubt it.—If Caron came to tell you," he went on, turning to the puzzled Abbé, "that you had intended to leave Mademoiselle Gamard, with the object of getting you out of her house … Well, you will have to go, willy nilly. That kind of man never risks a chance; they only play when they hold the trumps."

This old gentleman, a certain Monsieur de Bourbonne, epitomised provincial ideas as completely as Voltaire epitomised the spirit of his time. This withered little old man professed in matters of dress all the indifference of a proprietor whose estate has a quotable value in the department. His countenance, tanned by the sun of Touraine, was shrewd rather than clever. He was accustomed to weigh his words, to consider his actions, and he concealed his deep caution under a delusive bluntness. The very least observation was enough to discover that, like a Norman peasant, he would get the advantage in every stroke of business. He was great in œnology—the favourite science of the Tourangeaux. He had managed to extend the circle of one of his estates by taking in the alluvial land of the Loire without getting into a lawsuit with the State. This achievement had established his reputation as a clever man. If, charmed by Monsieur de Bourbonne's conversation, you had asked his biography of one of his fellow-provincials, "Oh! he is a cunning old fox," would have been the proverbial reply of all who envied him, and they were many. In Touraine, as in most provinces, jealousy lies at the base of the tongue.

Monsieur de Bourbonne's remark caused a brief silence, during which the members of this little committee seemed lost in thought.

At this juncture Mademoiselle Salomon de Villenoix was announced. She had just come from Tours, prompted by her wish to be of service to Birotteau, and the news she brought completely changed the aspect of affairs. At the moment when she came in, every one but the landowner was advising Birotteau to hold his own against Troubert and Gamard, under the auspices of the aristocratic party, who would support him.

"The Vicar-General," said Mademoiselle Salomon, "who has all the promotions in his hands, has just been taken ill, and the Archbishop has commissioned Canon Troubert to act in his place. The nomination to the canonry now depends entirely on him. Now yesterday, at Mademoiselle de la Blottière's, the Abbé Poirel was speaking of the annoyances Monsieur Birotteau occasioned to Mademoiselle Gamard, in such a way as to seem to justify the neglect which will certainly fall on our good Abbé. 'The Abbé Birotteau is a man who badly needed the Abbé Chapeloud,' said he, 'and since that virtuous Canon's death it has been proved that—' Then came a series of suppositions and calumnies.—You understand?"

"Troubert will be made Vicar-General," said Monsieur de Bourbonne solemnly.

"Come now," cried Madame de Listomère, looking at Birotteau, "which would you prefer—to be made Canon, or to remain with Mademoiselle Gamard?"

"To be made Canon," was the general outcry.

"Well, then," Madame de Listomère went on, "the Abbé Troubert and Mademoiselle Gamard must be allowed to have their way. Have they not conveyed to you indirectly by Caron's visit that, provided you consent to leave your rooms, you shall be made Canon? One good turn for another."

Everyone exclaimed at Madame de Listomère's acumen and sagacity; but her nephew, the Baron de Listomère, said in a comical tone to Monsieur de Bourbonne:

"I should have liked to see the battle between the *Gamard* and the *Birotteau*."

But, for the Abbé's worse luck, the forces were not equal, with the worldly-wise on one side, and the old maid upheld by the Abbé Troubert on the other. The time was at hand when the struggle would become more decisive, and assume a greater scope and immense proportions.

By the advice of Madame de Listomère and most of her adherents, who were beginning to take a passionate interest in this intrigue flung into the vacuity of their country life, a footman was despatched for Monsieur Caron. The lawyer returned with amazing promptitude, a fact that alarmed no one but Monsieur de Bourbonne.

"Let us adjourn any decision till we have fuller information," was the advice of this Fabius in a dressing-gown, whose deep reflections revealed to him some abstruse plan of battle on the Tours chessboard.

He tried to enlighten Birotteau as to the perils of his position. But the "old fox's" shrewdness did not subserve the frenzy of the moment; he was scarcely listened to.

The meeting between the lawyer and Birotteau was brief. The Abbé came in looking quite scared, and saying, "He requires me to sign a paper declaring my decession."

"What barbarous word is that?" said the navy lieutenant.

"And what does it mean?" cried Madame de Listomère.

"It simply means that the Abbé is to declare his readiness to leave Mademoiselle Gamard's house," replied Monsieur de Bourbonne, taking a pinch of snuff.

"Is that all?—Sign it!" said Madame de Listomère to Birotteau. "If you have really made up your mind to quit her house, there can be no harm done by declaring your will."—The *Will* of Birotteau!

"That is true," said Monsieur de Bourbonne, shutting his snuff-box with a dry snap, of which it is impossible to render the full meaning, for it was a language by itself. "But writing is always dangerous," he added, placing the snuff box on the chimney-shelf with a look that terrified the Abbé.

Birotteau was so bewildered by the upheaval of all his ideas, by the swiftness of events which had come on him and found him defenceless, and by the lightness with which his friends treated the most cherished circumstances of his lonely life, that he remained motionless, as if lost in the moon, not thinking of anything, but listening and trying to catch the sense of the hasty words everybody else was so ready with. He took up Monsieur Caron's document, and read it as though the lawyer's deed were in fact the object of his attention; but it was merely mechanical, and he signed the paper by which he declared himself ready and willing to give up his residence with Mademoiselle Gamard as well as his board, as provided by the agreement between them. When Birotteau had signed the deed, Caron took it, and asked him where his client was to bestow the goods and chattels belonging to him. Birotteau mentioned Madame de

Listomère's house, and the lady by a nod consented to receive the Abbé for some days, never doubting but that he would ere long be made a Canon. The old landowner wished to see this sort of act of renunciation, and Monsieur Caron handed it to him.

'Why," said he to the Abbé, after having read it, "is there any written agreement between you and Mademoiselle Gamard? Where is it? What are the conditons?"

"The paper is in my rooms," said Birotteau.

"Do you know its contents?" the old gentleman asked the lawyer.

"No, monsieur," said Monsieur Caron, holding out his hand for the ominous document.

"Ah, ha!" said Monsieur de Bourbonne to himself, "you, master lawyer, are no doubt informed of what that agreement contains, but you are not paid to tell us." And he returned the deed of "decession" to the lawyer.

"Where am I to put all my furniture?" cried Birotteau, "and my books, my beautiful library, my nice pictures, my red drawing-room all my things, in short!"

And the poor man's despair at finding himself thus uprooted was so guileless, it so perfectly showed the purity of his life, and his ignorance of the world, that Madame de Listomère and Mademoiselle Salomon said, to comfort him, and in the tone that mothers use when they promise a child a plaything:

"There, there, do not worry yourself about such silly trifles. We shall easily find you a home less cold and gloomy than Mademoiselle Gamard's house. If no lodging is to be found to suit you—well, one of us will take you as a boarder. Come, play a hit at backgammon. You can call on the Abbé Troubert to-morrow to ask his support, and you will see how well he will receive you."

Weak-minded persons are reassured as easily as they are frightened. So poor Birotteau, dazzled by the prospect of living with Madame de Listomère, forgot the ruin, now irremediably complete, of the happiness he had so long sighed for, and so thoroughly reveled in. Still, at night, before falling asleep, with the anguish of a man to whom a removal, and the formation of new habits, were as the end of the world, he tortured his mind to imagine where he could find as convenient a home for his library as that corridor. As he pictured his books astray, his furniture dispersed, and his home broken up, he wondered a thousand times why his first year at Mademoiselle Gamard's had been so delightful, and the second so wretched. And again and again this disaster was a bottomless pit in which his mind was lost.

The canonry no longer seemed to him a sufficient compensation for so many misfortunes; he compared his life to a stocking in which one dropped stitch leads to a ladder all the way down the web. Mademoiselle Salomon was left to him. But, losing all his old illusions, the poor priest no longer dared believe in a new friend.

In the *città dolente* of old maids there are several, especially in France, whose life is a sacrifice nobly renewed day by day to noble feeling. Some remain proudly faithful to a heart which death untimely snatched from them; martyrs to love, they learn the secret of womanliness of soul. Others succumb to a family pride which, to our shame, is daily waxing less; they have devoted themselves to make the fortune of a brother, or to the care of orphan nephews; such women are mothers though remaining maids. These old maids rise to the highest heroism of their sex, by consecrating every womanly feeling to the worship of misfortune. They idealise the concept of woman, by renouncing all the rewards of her natural destiny, and accepting only its penalties. They live enshrined in the beauty of their self-sacrifice, and men reverently bow their heads before their faded forms. Mademoiselle de Sombreuil is neither wife nor maid; she was, and always will be, an embodied poem.

Mademoiselle Salomon was one of these heroic creatures. Her sacrifice was religiously sublime, inasmuch as it would remain inglorious after having been a daily anguish. Young and handsome, she was loved; her lover lost his reason. For five years she had devoted herself with the courage of love to the mechanical joys of the unhappy man; she was so fully wedded to his madness that she did not think him mad.

She was a woman of simple manners, frank in speech, with a pale face not devoid of character, though the features were regular. She never spoke of the experiences of her life. Only, now and then, the sudden shudder with which she heard the narrative of some dreadful or melancholy incident betrayed in her the fine qualities evolved by great sorrows. She had come to live at Tours after the death of her companion in life. There she could not be appreciated at her true value; she was regarded as a "good creature." She was very charitable, and attached herself by preference to the weak and helpless. For this reason she had, of course, the deepest interest in the unhappy priest.

Mademoiselle Salomon de Villenoix, driving into town early next morning, took Birotteau with her, set him down on the Cathedral quay, and left him making his way towards the Close, where he was in great haste to arrive, to save the canonry, at any rate, from the shipwreck, and to superintend the removal of his furniture. He rang, not without violent palpitations, at the door of the house, whither for fourteen years he had been in the habit of coming, in which he had dwelt, and whence he was now to be for ever exiled after dreaming that he might die there in peace like his friend Chapeloud.

Marianne was surprised to see him. He told her he had come to speak to Monsieur Troubert, and turned towards the ground-floor rooms in which the Canon lodged; but Marianne called out to him:

"The Abbé Troubert is not there, Monsieur le Vicaire; he is in your old rooms."

These words were a fearful shock to Birotteau, who at last understood Troubert's character, and the unfathomable depth of revenge so slowly worked out, when he saw him quite at home in Chapeloud's library, seated in Chapeloud's fine Gothic chair—sleeping, no doubt, in Chapeloud's bed, using Chapeloud's furniture, contravening Chapeloud's will, in short, disinheriting Chapeloud's friend;—that very Chapeloud who had for so long penned him in at Mademoiselle Gamard's, hindered his advancement, and kept him out of the drawing-rooms of Tours. By what magic wand had this transformation been effected? Were these things no longer Birotteau's?

Indeed, as he noted the sardonic expression with which Troubert looked round on this library, Birotteau inferred that the future Vicar-General was secure of possessing for ever the plunder of the two men he had so bitterly hated—Chapeloud as an enemy, and Birotteau because in him he still saw Chapeloud. At the sight a thousand ideas surged up in the worthy man's heart and wrapped him in a sort of trance. He stood motionless, and, as it were, fascinated by Troubert's eye, which was fixed on him.

"I cannot suppose, monsieur," said Birotteau at last, "that you would wish to deprive me of the things that are mine. Though Mademoiselle Gamard may have been impatient to move you, she must surely be just enough to allow me time to identify my books and remove my furniture."

"Monsieur," said the Canon coldly, and betraying no sort of feeling in his face, "Mademoiselle Gamard told me yesterday that you were leaving; of the cause of it I know nothing. If she moved me up here, it was because she was obliged to do so. Monsieur l'Abbé Poirel has taken my rooms. Whether the furniture in these rooms belongs to mademoiselle, I know not. If it is yours, you know her perfect honesty; the saintliness of her life is a guarantee for it.

"As to myself, you know how plainly I live. For fifteen years I slept in a bare room, never heeding the damp, which is killing me by inches. At the same time, if you wish to return to these rooms, I am ready to give them up to you."

As he listened to this terrible speech, Birotteau forgot the matter of the canonry; he went downstairs as briskly as a young man to find Mademoiselle Gamard, and met her at the bottom of the stairs in the large paved passage which joined the two parts of the house.

"Mademoiselle," said he, bowing, and not heeding the sour, sardonic smile that curled her lips, or the extraordinary fire that gave her eyes a glare like a tiger's, "I cannot understand why you did not wait till I had removed my furniture before—"

"What?" she exclaimed, interrupting him, "have not all your things been taken to Madame de Listomère's?"

"But my furniture?"

"Did you never read your agreement?" cried she, in tones which ought to be expressed in musical notation to show how many shades hatred could infuse into the accentuation of every word.

And Mademoiselle Gamard seemed to swell, her eyes flashed once more, and her face beamed; her whole person thrilled with satisfaction.

The Abbé Troubert opened a window to see better to read a folio volume.

Birotteau stood as if thunderstricken.

Mademoiselle Gamard trumpeted at him, in a voice as shrill as a clarion, the following words:

"Was it not agreed that, in the event of your leaving my house, your furniture was to become mine to indemnify me for the difference between what you paid me for your board, and what I received from the late respectable Abbé Chapeloud? Now, as Monsieur l'Abbé Poirel has been made Canon—"

At these last words Birotteau bowed slightly as if to take leave; then he rushed out of the house. He was afraid lest, if he staid any longer, he should faint, and so give his relentless foes a too great triumph. Walking like a drunken man, he got back to Madame de Listomère's town house, where, in a lower room, he found his linen, clothes, and papers all packed into a trunk. At the sight of those relics of his property, the unhappy priest sat down and hid his face in his hands to hide his tears from the sight of men. The Abbé Poirel was Canon! He, Birotteau, found himself homeless, bereft of fortune and furniture.

Happily, Mademoiselle Salomon happened to drive past. The doorkeeper, understanding the poor man's despair, signaled to the coachmen. After a few words of explanation between the lady and the porter, the Abbé allowed himself to be led to his faithful friend, though he could only answer her in incoherent words. Mademoiselle Salomon, alarmed by the temporary derangement of a brain already so feeble, carried him at once to l'Alouette, ascribing these symptoms of mental disturbance to the effect naturally produced on him by the Abbé Poirel's promotion. She knew nothing of the hapless priest's agreement with Mademoiselle Gamard, for the excellent reason that he himself did not know its full bearing. And as it is in the nature of things that comedy is often mixed up with the most pathetic incidents, Birotteau's bewildered answers almost made Mademoiselle Salomon laugh.

"Chapeloud was right," said he; "he is a monster."

"Who?" said she.

"Chapeloud. He has robbed me of everything."

"Then you mean Poirel?"

"No, Troubert."

At length they reached l'Alouette, where the priest's friends lavished on him such effusive kindness, that by the evening he grew calmer, and they could extract from him an account of all that had occurred that morning.

Monsieur de Bourbonne, always phlegmatic, naturally asked to see the agreement which ever since the day before had seemed to him to contain the key to the riddle. Birotteau brought the fatal document out of his pocket, and held it out to the landowner, who read it hastily, presently coming to a sentence in these terms:—

"Whereas there is a difference of eight hundred francs a year between the price paid by the late Monsieur Chapeloud and the sum for which the aforenamed Sophie Gamard agrees to lodge and board, on the terms hereinbefore stated, the said François Birotteau; whereas the said François Birotteau fully acknowledges that it is out of his power for some years to come to pay the full price paid by Mademoiselle Gamard's boarders, and more especially by the Abbé Troubert; and, finally, whereas the said Sophie Gamard has advanced certain sums of money, the said Birotteau hereby pledges himself to bequeath to her, as an indemnity, the furniture of which he may be possessed at the time of his decease; or in the event of his voluntary departing, for whatever cause or reason, and quitting the premises at present let to him, and no longer availing himself of the benefits contracted for in the agreement made by Mademoiselle Gamard herein-before—"

"Heaven, above us! What impudence!" exclaimed Monsieur de Bourbonne. "And what claws the said Sophie Gamard has!"

Poor Birotteau, never conceiving in his childish brain of any cause which could ever separate him from Mademoiselle Gamard, had counted on dying under her roof. He had not the least recollection of this clause, of which the terms had not even been discussed at the time when, in his eagerness to lodge with the old maid, he would have signed all the documents she might have chosen to lay before him. His innocence was so creditable, and Mademoiselle Gamard's conduct so atrocious; there was something so deplorable in the fate of this hapless sexagenarian, and his weakness made him so pitiable, that in a first impulse of indignation Madame de Listomère exclaimed, "I am the cause of your having signed the act that has ruined you; I ought to make up to you for the comfort you have lost."

"But," said Monsieur de Bourbonne, "such proceedings constitute a fraud; there are grounds for an action—"

"Good, Birotteau shall bring an action. If he loses it at Tours, he will win it at Orleans; if he loses it at Orleans, he will win it at Paris!" cried the Baron de Listomère.

"If he means to bring an action, I should advise him first to resign his benefice in the Cathedral," said Monsieur de Bourbonne calmly.

"We will take legal advice," replied Madame de Listomère; "and we will bring an action if we ought. But this business is so disgraceful for Mademoiselle Gamard, and may prove so damaging to the Abbé Troubert, that we can surely effect a compromise."

After mature deliberation, everybody promised to assist the Abbé Birotteau in the struggle that must ensue between him and the allies of his enemies. A confident presentiment, an indescribable provincial instinct prompted every one to combine the names of Troubert and Gamard. But not a soul of those then assembled at Madame de Listomère's excepting the "old fox," had any accurate notion of the importance of such a conflict.

Monsieur de Bourbonne took the poor priest into a corner. "Of all the fourteen persons present," said he in a low voice; "not one will be still on your side within a fortnight. If you then want to call in help, you will perhaps find no one but myself bold enough to undertake your defence, because I know the country, men, and things, and, better still, their interests. All your friends here, though full of good intentions, are starting on the wrong road, which you can never get out of. Listen to my advice. If you want to live in peace, give up your office in Saint-Gatien and leave Tours. Tell no one where you go, but seek a cure of souls far from hence, where Troubert can never come across you."

"Leave Tours!" cried the Abbé, with unspeakable dismay.

It was to him a form of death. Was it not tearing up all the roots by which he held to the world? Celibates make habits take the place of feelings. And when to this system of ideas, by which they go through life rather than live, they add a weak nature, external things have an astonishing dominion over them. Birotteau had really become a sort of vegetable; to transplant it was to endanger its guileless functions. Just as a tree, in order to live, must always find the same juices at hand, and always send its filaments into the same soil, so Birotteau must always patter round Saint Gatien, always trot up and down the spot on the Mall where he was wont to walk, always go through the same familiar streets, and constantly frequent the three drawing-rooms where evening after evening he played whist or backgammon.

"To be sure—I was not thinking," replied Monsieur de Bourbonne, looking compassionately at the priest.

Before long all Tours knew that Madame la Baronne de Listomère, widow of a Lieutenant-General, had given a home to the Abbé Birotteau, *Vicaire* of Saint-Gatien. This fact, on which several persons threw doubts, cut short all questions, and gave definiteness to party divisions, especially when Mademoiselle Salomon was the first to dare speak of fraud and an action at law.

Mademoiselle Gamard, with the subtle vanity and the fanatical sense of personal importance that are characteristic of old maids, considered herself greatly aggrieved by the line of conduct taken by Madame de Listomère. The Baroness was a woman of high rank, elegant in her habits, whose good taste, polished manners, and genuine piety were beyond dispute. By sheltering Birotteau she formally gave the lie to all Mademoiselle Gamard's asseverations, indirectly censured her conduct, and seemed to sanction the Abbé's complaints of his former landlady.

For the better comprehension of this story, it is necessary here to explain how much power Mademoiselle Gamard derived from the discernment and analytical spirit with which old women can account to themselves for the actions of others, and to set forth the resources of her faction. Escorted by the always taciturn Abbé Troubert, she spent her evenings in four or five houses where a dozen persons were wont to meet, allied by common tastes and analogous circumstances. There were two or three old men, wedded to the whims and tittle-tattle of their cooks; five or six old maids, who spent their days in sifting the words and scrutinising the proceedings of their neighbours and those a little below them in the social scale; and finally, several old women wholly occupied in distilling scandal, in keeping an exact register of everybody's fortune, and a check on everybody's actions. They foretold marriages, and blamed their friends' conduct quite as harshly as their enemies'. These persons, filling in the town a position analogous to the capillary vessels of a plant, imbibed news with the thirst of a leaf for the dew, picked up the secrets of every household, discharged them and transmitted them mechanically to Monsieur Troubert, as leaves communicate to the plant the moisture they have absorbed. Thus, every evening of the week, these worthy bigots, prompted by the craving for excitement which exists in every one, struck an accurate balance of the position of the town with a sagacity worthy of the Council of Ten, and made an armed police out of the unerring espionage to which our passions give rise. Then, as soon as they had found the secret motive of any event, their conceit led them to appropriate, severally, the wisdom of their Sanhedrim, and to give importance to their gossip in their respective circles.

This idle and busybody assembly, invisible though omniscient, speechless but for ever talking, had at that time an influence which was apparently harmless in view of its contemptibility, but which nevertheless could be terrible when it was animated by a strong motive. Now it was a very long time since any event had occurred within range of their lives to compare in general importance to each and all with the contest between Birotteau, supported by Madame de Listomère, and the Abbé Troubert with Mademoiselle Gamard. In fact, the three drawing-rooms of Madame de Listomère, Mademoiselle Merlin de la Blottière, and Mademoiselle de Villenoix, being regarded as a hostile camp by those where Mademoiselle Gamard visited, there lay behind this quarrel a strong party spirit with all its vanities. It was the struggle of the Roman Senate and people in a molehill, or a tempest in a glass of water, as Montesquieu said in speaking of the Republic of San Marino, where public officials held their places but a day, so easy it was to seize despotic power.

But this storm in a teacup evolved as many passions in the actors as would have sufficed to direct the largest social interests. Is it not a mistake to suppose that time flies swiftly only to those whose hearts are a prey to such vast projects as trouble life and make it boil? The Abbé Troubert's hours were spent as busily, flew loaded with thoughts as anxious, and marked by despair and hopes as deep, as could the racking hours of the man of ambition, the gamester, or the lover. God alone knows the secret of the energy we put forth to win the occult triumphs we achieve over men, or things, or ourselves. Though we do not always know whither we are going, we know full well the fatigues of the voyage. Still, if the historian may be allowed to digress from the drama he is narrating, to assume for a moment the functions of the critic—if he may invite you to glance at the lives of these old maids and of these two priests, to investigate the causes of the misfortune which vitiated their inmost core—you will perhaps find it proved to a demonstration that man must necessarily experience certain passions if he is to evolve those qualities which give nobleness to life, which expand its limits and silence the selfishness natural to all beings.

Madame de Listomère returned to town, not knowing that for five or six days past several of her friends had been obliged to dispute a rumour concerning herself, and accepted by some, though she would have laughed at it had she heard of it, which attributed her affection for her nephew to almost criminal causes.

She took the Abbé to see her lawyer, who did not think an action an easy matter. The Abbé's friends, confident in the feeling that comes of the justice of a good case, or else dilatory about proceedings which did not concern them personally, had postponed the preliminary inquiry till the day when they should return to Tours. Thus Mademoiselle Gamard's allies had been able to make the first move, and had told the story in a way unfavourable to the Abbé Birotteau. Hence the man of law, whose clients consisted exclusively of the pious folks of the town, very much astonished Madame de Listomère by urging her on no account to be mixed up in such proceedings; and he closed the interview by saying that "he, at any rate, would not undertake the case, because, by the terms of the agreement, Mademoiselle Gamard was right in the eye of the law; that in equity, that is to say, out of the jurisdiction of the Court, Monsieur Birotteau would appear in the eyes of the Bench and of all honest folks to have fallen away from the meek, peace-loving, and conciliatory character he had hitherto enjoyed; that Mademoiselle Gamard, regarded as a gentle person and easy to live with, had accommodated Birotteau by lending the money needed to pay the succession duties arising from Chapeloud's bequest, without demanding any receipt; that Birotteau was not of an age, nor of a nature, to sign a document without knowing what it contained and recognising its importance; and that as he had ceased to live at Mademoiselle Gamard's after only two years' residence, whereas his friend Chapeloud had been with her for twelve years, and Troubert for fifteen, it could only be in accordance with some plan best known to himself. That, consequently, the action would be generally considered as an act of ingratitude," etc.

After seeing Birotteau to the head of the stairs, the lawyer detained Madame de Listomère a moment as he showed her out, and besought her, as she loved her peace of mind, to have nothing to do with the affair.

In the evening, however, the hapless Abbé, as miserable as a criminal in the condemned cell at Bicêtre while awaiting the result of his petition to the court of appeal, could not keep himself from telling his friends of the result of his visit to the lawyer, at the hour before the card-parties were made up, when the little circle were assembling round Madame de Listomère's fire.

"I know no lawyer in Tours, excepting the solicitor for the Liberal party, who would undertake the case, unless he meant to lose it," exclaimed Monsieur de Bourbonne, "and I do not advise you to embark on it."

"Well, it is a rascally shame!" said the navy lieutenant. "I myself will take the Abbé to see that lawyer!"

"Then go after dark," said Monsieur de Bourbonne, interrupting him.

"Why?"

"I have just heard that the Abbé Troubert is appointed Vicar-General in the place of him who died the day before yesterday."

"Much I care for the Abbé Troubert!"

Unluckily, the Baron de Listomère, a man of six-and-thirty, did not see the sign made to him by Monsieur de Bourbonne warning him to weigh his words, and pointing significantly at a town councillor who was known to be a friend of Troubert's. So the officer went on:

"If Monsieur Troubert is a rogue …"

"Dear me," said Monsieur de Bourbonne, "why bring the Abbé Troubert's name into a matter with which he has no concern whatever?"

"Nay," said the lieutenant, "is he not in the enjoyment of the Abbé Birotteau's furniture? I remember having called on Monsieur Chapeloud and seeing two valuable pictures. Suppose they are worth ten thousand francs? Can you believe that Monsieur Birotteau ever intended to give, in return for two years' board with this Gamard woman, ten thousand francs, when the library and furniture are worth almost as much more?"

The Abbé opened his eyes very wide on hearing that he had ever owned such an enormous fortune. And the Baron went on vehemently to the end.

"By Jove! Monsieur Salmon, an expert from the Paris gallery, happens to be here on a visit to his mother-in-law. I will go to him this very evening with Monsieur l'Abbé, and beg him to value the pictures. From thence I will take him to that lawyer."

Two days after this conversation the action had taken shape. The solicitor to the Liberal party, now Birotteau's attorney, cast some obloquy on the Abbé's case.

The Opposition to the Government, and some persons known to love neither priests nor religion—two things which many people fail to distinguish—took up the matter, and the whole town was talking of it. The expert from Paris had valued the *Virgin* by le Valentin, and the *Christ* by Lebrun, at eleven thousand francs; they were both choice examples. As to the bookcase and the Gothic furniture, the fashionable taste, daily growing in Paris, for that style of work gave them an immediate value of twelve thousand francs. In short, the expert, on examination, estimated the contents of the rooms at ten thousand crowns.

Now, it was obvious that as Birotteau had never intended to give Mademoiselle Gamard this immense sum in payment of the little money he might owe her in virtue of the stipulated indemnity, there were grounds, legally speaking, for a new contract, otherwise the old maid would be guilty of unintentional fraud. So the lawyer on Birotteau's behalf began by serving a writ on Mademoiselle Gamard, formulating the Abbé's case. This statement, though exceedingly severe, and supported by quotations from leading judgments, and confirmed by certain articles of the Code, was at the same time a masterpiece of legal logic, and so evidently condemned the old maid, that thirty or forty copies were maliciously circulated in the town by the opposite party.

A few days after this commencement of hostilities between the old maid and Birotteau, the Baron de Listomère, who, as commander of a corvette, hoped to be included in the next list of promotions, which had been expected for some time at the Navy Board, received a letter, in which a friend informed him that there was, on the contrary, some idea in the office of placing him on the Retired List. Greatly amazed by this news, he at once set out for Paris, and appeared at the Minister's next reception. This official himself seemed no less surprised, and even laughed at the fears expressed by the Baron de Listomère.

Next day, in spite of the Minister's words, the Baron inquired at the office. With an indiscretion, such as is not unfrequently committed by heads of departments for their friends, a secretary showed him a minute confirming the fatal news, ready drawn up, but which had not yet been submitted to the Minister, in consequence of the illness of a head-clerk. The Baron at once went to call on an uncle, who, being a député, could without delay meet the Minister at the Chamber, and begged him to sound His Excellency as to his views, since to him this meant the sacrifice of his whole career. He awaited the closing of the sitting in his uncle's carriage in the greatest anxiety.

Long before the end his uncle came out, and as they drove home to his house he asked the Baron:—

"What the devil led you to make war against the priesthood? The Minister told me at once that you had put yourself at the head of the Liberal party at Tours. Your opinions are detestable, you do not follow the line laid down by the Government, and what not! His phrases were as confused as if he were still addressing the Chamber. So then I said to him, 'Come, let us understand each other.' And His Excellency ended by confessing that you were in a scrape with the Lord High Almoner. In short, by making some inquiries among my colleagues, I learned that you had spoken with much levity of a certain Abbé Troubert, who, though but a Vicar-General, is the most important personage of the province, where he represents the ecclesiastical power. I answered for you to the Minister in person.— My noble nephew, if you want to get on in the world, make no enemies in the Church.

"Now, go back to Tours, and make your peace with this devil of a Vicar-General. Remember that Vicars-General are men with whom you must always live in peace. Deuce take it! When we are all trying to re-establish the Church, to cast discredit on the priests is a blunder in a ship's lieutenant who wants his promotion. If you do not make it up with this Abbé Troubert, you need not look to me; I shall cast you off. The Minister for Church Affairs spoke to me of the man just now as certain to be a Bishop. If Troubert took an aversion for our family, he might hinder my name from appearing in the next batch of peers.—Do you understand?"

This speech explained to the navy lieutenant what Troubert's secret occupations were, when Birotteau so stupidly remarked, "I cannot think what good he gains by sitting up all night!"

The Canon's position, in the midst of the feminine senate which so craftily kept a surveillance over the province, as well as his personal capabilities, had led to his being chosen by the Church authorities from among all the priests in the town to be the unacknowledged proconsul of Touraine. Archbishop, General, Préfet—high and low were under his occult dominion.

The Baron de Listomère had soon made up his mind.

"I have no notion," said he to his uncle, "of receiving another ecclesiastical broadside below the water-line."

Three days after this diplomatic interview between the uncle and nephew, the sailor, who had suddenly returned to Tours by the mail-coach, explained to his aunt, the very evening of his arrival, all the danger that would be incurred by the Listomère family if they persisted in defending that idiot Birotteau. The Baron had caught Monsieur de Bourbonne at the moment when the old gentleman was taking up his stick and hat to leave after his rubber. The "old fox's" intelligence was indispensable to throw a light on the reefs among which the Listomères had been entangled; he rose so early to seek his hat and stick, only to be stopped by a word in his ear:

"Wait, we want to talk."

The young Baron's prompt return, and his air of satisfaction, though contrasting with the gravity his face assumed now and then, had vaguely hinted to Monsieur de Bourbonne of some checks the lieutenant might have received in his cruise against Gamard and Troubert. He manifested no surprise on hearing the Baron proclaim the secret power possessed by the Vicar-General.

"I knew that," said he.

'Well, then," exclaimed the Baroness, "why did you not warn us?"

"Madame," he hastily replied, "if you will forget that I guessed this priest's occult influence, I will forget that you know it as well as I. If we should fail to keep the secret, we might be taken for his accomplices; we should be feared and hated. Do as I do. Pretend to be a dupe; but look carefully where you set your feet. I said quite enough; you did not understand me. I could not compromise myself."

"What must we do now?" said the Baron.

The desertion of Birotteau was not a matter of question; it was the primary condition, and so understood by this council of three.

"To effect a retreat with all the honours of war has always been the greatest achievement of the most skilful generals," said Monsieur de Bourbonne. "Yield to Troubert; if his hatred is less than his vanity, you will gain an ally; but if you yield too much, he will trample on your body, for, as Boileau says, 'Destruction is by choice the spirit of the Church.' Make as though you were quitting the service, and you will escape him, Monsieur le Baron. Dismiss Birotteau, madame, and you will gain Gamard her lawsuit. When you meet the Abbé Troubert at the Archbishop's, ask him if he plays whist; he will answer *Yes.* Invite him to play a rubber in this drawing-room, where he longs to be admitted; he will certainly come. You are a woman; try to enlist this priest in your interest. When the Baron is a ship's Captain, his uncle a Peer of France, and Troubert a Bishop, you can make Birotteau a Canon at your leisure. Till then yield; but yield gracefully, and with a threat. Your family can give Troubert quite as much assistance as he can give you; you will meet half-way to admiration. And take soundings constantly as you go, sailor!"

"Poor Birotteau!" said the Baronne.

"Oh! begin at once," said the old man as he took leave. "If some clever Liberal should get hold of that vacuous brain, he would get you into trouble. After all, the law would pronounce in his favour, and Troubert must be afraid of the verdict. As yet he may forgive you for having begun the action, but after a defeat he would be implacable.—I have spoken."

He snapped his snuff-box lid, went to put on his thick shoes, and departed.

The next morning, after breakfast, the Baroness remained alone with Birotteau, and said to him, not without visible embarrassment:

"My dear Monsieur Birotteau, I am going to make a request that you will think very unjust and inconsistent; but both for your sake and for ours you must, in the first place, put an end to your action against Mademoiselle Gamard by renouncing your claims, and also quit my house."

As he heard these words the poor priest turned pale.

"I am the innocent cause of your misfortunes," she went on; "and I know that but for my nephew you would never have begun the proceedings which now are working woe for you and for us. Listen to me."

And she briefly set forth the immense scope of this affair, explaining the seriousness of its consequences. Her meditations during the night had enabled her to form an idea of what the Abbé Troubert's former life had been. Thus she could unerringly point out to Birotteau the web in which he had been involved by this skilfully-plotted vengeance, could show him the superior cleverness and power of the enemy, revealing his hatred and explaining its causes; she pictured him as crouching for twelve years to Chapeloud, and now devouring and persecuting Chapeloud in the person of his friend.

The guileless Birotteau clasped his hands as if to pray, and wept with grief at this vision of human wickedness which his innocent soul had never conceived of. Terrified, as though he were standing on the verge of an abyss, he listened to his benefactress with moist and staring eyes, but without expressing a single idea. She said in conclusion:

"I know how vile it is to desert you; but, my dear Abbé, family duties must supersede those of friendship. Bend before this storm, as I must, and I will prove my gratitude. I say nothing of your personal concerns; I undertake them; you shall be released from money difficulties for the rest of your life. By the intervention of Monsieur de Bourbonne, who will know how to save appearances, I will see that you lack nothing. My friend, give me the right to throw you over. I shall remain your friend while conforming to the requirements of the world.—Decide."

The hapless Abbé, quite bewildered, exclaimed:

"Ah! then Chapeloud was right when he said that if Troubert could drag him out of his grave by the heels, he would do it!—He sleeps in Chapeloud's bed!"

"It is no time for lamentations," said Madame de Listomère. "We have no time to spare. Come—"

Birotteau was too kind-hearted not to submit in any great crisis to the impulsive self-sacrifice of the first moment. But, in any case, his life already was but one long martyrdom. He answered with a heartbroken look at his protectress, which wrung her soul:

"I am in your hands. I am no more than a straw in the street!"

The local word he used, *bourrier*, is peculiar to Touraine, and its only liberal rendering is a straw. But there are pretty little straws, yellow, shiny, and smart, the delight of children; while a *bourrier* is a dirty, colourless, miry straw, left in the gutter, driven by the wind, crushed by the foot of every passer-by.

"But, madame," he went on, "I should not wish to leave the portrait of Chapeloud for the Abbé Troubert. It was done for me, and belongs to me; get that back for me, and I will give up everything else."

'Well," said Madame de Listomère, "I will go to Mademoiselle Gamard." She spoke in a tone which showed what an extraordinary effort the Baronne de Listomère was making in stooping to flatter the old maid's conceit. "And I will try to settle everything," she went on. "I hardly dare hope it.—Go and see Monsieur de Bourbonne. Get him to draw up your act of renunciation in due form, and bring it to me signed and witnessed. With the help of the Archbishop, I may perhaps get the thing settled."

Birotteau went away overpowered. Troubert had assumed in his eyes the proportions of an Egyptian pyramid. The man's hands were in Paris, and his elbows in the Close of Saint-Gatien.

"He," said he to himself, "to hinder Monsieur le Marquis de Listomère being made a peer of France!—And then, 'With the help of the Archbishop, perhaps get the thing settled!'"

In comparison with such high interests, Birotteau felt himself a grasshopper; he was honest to himself.

The news of Birotteau's removal was all the more astounding because the reason was undiscoverable. Madame de Listomère gave out that as her nephew wished to marry and retire from the service, she needed the Abbé's room to add to her own. No one as yet had heard that Birotteau had withdrawn the action. Monsieur de Bourbonne's instructions were thus judiciously carried out.

These two pieces of news, when they should reach the ears of the Vicar-General, must certainly flatter his vanity, by showing him that, though the Listomère family would not capitulate, it would at least remain neutral, tacitly recognising the secret power of the Church Council; and was not recognition submission? Still, the action remained *sub judice*. Was not this to yield and to threaten?

Thus the Listomères had assumed an attitude precisely similar to that of the Abbé Troubert in this contest; they stood aside, and could direct their forces.

But a serious event now occurred, and added to their difficulties, hindering the success of the means by which Monsieur de Bourbonne and the Listomères hoped to mollify the Gamard and Troubert faction. On the previous day Mademoiselle Gamard had taken a chill on coming out of the Cathedral, had gone to bed, and was reported to be seriously ill. The whole town rang with lamentations, excited by spurious commiseration. "Mademoiselle Gamard's highly-strung sensibilities had succumbed to the scandal of this lawsuit. Though she was undoubtedly in the right, she was dying of grief. Birotteau had killed his benefactress." This was the sum and substance of the phrases fired off through the capillary ducts of the great feminine synod, and readily repeated by the town of Tours.

Madame de Listomère suffered the humiliation of calling on the old woman without gaining anything by her visit. She very politely requested to be allowed to speak to the Vicar-General. Flattered, perhaps, at receiving a woman who had slighted him, in Chapeloud's library, by the fireplace over which the two famous pictures in dispute were hanging, Troubert kept the Baroness waiting a minute, then he consented to see her

No courtier, no diplomate, ever threw into the discussion of private interests or national negotiations greater skill, dissimulation, and depth of purpose than the Baroness and the Abbé displayed when they found themselves face to face.

Old Bourbonne, like the sponsor, in the Middle Ages, who armed the champion, and fortified his courage by good counsel as he entered the lists, had instructed the Baroness:

"Do not forget your part; you are a peacemaker, and not an interested party. Troubert likewise is a mediator. Weigh your words. Study the tones of the Vicar-General's voice.— If he strokes his chin, you have won him."

Some caricaturists have amused themselves by representing the contrast that so frequently exists between what we say and what we think. In this place, to represent fully the interesting points of the duel of words that took place between the priest and the fine lady, it is necessary to disclose the thoughts they each kept concealed under apparently trivial speech.

Madame de Listomère began by expressing the regret she felt about this lawsuit of Birotteau's, and she went on to speak of her desire of seeing the affair settled to the satisfaction of both parties.

"The mischief is done, madame," said the Abbé. "The admirable Mademoiselle Gamard is dying." ("*I care no more for that stupid creature than for Prester John,*" thought he, "*but I should like to lay her death at your door, and burden your conscience, if you are silly enough to care.*")

"On hearing of her illness," said the Baroness, "I desired the Abbé to sign a withdrawal, which I have brought to that saintly person." ("*I see through you,*" thought she, "*you old rascal; but we are no longer at the mercy of your vagaries. As for you, if you accept the deed, you will have put your foot in it; it will be a confession of complicity.")*

There was a brief silence.

"Mademoiselle Gamard's temporal affairs are no concern of mine," said the priest at length, closing the deep lids over his eagle eyes to conceal his excitement. ("*Ah, ha, you will not catch me tripping! But God be praised, those cursed lawyers will not fight out a case that might bespatter me! But what on earth can the Listomères want, that they are so humble?*")

"Monsieur," replied the Baronne, "the concerns of Monsieur l'Abbé Birotteau interest me no more than those of Mademoiselle Gamard do you. But, unluckily, religion might suffer from their quarrels, and in you I see but a mediator, while I myself come forward as a peacemaker …" ("*We can neither of us throw dust in the other's eyes, Monsieur Troubert,"* thought she. "*Do you appreciate the epigram in that reply?*")

"Religion! madame," said the Vicar-General. "Religion stands too high for man to touch it." ("*Religion means me,*" thought he.) "God will judge us unerringly, madame," he added, "and I recognise no other tribunal."

"Well, then, monsieur," replied she, "let us try to make man's judgments agree with God's." ("*Yes, Religion means you.*")

The Abbé Troubert changed his tone.

"Has not Monsieur your nephew just been to Paris?" ("*You heard of me there, I fancy,*" thought he; "*I can crush you—you who scorned me! You have come to surrender.*")

"Yes, monsieur, thank you for taking so much interest in him. He is returning to Paris to-night, ordered there by the Minister, who is kindness itself to us, and does not wish him to retire from the service." ("*No, Jesuit, you will not crush us*," thought she; "*we understand your little game*.") A pause. "I have not approved of his conduct in this affair," she went on, "but a sailor may be forgiven for not understanding the law." ("*Come, let us be allies*," thought she; "*we shall gain nothing by squabbling*.")

A faint smile dawned, and was lost, in the furrows of the Abbé's face.

"He has done us some service by informing us of the value of those two pictures," said he, looking at them; "they will be a worthy ornament to the Lady Chapel." ("*You fired an epigram at me, madame*," thought he; "*there are two for you, and we are quits*.")

"If you present them to Saint-Gatien, I would beg you to allow me to offer to the Church two frames worthy of the place and of the gift." ("*I should like to make you confess that you coveted Birotteau's property*," thought she.)

"They do not belong to me," said the priest, well on his guard.

"Well, here is the deed that puts an end to all dispute," said Madame de Listomère, "and restores them to Mademoiselle Gamard." She laid the document on the table. ("*You see, monsieur, how much I trust you*," thought she.) "It is worthy of you, monsieur, worthy of your fine character, to reconcile two Christians, though I have ceased to take much interest in Monsieur Birotteau."

"But he is your pensioner," said he, interrupting her.

"No, monsieur, he is no longer under my roof." ("*My brother-in-law's peerage and my nephew's promotion are leading me into very mean actions*," thought she.)

The Abbé remained unmoved, but his calm aspect was a symptom of violent agitation. Only Monsieur de Bourbonne had divined the secret of that superficial calm. The priest was triumphant.

"Why, then, did you take charge of his act of renunciation?" he asked, moved by a feeling similar to that which makes a woman fish for compliments

"I could not help feeling some pity for him. Birotteau, whose feeble character must be well known to you, entreated me to see Mademoiselle Gamard in order to obtain from her, as the price of the surrender of—," the Abbé frowned— "of his *rights*, as recognised by many distinguished lawyers, the portrait—" the priest looked hard at Madame de Listomère—"of Chapeloud," she said. "I leave it to you to judge of his claim to it …" ("*You would lose if you fought the case*," thought she.)

The tone in which the Baroness uttered the words "distinguished lawyers," showed the priest that she knew the enemy's strength and weakness. Madame de Listomère displayed so much skill to this experienced connoisseur, that at the end of this conversation, which was carried on for some time in the same key, he went down to see Mademoiselle Gamard to bring her answer as to the proposed bargain.

Troubert soon returned.

"Madame," said he, "I can but repeat the poor dying woman's words. 'Monsieur l'Abbé Chapeloud showed me too much kindness,' said she, 'for me to part from his portrait.'—As for myself, if it were mine, I would not give it up to any one. I was too faithfully attached to my poor dead friend not to feel that I have a right to claim his likeness against anybody in the world."

"Well, monsieur, do not let us fall out over a bad picture." ("*I care for it more than you do,*" thought she.") "Keep it; we will have it copied. I am proud to have brought this sad and deplorable lawsuit to an end, and I have personally gained the pleasure of making your acquaintance.—I have heard that you are a fine whist player. You will forgive a woman for being curious," she added with a smile. "If you will come and play occasionally at my house, you cannot doubt that you will be heartily welcomed."

The Abbé Troubert stroked his chin. ("*He is caught; Bourbonne was right,*" thought she, "*he has his share of vanity.*")

In fact, the Vicar-General was at this moment enjoying the delicious sensation which Mirabeau found irresistible when, in the day of his power, he saw the gates of some mansion which had formerly been closed against him, opened to admit his carriage.

"Madame," replied he, "my occupations are too important to allow of my going into society; but for you what would not a man do?" ("*It is all over with the old girl; I will make up to the Listomères, and do them a good turn if they do me one,*" thought he. "*It is better to have them for friends than for enemies.*")

Madame de Listomère went home, hoping that the Archbishop would complete a pacification so happily begun. But Birotteau was to gain nothing even by his renunciation. Madame de Listomère heard next day that Mademoiselle Gamard was dead. The old maid's will being opened, no one was surprised to learn that she had constituted the Abbé Troubert her universal legatee. Her property was estimated at a hundred thousand crowns. The Vicar-General sent two invitations to the service and burial to Madame de Listomère's house—one for herself, and the other for her nephew.

'We must go," said she.

"That is just what it means!" exclaimed Monsieur de Bourbonne. "It is a test by which Monseigneur Troubert meant to try you. Baron, you must go all the way to the grave," he added to the navy lieutenant, who, for his sins, had not yet left Tours.

The service was held, and was marked by ecclesiastical magnificence. One person only shed tears. That was Birotteau, who, alone in a side chapel where he was not seen, believed himself guilty of this death, and prayed fervently for the soul of the departed, bitterly bewailing himself because he had not obtained her forgiveness for having wronged her.

The Abbé Troubert followed his friend's body to the grave in which she was to be laid. Standing on its brink, he delivered an address, and, thanks to his eloquence, gave monumental dignity to his picture of the narrow life led by the testatrix. The bystanders noted these words in the peroration:

"This life, full of days devoted to God and to Religion—this life, adorned by so many beautiful actions performed in silence, so many modest and unrecognized virtues, was blighted by a sorrow which we would call unmerited if, here, on the verge of eternity, we could forget that all our afflictions are sent us by God. This holy woman's many friends, knowing how noble was her guileless soul, foresaw that she could endure anything excepting only such detraction as would affect her whole existence. And so perhaps Providence has taken her to rest in God only to rescue her from our petty griefs. Happy are they who here on earth can live at peace with themselves, as Sophie now reposes in the realms of the blest, in her robe of innocence!"

"And when he had ended this grandiloquent discourse," said Monsieur de Bourbonne, who reported all the details of the funeral to Madame de Listomère that evening when, the rubbers ended and the doors closed, they were left alone with the Baron, "imagine, if you can, that Louis XI in a priest's gown giving the holy-water sprinkler a final flourish in this style"—and Monsieur de Bourbonne took up the tongs and imitated the Abbé Troubert's movement so exactly that the Baron and his aunt could not help smiling. "In this alone," added the old man, "did he betray himself. Till then his reserve had been perfect; but now, when he had packed away for ever the old maid he so utterly despised and hated, almost as much perhaps as he had detested Chapeloud, he, no doubt, found it impossible to hinder his satisfaction from betraying itself in a gesture."

Next morning Mademoiselle Salomon came to breakfast with Madame de Listomère, and as soon as she came in she said quite sadly:

"Our poor Abbé Birotteau has just been dealt a dreadful blow which reveals the most elaborately studied hatred. He is made Curé of Saint-Symphorien."

Saint-Symphorien is a suburb of Tours lying beyond the bridge. This bridge, one of the finest works of French architecture, is nearly two thousand feet long, and the open squares at each end are exactly alike.

"Do you understand?" she added after a pause, amazed at the coolness with which Madame de Listomère heard this news. "The Abbé Birotteau will there be a hundred leagues from Tours, from his friends, from everything. Is it not exile, and all the more terrible because he will be torn from the town that his eyes will behold every day, while he can hardly ever come to it? He who, since his troubles, has hardly been able to walk, will be obliged to come a league to see us. At the present moment the poor man is in bed with a feverish attack. The priest's residence at Saint-Symphorien is cold and damp, and the parish is too poor to restore it. The poor old man will be buried alive in a real tomb. What a villainous plot!"

It will now, perhaps, suffice in conclusion of this story to report briefly a few subsequent events, and to sketch a last picture.

Five months later the Vicar-General was a bishop; Madame de Listomère was dead, leaving fifteen hundred francs a year to the Abbé Birotteau. On the day when the Baroness' will was read, Monseigneur Hyacinthe, Bishop of Troyes, was about to leave Tours and take up his residence in his diocese; but he postponed his departure. Furious at having been deceived by a woman to whom he had offered a hand, while she was secretly holding out hers to the man whom he chose to regard as an enemy, Troubert again threatened to mar the Baron's career and hinder the Marquis de Listomère from receiving his peerage. In full council, at the Archbishop's palace, had uttered one of those priestly speeches, big with revenge, though smooth with honeyed mildness.

The ambitious lieutenant came to see this ruthless prelate, who dictated hard terms no doubt, for the Baron's conduct showed absolute subservience to the terrible Jesuit's will.

The new Bishop, by a deed of gift, bestowed Mademoiselle Gamard's house on the Cathedral Chapter; he gave Chapeloud's bookcase and books to the little Seminary; he dedicated the two disputed pictures to the Lady Chapel; but he kept the portrait of Chapeloud. No one could understand this almost complete surrender of all Mademoiselle Gamard's property. Monsieur de Bourbonne imagined that he secretly kept all the actual money to enable him to maintain his rank in Paris, if he should be called to sit on the Bench of Bishops in the Upper Chamber.

At last, on the very day before Monseigneur Troubert left Tours, the "old fox" detected the last plot which these gifts had covered, a *coup do grâce* dealt by the most relentless vengeance to the most helpless of victims. The Baron de Listomère disputed Madame de Listomère's bequest to Birotteau on the ground of undue influence! Within a few days of the first steps being taken in this action, the Baron was appointed to a ship with the rank of captain; the Curé of Saint-Symphorien was, by an act of discipline, placed under an interdict. His ecclesiastical superiors condemned him by anticipation; so the assassin of the late Sophie Gamard was a rogue as well! Now, if Monseigneur Troubert had kept the old maid's property, he could hardly have secured Birotteau's disgrace.

At the moment when Monseigneur Hyacinthe, Bishop of Troyes, was passing in a post-chaise, along the quay of Saint Symphorien on his way to Paris, poor Birotteau had just been brought out in an armchair to sit in the sun on a terrace. The unhappy priest, stricken by his archbishop, was pale and haggard. Grief, stamped on every feature, had completely altered the face, which of old had been so blandly cheerful. Ill health had cast a dimness that simulated thought over his eyes, which had been bright once with the pleasures of good living, and devoid of any weight of ideas. This was but the skeleton of that Birotteau who, only a year ago, vacuous but happy, had waddled across the Close. The Bishop shot a glance of contempt and pity at his victim; then he vouchsafed to forget him, and passed on.

In other times Troubert would certainly have been a Hildebrand or an Alexander VI. Nowadays the Church is no longer a political force, and does not absorb all the powers of isolated men. Hence celibacy has this crying evil, that by concentrating the powers of a man on one single passion, namely, egoism, it makes the unwedded soul mischievous or useless.

We live in a time when the fault of most governments is that they make man for society rather than society for man. A perpetual struggle is going on between the individual and the system that tries to turn him to account, while he tries to turn it to account for his own advantage; formerly, man having really more liberty, showed greater generosity for the public weal. The circle in which men move has insensibly widened; the soul that can apprehend it synthetically will never be anything but a grand exception, since, constantly, in moral as in physical force, what is gained in extent is lost in intensity. Society cannot be based on exceptions.

Originally, man was simply and solely a father; his heart beat warmly, concentrated within the radius of the family. Later on he lived for the Clan or for a small Republic; hence the grand historical heroism of Greece and Rome. Next, he became the member of a caste, or of a religion, and often was truly sublime in his devotion to its greatness; but then the field of his interests was increased by the addition of every intellectual realm. In these days his life is bound up with that of a vast fatherland; ere long his family will be the whole human race.

Will not this moral cosmopolitanism, the thing the Roman Church hopes for, be a sublime mistake? It is so natural to believe in that noble chimera—the brotherhood of men. But, alas! the human machine has not such godlike proportions. The souls that are vast enough to wed a sentiment that is the prerogative of a great man will never be those of plain citizens, of fathers of families.

Certain physiologists opine that if the brain expands, the heart must necessarily shrink. That is a mistake. Is not what looks like egoism in the men who bear in their breast a science, a nation, or its laws, the noblest of passions? Is it not, in a way, a motherhood of the people? To bring forth new races or new ideas, must they not combine in their powerful brain the breast of the mother with the force of God? The history of an Innocent III, of a Peter the Great, of all who have guided an epoch or a nation, would at need prove to be, in the highest order of minds, the immense idea represented by Troubert in the depths of the Close of Saint-Gatien.

SAINT-FIRMIN, *April* 1832.